BLACK MAN'S
KIDS

A NOVEL BY
AUTHOR ZEE. W

www.zbookpublishing.com

Black Man's Kids© 2025 by Zee. W

ZBook Publishing, LLC
Conyers, GA
www.zbookpublishing.com

Editing & Formatting: Carla M. Dean, U Can Mark My Word Editorial Services

First Edition

Paperback **ISBN**: 978-1-941689-13-4

PRINTED IN THE UNITED STATES OF AMERICA

DEDICATED TO "CLOCK-MAN"

This book is dedicated to the Black man and woman that taught me to love myself, my culture, my family, my talent, and my God. I love you Abah (Father) aka "Clock-Man" and Emah (Mother).

And to my five siblings, Chyah, Hahnah, Beulah Yamemah, Deborah and Matthew Zadok. My protectors. My counselors. My guardians. My soulmates. Thank you for always concerning yourself with me. Caring if I'm happy or sad. Routing for me. Encouraging. Always saying sorry even if it was my fault. Laughing when I laugh and wiping my tears when I cry. And, giving me unconditional love. The most valuable type of love there is.

We are a tribe. The daughters and son of Matthew Mark and Chris Ann. Together we can get through anything. We can conquer the world.

And especially to you my beautiful, Matthew Zadok. You will forever be my big little brother. In this life and the next. I will never forget your loving smile. How you made me feel bigger than what I am. How you supported me. How you listened intently and loved me without a cause. Keep making intercessions for us up there. We feel it down here.

Until we meet again, Zadok Forever!

Author Zee. W

"The Righteous Suffer Violence and The Violent Take it by Force."

—Matthew 11:12

#JUSTICEFORZADOK
#JUSTICEFORZADOK
#JUSTICEFORZADOK
#JUSTICEFORZADOK
#JUSTICEFORZADOK
#JUSTICEFORZADOK

BLACK MAN'S
KIDS

PROLOGUE

JANUARY 2011

I love my children more than I love myself—but Lord, sometimes they get on my damn nerves. They don't seem to understand that their image, regardless of how grown they are, still reflects on me and their father. And lately, they're making us look bad. All six of them. Yes, six. And no, none of them were a mistake. When people hear that I have six kids, they stare at me like they're waiting for an explanation. The only explanation is love.

If you really want to know the truth, I would have had ten kids if my king hadn't gotten locked up. When you have a man like him, having babies is like giving birth to diamonds. Their worth is wrapped up in his worth, and my king is a priceless man. All my children have the same father and were conceived in love, within an honest, faithful marriage—not one of those slave-master weddings with the white pastor and white piece of paper granting you "permission" to love. No, we had our own ceremony, reciting our vows before God with one of my king's disciples as the witness.

Our children had a better upbringing than we did while growing up, and despite all that he and I had been through, we still had enough love to pour into them.

1
THE MAMA
"The Strong One"

Today's one of those days—I've got a bottle of red wine, an old photo album, Sade playing softly, the phone off, curtains drawn, and my house clothes on. I'm lying on a cot that I made of couch cushions, pillows, and bed sheets spread across my wooden floor. The flames of the fireplace glow, casting dancing shadows that momentarily entertain me as they shift and morph into abstract shapes on the walls of the small, dark room; I try to guess what they resemble. The calming reddish-orange flame is mesmerizing, transporting me to another place, and the crackling of the wood is as soothing as the sounds of the ocean. Sipping my wine, I flip through the pages of the photo album and wonder how thirty years flew by so fast.

I see the evolution of my children from when they were babies until now as adults. Their smiles have changed over the years—from effortless innocence to something forced. The white of their beautiful almond- and marble-shaped eyes, once bright and full of wonder, grew duller with each passing year as they came to realize what a cruel world they lived in.

I flip back and forth between their baby photos and grown-up ones, looking for signs. Warnings. Something I missed. Was there a weakness within them that I could have strengthened before they got older? Was there something I could have done to raise them better? I search their faces in the pictures to see if there is anything I overlooked that would have given me a hint of what kind of adults they would become. But no matter how closely I study their baby pictures, I see nothing but hope—high, high hopes. Maybe I set my hopes for my children too high. When they were younger, I kept things they shouldn't touch on the top shelf, out of reach. Did I place their dreams up there, too? When they were determined to get what they wanted from that top shelf, they would make a ladder to help them reach it. They are still doing that now, except the ladders they are using to try and reach what they want ain't sturdy, and I'm afraid that if they fall off, they are really going to hurt themselves.

Closing the photo album, I take another sip of wine. The fire's too hot, so I scoot my makeshift bed back a few inches and untie my satin robe. I sigh. I did the best I could with all six of them. I loved them like my own skin, but love wasn't enough when it came to raising them. Love is great, but it can't protect them from themselves now. It can't predict outcomes. Maybe love can shape their outcomes, but the world has its own way of shaping outcomes, too. I worry that pretty soon my love for them will be in competition with the world, and even though I know there ain't no love in the world stronger than what I have for my children, I also know it ain't about the strongest love. It's about which has the most influence—and the world's got me on that one.

The world is corrupt and brainwashing. I tried to teach my children what their father taught: family and love matter more than riches and wealth. But, having seen me struggle so much, my words lost their impact. They didn't want to be like me, and honestly, I prayed they would do better.

I stole to feed them and taught them how to do the same, but I didn't see it as stealing. Back then, it was survival. What was I supposed to do? Beg the government for a handout? Pretend to be a helpless, husbandless Black woman waiting for the government to support me and my six kids? Hell no! I wasn't lying, apologizing, or begging for anything, not even a monthly check. If my king hadn't been arrested, our lives would've been different. But after they sent him away, I had to wear two hats—mama and daddy.

Before going to prison, my king made money doing speaking engagements and selling his artwork. That paid our bills, put food on the table, and kept clothes on our backs. We were really on our way up, and my king had big plans for our family, but things shifted after his arrest. The same people he had helped were nowhere to be found when we needed them. All the services he provided for the community were done out of love, and he didn't take or expect any money in return. So, you would think folks would've shown their gratitude or some sort of loyalty to his cause by chipping in to help us, but they didn't. Nobody lifted a finger or offered a dime. Not even his snake-ass friend Sir Zion. So, I did what I could.

Back then, nobody was hiring a Black woman who didn't have a college degree—or, as I like to say, a prepaid education. I had knowledge but no paper to prove it, so I couldn't get a job that was worth a damn! And I wasn't about to scrub some white woman's floor like this was the damn 40s and 50s. That's all that seemed to be out there for me. So, I felt stealing was my only option to provide for my children.

In addition to groceries, I stole my kids' school clothes and supplies. Then I got bold— faked tax returns and received huge refunds every year despite never having worked a day in my life, forged social security checks, and even collected disability for a father I never met. I was pulling in nearly $4,000 a month, plus a $7,000 tax return each year. I didn't give a damn about stealing from a government that stole from me. They stole my family from Africa! Stole my ancestors' labor for years. Hell, they even stole the land we live on. The way I looked at it, my stealing from them was my creative way of getting the forty acres and a mule they promised us, and it supported me and my children for years until I got arrested. *Shit!* After years of scheming and fraud, one stupid move got me two years in jail. But something I will probably never forgive myself for doing is pulling my oldest daughter into my mess.

When my landlord's dead wife's social security check of two grand accidentally got sent to our address, I took Balanah, got her a fake I.D., and had her forge the check. I didn't need the money—we were good. But I got greedy. We didn't even put a dent in that money before the cops came knocking on our door, looking for Balanah. I tried to take the rap for her, saying I forced her to do it so they would let her off, but they only ended up arresting both of us. Greed—that's what did me in. I flirted with one of the seven deadly sins and got burned.

That was a painful time, and everything spiraled out of control from there. The kids were scared, and I didn't know how they would make it without me. But my oldest, Malichai, had his own way of figuring things out. Unfortunately, his solution involved selling drugs—the very thing his father had fought against and sacrificed his life for.

Two years away from my children felt like a lifetime, and I feared what my absence would do to their development. When I got out, I saw my fears were valid. Those two years spent away from them had changed everything. My kids were different. They were still young, but it was like they didn't need me anymore, and my influence seemed to fade away. Malichai had spoiled them to the point of ruining them. They wore fancy clothes, talked differently, and I could tell by their eyes that they were looking at the world through a lens I didn't give them. There was nothing I could do. They became materialistic and accustomed to easy money—the lifestyle I spent years trying to shield them from. I never would have imagined their own brother would be the vessel that led them to it. Now, he's paying for it, but it ain't entirely his fault. He was doing what he thought he had to do. And the worst part is that Sir Zion—that snake, that weasel, that corrupt imposter of a Black man—is the one who got him started. He made it seem alright for Malichai to go down that path. Some godfather he turned out to be. I hate him for that, among other things.

I grab the wine from the coffee table, pour another glass, and take a sip. Just the thought of Sir Zion's slimy ass makes my skin crawl, and I take another swallow from my glass. This time it's more of a gulp. I can't think of him without recalling that shameful night—one I'll regret for the rest of my life.

I curse the day I let that weasel of a man touch me. He wrapped his weak arms around me and put his venomous lips on mine, poisoning my soul. His dry locs felt like sandpaper against my neck as they fell from his head and landed on my chest. *Lord, what did I let him do?* I never liked him. I never trusted him. Yet, I allowed him to enter my soul through the same door my king used to enter me. I wasn't drunk. I wasn't high. I was just an emotional wreck and did a foolish thing. That was over fifteen years ago, and I still regret it.

My king had just been sentenced to life, and I was feeling the weakest I had ever felt in my life. Weak for my six children, weak for myself. What were we going to do without him? Sir Zion, his so-called partner who he had been friends with since elementary school, saw my vulnerability and made his move...and I let him. I can't believe I betrayed a man who never betrayed me. A man who loved me and his children more than life itself. A man who gave his entire life to keep not only his family safe but others, as well. I'll never forgive myself for dishonoring him the way I did. Never!

And it didn't even feel good! No matter how tight I closed my eyes, Sir Zion wasn't my king. His touch, his kiss, his length, width, and girth—none of it came close. It was such a waste that I stopped him mid-act and told him to get the fuck off me. When he acted like he didn't hear me, I bit his ass on the neck hard, breaking the skin. He screamed, jumped up off me, and drew back his arm like he was about to slap me, but I had a surprise waiting for him. See, not long after my king went to prison, he told me to keep a knife at the side of my bed for my protection, and Sir Zion found that same knife pointed at him.

"You ain't shit, Akimah!" he yelled at me, wiping the blood from his neck.

Reflecting back on the night, I can't help but think I cursed my six children's lives by laying with that snake. My new faith teaches that curses can be broken, but I don't know the remedy. All I know how to do is love my kids hard and keep reminding them of who their father is, in the hope that they will learn the power of their true selves.

Before my king was called Akimbo Sedah, he was known as Charles Soyer, and before I became Akimah Sedah, I was Rachel Johnson. Both of us were raised by Uncle Sam, in and out of group and foster homes—our parents being as much an enigma to us as we were to ourselves. I met him in the last foster home I lived in. I was just sixteen when we met, and he was about to turn eighteen, facing aging out of the system. He wasn't scared, though. At eighteen, he was more of a man than most fully grown men, fearless and bold as a lion. I fell for him immediately when he showed interest in me, teaching me everything he had learned over the years. It was during this time that I realized he was wise beyond his years; he shared that wisdom with me, freeing me from the invisible social blindfold I had unconsciously worn.

When I referred to him as Charles, like our foster mother, he corrected me and told me that he had renamed himself Akimbo. He explained that he no longer accepted his government name because naming a child is an honor that only belongs to someone who loves, cares for, and will protect that child at all costs. He assured me that the system would never love him in that way, so he gave himself a new name, and I followed suit by renaming myself, as well.

Akimbo and I bonded instantly through our shared pain and experiences as wards of the state. He was the one who taught me to forgive the mysterious parents who had abandoned me and to be grateful that they hadn't ended my life before I was born. "Even though they placed you in a system as irresponsible and corrupt as this one, at least they loved you enough to let you live. So, hold on to the last bit of love and honor they had for you," he told me. "But don't waste your time searching for your mother," he advised. "Look to yourself and you'll find her, just as I have looked to myself and saw my father. I am him, and he is me."

I didn't always understand everything Akimbo told me, but the passion in his voice touched me so deeply that I believed every word he said. He was unlike any guy I had ever met. He read books. He didn't hang out on the corner shooting dice, smoking weed, or getting drunk. He didn't chase after every young girl who pursued him, and he was the only young man I knew who could hold a conversation with an adult and actually be listened to, as if he were their equal. His vocabulary was vast, and he carried himself like a king. He truly is one in his own right. Just four weeks after meeting Akimbo, I knew I was going to marry him. I also knew that when he turned eighteen and left, I would follow him wherever he went. I was down for him from day one.

My king was a beautiful man—striking, even. He stood six feet one and walked with the stride and confidence of a soldier fighting for a cause of his own. His skin was the color of tar but gleamed like silk. That blackness was as breathtaking as the midnight summer sky, and his big, bright eyes sparkled like the stars. His confidence in his skin tone gave me the courage to wear mine the same way. We shared a similar complexion, and being with him made me ashamed of the times I tried to scrub the black off my skin with Clorox because, according to my foster mother, dark-skinned folks always looked dirty. But Akimbo told me my skin was beautiful—that I was blessed to be so uniquely colored. I had never thought of my skin tone as unique or beautiful, but he changed that. Before long, I was walking with the same pride he did.

People on the street called him "Black Man," not just because of his skin tone but also because of the pride he carried and the constant philosophies he shared with others about the Black race. My king appreciated the changes brought about by the civil rights movement, but he believed the fight was far from over. He felt that Blacks got too relaxed after the government granted us our rights.

"We need more than rights," he'd preach. "We need to dissociate from their way of thinking and reintroduce ourselves to our true selves. If we don't know who we are, our children won't either. And if that happens, our generations are doomed. We still are a part of their discriminatory system, regardless of what their law books say!"

He believed that while everybody else was settling down, we should have been preparing for part two of the revolution—a deeper, internal war. A battle for the mind. He saw the next step as reconstructing our lives and our thinking—rebuilding our communities, our families, and our sense of manhood.

He started his own movement and quickly gathered followers. People were so inspired by his philosophies on family and manhood that they flocked to him—sometimes showing up at our door in droves just to hear him speak. He became our community's hero almost overnight. Whenever there was a crisis—a woman being beaten by her husband, an elderly person harassed by drug-dealing youth, or another police killing without justice—people came to my king. And he stood up bold, turning up the heat. He led rallies in front of police precincts, demanding they do something about the drugs destroying our neighborhood. And when the police didn't do their job, he did it for them. He fought the war on drugs fearlessly—organizing community-led raids on drug houses, pulling strung-out people off the streets to get them help, and even convincing young dealers to walk away from the game. It was a dangerous time for us, but the entire community stood behind him. He told me not to fear, because fear is just as powerful as faith—and he didn't want the two to collide.

My king believed we couldn't rebuild families without removing the poison that was destroying them—and at the time, that poison was drugs. If a father wasn't using, then the son was selling. He said drugs were a form of slavery that killed and enslaved more Blacks than slavery ever could. It affected entire generations. He felt there was a hidden social order behind it all—that the police weren't there to stop the problem, only to monitor it. And that wasn't enough for him.

Akimbo became like a Black Robin Hood in the way he handled those street vigilantes, and after a while, we started seeing less crime. That's when the politicians took notice. Mayors, senators, police commissioners, and other "glorified" government officials began calling him into meetings to see how he could assist them further in this war. He humbled himself and went, each time returning home more motivated than before. While they tried to steal some of his limelight, he used those meetings to solicit government funding—money for more rehab centers, women's shelters, youth programs, counseling centers for families at risk, and better housing. They all made false promises to him. Still, he kept hope alive.

At the top of his list was getting rid of the last drug house left in our community—an abandoned box warehouse that had become a place for addicts to shoot up, drug dealers to make their drops, and women to sell their bodies. It was the thorn in the side of his movement and his future plans for creating facilities to help our community, but the government officials did nothing about the building. At first, they claimed it was a historic monument and couldn't demolish it. When that excuse grew old, they said they didn't have the funds to tear it down. That's when Akimbo offered to do it himself, only to be threatened with the same life sentence they gave him. The truth was, many of those officials didn't want that building gone because they were making money off it. Drug dealers were greasing the palms of those corrupt politicians, and they regarded that abandoned building as a second income—a dirty investment to pad their underpaid salaries. My king grew to hate that building so much that he lost sleep over it. He couldn't rest until it was gone. He couldn't see his vision for our community manifest as long as it was still there.

And then the worst happened. A little girl was raped and killed inside that building on her way to school. My king took it hard. The girl's mother stayed with us for two weeks—too broken by grief to even move. Everybody looked to Akimbo, waiting for him to act. They expected him to do something, and he did. He blamed himself so much that he took matters into his own hands.

He began plotting with Sir Zion. He didn't tell me what he was thinking until he had already planned everything out because he knew I would try to talk him out of it. But we both knew once Akimbo had his mind made up about something, there was nothing I could do or say to dissuade him. He was going to do what the city wouldn't do––blow up that building. I didn't waste my time trying to change his mind, but I didn't think about the consequences either.

When the day came, everything seemed to go according to plan. Akimbo got the explosives he needed from a retired Vietnam vet he grew up with in foster care. Sir Zion's job was to make sure everyone was out of the building, which took weeks. Then, in the early morning, when no one was around to get hurt or affected by the blast, my king pressed the button, causing the building to crumble like a cookie. When he returned home, it was like the weight of that building had finally been lifted from his shoulders. He was no longer haunted. We made love that night for hours. I could feel the victory in his kisses, the triumph in the way he held me. His energy was contagious, and I was proud to be part of it.

Before the sun could set good, our house was surrounded by police officers and the news media. My king wasn't nervous, though. After all, it wasn't like he had killed anybody. In fact, he saved a lot of people by getting rid of that building. He already had his lawyer lined up, so he didn't think they could hold him long. Or at least, he thought.

After exiting the front door of our home, Akimbo spoke into the cameras with confidence, relaying his best speech yet for thousands of others to hear and offering inspiration. As the officers proceeded to take him into custody, hundreds of his followers rallied behind the police cars, holding up signs that honored his cause and applauding him. They then followed behind, marching all the way to the precinct to continue their protest.

With my king behind bars, it was my turn to stand in front of the cameras and speak. I let them know what my husband was trying to do. I let them know his motives, and I spoke just as fierce and powerful as he did. I knew he'd be proud of me.

We stayed outside the police station all night and into the next day—until they threatened us with their dogs and tear gas. So, we finally went home, still feeling high and victorious. Every news station was covering the explosion caused by my husband. As I watched the news clip of my Akimbo, his voice was so powerful and motivating that I got chills. I just knew that when he got out, everything he envisioned for our people, for our community, was going to happen.

My phone rang nonstop with interview requests, but I ignored them all. I wasn't going to speak to anyone until my king gave the word. Whatever message he wanted me to put out there, I would—but only when he was ready. Sir Zion, on the other hand, was loving all the attention. My stomach turned every time I saw his face on TV, smiling like some kind of superstar instead of a man with a noble cause. I tried not to let it bother me too much, though. Our voices were finally being heard from a mountain top, and I was too excited for the rest of the world to hear.

Then, the next night, a story broke—the one that changed my family's lives forever. While the city cleared away the debris, they found a body. A man had been inside the building when it blew. Everything changed in an instant. My husband went from hero to murderer in less than forty-eight hours. They gave him a life sentence because of that man who was probably a junkie, but even junkies deserve to live. I couldn't blame nobody but that damn Sir Zion! He had one job—to make sure everybody was out. He failed, and I hate him for it.

My husband's movement died too soon, like it never happened. The drug dealers he spent years chasing away were back terrorizing the streets. Nobody else stepped up to take his place—not even that weak-ass Sir Zion. Sometimes, I feel like it was all in vain. What did we really accomplish? Then I have to remind myself we did a lot. Akimbo touched lives. He encouraged the union of several families. He provided help to addicts. But where does that leave us—his family?

The last time I saw my husband was on TV. He didn't let us come to court or visit him in jail. I wish he would allow us to see him or at least let his sons talk with him, but he won't. He wrote me one letter, saying he didn't want me or his children to see him like that and it was best to remember him as the man he was before he left. He doesn't write or call. It's like he's dead.

So, what else could I do besides live my life? I considered continuing his movement, but my voice was weak, and I had six children to raise. In that same letter, he assured me that Sir Zion would look after us. And boy, did he.

He fucked up Malichai's life, and he thinks I don't know he's got his claws in the rest of my children, too. It's like he's after them, and I don't know why. The last time I saw him, he cursed me and my kids. Said they'd never be shit. Said they were nothing more than a dream deferred. He called Malichai broke and hopeless. Balanah spineless and weak. Called Sahara a conforming sellout. Said Ebony was crazy and unbalanced. Said Kwame was worthless and lazy, and called Essence selfish and destructive. He told me Akimbo would weep if he saw the way his children turned out on account of my upbringing. His words stung me like a million bee stings.

Could he be right? Did I do a horrible job raising my children? Had I failed them?

I thought about each one—and what I saw wasn't pretty. Malichai is one step away from being strung out on crack like the girlfriend he let drag him down. Balanah is wasting her life, expecting a miracle to fall in her lap without putting in no effort. She's getting so resentful that sometimes I wonder if she will just walk away from all of us. Sahara is so busy trying to conform to her husband's idea of perfection that I fear she's gonna snap any day now. Ebony's got secrets, and I have a feeling it has something do with that no-good ex-fiancé of hers and my granddaughter, Zena. Kwame's drowning in depression, turning into something that ain't him. I know he's whooping that wife of his. I can tell by how jumpy she is around him. And his son? That child don't look shit like him. Lastly, there's Essence. She's so spoiled and stingy that I know it's not going to be long before she learns a hard lesson.

All of that made Sir Zion sound right. *But then I remembered who my children really are.* They're not their situations. They're powerful, strong, and determined, even if they don't know it yet.

After Sir Zion said those things, I laughed, spat in his face, and walked away, my stride conveying a message of strength and confidence. I should've cut him, but the spit was enough.

Sweet memories. Hell, I'll drink to that.

While taking another sip of my warm wine, I stare at the dancing shadows on the wall.

My kids are going to be alright—even if they're still out here making me and their daddy look bad.

2

MALICHAI

"The Broke One"

Meka ain't been home in a week. I can't find her skinny ass nowhere, and I've looked just about everywhere. I hit up every crack house in the city, called the hospitals, even checked behind the dumpsters. Nothing. I pray ain't nothing happened to my girl. I need to find her before we get evicted next Friday. If I don't, I might not ever find her.

I'm frustrated, but I'm taking it. After all, I brought all this shit on myself. I'm really paying heavy for the mistakes I made. But how long does a person have to keep paying for their fuck-ups?

Back then, how in the hell could I say no? I would've been one dumb Black man to turn down that kind of money. And one thing this country don't need is another broke, dumb-ass Black man dragging the rest of us down.

All I had to do was make one little drop. Jumpstart the battery on my old, washed-out Caprice. Pray the lion under the hood stopped coughing long enough to roar. Cross my fingers and hope I would make it down I-20 without breaking down or attracting the attention of the Atlanta police. Get to the spot, pop the trunk, close it, and collect five grand from Sir Zion. Seemed simple enough.

That was almost twelve years ago. I was only eighteen. Now that I'm older, I know ain't nothing that simple. The easier something seems, the heavier the consequences. That's the Catch-22 of the drug game. But I ain't really have a choice. Mama had finally gotten arrested, taking my sister Balanah with her. So, being the oldest of six kids, I was left to fend for the rest of us, but it was kinda like that even before Mama went to jail.

I'm the spitting image of my father—look just like him—but I ain't him. Couldn't fit in his shoes no matter how hard I tried. I ain't like him, and I'm sick of everybody expecting me to be. Maybe that's why I started selling drugs. Then again, if I hadn't, social services would've come, taking my younger siblings to be raised by that molesting bastard they call Uncle Sam. And I wasn't having that. Hell nah!

I hate that Mama dragged Balanah into her scamming mess. She was the second oldest. If she hadn't gotten locked up, who knows where I would be? I wouldn't have had to play daddy to my bad-ass siblings, that's for sure. Balanah's life has been fucked up ever since. First offense, seventeen years old, and they charged her as an adult. That shit is still on her record, and it's why she can't get a job despite having a college degree. That happened years ago, and she has been clean ever since. So again, I ask, how long does a person have to pay for their mistakes? Half a lifetime? Forever? How fucking long?! Balanah wasn't built to be a thief. Mama taught all of us how to steal, but Balanah was the only one who felt guilty about it. She'd whisper to me, "This is wrong," and I would tell her, "Starving is wrong." She did whatever Mama told her. Hell, she still does whatever anybody tells her to do.

I love my brother and sisters more than anything, but it was easier to express that when they were younger—before they got all high and mighty, judgmental, and ungrateful. Hell, if it wasn't for me, they wouldn't be where they are now—sitting high, looking down low on me. That one little drop I made saved us. And when I saw how quick and easy that money came, I went back to Sir Zion requesting more work. The hustle paid the rent, bought groceries, and kept the heat on. I could've been selfish and fixed the Caprice—got a two-tone paint job to cover the rust spreading like cancer, dressed it up with some chrome wheels, and changed the engine so the bitch wouldn't stop on me every time I put my foot on the brake. But I didn't. I took care of them instead. Shit, I was a real sucker.

I was buying school supplies and handing out lunch money like I was their damn daddy. And now I can't call and ask for fifty cents without getting a lecture.

"You sure you looking for a job, Malichai? Seems like you should've had something by now. You keeping your pee clean, right?"

That's what my youngest sister, Essence, said when I asked for twenty dollars for gas. I didn't ask for a down payment for a house. Just twenty dollars. And yeah, I've been looking for a job. And no, my piss ain't been clean. But that ain't none of her damn business. A broke Black man gotta find peace where he can. For me, it's firing up a fat one and getting blazed from time to time. I've been searching hard. But corporate America won't see me, and blue-collar jobs want to work me like a slave for little pay. And I ain't no fucking slave!

It's been five years since I slung any dirt. I've been trying to stay on the straight and narrow, but I'm starting to think that the system wasn't created for everyone to stay straight. They need some of us poor, some of us working, and some of us doing illegal things to make money. That's how they maintain the social order in this country. I've been broke for so long that I'm about to lose my balance and go back to what I know. But I promised myself I wouldn't.

That one drop turned into an entire operation, and I was the CEO. *It was the best of times; it was the worst of times*—whoever said that must've been watching my life back then because there is no other way to describe it.

By the time Mama and Balanah got out of jail, they returned to a posh condo that I paid for outright. Mama still lives there. And me? My ass is in a hotel. I ain't tripping. I bought it for her unconditionally, and I'm no Indian giver. But it would be nice if she at least offered for me, Meka, and my son to stay there until we get back on our feet. She ain't said a word. Hell, she barely even asks how I'm doing. Probably don't want to hear the answer. My life is fucked up. I'm broke. I'm beat down. And I'm two days away from being evicted— for the third time this month.

Kwame, my younger brother, offered to let us stay with him. But out of all the houses on the market, he had to go and buy the house me and Meka got kicked out of years ago. The same *dream* house that started this nightmare I'm living in now. That house holds too many unpleasant memories; I can't go back there.

Mama appreciated the condo, but she hated how I got the money to pay for it. Just like she despised welfare, she despised drug dealers.

"You're worse than the white man. Killing your own people? That's genocide, Malichai! Lord, your daddy would be ashamed," she said, shaking her head and turning up her nose like I smelled like shit.

Mama always brought up my dad whenever she wanted me to feel low about what I was doing. I used to worship my dad, honoring him with the same respect I had for our Black leaders, Malcolm X and Martin Luther King, Jr. To me, he wasn't too different from them. But by eighteen, I stopped caring about what he thought of me. Hell, if he was smart, he wouldn't give a damn about what I was doing either. The only thing he needed to concern himself with was making sure he didn't drop the soap while serving time somewhere in a maximum-security prison in South Georgia.

Mama hated what I did, but she didn't mind when I greased her hands with cash. She would take the money while lecturing me, like her words washed the cash clean.

"You don't want that kind of blood on your hands," she would say. "That blood stains forever. It's a curse and can follow all your generations."

Well, that "cursed" money helped put two of my siblings through college and provided enough support to the others so they could become the *outstanding* citizens they are today.

What made it worse for Mama was the fact that Sir Zion was the one who got me into the game. He and my dad were both rebels fighting for Black empowerment, and together, they rallied hundreds of frustrated, socially emasculated Black men to join them in making a change. This was long after the Black Power movement faded. At the young age of nine, I bought into it all. Now? It feels like over-righteous bullshit. Folks are out here trying to survive—we ain't got time to tap into the powers of our royal blood. My royal blood's still Black, but in a country where the color of royalty is white, I ain't got a chance with that rhetoric. That's why I did what I had to do—though I regret it now. I don't know what made Sir Zion change, but maybe he was just trying to survive, too.

The thought of him makes Mama gag. She calls him a phony and a hypocrite, blames him for Dad being incarcerated, and says he should've been the one locked up instead. She never trusted him, even during their movement. But that didn't stop her from sleeping with him a year after Daddy got arrested. She doesn't know I saw them. I wasn't sleep. I heard her crying about how weak she felt without her king—my daddy—and Sir Zion wrapped his arms around her and became her king for that night. Mama despises hypocrites, but she can't see that she's one herself. If I ever said that to her, she'd probably have a heart attack.

She may be a hypocrite, but she wasn't wrong about one thing––I'm cursed for selling that poison. I haven't been shot, never been robbed, never spent a night in jail, and never got hooked on drugs. But that curse skipped right over me and attacked my family, and I can't help but blame myself. Not the white man, not the next man, not God—just me. I've always accepted responsibility for my mistakes, and I fucked up my family's life. I'm the reason my girl is cracked out, and my son was born with a disability because of it.

I'm thirty but feel sixty, and probably look it, too. I used to be handsome, but not anymore. To be honest with you, I couldn't give a fuck how I look these days. I'm worn out. Beer belly, yellow teeth from smoking weed all day, bags under my eyes from sleepless nights, and a receding hairline already. I'm tired.

My son is five years old, and with his height, he would be perfect for shooting hoops. But he can't focus and has fits almost three times a day—falling to the floor and screaming at the top of his lungs like he's possessed. Doctors say he's never gonna have more than a third-grade education. So, getting drafted into the NBA is out for him. So is becoming a doctor, a lawyer, or even a grocery store bagger. I'm gonna have to take care of him for the rest of my life.

His mama, Meka, has been strung out for five years. It started with her smoking high-grade weed—that loud-loud—but it wasn't enough for her. That's just like Meka. Nothing is enough, and she always wants more. She's always been curious, always chasing something. Being with her, you never knew what kind of shit was going to happen. She's determined, wild, fearless—living life on the edge. That's what made her exciting to me. That's why I love her. That's why I'm by her side to this day and not going anywhere, no matter what Mama and my sisters say. They can go to hell.

She started sprinkling that powder in the blunts. I had it lying around like flour, so it was easy for her to try. Like I said, Meka is a curious person, but I didn't expect her curiosity to lead to her getting hooked. I tried that shit once, but I wasn't made out to be that damn high. Based on her reaction the first time, I thought she wasn't either. She complained about her high taking too long to wear off and said she'd never try it again. A month later, she was snorting it straight, burning through my supply. She became so dependent on that shit she couldn't do nothing without it. It became her oxygen, her energy, her reason to wake up—or lie down. She snorted before cooking, eating, watching a movie, and before sex—which, I won't lie, made things interesting.

I didn't know how to stop her. That was my business, and I had nowhere else to keep the powder. I told myself she'd grow out of it, but I guess I was lying to myself to justify what I was doing. I wish I had stopped her back then when she still had a chance.

We were young, and with so much money, our lifestyle became like a drug, too. We partied for days, shopped like the world was ending, ate out every night of the week, and frequented the hottest nightclubs' VIP sections. We even went to strip clubs together, and she would pick out girls for us to take home. I don't know any woman who would encourage threesomes, and sometimes even foursomes, with her man. Nobody could touch us. It was the best of times with her, which is why I have to endure the worst of times with her, too.

Meka was always thick—curves like a biscuit and round as a rump roast—but the drugs wasted her. She went from being a double D cup to a full B, and her size 12 jeans were now a 6. Still, she was sexy as hell. Then one day, she stopped breathing. I came home and found her on the kitchen floor, foaming at the mouth with her eyes wide open and only the white part showing. I nearly lost my mind. The doctor said if I had come home one second later, she'd be dead. That's when I said enough was enough. While she recovered for two weeks in the hospital, on a ventilator, I cleaned house. Sold the last of my stash and got out of the business. I was done. Let's just say when she got home, she wasn't too thrilled about what I did.

"How the fuck we gonna live now, Mal? How you gonna do some shit like this without consulting with me first? I thought we was in this shit together?"

"We are," I told her. "I'm doing this so we can live. Both of us."

It was some hard months after that, but I stuck to my decision. That didn't stop Meka from still being a junkie, though. I tried getting top-paying jobs to maintain our lifestyle. Of course, nobody would hire me. We blew through the last of our money like we still had it like that. We didn't think to save for the rainy days ahead of us. Meka even stole a few bucks from our funds to get high.

One thing about having a lot of money is that you live in the moment. You don't think about tomorrow; you just think about the day. We didn't plan shit. We didn't own our house—it was rented for show. The luxury cars we drove? They were all leased and eventually got repossessed. At least I bought Mama a condo outright. I don't know why I couldn't think like that for Meka and me. Meka wanted that three-level house with five thousand square feet and an indoor pool that cost thousands to maintain. I just wanted to give her the best, but my idea of "best" was childish and materialistic. Meka wasn't the only one spending my money. I was forking out thousands of dollars a month to my brother and sisters, not to mention Mama. I never kept count. Whatever they needed, I just gave it. The powder I was selling was a white money tree...until I chopped it down.

We were evicted in less than a year, all our shit thrown out on the street. By the time we came back with a moving truck, all of our big-screen TVs, leather couches, and expensive clothes were gone. Our so-called friends were probably the ones who took our stuff. We lost it all in one day, but I still didn't regret my decision. At twenty-five, I finally felt like a man making such a life-changing decision. Meka couldn't handle the stress and was pissed off at me, but she stuck by my side. People can say what they want about Meka, but she always respected my decisions as a man.

When we couldn't afford her drug of choice, Meka started smoking crack. It was cheaper and easier to find on the street than powder. That's when everything started to go downhill. We began bouncing from hotel to hotel. I took on whatever odd jobs I could—detailing cars, raking leaves, selling scrap metal. Anything that would bring in chump change so we could get by. But sometimes, Meka would steal what little money I had to get high.

When she got pregnant, she went to rehab. For a few weeks, everything seemed so promising. I really believed she was going to make it. It made me feel better about my decision, especially now that I was going to be a father, but she couldn't stay clean. I couldn't watch her every minute—I had to keep a roof over our heads. But every time I came home, I feared I'd find her and my baby dead. Then one day, she was just gone. I gave Zachery to Mama when he was still an infant, but as he got older, he got to be too much for her to handle, so I took him back. After all, he was my responsibility.

I spent so much time searching crack houses for Meka, it felt like I was a fiend myself. I had to bail her out of jail a few times after she got caught stealing, trying to get money I refused to give her for crack. One day, I walked into the hotel room and found her sucking some dude's dick. I didn't even get mad. I just felt sorry for her. It was my fault. I'd dragged her into that life. That's when I decided just to give her what little money I had so she wouldn't end up in jail or turning tricks for that shit. I figured if I created the monster, I might as well try to control it. But once Zachery was born, I had two monsters on my hands. When I ain't chasing behind Meka to keep her off the streets, I'm chasing after my son.

I hate to admit it, but I ain't got the patience for my son. Meka's so high most days, I don't even think she knows he exists. I feel so relieved when I drop his hyper ass off on that short bus that it feels like a holiday. Don't get me wrong, I love that boy like my own skin, but I just need a break. The doctors want me to give him some drug to calm him down, but I ain't doing that shit. Hell, he was born with drugs in his system because of his parents—I'm not adding more. This is my penance.

The teachers at his school ain't too thrilled with my decision not to drug him, but the hell with them, too. They just need to do their damn jobs, and they bet not touch him either. One day, I hit him so hard across the head that he lost consciousness for a few seconds. When I saw him fall out, I felt awful. But I felt even worse when he came to, too quickly. I just wanted thirty minutes of silence, but he was up and bouncing off the walls again like it never happened.

Right now, he's with my sister Balanah. I dropped him off a week ago, promising I'd be back in an hour. She's been blowing up my phone ever since, but I need the break. I can't take him with me while I'm out looking for his mama. I know my sister is pissed at me because I'm always dropping him off and leaving him longer than I say I will, but I need help with that boy sometimes. I wouldn't have to do that if they offered to help me more, or if Meka wasn't lost to crack.

Sometimes I wonder if I quit the game too soon. Other times, I wonder if I should've never got into it at all. But like I said, I didn't feel like I had a choice. I had to do what I had to do. What started as desperation turned into greed. I was young, but I'm still paying for my mistakes. How long? How long do I have to keep paying for my mistakes?

3

BALANAH

"The Weak One"

I'm suffocating. I can't breathe. Out of all the air in the world, somehow mine is being stolen from me. It's free and abundant, yet they want mine. How greedy of them! You'd think I would fight back, but I don't even have the energy. My family—my husband and three daughters included—is like leeches, sucking me dry. And I'm allowing them to. Soon, I won't have the strength to blink, and then I'll be completely helpless.

I feel betrayed—by myself. All the faith I once had has turned on me, disguising itself as hope, leading me down roads of delay, pain, and disappointment. Disappointment has been the one constant in my life, and I feel trapped within it. Its shell is thick and made of steel, so strong that not even a bomb can set me free. I'm wasting away inside, screaming for someone to save me from myself. But no one hears me—not even God. I wish they could hear me. I wish someone would just listen. But no one ever does.

It's all taking a toll on me—fast. Some days, I just want to get up and leave. Disappear. Begin again with a new identity, away from everyone's constant needs, especially those who never consider mine.

I've been disregarded for so long that I'm starting to believe I don't matter. Maybe if I leave, I'll have a chance to start over.

It's funny. The most peace I've ever felt was during my greatest fear—prison. Before being sentenced to two years, I feared the outcome more than death. But once the sentence was handed down, the fear disappeared. I felt at peace. I was alone in a quiet space, and I finally got to know myself. When I was *set free*, it felt like walking into bondage again; my freedom took on a reversed meaning. I went back to a life where I wasn't myself, only what everyone else needed me to be. And I'm still stuck in that place after all these years.

I tried to climb out of the hole I helped the world dig for me. Every time I thought I was getting close—like when I landed a job interview—I fell right back in. The background check always gets me. I was seventeen when Mama made me forge a signature on that Social Security check, and I'm still paying for it. Sometimes I wonder if things would've been different if I had never gotten locked up.

I feel worthless. Yet something inside keeps pushing me to keep going. Maybe I like the pain from my failures. Maybe it's the only way I can feel alive. To feel the hurt. I bury all that pain deep in my gut. It rises, tightening in my chest, trying to kill my heart. But I keep pushing it back down—like I do everything else. One day, I'm gonna explode. And maybe that won't be such a bad thing.

It's easy to blame others for the way I am, but the fault lies entirely with me. I allowed them to walk all over me. I never stood up for myself. My low self-esteem overshadowed my hidden confidence. And I never said no. I volunteered when I didn't have the time or didn't want to, and now, no one asks—they just assign me tasks. I'm expected to do everything and be everything to everyone without any thanks.

All I want is to live before I die. Really live—for myself. Right now, I'm just existing. I want to be seen, heard, and considered—not out of pride, but out of a humble, basic human need. I don't crave fame, just recognition. That's all.

My purpose can't be just to help others get to the top so they can look down on me. I've been watching Sahara's kids for six months now while she secretly finishes her last year of law school. Malichai's son has been here for three weeks, and he's a handful, too. I've got three kids of my own, clinging to me and pulling me back down when I try to get up and do something. I spend hours on the phone talking to my other brother, Kwame, about his grievances, but he's never asked about mine. He even told me a secret—that he hit his wife. I kept it, even though everyone can see how that girl walks on eggshells around him. For once, I would like to be the one on the phone who is listened to, heard, and understood. For once, I would like to entrust someone with a secret of my own. I'm tired of keeping everybody's secrets *and* my own. Secrets carry too much weight on the soul.

I'm helping my youngest sister, Essence, with a marketing plan for her new business ventures—again, sacrificing my time—only for her to question my advice. "Are you sure about that, Balanah?" she will ask, but still uses it. I want to start my own business, too, but no one ever brings that up. I have a degree in Business Administration, but it holds no value to them.

Being part of a large family is both a blessing and a curse. It's a blessing because you're never alone, but it was a curse for us because with six siblings, everyone was assigned an unspoken role before we were old enough to talk. It doesn't matter if it fits or not—you wear it anyway.

I was the first to graduate, but since I'm not working for some Fortune 500 company, my degree feels like the elephant in the room. It hurt my feelings when Mama asked my sister, Sahara, to help her with a business plan, even though I had taken many courses on it. Sahara was studying to be a lawyer; I didn't see the connection between the two. "I always knew she'd be successful," Mama always says when bragging to others about Sahara's success.

Kwame sought advice from Ebony on which school to attend after she got accepted into that hotshot art school. I graduated at the top of my class, but that means nothing to them because I'm not working. I'm nothing but a glorified housewife, babysitter, and secret advisor helping folks as they pursue their dreams. Once they achieve success, I'm forgotten—a mere afterthought, never to be mentioned again. I don't need them to shout from the mountaintop that I helped them, but a simple thank you would be appreciated.

I helped my husband start his property management business. When we met, I set my own dreams aside so he could shine—just like Mama always said: "A man got to be able to shine, Balanah. You've got to be his helpmate. That's how your father became the man he was—because I let him shine." My husband's business thrived a few years ago, and I know it was largely due to my dedicated efforts. I was proud of what we built together. But while he got to be the face of it, I became his glorified secretary. Despite being listed as a partner on the incorporation papers, I was pushed into the background, working from home and putting in extra hours. He promised me that once the business took off, he would support my dreams in the same way that I supported his, but that support never came. I truly believe the reason is that he didn't like the idea of me being more successful than him. Anyone who is successful intimidates him.

Now, with the market shifting and clients pulling out, the business is struggling. I could help more by trying to come up with a solution to save it, but I'm bitter. I feel used. Disregarded. And that kills my drive. He's so cocky; he hasn't even asked for my help. Instead, he seeks advice from people who have never done a damn thing for him. He knows what he did to me, but saying he's sorry means having to support me the way I supported him, and he's incapable of it; he's selfish in the worst way because he doesn't realize it. Yes, he pays the bills and is a great provider, but that doesn't mean he's not selfish. And I've had enough. I'm going to let him fail; I have nothing to lose. Besides, I'm going to be out of here pretty soon anyway. My bags are already packed.

There's nothing worse than feeling used. It breeds resentment, regret, and even hatred. And hate? It's like poison, traveling through your veins, spreading through your body like a plague, rotting you from the inside out. That's why I think about leaving so much. It's my only hope of saving myself.

I don't have much money, but I have a plan. I borrow small amounts from my siblings—$50 here, $40 there, nothing that can be missed—and deposit it into an account. So far, I've saved about $3,000. It's not much, but it'll have to do. If that's not enough, I'll be taking Sir Zion up on his offer of an interest-free business loan. I hate to do business with a dog, but it might be my only way out.

Lately, my husband has been home a lot more, and I can't stand it. Before, he would work late hours and come home too tired to talk. Now, he looks for anything to complain about—the heat is too high, lights left on, Zionah's bookbag on the table. His complaints about Zionah are the hardest for me to handle. Zionah isn't his biological child, and it shows in how he treats her. They clash constantly, dragging me into their fights like a referee. I try to mediate between them, but honestly, sometimes I just want to disappear. I never want my daughter to feel like the black sheep among her half-siblings. I wish my husband were more sensitive to how she might feel, given that she doesn't have the same father as her other siblings, but he can only empathize with things that directly affect him. It's just who he is. That's why I call him selfish.

Zionah is fifteen—willful, emotional, and transitioning into womanhood. I know most of her mood swings are due to her changing hormones, but he talks about her like she's already a lost cause. I can't wait until his younger kids go through the same stage so I can throw it in his face. But by then, it may be too late. Zionah might already hate him—and resent me for staying with him.

She's headstrong and a natural rebel. That's in her genes, and I'm not going to punish her for it or make her feel like something's wrong with who she is. One day, I'm certain those same characteristics will take her farther in life than I ever dreamed. Instead, I'm trying to teach her how to channel them, but that's not enough for him. Sometimes, he's right. The other day, when he tried to take her cell phone away as punishment, she shattered it at his feet—a $600 phone she begged for. I believe that was her way of saying, *You can't hurt me more than I can hurt myself.* He just looked at me with his mouth hanging open, waiting for me to do something—but what could I do? Then he stormed out the front door and didn't come home for three days.

I hate when he puts me in a position where I feel like I have to choose between him and her. It's childish. But if I had to choose, it would be her—she's my child, and she needs me. I think he knows that. Between them, I'm caught in a constant tug-of-war. Those two seem to lock horns every day like it's a sport. She pushes his buttons, and he pushes hers right back. Then an argument ensues, and I'm yanked into the middle.

Sometimes I wonder if he treats her the way he does because of how she looks. Zionah is dark-skinned. He's high yellow, and so are our other kids. She gets her complexion from me. And I know how we're treated—by our own people. Not just white folks. Dark skin gets you labeled angry, defiant, and difficult. I never wanted Zionah to feel insecure about the color of her skin like I did growing up. My mama raised six beautiful dark-skinned kids and taught us that Black is beautiful. But not every Black household does that. Some children are taught to believe that the brighter the complexion, the shinier the beauty.

Come to think of it, I've never heard him call her beautiful. He's been raising her since she was four, so you'd think they would have a bond. At first, I thought he just wasn't the type to give compliments. He tells me all the time that I'm sexy, but that's different. I'm a grown woman. Sexy isn't the same as beautiful, and every young girl needs to hear she's beautiful—from a man, especially. It's important for their development. My daddy always told us girls that we were beautiful. That's why we all walk around like we're supermodels now.

When one of his half-white nieces visited, he couldn't stop complimenting her looks, and right in front of Zionah, who has ten times her beauty. She just didn't have the straight, wavy hair that hung past her shoulders and the yellow complexion he found so pretty. Zionah is as gorgeous as they come, though, with her flawless, smooth skin, unique high cheekbones, and eyes so big and bright that you can see heaven in them. If she weren't such a rebel, maybe she'd call back one of those modeling scouts who are always hunting her down in the malls. "Beauty isn't a talent, Mama," she tells me. "It's a deadly vanity. If I'm gonna make money, it's going to be for something more honorable than how pretty I am." The girl is so smart and gutsy. She doesn't understand how not using those two characteristics wisely can intimidate others, including my husband— the man she now reluctantly calls Dad.

When he's not complaining about Zionah, it's my brother Malichai and his son, Zach, who runs wild—tearing shit up, screaming at the top of his lungs, crying, and even peeing on the furniture. He can't help it; he has problems. Still, my husband acts like he wants me to kick him out onto the streets. But I'm not going to do that. He's family.

Besides, I owe a lot to Malichai. He paid for me to go to school and get my degree. When no bank would help us, he loaned us $25,000 to start the business. So, whenever he mentions Zach being at our house too long, I remind him that sometimes you have to return favors. But then he'll blow up, screaming he's tired of me throwing that in his face and that we paid him back. Yeah, we did pay him back, but it took us three years of interest-free installments. That's not the point, though. Malichai gave us an opportunity without us having to beg. But because we paid him back, my husband feels like we don't owe him shit. And he wants Zach out.

When Malichai was balling, those two were tight. They used to hang out and chop it up. Now, whenever my brother comes over, he acts annoyed by his presence—walking right by him without a word, stomping up the stairs, and slamming our bedroom door loud enough for Malichai to hear. Malichai doesn't come around anymore, and I don't blame him. I know he needs someone to talk to sometimes, a meal, or a few bucks. But I can't offer anything without creating tension. My husband makes me feel guilty for helping him. Malichai isn't a stray dog—he's my brother. I think my husband feels bigger when others are down. It's sad.

He's jealous of how close I am with Malichai. I can feel it when we talk on the phone. He lurks around, pretending not to listen to a conversation that has nothing to do with him. Some days, I swear I just want to leave.

His family never treated me like one of them, not even after nearly fifteen years of being his wife. I've felt more like the help. I can count on one hand—minus a finger or two—how many times they visited us or even called. But when the money started rolling in, the phone started ringing more with family members who were suddenly interested in how he was doing, claiming they were "just thinking about him." Not about me or the kids. Just him. Now that the business is going belly up, I doubt they'll keep calling. He brags about how well-off they are, but back when we needed help, they were nowhere to be found. That's why we had to go to Malichai— the one he now treats like trash.

Of all my siblings, I was the one most affected by our dad getting locked up. I remember how good things were with him around. The house felt alive—swarming with people who listened to him talk as if he were some kind of prophet. Mama would gleam with pride the whole time. He treated us girls like princesses and his sons like princes. All eight of us would eat dinner together on the floor, sitting in a circle as we passed around Mama's nutritious dishes, African style, with the sounds of Bob Marley serenading us and incense burning. I felt royal and significant—like my life had meaning.

We were far from rich, but Mama's creativity made our home feel and look like a presidential suite. Most of the furniture came from dumpsters, thrift shops, or Goodwill. Daddy would sand and paint it until it gleamed like new. Mama sewed pillows, curtains, and other fabric from used bedding to bring color and life to every room. After Daddy splashed vibrant paint on the walls, our little three-bedroom house looked like something out of a magazine. I never felt poor. Daddy always said that being rich wasn't about how much money you had but how much love and honor you held in your heart. And by that measure, we were wealthy.

I try to explain how I lived to my husband, but he doesn't understand. He doesn't try. When I cry about my father being locked in a cell no bigger than a broom closet, he tells me, "At least he ain't dead," like that's supposed to comfort me. He shuts me down, ending the conversation. I wish I had someone who would listen to me. Someone who understood my pain—or at least tried to soothe it. But I don't. I'm the listener while everyone else talks.

I've listened to my husband tell his life stories so many times that I could ghostwrite his autobiography. He loves it when I listen to him, but he can't do the same for me. Talking about my past helps me get a clearer idea of my future and cope with the void left by my absent father. Even as a child, I knew who I was and what I wanted. I want that back. But I dare to share my past with him. He never seems interested in hearing it and usually changes the subject to a story about his past that I've heard a hundred times before.

I can't help but wonder if he even knows me—what I like, what

I need. He says he does, but I learned in a college writing class that it's better to *show* than to *tell*. Anyone can talk, but the proof is in a person's actions. I would love for him to take some kind of regard for me—to ask how I'm doing, how my day went, what my dreams are, and how he can help me accomplish them. He treats me like the only aspirations I have in life are cooking, cleaning, and watching our kids—and sometimes, someone else's too.

I wish I could share my secrets without fearing he'll throw them back in my face or turn a deaf ear to me. I wish I could show him my business plan without him picking it apart, feeding my fears. I wish I could tell a simple story without him interrupting me, blabbing about a similar experience of his. I wish he knew I have a voice that is dying to be heard. I wish they all knew.

You don't need a degree to understand that if someone isn't getting joy, pleasure, or support in a relationship, they will want out. That's where I am with my husband, and honestly, with my family, too. That's why I packed two bags a few weeks ago and hid them in the closet. I also purchased a plane ticket to Chicago but keep changing the flight dates every week. I don't know what I'd do there, but for some reason, it calls to me every day.

One day, if nothing changes, I'm gone. I'll hop on that plane and leave. I'll find fresh air to breathe and someone to listen to me. Start a new life. I think I deserve that. Actually, I *know* I do. It would be easier for me to leave if my husband cheated on me, physically abused me, or if we didn't have kids together. But that's not the case.

Is it selfish to want more than just loyalty and love? I don't think so. I need to exist, too. I'm a good person, but if I keep being ignored, I'm going to disappear. I'll become invisible to everyone who needs me but has used me, abused me, or taken me for granted.

Come to think of it...maybe I'll leave today.

4

SAHARA

"The Sellout"

I'm losing my mind—seriously—and that's not like me. Nobody's more mentally stable than I am. If I didn't know better, I'd say I'm on the verge of a nervous breakdown. But I don't believe in those; they're just overrated outbursts—emotions that people could control if they simply focus and take deep breaths.

So, let me take two deep breaths: quick inhale, slow exhale. And another. There. I feel better already.

I don't know what the fuck—oops, I mean hell. Dammit! I'm supposed to be working on not cursing. You can see how well that's going. John says it makes me look classless when I curse, and Lord knows I'm gonna need all the class I can get when I stand in front of those cameras while he announces his run for State Senator. No cursing—just breathing. *Ahh...better.*

Anyway, what I was trying to say is—I feel like there's a ticking time bomb lodged in my brain. I literally hear it. *Tick...tick...tick...* threatening to explode. Lately, I've been so irritable, and my chest stays tight. Sometimes, it feels like something is squeezing my chest, making it hard to breathe, and then lets go. It started two weeks ago when one of the girls accidentally bumped into me. *Tick...tick...tick.*

When my son, Michael, tapped me on the shoulder while I was deep in thought, startling me. *Tick…tick…tick.* When my caterer cancelled last minute for the Christmas Eve party I host every year—the party where John's announcing his candidacy—saying she had a "family emergency." Left me in a hole full of crap. *Tick…tick…tick.*

Then my sister Essence called and told me not to be mad when I see her at the party, but she wouldn't say why. *Tick…tick…tick.* With her, it could be anything, but I pray it's not anything that will damage me and John's image. I also pray it doesn't have anything to do with her and her husband, Dr. Lawrence McCall—John's friend, whom she married two weeks ago. God, I hope everything is okay between them. But whatever it is, why can't Essence just skip coming to the party or wait until after to stir up drama? That girl can be so selfish. She knows how important these parties are—they're more political than festive.

Then there was my sister, Ebony, calling me phony. Nothing stings like being called a sellout! *Tick…tick…tick.* I only called to check on her after I saw her get off the bus with a cast on her foot. I don't know why she's even riding the bus when she paid cash for a Benz. And what happened that she's wearing a cast? Another reason for my call was to make sure she received her invite. She was the only one who didn't RSVP, but that's just her: a rebel without reason and always mad. Such a tortured artist. She's probably mad because I ignored her last week, but it wasn't personal.

When I saw her getting off the bus, John and I were heading to lunch with a wealthy businessman and his wife, who could be potential campaign donors. At first, I didn't think she saw us. John gave me the look as if to say, *Not now.* So, I kept walking. I couldn't stop to say hi; I was on a business lunch, for God's sake. And honestly, she looked a mess. My sister used to be striking. Now she looks like a homeless person who just escaped a mental ward. The extra pounds she's packed on were stuffed into a dingy black jogging suit that had holes at the knees and bleach stains, and she was wearing a house shoe. Her afro was matted and full of lint, and she looked like she hadn't washed her face in weeks. She's been like this ever since her fiancé left her five years ago. She needs to get over it. He only used her for her money and fame. She couldn't see it back then, but once she finally realized it, that's when she started spiraling.

Then my oldest brother, Malichai, called, asking for three hundred dollars, never mind that I had just given him a hundred dollars the week before. I hate giving him money for his cracked-out girlfriend to smoke up or for him to buy dime bags. Honestly, the party would go much smoother if he and his junkie baby mama didn't show up this year. Too many high-profile guests will be there, and John already "suggested" I not invite him. I've thrown this party for five years straight, and he's only come to one. I didn't even send him an invite this year. Besides, he gets evicted so much that I wouldn't have known where to send it anyway.

Malichai asks for money like I print it in my basement or something. They all do! My family thinks I'm rich because of the way John and I live, and Malichai feels I owe him the world just because we're blood. Well, I don't owe him a damn thing! Sure, when Malichai had money, he gave freely to me and my siblings. But that was years ago when we were kids and unable to take care of ourselves. I paid for my own education. I could have taken his money to pay for school like Balanah and Kwame, but I chose to make my own path——one that didn't involve bloody drug money. Besides, my money isn't mine alone; it's mostly John's. My husband didn't have it easy either. He earned every dollar. And when it's hard to earn, it's hard to give. When I told Malichai I didn't have it, he hung up without so much as a goodbye. *Tick…tick…tick.*

But the biggest tick? That came about an hour ago when John texted me: *I might want a divorce, but don't go getting all upset because I'm not sure yet.*

How *formal* of him. The coward texted that to me. *Tick...tick...tick.* Divorce? Don't get upset? Easy for him to say—he owns everything: the house, the cars, the bank accounts. Everything we've accumulated over the five years we've been married is in his name. What the fuck? I'll give myself a pass on that one. Hell, I deserve two. What. The. Fuck.

This came out of nowhere and at the worst time. I was stuck in traffic when I got the text—just like I am now while running errands for him. I have to drop off his suits at the cleaners so he can look crisp for the numerous political events and parties he attends weekly, take lunch to his campaign volunteers who are pickier eaters than my toddler son, go to the grocery store to get something to cook for the kids, take my twins to cheerleading practice, and pick up Michael from tutoring. And he wants to hit me with *this*? He's tripping. And as tired as I am, I almost said, *bring it on!*

I called him three times, but he didn't answer. Finally, he picked up and immediately said he was sorry—claimed he didn't know what he was thinking. I almost believed it was stress from the campaign, which is heavy on both of us. But then...he mentioned there was another woman.

Tick...tick...tick.

A *white* woman.

Tick...tick...BOOM!

What. The. Fuck. It doesn't matter if she's white, Black, blue, or green. It's fucked up!

I've been a faithful wife for years. Even after all his "*slip-ups*", as he calls them, I stayed. I dropped out in my last year of law school when his biological clock started ticking, and he just *had* to have kids. First, the twins, Tiffany and Amber, then Michael, two years later. When they got old enough for me to go back to school, somehow it was never the right time. First, he was making partner and needed my support. Then he started a non-profit—one that he makes a killing off of with government funding, giving free legal services to the underprivileged. Whenever I mentioned wanting to finish law school, he would say there wasn't enough time for us both to be ambitious. And now? He's running for Senator. Fuck him and his white woman.

I've sacrificed so much for him. What the hell has he done for me except selfishly put himself first? I nearly lost myself trying to be who he needed. Maybe that's why the word "sellout" cuts so deep. I didn't see myself as selling out but rather compromising for my husband. The biggest compromise? Becoming a Republican like him. No—actually, it was putting a perm in the full, thick Afro I'd been growing since birth. That almost killed my mama, and my siblings shamed me as if I had bleached my skin. John insisted I perm my hair, saying I was too dark-skinned to sport an Afro in the corporate world and that my Afro perpetuated stereotypes that evoke fear. He also threw in that he preferred a straighter look.

When we met at the AU Center, he didn't mind my fro. But once he graduated, his Blackness became something he tried to hide. I started hot combing my hair, but that wasn't straight enough for John. And I got tired of feeling like my hair dictated my Blackness. The truth is, I get more respect with my straight hair. What's the big deal? I wasn't selling out; I was buying in.

I moved from the West Side of Atlanta to Buckhead. Most of our friends are white. My kids talk proper. Am I phony because of these things? I can't help it if we live in a white neighborhood and my kids go to white schools. People rub off on you, but my family doesn't see it that way. To them, I'm as phony as they come.

John said this side of town offered more opportunities for our family, and he's all about opportunities when it comes to our children. He wouldn't even let me name them, afraid I would choose names that were *too ethnic*. His reasoning? *"In America, your name is your bond. We have to give them names that will help them thrive in society, not be judged before being given a chance to show their true potential."* That sounded like bullshit to me, but I let him have his way.

There are some things John was right about, though. For instance, the schools here are better. It also didn't take John long to climb the ladder at work, making partner partly because he played golf with the senior partner's nephew. But I'm not stingy with the opportunities I've gained; I help my family out every chance I get.

I connected Essence with a reputable real estate investing firm, where she's thriving. John helped Malichai's girlfriend beat a bank robbery charge. I introduced Kwame to the sports agent who got him drafted into the NFL—because his daughter attends the same daycare as Michael. And Ebony? She's a mini-celebrity in Atlanta because of what I did for her. Her paintings—women hanging themselves, burning buildings—are a bit disturbing to me, but the white folks love them. I organized her first show, pulling out John's Rolodex and inviting everybody who was anybody, and she blew up almost overnight. Mama is practically living like a queen off the money I give her every month. Ebony, Essence, and Kwame make enough to help out, but do they chip in? Never. It's always my responsibility. And do I ever get a thank you from any of them? Of course not. Instead, I'm labeled as a phony and a sellout.

Every time there's a problem, who do they call? Me, the "phony." I'm the one who keeps everything together. When Mama and Balanah got arrested, I stepped up, too. I held the family down while Malichai sold drugs and got all the praise. I helped with homework, nursed them when they got sick, and cooked meals. Me, the "sellout."

They really lost it when I became a Christian. They blamed John and said he "brainwashed" me. He influenced me, not brainwashed me. I had my own experience going to church with him that day for the first time ever. Mama acted like Christianity was a cult. "You know what your daddy said about them Jesus freaks?" she asked when I broke the news to her. I didn't want to hear the answer, but she told me anyway. According to her, Jesus was just another tool of white supremacy. "Same Jesus lovers killed your ancestors," she said. "That ain't right, Sahara. What kind of religion believes in murder?"

To me, Jesus isn't a color—He's a Savior, love, and peace. Besides, everyone sees God in their own image. Scripture does say He had feet of brass, which sounds pretty Black to me. Maybe if the revolutionaries looked into that, they'd stop judging us Black Christians. You ready for the twist, though? Mama ended up converting, too. I was shocked when she became a Christian. I wonder what Daddy would say about *that*.

According to Mama, Daddy had an opinion about everything— a modern-day Solomon. In Mama's eyes, he was almost always right and wiser than any man walking the earth. I used to respect him; now I resent him. He left us in a mess. I didn't need a hero—I needed a dad. And I still do. No letters. No calls. We can't even visit him. It's like he never existed.

But on the West Side where I was raised, everyone acts like my daddy is a hero. Some of the local, black-owned restaurants even have his picture hanging on the walls alongside Malcolm, Martin, and Barack. I should feel proud, but I don't. John makes me feel ashamed. Before we walk into one of his dull office parties, he tells me, "Don't mention your...you know...dad. Too controversial." He didn't have to worry about that. I've been overshadowed by my father's legacy long enough. I just want to be seen as *me*, not as Akimbo Sedah's daughter.

When John said he was running for senator, the first thing he asked was if my dad would be a problem. At first, I felt insulted. My father's in prison, paying his debt to a white society. What the hell does my father have to do with John being a senator? Back in college, John used to name-drop him to gain political connections in the Black community while in law school. Now he's ashamed.

He doesn't know it, but I saw him the other day with Sir Zion, sitting in the back of his limo, probably discussing money. Sir Zion is the real phony and sellout. He got Malichai into the drug game, yet he's worried about my dad's name being a problem. Still, I get it. Campaigns get ugly. To answer his question, I just smiled and told him that I hoped my dad wouldn't be an issue. The last thing I need is the election bringing up my family's dirt.

Becoming a senator was John's lifelong dream, but after Obama won the election, he added becoming President of the United States as another one of his life goals. John's family breeds Black lawyers; his great-grandfather was even one. Now that John is running for senator, he's taking it up a notch. He sees himself in the White House, and I assume he would prefer a white woman to accompany him there instead of me, given the bullshit he just told me.

I don't know why he had to tell me she was white. Like the fact that she was white was the consolation prize for my humiliation. Was I supposed to pat him on the back? Congratulate him? *Tick…tick…tick.* Maybe he's just proud that this time, when he rolled in the mud, he came up white.

When I finally got off that purgatory of a highway, I found myself right back in more traffic. *Tick…tick…tick.* I'm sure I'll be late dropping off lunch to the volunteers, and I had half a mind to spit in their food. Those young white kids look at me like I'm the damn help—but who can blame them? Especially when John treats me like the help. His suit might just not make it to the cleaners today, and I'm tempted to leave those kids where they are. To hell with everybody. *Tick…tick…tick.*

Okay, I don't mean that. Let me take a deep breath. I can handle this shit…I mean, mess. *Another deep breath.* I've been through worse. I try to convince myself that John's just under a lot of stress and doesn't know how to handle it like I do. *Deep breath.* Everything is going to be fine. All I have to do is breathe and stay calm.

This isn't the first time he's threatened to leave me. The last time, it was about the fifteen pounds I gained after having Michael. Fifteen pounds! After that, I was a size 12. Where I'm from, that's a ten! But John didn't see it that way.

"Sweetie, you know what I like," he said, stroking my back. "I've always liked thinner women. It's just what I'm attracted to, and in our world, you can't be bigger than a six." I was a ten when I met him, but I got down to a six for the wedding and kept it off—until Michael.

"I understand you just had the baby," he said. "But it's been a year. I've been patient, but I'm starting to lose interest. I've even had thoughts of leaving."

What I should've said was, *"Fuck you and your interest,"* but instead, I just smiled and nodded like the perfect Black Stepford wife he molded me into. Maybe I *am* a sellout! *Tick…tick…tick.*

That squeezing in my chest started again when I tried calling John back, and he answered like I was his annoying intern. No hello. Just barking.

"Didn't I say we'd discuss this later? I'm in a meeting! Just disregard the damn text!" *Click.*

After the squeeze came more ticking. Then, a Range Rover cut me off, and I slammed my brakes so hard that I got whiplash and dropped my phone underneath the gas pedal. *Tick…tick…tick.* I leaned over to pick it up, and the car behind me laid on the horn for me to move up the lane. *Tick…tick…tick.*

Of all the days and times to repave the roads, they pick lunch hour on a Monday. I sat through three green lights before finally getting the chance to free myself from it. After retrieving my phone, I called John again. *I don't give a damn about his meeting; I need to talk to him.* But he sent me to voicemail. Then came his polished message, every word pronounced like he was trying not to sound Black. I'd watched him re-record that greeting a dozen times until it was perfect. *How do I sound now?* he would ask. What he really wanted to know was, *Can you tell I'm Black?*

My phone buzzes with another text. I know it's John. He's the only one who texts me when he could just pick up the damn phone and call. So fucking annoying.

Tick...tick...tick.

Breathe, Sahara. Breathe.

I glance at the message. Yep, it's John.

Instead of harassing me, focus on bringing my team lunch. I received a call saying you haven't arrived at the office yet. My volunteers need their lunch! Can you complete one simple task?

"Fuck you, Negro! I can complete plenty!" I shout out loud.

I was so busy reading the message that I missed the light again. Now, I'm stuck another round while the cars behind me honk like they want me dead, treating their horns like bullets. I can't take the noise. Suddenly, everything seems too loud. *Tick...tick...tock!* I finally lost it.

Next thing I know, I'm out of the car. My vision is blurred, hands flailing in the air, and my heart is pumping fast. My mouth is going a mile a minute. I'm talking so fast I bite my tongue a few times, spittle flying through the air like mist. I don't know what I'm saying. My chest is tight—so tight that it feels numb. Then I hear myself.

"Fuck! Son of a bitch!"

Balling up my fists, I storm towards the closest honking car and start kicking the driver's door. I feel something crack in my foot, but I keep going. The driver's yelling, but he doesn't get out. My chest gets even tighter, and I'm forgetting to breathe.

Wait a minute! Am I really having a nervous breakdown? How weak of me!

Then someone yanks me back. They grab my arm so hard that it feels like they're trying to rip it off. I snap—*tick...tick...tick*—and punch them in the face. It feels good, so I do it again. And again. Then I kick them. I don't even know who it is. I'm yelling, cursing, flailing. My limbs are out of control, mostly hitting air. *Tick...tick...tick.*

Then I fall—or at least I think I do. Could've been a billy club that knocked me down. Tears run down my cheeks. Wait. No, it's not tears. It's blood. I see the bright red color saturating my boring, white blouse that John insists I wear when I go to his office.

What the fuck? I'm bleeding.

Suddenly, I remember to breathe—but it's too late. I breathe anyway, snapping myself back into reality. I now realize I'm on the ground being handcuffed. And the person who I was beating on? It was a cop. Shit. I done fucked up now, but did he have to hit me with his billy club?

Tick…tick…tick.

5
EBONY
"The Crazy One"

I'm about to commit murder in less than an hour, and honestly, I don't have shit to lose. Just two weeks ago, I tried to kill myself. Tied a drop cord into a noose, put it around my neck, and jumped from my two-story catwalk—no hesitation. But apparently, I didn't die. The universe had other plans for me. I wasn't the one who needed to die. That was Kenton. And I can't wait to do it.

When I jumped, one of the metal pickets snapped, and I broke my foot instead. While lying there in pain, I had an epiphany: *kill that motherfucker!* Sure, I'll probably spend the rest of my life behind bars, but I don't give a fuck. Locked up in a slammer is better than spending a lifetime breathing the same air as the devil himself. If I'm lucky, the judge and jury will take it easy on me, considering Kenton's worthless ass raped my teenage daughter—repeatedly.

And let's be clear—this ain't no impulsive *"crime of passion."* I've thought this out all the way down to how many times I'm gonna shoot him. First, I'm shooting him in the dick. Then both knees. When he looks up, begging me to spare his life, I'm gonna blow his fucking brains out and then have a good laugh. I'll wait at least three minutes between each shot so he's tortured by the pain I'm going to inflict on him. When he finally drops, I'll kick him in the ribs and spit on what's left of his splattered head.

Oh, and I'm not gonna run either. I'll wait for the police and own my crime. I'm not like him. He never took accountability, but I know my baby didn't lie. I saw it in her eyes—the pain, the hatred where her innocence used to be.

They said there wasn't enough evidence, and because Zena refused to testify, he got off. I didn't blame her for not wanting to confess Kenton's filth in front of a jury of strangers. She would've had to experience the pain and humiliation of reliving the rape all over again. I didn't want that for my daughter. So, now I'm the judge. And as soon as I get off this bus and kill him, I'll be God. Then when I send his ass to hell, I'm gonna be the devil.

People keep staring at me. I can understand why—because I'm out here looking a hot mess. Limping around in a cast that feels like concrete, carrying a bag that clearly holds a gun. I didn't bother to comb my hair. I'm wearing the same raggedy housecoat I've worn all month with my pajamas underneath. My nappy Afro is lopsided, and my one house shoe on my free foot has a hole at the toe. I figure I'll be thrown in a holding cell for a while before they process me, so I dressed for comfort, not fashion.

Folks have been calling me crazy my whole life. I can't totally disagree with them, but I think they just don't understand. See, what they call crazy, I call brave. When I was young, I threw a can of black beans at a police officer's face so Mama could escape when she got caught stealing groceries. Then there's the time we got evicted by our Arab slumlord when I was twelve years old. I burned down the apartment because he refused to give Mama back the security deposit. I've always done the things that other people don't have the guts to do. And I definitely got the guts to do what I'm about to do to that disgusting bastard.

I can't live knowing what happened right under my roof. Zena was just thirteen when Kenton, my so-called fiancé at the time, violated her. For two years, she was being raped. I didn't see it. I didn't know. And I feel I failed as a parent at protecting her. But I will get revenge for my daughter, and although it's taken me five years to get to this point, the timing is perfect. Kenton just got married and recently had a baby girl. I also heard his photography company is booming. Seems like he's at the peak of his life, but I'm about to put an end to all of that—and I plan to make it as painful as possible for him.

Zena thinks she's the only victim, but I feel violated, too. I've been holding this secret for five years. She made me promise not to tell anyone, and back then, it seemed to be an easy secret to keep. I wasn't ready to let my family know what I unknowingly allowed to happen in my own home.

As mother and daughter, I believed we shared a bond so deep that I would be in tuned with her every emotion. But something happened over the years. My art started taking over. My work became my baby. And I lost my intuition. That made Zena an easy target for Kenton.

After he violated her, me and my daughter's relationship changed, but I didn't know why. I thought Zena was just going through that period of "smelling her ass" since she was now a teenager. We used to be best friends. She used to tell me everything. She would hold my hand, talk to me about her dreams, and even sleep in my bed some nights. Then it seemed like she became distant overnight, and I noticed a change in her behavior. After Kenton, she spiraled. She started drinking, stealing, smoking weed, and fighting in school so much that she got expelled and had to settle for getting a G.E.D. She even got arrested for stealing a car. She had so many plans for her future; my baby was really going to make something of her life. But Kenton stole her dreams when he robbed Zena of her virginity. She even lost her creativity and stopped drawing. She's a better artist than me. She inherited it from me, like I did from my father. I wonder what he would say if he knew what happened to his granddaughter. What would he think of Black men then?

Nobody in my family knows. I couldn't bring myself to tell them. To be honest, when she finally opened up to me, I wasn't ready to hear it. Not because I didn't believe her or because I didn't want to lose Kenton, but because it was too damn heavy. She told me the day before a big art show where my work was being featured at a popular gallery. Let's just say I never made it to the show that day or any other show after that. Haven't picked up a brush since. Her news shook my whole world, and it's still shaking. I punished myself for what my daughter endured up until the day I tied that cord around my neck and jumped. I used to be somebody. I worked out, attended private parties, and performed poetry at open mic nights. Now my fat ass lays around the house all day—drinking, eating, and plotting murder.

My siblings judge me enough. I don't need to give them anything else to add to their list. Sahara had the nerve to say to me one day, "Why'd you stop working, Ebony? All that trouble I went through to get your work noticed, and you throw it all away. Is this about Kenton? Move on already." She can kiss my ass. I called her a sellout the other day, and she damn near chocked on her own ego. She was livid. Then I saw her and her uppity husband about to go inside a restaurant, and they walked right past me like they didn't know me. Guess I'm bad for her image now that I ain't the hot artist she can brag about.

I never took criticism well and have no idea how I lasted as a working artist, but I managed. Yet, when it comes from family, it cuts deeper. There's so much pressure to be strong, especially because of who Daddy was back in the day. His warped legacy that Mama is always bragging about is almost impossible for us to live up to. He's still got a name in the streets, still got followers even while in prison. I wonder what having a cold-blooded killer as a daughter is going to do to his image. I know what they said when Malichai started dealing. Some of his zealous followers called us hypocrites, but if it wasn't for Malichai, we'd be worse off.

I'm not my daddy. And I can't keep pretending. My family coined me "the strong one," but I'm not. I never was. I just learned to save face. You can't ever have a weak moment when you're looked at as the strong one. But I've been broken for years. Mama can see through me—through all of us—but even she doesn't know the real source of my pain. I know how to hide it—just like Zena did. Besides, she would only blame me, and I already blame myself enough. I don't need to hear it from her, too.

None of them ever liked Kenton. They thought he was a freeloader. And I hate to admit it, but I used to be in love with him. I don't even know why. His ass came at me with that fake *"I really admire your dad"* line, claiming he was writing his thesis on my dad's teachings. It was all bullshit. But somehow, I let that bullshit make me feel important.

In my defense, I fell out of love with him long before Zena made her confession—not that it matters. When I kill Kenton today, that secret among others I've been keeping will be revealed. Starting with the biggest one: Sir Zion is Zena's father. I've carried the weight of that secret long enough. What happened to Zena didn't exactly happen to me—but it was close. My so-called godfather, my daddy's best friend, preyed on me when I was young and vulnerable. He didn't force himself on me physically, but he manipulated me. Mentally raped me. And I got pregnant with Zena. As far as I'm concerned, it's the same thing as being raped.

After I kill Kenton, I'm sure it's going to make news considering my local fame. My family will be shocked. And I'm sorry for the pain this'll cause them. At least they'll have something else to gossip about over Christmas dinner. That's one thing I won't miss—Sahara's phony holiday charades. Just because she married some big-shot lawyer, she expects us to play nice and fake our way through dinner to impress him and their bougie guests.

I wonder how my actions will affect her husband's reputation with talks of him running for Senate. The hell if I really care. I'm pretty sure Sahara will somehow make it about her—like she did when Malichai's cracked out girlfriend was suspected of robbing a bank. But I won't be there to see it. I can't keep up her image, daddy's image, and this strength I've been faking. All those walls fall today.

Sarah once told me during an argument that I'd never do anything to make a change like Daddy did. Well, she can shove that theory up her tight ass. Killing Kenton *will* change lives. His newborn daughter will never know him or be defiled by him. Hopefully, Zena will finally feel vindicated. As for me—well, I'll finally be free to a degree.

And when this is all over, I don't want no help from Sarah's husband or his legal buddies. This shit is all mine to deal with, and I'm gonna take my jail sentence in stride. Daddy's been in prison over twenty years for standing by what he believed. Maybe he'll understand. Maybe he'll even be proud. Now that Mama's found Jesus, I'm sure she won't approve of the way I got justice for my daughter. She might even disown me—but truthfully, I've already felt disowned for quite some time now. I wanted to tell Mama what happened so many times, but I just couldn't make myself do it. So the pain became mine and Zena's to carry alone.

Things got worse when Zena came out to me as a lesbian. Not because I'm homophobic, but because I blamed Kenton. After what he did, who could blame her for not trusting men? I don't even know how the family will handle it. Sarah's newfound religion is the worst kind—judgmental and cruel. The kind that damns beautiful souls to hell over who they love. What kind of faith is that?

The doctors told me after I had Zena, I wouldn't be able to have no more kids because of some disease in my fallopian tubes. They had to remove them both. I thanked God for Zena, assuming she would get married and give me some grandbabies. But now, I know that won't happen. And it's all Kenton's fault.

Unless Zena changes her mind about her sexuality or decides to have children through artificial insemination, my bloodline will stop with her. If I had known she'd be my only child, I wouldn't have had those two abortions. But I was only fifteen the first time I got pregnant and sixteen the second time. Too young to have children. I didn't want to upset Mama, and I didn't want to tarnish Daddy's name. But then, I had Zena at seventeen. So much for saving face.

The bus is coming to my stop, and my trigger finger is throbbing with anticipation. I wonder how he's going react when I walk up into his photography studio and aim my gun at him. Will he cry? Scream? Beg? I don't care. I just want to see him bleed. I've had plenty of practice shooting my gun. I went to a shooting range a few weeks ago and learned how to hit a winner real quick. The prosecution team will probably use that against me when I go to trial, but I don't care. Jail doesn't scare me. To be honest with you, this is the freest I've felt in a long time.

The bus stops. I throw my heavy bag over my shoulder and limp off like a crazed bag lady. Some people watch me out the corner of their eyes and others look away, avoiding eye contact with me all together. They're the least of my concerns. I'm focused.

As I get off the bus, my eyes lock on Kenton's studio that is only a few feet away. I would've driven my car if it hadn't gotten repossessed. I had the money to pay the note—just not the energy. Like I said, all I've been doing lately is eating, drinking, and plotting Kenton's death. I've been surviving off my prints, which still sell commercially. Two days ago, I transferred all my assets to Zena. I ain't wasting a dime on some slick, money-grubbing lawyer who will probably try to get me to plea insanity. I'll never do that. I'd rather rot in jail than deny myself and my daughter our due vengeance. I even set it up so Zena can profit off my art. Maybe I'll do one last piece—Kenton's headless body holding his severed dick. Or maybe I'll write a book. I'm sure people are gonna want to hear my story considering who my family is—especially my dad—and I'll tell it to publicly shame Kenton the way he should've been shamed years ago.

My foot is itching something awful inside the cast, but I don't stop to scratch it with the thin stick I carry around just for that purpose. I keep on limping. The closer I get to the door, the more anxious I become. My heart pounds. My stomach is knotted and gassy. But I keep on walking. Nothing is going to stop me.

His studio is in the heart of downtown Atlanta, surrounded by trendy shops, bars, and other artsy places. I heard his wife is wealthy and footed the bill for him. Lucky for her, she doesn't have any children old enough for him to rape yet. Or does she? The front doors are glass, with "Kenton Jones Studio" etched in black, gray, and white. I considered shooting my way through the doors but decide against it. The sound of gunfire would attract too much attention, and I don't need anything or anyone stopping me from blasting his kneecaps.

I see my reflection in the glass and hardly recognize myself. I'm one French fry away from a size sixteen, and my once smooth, copper complexion is blotchy. My lips are cracked. My eyes look swollen. I used to turn heads. I still do—but now it's for all the wrong reasons.

As I step inside the studio, the warm air rushes under my flannel pajamas. Elevator music is playing lightly through the speakers, and the scent of lavender from a candle burning on the receptionist's desk fills the air. My eyes quickly scan the room, and I notice photos of children he took. I start to wonder if those children's lives have also been affected by his sick-ass perversion.

A pale, skinny white girl with dyed blue-black hair is sitting behind the desk, flipping through an appointment book. So much for hiring more Black folks like he promised. She gives me a bewildered look when she sees me approaching. I'm still scanning the room as I walk up to her. I don't see anybody else, but I do see the door with his name on it. It's closed, but I know he's inside because I saw his silver BMW parked out front.

"Can I help you?" she asks, her hand inching toward the phone like she's ready to dial 911.

"Ebony Sedah, here to see Kenton Jones," I reply, name-dropping.

I'm hoping if she doesn't recognize my face that she's at least hip enough to know the name. From the expression on her face, she doesn't seem to recognize either.

"He's in a meeting," she says quickly, as if she has given that same excuse to many others. "Who should I tell him stopped by?" She gives me a strange look.

"Ebony Sedah," I repeat for the second time. "But you don't have to do that. I'll tell him myself. He's expecting me."

"Ma'am, you can't go in there," she yells to me, getting up from her desk as I walk past her.

I ignore her as I follow the black tiled floors to his door. Instead of knocking, I walk right in.

"I'm sorry, Mr. Jones. She just walked in. Do you want me to call the police?" Ms. Scary Ass says as she rushes through the door behind me.

He looks at me and grins like my presence is amusing him.

"No, it's fine," he replies, waving her off.

Photos cover his desk—kids, buildings, dogs. He's wearing a silk-looking black button-up shirt and khaki pants, just like I hoped. Easier to see the blood saturate them when I shoot his dick off. He quickly clicks off something on his computer. I wouldn't be surprised if he was looking at child porn. *Nasty bastard. His seconds are numbered.*

"Well, well, well... If it isn't the great Artist Ebony Sedah." He claps in a slow, sarcastic way. "Haven't you become the poster child of worthlessness. What a waste. What a waste it all was," he says, giggling.

His words don't bother me. I barely can hear him. He's so busy amusing himself that he doesn't notice as I unzip my bag and reach inside for my gun.

"How's Zena?" he adds, smug.

How dare he speak my daughter's name. Now, I'm even *more* ready for the kill.

The second I feel the handle, I pull the gun out. He freezes. My eye is twitching, my mind goes blank, and my body feels numb—like I'm no longer inside of it. He's quiet and trembling. Just the way I want him, but I need more—I need to see blood.

I aim the gun at his crotch. He sees the look in my eyes and knows I'm serious. He knows it's over for him. Jumping up from his chair, he raises his arms high in the air. I come around the desk, backing him into the corner. I'm so close to him that I can smell the coffee and stale cigarettes on his breath. Shooting him at close range was my plan. I put the nose of the gun against the little bulge in his pants and jab him with it.

"What the hell?! You crazy bi—"

Before he can finish his sentence, I close my eyes, pull the trigger, and exhale. Then prepare to do it five more times.

6
KWAME
"The Lazy One"

I think my wife is trying to kill me. Honestly, she's got a damn good reason—well, quite a few. For one, I ain't worked in over two years and have gained about sixty pounds. We ain't hurting financially, but I know she'd rather see me do more than lay around all day eating chips and chugging beers. On top of that, I treat her like a maid. She's so used to my demands that all I have to do is snap my fingers and she comes running. I ain't gotta do shit, and sometimes I feel justified in that given how hard I used to work. But the biggest reason of all? Lately, I've started hitting her. And as much as I hate to admit it…it feels good!

Maybe I watch too much TV, but I swear she's poisoning my food. The last three meals she brought me had me sick as a dog, stuck on the toilet for almost an hour with everything coming out both ends. When I came out of the bathroom, she was standing there with a strange look on her face—almost like she was surprised I was still breathing. Didn't even ask me if I was okay, and I know her ass heard me in there gagging and moaning. If I cared about life or death, I would stop eating her food, but I don't, so I continue to eat the shit. I told her I want hot wings tonight, and since I don't let her buy takeout anymore, she's gotta make them from scratch—fried extra crispy, made wet, and minus the poison. If I get sick again, she's gonna feel my hand—and not in a good way.

The first time I hit her, I was more shocked than she was. I'd called her to the living room three times before she came. She claimed not to hear me, but I wasn't buying it. I just wanted another beer, and this time, I wanted it to be frosty cold and not lukewarm like the last one she'd brought me earlier.

When she finally came in the living room, rolling her eyes and sucking her teeth, something in me snapped. I thought back over the course of our relationship, and before I knew it, I jumped up from the couch and smacked her across the face so hard it left her weave messy. I felt bad for a second, but she barely flinched. I was raised better, and my dad wouldn't be pleased with me. But the way she took it—like she *expected* it—made me feel empowered and like my reaction was justified. No, it's not the best excuse, but it's definitely a good explanation.

After that, I couldn't stop replaying the past, which has led to my resentment toward Tammy. I saw myself on the field, getting clobbered by burly dudes just to keep her dressed in Gucci, driving luxury cars, and laced in ice. I never cared about having all that. I just loved playing ball. But Tammy? She was all about the dollars. That one flashback had me asking myself: *what's she ever done for me?* Nothing but fuck me when I want it, and the sex ain't even that great. Then I married her, thinking she was carrying my child—turned out the kid wasn't even mine. When the baby came out looking nothing like me, she hit me with a weak-ass sorry. *Sorry my ass! We done already jumped the broom.* Now I'm raising somebody else's son. My family doesn't even know Lucas ain't mine. I should've left her ass, but she looked so damn helpless. And I didn't want a public divorce fucking up the endorsements I had coming my way.

At the end of the day, it was cheaper to keep her. All I ask for is three meals a day, a clean house, peace, and cold beer—and she got the nerve to roll her eyes at me? It's because of her that I'm in this situation now. So yeah, when she pisses me off, I hit her. Not often, but enough. I thought about going to anger management classes, but that means getting off the couch and admitting I'm a woman-beater. I ain't ready to do either.

I got hurt playing football two years ago. Even before the injury, I was breaking down. My body always ached. People don't realize how hard those hits are we take out there. Tammy sure didn't understand. Couldn't even get her to rub Icy Hot on me. She only came to my games for social appearances, box seats, and the free champagne. *Fucking Hollywood wife!*

When I mentioned retiring early and maybe doing commentary, she flipped.

"You a ballplayer, Kwame! You can't quit your passion," she said, holding her Fendi bag in one hand and the keys to her Benz in the other. "Commentators don't get paid like players. We'll have to downgrade our lifestyle, and all our friends will laugh at us. Baby, you're made of steel. Ain't nothing gonna happen to you. And if something does happen…well, you got that insurance package." She then patted me on the shoulder and left, probably to go shopping. Didn't even see the desperation in my eyes.

The truth is, I was thinking about quitting because of guilt. Nobody knows Sir Zion paid me to throw a game. Cost my team a Super Bowl spot. I thought I'd get a chance to make it right, but I got injured shortly after. I was a rising star, and if I'd waited my turn, I would've had more than the pocket change Sir Zion gave me. But no! I was trying to keep up with the other players, buying shit for me and Tammy that we didn't need just so we could fit in.

I'm sure Tammy has considered divorcing me now that I'm viewed as a washed-up athlete, but we ain't been married long enough for her to get alimony, and since Lucas ain't mine, no child support either. In three years, she could attempt to collect alimony, but by then, I'll be broke and her ass won't get a dime. Where's she gonna go anyway? Her family doesn't want anything to do with her, and she's too snooty to go back to the stripper pole I met her on. So, for now, she stays. And while she's here, she better be at my beck and call—minus the attitude—or she'll catch the back of my hand. She owes me. I paid enough already. I'm not the same Kwame she met two years ago. Hell, I barely recognize myself sometimes.

I should've taken that sports commentator job and told Sir Zion to go fuck himself. It wouldn't have paid as much as playing ball, but at least I'd still have some dignity. It would've also been better than what I'm doing now, which is virtually nothing but existing. But it's too late. Nobody cares what a fat has-been thinks. So, I sit here, flipping through games, commenting to myself. That's the closest I'll get.

My family thinks I'm wasting my life. They hate that I've gained weight and don't do anything but watch college ball and old NFL reruns on TV all day. Hell, I did the same shit when I was younger. Right now, I'm spread out on the couch, the heat from the leather cushions creating a nice contrast with the slight chill coming from the ceiling fan spinning on low. My body is the perfect temperature underneath the plush blanket I'm wrapped in. I'm comfortable as hell and ain't got no reason to move except if I have to piss. And I wish Tammy could do that for me.

I flip back to the college ball channel, prop my head on a toss pillow, and curl up more under the covers. I would ask Tammy for another beer, but it makes me have to go to the bathroom too much, and I don't feel like getting up. So, I'll just snack on the last of the Doritos she brought me earlier.

Balanah had the nerve to call me lazy for turning down some office job Sahara found. I always told myself if I ain't playing ball, I ain't doing nothing at all. I don't know why they're so concerned about how I spend my time. It ain't like I'm asking them for shit. I ain't got my hand out like Malichai, and Sahara ain't controlling my life like she does everybody else. So, they can just lay off me.

True enough, this ain't how I pictured my life after getting drafted. I thought I'd play a few seasons, snag major endorsements, then move into commentary or scouting. But shit never works out the way you plan. Hell, I never even thought I'd make it to the NFL—until I did. Even after much planning, sometimes things go left. I ain't too worried, though. I've still got good money coming in from my insurance and old endorsements—cereals, sports drinks, shit like that. So, if I'm gonna live like a fat cat, I choose to be like Garfield and lay around all day. Maybe I'll have Tammy make me lasagna tonight instead of wings.

Mama always tells me, "Your daddy didn't have a lazy bone in his body. Never felt sorry for himself either." That's why I barely talk to her—or any of them. I stay secluded in my little nest. Only seeing them during the holidays, if that. Okay, so my father wasn't lazy, but I bet he's somewhere lying on a cot right now in prison. Ain't much else to do in the pen. So, I guess we're similar after all. I don't like hearing all that shit about my dad, though. It gets me depressed. If a man with his vision ended up behind bars, what hope is there for the rest of us? This couch is the safest place I've got.

Now that I think about it, I haven't left the house in two months. Two whole months without sunlight. Damn, maybe I'm a vampire now. Then again, I'd probably starve to death—unless someone came and leaned over this couch for me to bite and suck their blood. But two months ain't that bad. We just moved in two months ago. I'm still adjusting...getting used to the place. Shit, who am I kidding? I'm voluntarily couch-ridden.

I like this house. Always have. Malichai and his girl used to rent it years ago. When it went up for sale, I bought it immediately. I guess it was because of the way it made me feel. It gave me hope back then.

When I'd visit him here, I started believing I could make it big. Maybe all that dreaming paid off because I got to where I wanted to be. I bought the house hoping it'd bring me back to that mindset, but so far, I don't think it's working. It still feels good to be in a familiar place, though—a place that reminds me of my happier, more hopeful self.

I think Malichai's salty because I bought this place. He won't answer my calls, and he's the only one who ain't been by here to see me. He should be honored, not upset with me. And if he would let me explain why I chose it, he'd get it. Of course, Essence is pissed at me. When I told her I was looking to buy a new house because I wanted to downgrade, she assumed I'd use her since she's top dog at that bougie real estate firm. But I went with somebody else. Her ass needs to know how it feels when somebody tells her no for once. She's always saying no to everybody else. Now she ain't talking to me, but I don't care. It's been peaceful not having her blow up my phone telling me to get up and go find a life. Essence needs to learn to give in order to receive. I hope I taught her that lesson. If not, maybe someone else will.

Mama didn't raise us to be spoiled and self-centered, but somehow, that's how Essence turned out. Then again, she didn't raise me to be a woman-beater either...and look at me now. She didn't raise Ebony to be a tortured artist or Sahara to be a phony. She didn't raise Malichai to be a drug dealer or Balanah to be such a damn push over. Yet, we turned out this way. I wonder what my father would say about us. Mama tried to mold us into his vision of what a true Black man's kids should be—confident, respectful, honorable leaders for the next generation. But I don't think any of us lived up to that. I know I haven't.

Could I change? Maybe. But I feel too stuck in my ways now. I do get scared thinking about the future, but I just tell myself there's no use fearing tomorrow when I'm still trying to survive today. I'll deal with tomorrow when it comes.

Until then, I'm gonna continue to be me. If Tammy don't like it, she can leave. I don't mind being alone. As long as I got my 72-inch flat screen showing ball games, a cooler full of ice-cold Heinekens, and this leather couch, I'll be alright. Speaking of which, where the hell is Tammy? She knows I like lunch at noon sharp. I swear that girl likes to get slapped.

7

ESSENCE
"The Selfish One"

U gh, I hate when people ask me for money—especially when I don't have it. It feels like getting a Pap smear or a root canal. I can't stand it! Folks love to say I'm selfish or stingy, but I'm not. I prefer the term *financially possessive*.

Beggars, beggars everywhere! That's why I hate walking through Woodruff Park—it's like a playground for bums. "You got a dollar?" "Can you spare fifty cents?" "Please, ma'am, I'm hungry." Hell no! I don't got shit for your funky ass. And newsflash: everybody in America is hungry, whether they eat or not. Sometimes I flip it on them. Before they can ask me for change, I hit them first—"You got a dollar?" Ha! You should see the looks on their faces. Even they don't like being asked for money.

And just when I get past them, I have to dodge the damn Salvation Army. I can't stand them either. This time of year, they're unavoidable—dressed in their dingy Santa suits while standing outside grocery stores, on street corners, and even in front of my favorite consignment boutique that I'm about to walk into. All I want is to sell this damn wedding dress, but I have to hear that damn bell. And they ring it extra loud when I walk by, like they're trying to shame me into donating. *Ring! Ring! Ring!*

Then there's my broke-ass siblings, Malichai and Balanah. Always calling, always needing something. Honestly, I don't even know why they bother. They already know what I'm going to say: *I don't got it* or *I can't do it.* And I really don't got it. I haven't sold a house in months! Just because I have a pretty nice savings doesn't mean I have money to give away. Hell, I work hard, and if I want to enjoy a spa day or buy myself a nice pair of shoes, I'm going to do it.

Now, if they were disabled or sick, maybe I'd feel differently. But they're able-bodied. Balanah needs to lower her standards and accept that she has to start from the bottom, regardless of her degree. Malichai needs to raise his because raking leaves and selling junk don't count as real jobs. And he needs to quit smoking weed so he can pass a piss test. Shit, I worked at McDonald's, as a mall janitor, and at a daycare center. If I did whatever I had to do to stay afloat, they can, too.

And now Balanah's mad because I won't babysit for her this afternoon. Girl, please. I got a date. Yeah, I used to work at a daycare center, but watching kids isn't my idea of fun—especially not Zach, Malichai's wild-ass son. Zach has been at her house for over two weeks now. She needs to call his dad instead of calling me. Kids are work; that's why I don't have any. They assume that since I don't have children, I have free time on my hands. The truth is, I don't have children because I *don't* have the time.

Truth is, all that free time helped me get the good job I have now—that along with my determination. I'm a realtor at one of the best firms in Atlanta. The houses pretty much sell themselves. All I have to do is show up looking good in my Cadillac STS, but given the current state of the housing market, I haven't sold shit. I've got the same subprime loan on my loft as everyone else, and my car note is damn near as much as my mortgage. If I don't close a deal soon, I'm going down with the rest of 'em.

I guess that's why I married Dr. Lawrence McCall. Desperation. Though the market is down, the firm still gets clients, but they're all white and don't come to my desk. Maybe it's my natural hair or chocolate skin. I know the company hired me to be the token Black realtor—the one every Black person preferred to deal with—and I was fine with that because Black money ruled Atlanta. Because of that, I dominated the firm. But now? Everyone's foreclosing. No clients. Nothing.

Then Sir Zion comes into my office, asking me to find him a house. I'm desperate, but I'm not that damn desperate. I don't care if he's my godfather—he makes my skin crawl. And I don't care where his money came from; I want no part of it. So, I turn his ass down quick, but that leaves me with no clients once again.

Which brings me to Kwame. I want to kick my brother's ass right now. I'm one sale away from joining the Million Dollar Club, and he went with another realtor. That's why I'm not talking to him now. He knew I needed that commission. What a fucking asshole!

Sometimes I think my siblings are jealous of me because I don't try to live up to the standards set by my father, the great Akimbo Sedah. I make my own choices. If I want something, I go for it. If I don't want to do something, I say no—and I don't care who doesn't like it. That kind of freedom has taken me far in life. I'm relentlessly ambitious, steadfast, and about my business.

They call me selfish, but I've always had their backs. Like when Sahara's trifling husband's side chick slashed her tires. I tracked that heifer down and wore her ass out like she stole something. When Kwame got cut with a razor by a stalker? I beat her down so bad that she left athletes alone for good. And when I found Meka wandering the streets all cracked out? I had a client with me at the time, but I didn't care what they thought. I put my nephew's mother in my car, took her home, cleaned her up, fed her, and called my brother to come and get her stank ass. I'm down for my family. Just don't ask me for money or to babysit. I draw the line there.

I roll my eyes at the perverted Santa ringing the bell and staring at my ass. *Gross!* As soon as I enter the boutique, I spot at least five things I want right off. I hope I get a good offer for this wedding dress—a top-of-the-line Vera Wang. I looked amazing in it when I walked down the aisle. I drop it on the counter. The clerk looks at the tag and then back at me like she's about to lowball me.

"I can't sell this dress for more than eight hundred dollars," she says.

"But I paid three times that!"

"Ma'am, this is a consignment boutique. People come here for deals, not to pay retail prices. Don't you like the prices when you shop here?" she says, rolling her eyes and handing it back.

"Come on. What about fifteen hundred?"

"Eleven hundred. That's the best I can do."

It's a deal. I leave the dress with her and start shopping. I'm buying something for the date I have tonight. I can't wait. I landed myself a sexy man in uniform—a cop. Yes, I had a wedding two weeks ago, and now I'm going on a date. Like I said, if I don't want to do something, I say no. That's what I should've said to Dr. Lawrence McCall when he proposed—*No.*

I don't like feeling misled. I'm nobody's fool. Don't offer me the world, then on the honeymoon flip the script and hand me the bitter truth and a crooked penis to boot. He done lost his mind! This is my third marriage, and whoever said "third time's a charm" didn't know what the hell they were talking about. After my second wedding, my siblings started calling me the runaway bride. But I didn't run—I walked away. My first marriage? I was too young. The second? He lied about his age. Said he was thirty-one, like me, but was really twenty-one. What the hell can I do with a 21-year-old? Both were broke anyway. Cute, but broke.

Then there's Dr. Lawrence McCall. I was introduced to him by my sister, Sahara. She's going to be pissed when I show up to her snooty Christmas Eve party with Marco instead of my husband—well, soon-to-be ex-husband. She and her husband paid for half of my extravagant wedding. Dr. McCall is a friend of John's, her husband. Their families go way back. Honestly, I think they only introduced us for political and social gain. He probably just wanted campaign donations. Sahara should have told him I was a risk given my track record. Maybe she thought I'd stick it out this time because of his status—and maybe I did, too. With the market the way it is, I needed some financial security before I lost everything. I figured that being his wife would help me make some good connections with all the rich people he knew. You know, sell a few million-dollar properties, climb the ladder, and bust through that glass ceiling by starting my own firm one day. But that wasn't the case.

He comes from a wealthy family, but apparently, that doesn't pay the bills. Neither does his expensive medical degree. What a waste. When I pictured being a doctor's wife, I imagined a condo in Aspen, weekend vacations at the beach house, and spa days. What I got was bad credit, student loans, and what he called his "ten-year plan." On our honeymoon, he told me, "Essence, in ten years, most of my loans will be paid down. Then we can put a down payment on your dream house and start living." Translation: he wanted to move into my loft. Um…I don't think so.

Worse than that, I might get garnished for all the damn loans he took out to put himself through school. If your rich family can't put you through med school, what good are they? I'm not about to foot the bill. Ten years? Hell, I only planned to stay married to him long enough to qualify for spousal support—and that isn't ten years in Georgia.

"When I'm done with my residency, I'll start making better money," he said. *Residency? What the hell is that?* I soon found out it's something like an internship for doctors. They work you like a dog and pay you like dog shit. How misleading of him! He should've introduced himself as Resident McCall, not *Doctor*, considering the big difference in pay. Residents should have to wear off-white coats so we common folk don't get bamboozled. Hell, give 'em blue coats. He's a con artist as far as I'm concerned. And who the hell would stay with a con artist? Not me.

And don't get me started on his snooty-ass family. They treated me like some kind of fucking case study, talking about my dad like he was some terrorist and my family were refugees.

"How many of you are there?" his mother asked like she was counting sheep. When I told her six, she turned up her nose and replied, "Oh…all by the same woman?" Of course. My dad didn't get down like that. Then one of his brothers said, "I heard he had two other sons by different women and a wife in another state," as if I weren't standing there. Gossiping clowns. They didn't know what they were talking about. For the record, my sisters and brothers are my dad's only children, and my mother is the only wife he has ever had.

They acted like I was some sort of charity case. His father bragged about how his great-grandfather passed for white to get ahead and left them land in Connecticut. He boasted about owning beachfront property and a slew of profitable vineyards in California. "Taking on this family name will finally give you something to be proud of. I hope you're worth it," he said while looking at me, but he was really talking to Lawrence. I wanted to punch him in his pointy-ass nose. And Lawrence just smiled like his dad was right. They really thought they were saving me. I'm not denouncing my father's name for nobody. My dad may not have been rich, but he made a difference—by encouraging people and leading by example, not passing for white. That's not pride—that's cowardice.

Besides his unbearable family, Dr. McCall—sorry, *Resident* McCall—was boring as hell. Worked my last damn nerve. And with that breath? He should've been a dentist. Gross. Maybe it was his news of being broke, or maybe I finally saw him for who he really was. Either way, the man repulsed me. On our honeymoon night, he gave me this sappy look, held my hand, and said, "Tonight is going to be special, my love." Ew. Sounded like a Hallmark card. He was too soft for my liking—not just his personality, but physically. Sweaty palms, soft hands—ugh. His voice was even soft. Put some bass in your voice for crying out loud. He didn't have to sound like Barry White, but damn—at least better than Mike Tyson.

Then I saw him naked...Lawd. His toes pointed downward like a ballerina whenever he was lying down. Looked like he was ready to jump up and do a twirl. His knees buckled like he had arthritis, and he couldn't stretch his legs out. Every time he moved, something cracked like he needed some WD-40. Who did I marry? The Tin Man? I didn't notice all of this shit about him before. The credit cards he threw in my face must've blinded me to his imperfections, and had he not maxed them out buying things for me, I'd still be blind. But now? *Harpo, I sees the light.* And it's too bright. I never liked solar eclipses, so I didn't stay to watch. I left that night. Most marriages are business deals nowadays anyway, so I don't feel bad backing out. He'll find someone else. She'll never be me—but hell, I'm fabulous, and that's hard to find.

It was slick the way I left Lawrence in that hotel room with a hard-on. The second I knew that it wasn't going to work, I planned my exit. I didn't want to outright tell him to his face that I wanted a divorce, though. He might've snapped and tried to choke me out. Not that he seemed the type, but you never know. Then again, with those soft, sweaty hands, I doubt he could've gotten a grip on my neck.

"I got something special for you," I told him.

Of course, he thought I meant sexually, and his small dick quickly swelled to a small-medium.

I forced myself to kiss his cold, wet lips and whispered, "It's in the car. Give me a minute."

That threw him off.

"Just wait until tomorrow. Tonight's too special. I don't want you to go anywhere," he insisted, pulling me closer to him.

Pouting, I told him the night wouldn't be as special without it. Then I pulled on my pants, threw on my shirt, and grabbed my purse. "Just be patient."

I flashed him a flirty smile, and after another kiss on the lips, he gave in. The fool never even asked me what the surprise was. I blew him a kiss and was out of there so fast my head spun. I went straight to his place—still had a key from when we were dating. Unfortunately, he had a copy of mine, too. I packed up what I considered my share of the wedding gifts, hit the highway, and called a locksmith to change my locks before Lawrence showed up at my door in a rage, trying to get in.

I pulled all that off in under an hour, locks included. When Lawrence started blowing up my phone, I finally answered and told him it wasn't going to work. He cursed me out something proper: "You selfish whore! You cold-hearted bitch! Do you know what I went through to get my family's blessings to marry your nappy-headed self?!" He started making threats until I reminded him that I had brothers who wouldn't hesitate to whoop his ass if he touched me. He was scared of them the way white folks are scared of Black folks, even though he's Black himself.

He still came to my place and tried to use his key.

"I want my money back, you money-grubbing wench! I maxed out my cards on you, and my parents spent a fortune on our wedding! You've shamed my family! I knew you were just jealous! Dark-skinned people always have problems with light-skinned people!"

Jealous? Of him? Please. Light-skinned brothers haven't had any real play since the '80s, and I didn't tell him to max out his credit cards—he was just trying to show off. He sold me an image he couldn't afford, so now he's stuck with the debt. And his parents were the ones who insisted on the extravagant wedding to impress their family and friends, so they were supposed to cover the costs.

He stood outside my door yelling for so long that I had to call the police. And that's how I met Marco. Isn't that ironic? I met the man of my dreams on my honeymoon night. When Marco showed up, Lawrence tried to intimidate him with his posh accent and "high society" connections.

"This woman has stolen from me in more ways than one, and you need not interfere! My father is properly acquainted with every police chief in this county, and I'll have your badge. So, I suggest you go write some tickets or something," Lawrence said to Marco, shooing him away as if he were insignificant.

Unmoved by Lawrence's threats, Marco didn't budge. "Actually, is that your silver Lexus parked out front, sir?"

"Yeah, why?" Lawrence said with pride.

"Well, I'll have to write you a ticket for being parked in front of a fire hydrant, but first…" He cracked his knuckles. "…you got to go."

He twisted Lawrence's arm behind his back so fast I thought it might pop off. Lawrence screamed like a little punk, still verbally threatening him using his father's name. Marco roughed him up just enough to make a point; he slammed him against the wall and then pushed him into the metal stair railing, each time apologizing like it was an accident. By the time Lawrence finally reached his car, he was almost in tears. And Marco still gave him a ticket for being illegally parked. Ha!

After Lawrence drove off, Marco looked at me and smirked. "I hope you didn't really steal from him."

I shook my head.

"What the hell were you doing with a guy like that anyway?" he asked, then flashed a smile before adding, "I don't know you from Adam, but he doesn't seem like your type."

"It's a long story. But if you've got time, maybe you can come up, and I'll tell you all about it," I replied flirtatiously.

Lucky for me, he had time. We kicked it in my loft for almost two hours—and didn't mention Lawrence's corny ass once. I even invited Marco to Sahara's Christmas Eve party. I know I'm moving fast, but as I've already mentioned, I'm ambitious. When I see something I want, I don't waste any time getting it. He didn't say for sure if he'd come, which annoyed me a little, but I have a good feeling he will. He stayed until he got a call on his radio, and we exchanged numbers before he left. I can't wait to see his sexy ass again tonight.

Marco is *movie star* fine. Think Denzel Washington in *Training Day*—same swagger. That uniform hugged every muscle, and his skin looked like it had been dipped in melted Hershey's chocolate. His jawline was broad and strong, perfectly chiseled to the symmetry of his V-shaped face, and he looked like he worked out for a living. If he looked that good *in* uniform, I can only imagine what he looks like *out* of it. Maybe I'll find out tonight. Who knows? *Whew.* I'm getting flustered just thinking about him. I've never had a man that fine. Real-life men don't usually come that sexy, only in the movies. But Marco is real.

I know cops don't make a lot of money, but I'm not thinking about that right now. If I'm lucky, maybe he's one of those crooked ones—the kind that takes drug money and backdoor payoffs. He *did* rough Lawrence up like he didn't care about the consequences. He definitely has that *I don't give a fuck* attitude. Ooh, I hope that's the case. Please, please, please let him be a dirty cop. Damn, now I'm begging.

I can almost hear Mama's voice: *Be careful what you wish for, Essence.*

I feel a chill, but I shake it off, cross my fingers, and kiss the sky in gratitude anyway.

8
MALICHAI
"The Job Offer"

If there's one thing I'm glad I've held onto over the years, it's my old box Chevy. I kept her on ice while I played with Benzes, Lexuses, Porsches, and whatnot, but you always go back to your roots when shit gets tough. That old faithful lady you thought wasn't good enough—until you need her and realize her worth. Only problem is, now she won't start.

I pump the gas and crank her for the third time—still nothing but choking sounds. It can't be the oil 'cause I changed it two weeks ago. The starter's good, too; I replaced it last year. But with how often I've been driving on empty lately, it might be the fuel pump. Damn, I hope not. I can't afford that repair, and if I get evicted from this hotel, she'll be left in the parking lot until they tow her away. That would be the end of her for sure because I won't be able to afford the impound fees either.

"Come on, girl," I whisper.

I try again. This time, I'm gentle on the gas. She sputters, coughs, then—bingo!

"Thank you, God," I say as I swerve out of the parking lot to go make some money.

It's early—about 6:15 a.m. I love this time of day because there's a calm in the air that gives me hope for a better tomorrow. The streets are quiet, and the birds are singing. It makes me think if they have something to sing about, maybe I do, too.

I come to a red light and notice I'm the only car on the road. An old man shuffles across the street, hunched over and walking like he's stepping on hot coals. Watching him makes me wonder if he used to walk tall like I do—upright and effortlessly. Maybe age has bent him, or maybe it was years of heavy burdens. I'll place my bet on the burdens. Hell, I'm already in the early stages of walking the same way. I don't stand as upright as I used to; I can't help it. I got some heavy shit weighing me down. Sometimes my chest hurts like I'm bench-pressing my problems. All I can do is pray for the strength to stand tall again—and stay that way.

It's Monday—the hustler's day. The early bird gets the worm, and I'm on the hunt for one fat enough to feed all my bills. I need about five hundred dollars—enough to keep from getting evicted, pay my cell phone bill, and fill up my tank so I can get around to do all this shit again next week. I also gotta find Meka. Still no sign of her, and the images I keep pushing out of my head—her lifeless, cracked out in a dumpster somewhere—are eating at me. God, I hope I'm wrong.

I shake away the horrible image and bust a left on Glenwood Road to try to find some money. I consider myself an entrepreneur. I don't get no respect for it, but it's what I am. I hustle every day from sun up to sun down—honest hustle, too. On Mondays, I pick up cans. Mostly beer cans. One full contractor's bag brings at least thirty dollars. It adds up. People don't realize how much you can make recycling metal. Mondays are best because folks blow their Friday checks on six-packs and keep drinking through Sunday. I know the best spots to find these cans—in park bushes, behind nightclubs, and along highway shoulders. I just gotta beat the garbage men and jailhouse cleanup crews to the punch.

Glenwood Park is my first stop. Folks hang out there on the weekends, getting drunk and high. Hell, if I could make money collecting blunt roaches, I'd be rich from all the ones I see mixed in with the beer cans. But that would be too easy, and nothing ever comes easy for me.

When I ain't hunting for cans, I'm searching through folks' trash for scrap metal. Yep, I ain't too damn proud to dumpster dive to support my family. I even called the county for trash pickup schedules so I can beat the trashmen to the gold. I find old desks, metal bed frames, and filing cabinets—especially when folks are updating their home offices or redecorating. I pulled the back seats out of my Chevy to make room, but sometimes, I still have to leave some stuff behind. What doesn't fit in the back is crammed into the trunk. Sometimes the items stick out so far that it gives the cops a reason to pull me over, as if they needed one anyway.

On the weekends, I rake leaves. It's hard competing with them damn Mexicans, so I lower my prices to stay in the game—twenty-five bucks for the whole yard, front and back. Some folks still try to Jew me down from that. It's like they smell the desperation on me, and I usually end up doing the work for fifteen. Shit, I ain't in no place where I can turn down money. I make up the difference detailing cars, which is something I actually enjoy doing. I don't stop shining the rims until I see my reflection in them, and the windows are streak-free. I vacuum obsessively, Armor All the dash, and spritz the interior with my own special car spray. All that in under thirty minutes. I only charge thirty-five dollars to clean inside and out. On good days, I'll do at least five cars. On slow days, like I had all last week, maybe two, if that.

If I had my way, I would be running a business that isn't so mobile and doesn't pay like dog shit. But for now, this is what I've got. And it pisses me off when folks act like I ain't trying—like this isn't real work. It is. I work so hard that my feet throb and my fingers ache by the end of the day. I can barely bend over without a sharp pain shooting from my tailbone up to the top of my spine. I need to get that checked out. If I end up bedridden, who's gonna take care of us then?

When I pull into the park, it's empty. Perfect. The kids are in school, and the street hustlers are still sleeping off their weekends. I park, grab a trash bag from the passenger seat, and pray I fill it before I leave. Hunting for cans feels like a treasure hunt—aluminum is my gold.

I put on gloves and pop the top of the first trash can filled with all kinds of nasty shit—condoms, bloody tissues, tampons, and other foul-smelling wet objects. But I do find a few scratch-off tickets. I always keep them. One time, I found an unclaimed ticket worth two hundred and fifty dollars. Hasn't happened since, but I keep hoping I'll be lucky like that again. I pocket the ticket and continue searching through the trash. I used to feel ashamed, but not anymore. Passersby look at me like I'm a bum. Truth is, I'm only a few bucks away from being one.

I come across crack pipes and empty baggies—triggers from a life I left behind five years ago. Sometimes the urge creeps up to go back to making my money the easy way, but then I think about my son, Meka, and the mess I'm dealing with now. I've cursed myself enough. Returning to that lifestyle might kill one of us, and that's not something I'm willing to risk. My hustle now is cans, not dope. I find over a dozen crushed cans in one bin and feel hopeful. I ain't even hit the bushes yet.

A rat jumps out of the next trash can I open and nearly gives me a heart attack. It had white streaks in its dark grey fur—an old rat— and jumped like a damn rabbit. Shit, I didn't even know rats could jump. I've dealt with possums before, but never airborne rats. After that, I kick over the next few cans, so if there are any rodents inside, they have a chance to escape before I start rummaging through the trash. By the last can, my bag is almost a quarter full. That's a good start. Now it's time to hit the ghetto jungle—the bushes and woods.

Sometimes I feel like a Black, hood version of Tarzan walking through these woods. I got bit by a damn fox out here—yep, a fox. Folks look at me like I'm crazy when I tell them, like I said a lion or something attacked me. You'd think they never heard of a fox. It barely got me, just nipped at the hem of my pants before I kicked it off and sent it flying halfway across the woods. I was about to squash that little bastard like one of those cockroaches in our hotel, but it got away.

The other day, a damn pit bull came at me outta nowhere and bit the hell out of my hand. It looked like one of those fighting dogs—probably escaped from some busted-up ring. I had to get seven stitches, but I was lucky it wasn't rabid. I was right back in the woods the next week, hunting cans with my hand wrapped in gauze.

If I ain't dealing with wild animals, it's wild Negroes trying to rob me for the little change I got. But I know how to deal with them, too. I carry a switchblade in my boot for the wild Negroes, mace for the pits, and a pellet gun in my waistband. The only thing I used so far is the pellet gun, and that was on a squirrel. Not 'cause I was in danger. I was bored and wanted to test my aim. Hit him right in the head. Dropped him like a rock. I can't stand squirrels anyway— annoying-ass creatures.

Today, I hit the jackpot. There are cans everywhere—littered on the dirt and hay like shiny coins. I start picking them up like I'm harvesting crops, clearing the entire area as I kick up leaves and turn over rocks to make sure I ain't miss any. Then I throw the bulging black sack over my shoulder like ghetto Santa Claus and head back to my Chevy, planning to check the dumpsters behind the bars down the road.

As I step out of the woods, I notice a white Ford pickup truck parked behind my vehicle, blocking me in. I'm not in the mood for no bullshit. Out here, folks try you just because they can and for no other reason. Usually, when they recognize who I am—or should I say, who I was—they back off. They'll say things like, "My bad, Mal…didn't know it was you. How you holding up, man?" Or worse, "Keep your head up, man," or the tempting, "I know a dude selling heavy. Maybe y'all can link."

I drop the bag on the ground, reach into my boot for my switchblade, then pick the bag back up and throw it over my shoulder like a dead body as I walk towards my car. I got that *"don't fuck with me"* expression on my face, and I'm ready to fuck a man up if I have to. I can't see who it is through the tinted windows, but the closer I get, I notice movement inside. Then the door opens. I drop my bag and flip open my blade, ready to slice somebody up—until I see it's my man, Darrel.

"Yo, what's up, folk?" He smiles ear to ear, anxious to greet me with our signature handshake.

"Damn, man. Why you stalking me?" I laugh and give him dap.

Darrel and I go way back, back to the slanging days. He got out the game after snorting up someone's supply and getting beat damn near to death. He was in a coma for six weeks. The scar on his face still runs from his left brow to the tip of his chin like a thick rope of dead skin. He loves his scar; it makes him look and feel fearless. Dudes seldom mess with you when you got a scar like that.

"Never that," he says, still cheesing.

I can see all his golds, maybe a few new ones on his bottom teeth. He looks good. He's even wearing new clothes—a pair of jeans and a navy-blue hoodie.

"So that's you?" I ask, looking at the truck.

It's as old as my Chevy, but its body is clean. Still, I was shocked. Darrel hustles like I do to survive these days, and we don't make truck money. Then, I wonder if he has started back selling dope. We keep each other on the straight, and if he's slinging again, it'll be hard for me not to do the same.

"What you got yourself into, man?" I say, convicting.

"It ain't what you think, man. I got a legit job making good money. I bought this off some old cat the other day for three grand."

"Three grand? Where'd you get three grand? You sure you ain't—"

"Come on now," he cut me off, shaking his head. "You know better than that."

"Three grand, huh?"

I check out the truck's inside—vinyl seats, one already ripping, no radio, hole in the floorboard, and it smelled like old man. I bet it ain't got no heat or A.C. either, but it's still a truck. Darrel ain't had a ride in years. Last time I saw him, he was riding on the Marta bus.

"I've been trying to catch up with your ass for weeks," he says. "You a hard dude to keep up with. Even came by your spot."

"What for? You trying to pay me back that twenty I let you hold? I sure could use it right now." I pop my trunk and toss the bag of cans inside.

Darrel walks over and peeks inside my trunk. He lifts up the bag of cans.

"What's this?" he asks. "About fifteen dollars?"

"I ain't done. Still got the clubs and the highway to hit. Might make about— "

"Forty dollars?" he says sarcastically, like it ain't good enough for him no more.

"I pray."

"That ain't shit, man."

"Well, everybody can't work at the White House like you," I joke. We both laugh.

"It ain't like that, but it's better than this."

"Oh yeah?" I attempt to close my trunk, but it doesn't latch. "Shit."

Too much stuff—metal desk, rails, bedpost, box of fixtures. Darrel helps me rearrange some things, and I can finally slam it shut. Then he pulls forty dollars out of his pocket and hands it to me like it's nothing. I take the twenty he owes me and try to give the rest back.

"You only owed me twenty, man. I don't take handouts."

"Consider it interest," he says, smiling.

"Interest, huh?" Now I'm really suspicious. Darrel ain't the type to give away money. It comes too hard for us. Something's up.

"For looking out. I mean, if it wasn't for you…"

His drifted off. I didn't press. Neither one of us are for that soft and mushy shit.

"I'd probably be on the street holding a can and a sign if you hadn't shown me there was other ways to hustle besides selling dope. I promised my mama that I was finished with the game, and you helped me do that. I appreciate you, man."

"Respect," I respond, giving him dap.

"Anyway," he says, his tone changing, "I ain't got all day. I got to meet my boss in a few."

"Look at that. Your boss, huh?"

I walk over to the driver's side and unlock the door. Darrel follows me. After sliding behind the steering wheel, I cross my fingers as I try to crank her up. She chokes a few times, but after pumping the gas and revving the engine, she finally starts.

"What's going on with her?" he asks, leaning over to talk to me through the window.

"I can't even afford to think about it, man." I sigh. "Might be the fuel pump."

"You been driving on fumes, huh?"

"Can't help it. I gotta get out here and treasure hunt. Gotta make that money."

"Look, man. Why don't you come work with me." He finally gets to the point. "You can make at least two grand a month."

"Two grand a month?" I repeat like he said a million.

To me, it might as well be. I couldn't imagine making that kind of money consistently. There had to be a catch.

"Doing what?" I ask, my curiosity at an all-time high.

That's when he breaks it down. His new boss is a real estate investor who buys up foreclosed homes dirt cheap. The reason he's able to get them so cheap is because before the bank officially takes them over, he hires people like Darrel to strip them—knock down the walls and steal the copper pipes, HVAC units, water heaters, everything. Daryl says it pays triple what I make collecting cans and raking leaves, and in half the time. Still sounds risky, and I can't afford to get locked up.

"Man, trust me. It ain't robbing like you think. These houses sit vacant for years, and when the banks finally deal with them, they got insurance to cover all that shit. Hell, they benefit from it. It's a write-off. You know how much those AC units go for? More than all that junk you got in your trunk. And the copper pipes?" He slaps the roof of my car. "That shit's like gold. One pipe is worth more than everything you can sell in a week, man." He holds up crossed fingers to the sky. "No lie. That's how I got this truck and this gear." He smooths his sweater, prideful but humble.

I look at his truck again. Temptation starts creeping in.

"Come on, man. With a brain like yours, we could double what I make. I need your help, man. Besides, those banks are thieves. They stealing folk's houses left and right. Shit, the way I see it, it's due justice. They got my mama's house a few months ago," he says, his voice dropping.

"Damn. Sorry to hear that."

"Yeah, man, she raised all us in that house and finally had it paid off—until she had to take out a second mortgage to help with my medical care." I see the remorse in his eyes. "Signed away her life just to save my sorry ass. Her mortgage almost tripled, and after five years, she just couldn't keep up the payments." He stares off. "But I'm gonna buy her house back. I don't know how yet, but I'm gonna do it."

"I know you will," I say, encouraging him.

He snaps out of it when I rev the engine again.

"So, what you think?"

"I don't know. I gotta think about it."

"Come on, man. Sell this last bit of scrap today, then ride with me tomorrow. I promise, we gonna get paid."

"I said I'll think about it," I reply in a firm tone.

"Alright, but don't wait too long."

I throw him up the peace sign and pull off. In the rearview, I see him raise his hands like, *What's there to think about?* He knows I'm watching him.

I spin back around and park beside his truck.

"What time you want me to pick you up?" he asks, excited.

"I don't know. But...have you seen Meka?"

His expression turns from hopeful to a look of disappointment. I don't know if it's because I haven't given him a definite answer on the job or because he knows what Meka being gone could mean.

"Damn...last time I saw her was maybe a few weeks ago at Dudley's," he says, squinting like he's trying to remember clearly. "Yeah, it was Dudley's. She was with that crazy-ass bitch Wavy."

"Shit!" I punch the steering wheel.

Wavy and Meka together is a disaster. Wavy is like gasoline, and Meka is a lit flame. No telling where she is now if she's with that wild-ass girl.

"When's the last time you saw her?" he asks.

Darrel knows my history with Meka. He's even helped me look for her before, but she ain't never been gone this long.

"Two weeks."

He tries to hide the worry in his eyes, but I see it.

"Damn," he mutters, shaking his head. "You check the county?"

He means the jail. I nod my head.

"What about the...the hospitals?"

He means the morgue, but he won't say it. I ain't ready to go there either.

"Naw," I reply quietly.

"Well, I'll ask around and keep my eye open. She'll turn up. You know Meka."

"Yeah…I know."

This time, I drive off for real. I got more cans to collect and maybe two cars to detail today. After that, I'll look for Meka some more. *Too much shit to do today.* I sigh, wondering when a break from the heaviness of life will come.

9

BALANAH
"The Free Seminar"

As soon as I pull into the parking lot of the Comfort Stay Inn, my car starts dipping in and out of potholes, tires scraping against torn-up cement and broken glass. I can't believe this is where my brother—and more importantly, my nephew—lives. How does he do it?

If it weren't for the shady-looking folks sitting on the concrete steps, hanging over the railings, and peeking outside their door to watch my car like I'm a robbery suspect, I'd think the building was abandoned. Some are smoking, others sipping from bottles, and some just pacing around, looking worn out. The four-story building, held together by crumbling bricks and cracked mortar, looks haunted—even this early in the morning. I'm almost afraid to get out, but I remind myself that these still are my people. If I'm scared of them, I might as well be scared of myself— and that's just ridiculous.

It's my first time here. Usually, Malichai comes to visit me. Today, I decided to stop by after dropping Zach off at school. I live in Lithonia, and this is Decatur, about 15-20 minutes away. I've been doing the back-and-forth commute for weeks now. Since Malichai won't answer his phone or return the messages I left with the front desk, I came to find out when he plans to come and get his son. I hate feeling like the bad guy for needing a break, but I need to get back to my own life before I end up in a place like this myself.

Zach only goes to school for half a day, so I'll have to pick him up in a few hours. Then it's home to cook dinner, help the kids with homework, and play referee for whatever fight Zionah and Stephan are going to get into. I've got two free hours, and after I leave here, I'm heading to the library for a free business branding seminar that I think will be helpful in pushing me to start my own business. I missed the last one. Not today. I'm actually excited about it. But first, I need to deal with my brother.

I park next to a minivan with no tires and a shattered windshield. There aren't many cars in the lot. When I step out of my Acura in a pair of fitted khakis and a leather coat, people stare harder—some sneer, others go inside their rooms only to watch me from behind the window blinds. I hear someone mutter, *"I hope she ain't no damn social worker."* Another says, *"She look like a probation officer."* Then somebody else adds, *"Shit, she might be undercover."* With that last comment, people scatter as I head toward the motel lobby.

The closer I get to the building, the more I smell urine—dog, human, who knows. Either way, the stench is burning my nostrils. Just as I reach the door, a thin, leathery-skinned middle-aged Black woman calls out to me.

"Ma'am, you ain't here to see Lexy Hamilton, are you? 'Cause that ain't me, and she don't stay here no more, and I ain't got shit to—"

I cut her off, telling her she got the wrong person, but she continues to stand there and stare like she doesn't believe me. When she starts cursing under her breath while nervously puffing on a cigarette, I ignore her and walk into the lobby.

Behind the front desk, a Middle Eastern—or maybe Indian—man is standing behind what looks like bulletproof glass. He looks solemn and unfriendly, or maybe he's just constipated. Hard to tell.

As I approach, he squints his eyes, lowers his brows, and gives me that familiar suspicious look.

"I'm looking for Malichai Sedah," I say firmly.

"You police? I don't know anything, ma'am. I just run honest motel," he says with a thick accent and attitude.

"I'm his sister. I just need to speak with him. What room is he in?"

"Sister?" He frowns. "Sister need to help brother, or he get evicted in one week." He holds up one long, hairy finger in my face. "You pay for him. You pay seven hundred and fifty dollars right now and he stay." He slaps the counter.

Damn, Malichai's about to get evicted. Looking at this place, that might not be such a bad idea, but then, where would he and Zach go? Guilt hits me. I think about the three thousand dollars in my savings account—my escape money. For a second, I feel the urge to pay it. But I don't. And I'm actually proud of myself. Saying no is something I'm learning.

"I'm not here to make a payment. I just need to know his room number so I can chat with him. Is that okay?" I snap at him.

"Room 220. Go now!" he barks. "Tell him to pay or he leave. No more favors for him or son or girl."

I know he's talking about Meka. I push the thought of her trifling ass aside and head to the stairs right outside the lobby's entrance. People are still watching me like I'm the law, but I ignore them.

When I get to Malichai's door, I knock hard, even though I didn't see his Chevy in the parking lot. Maybe Meka's home. Last I heard, she was missing again, but that was almost two weeks ago. Usually, it's only over the weekend or a few days, give or take. She has to be back. Probably cracked out.

The door's steel, and my knuckles hurt after knocking. After about five tries, it's obvious no one is inside. Curious, I peek through the blinds that are open a bit, and my heart sinks. The room is tiny--almost smaller than my master bedroom. It has two full-size beds, and the sheets are a mess. In the back, there's a small kitchenette—

more like a sink attached to a countertop that's no longer than my arm span and a mini fridge positioned against a worn wall. The table is barely bigger than a coffee table. I assume they use it to eat on because it's covered with stale TV dinners, fast food bags, and busted cigar guts. The sight of my brother's living conditions breaks my heart, and once again, I think about the money in my savings account. *Maybe I should give it to Malichai, but would it even be enough to help him?*

"You lookin' for Mal?" a woman's voice calls from the room next to his.

"Yeah," I respond, looking in her direction.

She's smoking a cigarette and leaning against the door while wearing a half-open silk robe and no bra. She doesn't seem to care that her body is exposed. A passerby whistles at her, and she blushes.

"You don't look like his type," she says, tapping ashes on the ground. "But with that sloppy girl he's always running behind, I guess he don't got no type."

"He's my brother."

"Oh." She perks up and takes one last draw of her cigarette before flicking it on the ground among dozens of other cigarette butts. "He probably out working."

"He got a job?" I ask, surprised.

"He do something to make money. Don't we all?" She shrugs. "I see him leave early every morning, and he don't get back till late at night. Now, that's my kind of man—hardworking and sexy. Mmm." She sighs. "That girl don't deserve him, but ain't that how it go? We never get what we deserve."

She pulls another cigarette from somewhere in her robe. I don't even want to know where she was holding it.

"Can you let him know his sister Balanah came by?"

"Ba...who? All y'all got them crazy names, huh?"

"Just tell him B came by."

"Now that I can remember." She grins, revealing red lipstick smeared on her front teeth. She scratches her head, and her wig shifts from side to side.

"Tell him I need to talk to him about Zach."

"His son? He okay? Ain't seen him around lately. Poor kid. He's cute but not right in the head. That chile puts on a good fuss—screaming and pounding on them walls. I just want to shake his little ass sometimes. Missing all my beauty sleep 'cause of that boy. Shit."

"Thanks," I mutter as she finally lights the cigarette and takes a puff.

"Uh-huh," she hums.

Back in my car, I take a deep breath. Maybe I should lay off Malichai for a while. He's clearly struggling. I guess I can handle Zach for a little while longer. Stephan's just gonna have to deal with it. Hell, I deal with a lot of things that he won't lift a finger to do anything about, so why am I hurting my head over this?

I put on my *Best of Curtis Mayfield* CD to lift my mood and head to the library, bobbing my head to "We Got to Have Peace" while speeding down I-20. My cell phone vibrates. Right away, I assume it's Malichai and don't even look at the caller ID before I answer.

"Mal?"

"No, heffa…it's Essence."

Shit. What does she want now?

"What's up, Ess?" I ask, already bracing myself.

"I need you to do me a favor," she dives right in.

I sigh. *Be nice if she did me a favor for once.*

"A favor?"

"Yeah," she whines like a kid.

"What's up, Ess?" I say again, unenthused.

"Damn, why you sound like that? You making me feel bad."

"Essence, just tell me. I have an appointment."

"Appointment?" she scoffs. "Where *you* going?"

My chest tightens. I'm already irritated by the sarcasm in her voice. Like I got nothing better to do with my life than do favors for her.

"Business?" I say sharply, but she doesn't catch my attitude.

"Oh…" She ignores my response and doesn't bother to follow up on it. "Well, I need you to talk to Sahara for me."

"About what?"

"The *doctor.*"

"You mean your husband?" I say, referring to the man she just married a few weeks ago.

"He's no husband of mine," she snaps.

"What?!"

"Yes!"

"Damn, girl. What was wrong with him?"

"I don't even feel like getting into all that. But I know Sahara's gonna be pissed since she and John paid for half the wedding, and I just can't bring myself to tell her. I was just gonna show up to her boring little party with my new man, but—"

"New man? Damn, Ess, it's only been a few weeks since you exchanged vows."

"And?" she says, like my statement went over her head. "Look, I don't want to ruin her little party, and I don't want Mama and the rest of y'all to be too surprised. So, just let everybody know that the fake doctor and I are done. I don't even look at it as getting divorced since we weren't married twenty-four hours before I changed my mind. To me, it ain't that big of a deal. Besides, it's *my* life."

"Yeah, it is your life. Which is exactly why I don't see why I have to be the one to tell everybody your business."

"Come on, Balanah. People won't be so mad if they hear it from you."

"Call Kwame and tell him to do it. He's the peacemaker."

"I ain't talking to Kwame's sorry, lazy ass!"

"You still mad at him?"

"Hell yeah! So you gonna do it or what?"

I say nothing. She takes my silence as a yes.

"Good!" she squeals, and I imagine her clapping her hands like a spoiled kid. "Oh yeah, before I forget—I ran the business plan you helped me with by Sahara. She said it looks good. Just made a few small changes. Isn't it great having a lawyer in the family?"

My chest tightens more. If she can run my work by Sahara, she can damn sure tell her about her broken marriage.

"When are you gonna be available to look at it again?"

"I don't know," I respond quickly.

"What about now? I got a few minutes. I can stop by."

"I just told you I'm on my way to an appointment."

"Oh yeah. Where?"

"The library."

"What kind of business you got at the library? You gotta pay an overdue book fine or something? That shouldn't take long. I can meet you there. I heard there's a good seminar going on today. I'd love to get in."

"That's where I'm going, Essence."

"To the seminar? For what?"

"The business I'm trying to start."

"You are?" She sounds dumbfounded. "Maybe I should come, too."

"Can't. You had to be on a waiting list, and there are no more seats."

"Please give me your seat," she begs, sounding like a child again.

"Are you serious?"

"Yes! Come on, Balanah. I really need this. With all that money Stephan makes, you don't need it like I do. Please…"

"I gotta go, Essence."

"So you're not gonna give me your seat?"

She really is serious.

"Bye, Essence."

"What's wrong with you?" Now she sounds offended.

"Bye, Essence," I repeat, then hang up.

My heart races. I can feel myself getting angry, but I crank Curtis Mayfield and blast it loud—so loud I can't hear my own thoughts. I have to stay focused. Today is *my* day, and I'm not going to let anyone or anything ruin it.

The seminar got amazing reviews online. I have so many ideas about what I want to do; I just need to narrow them down. Maybe I'll open a shop that sells quirky, trendy things. Or maybe a marketing firm. After all, I do have a degree. Or catering. Or party planning. Something will stick. If nothing else, maybe I'll finally step out of my shell today and benefit from the networking.

I pull into the crowded library lot. My briefcase, laptop, and notepad are on the passenger seat. I smile at the briefcase—a sleek brown leather find from a thrift store. Feminine, contemporary, pleated sides. Holding it makes me feel closer to the woman I'm aiming to become. It's like carrying my confidence.

As I reach for my things, my phone vibrates. *Damn.* If it's Essence again, I'm sending her straight to voicemail. I turn the engine off and look at the screen. It's Stephan. He never calls at this hour.

I answer. "Yes?"

"Did you know Zionah's home?"

I hesitate before answering because I didn't know she was home. I saw her leave for school this morning.

"Yes," I lie to save myself from a future argument.

"Why?"

"She wasn't feeling well," I lie again.

"She doesn't look sick. If she's sick, why is she on Facebook and not in her bed? Here, I'll give her the phone so you can tell her. She won't listen to me."

I hear him calling her, then her snappy voice in the background. I can't make out what she said, but I can tell by her tone that she's giving him attitude.

"Hello!" she barks.

104

"What are you doing, Zionah?"

She sighs.

"If your dad told you to go lie down, do it. And no computer."

She sighs again—this time heavier.

"Did you hear me?"

"Okay!" she yells. "But he didn't have to talk to me like that. I didn't even say nothing to him, and he just started going off—calling me a dropout and saying he ain't gonna be paying my rent when I can't find a good job when I'm older. I make good grades, Mommy! I just didn't feel like going to school today. I had perfect attendance until now."

Now I'm sighing. I wasn't prepared to play referee this morning. I glance at the time. Ten minutes until the seminar starts.

"We'll talk about it later," I say, trying to stay calm.

Then Stephan gets back on the line.

"You really need to talk some sense into this girl. She ain't sick. I should take her behind back to school."

I hear Zionah yell, "I ain't getting in the car with you! You'll probably drop me off at a boarding school or leave me in the woods somewhere just to get rid of me!"

"You hear that? That's how she talks to me!"

I sigh again. I'm so frustrated, I'm on the verge of tears. It's now seven minutes until the start of the seminar, and I see people gathered in the parking lot—networking and exchanging business cards. I want to be part of that.

"I'll deal with her when I get home," I say as calmly as I can.

"Yeah, right," he scoffs. "Where are you?"

"At a business meeting."

"A business meeting?" He sounds as confused as Essence.

"Yes!" I snap.

"Why are you yelling? You mad I called her a dropout? I didn't mean it like that. I'm just showing her tough love because I want the best for her. I've told you that."

That's part of why I'm mad, but not the whole reason. Of course, he doesn't know this.

"I need you to come home anyway. Can't you reschedule your *business* appointment?" he says in a cynical tone.

"No. Why?"

Now there are five minutes left. People are shaking hands and starting to go inside. I feel like I'm missing out on the total experience.

"Because we just lost our last contract, and I'm shutting the business down. We need to discuss our options—and I need you to write some letters. I'm suing every last one of them who broke our contracts early. We need to prepare now before it's too late."

"Why don't you get one of your employees to do it?"

"You mean *our* employees."

Funny how his "I" becomes "we" when there's a crisis. Now they're *our* employees.

"Not really."

"Come on, B. I need you. We're about to lose everything. Besides, I had to let everyone go today. Can't keep them if you can't afford to pay them. I know you've got your own things going on, but you need to wake up and see what's happening. As of today, we don't have any income!"

He sounds stressed—and for some reason, that gives me a tiny bit of satisfaction.

"I'll be home later," I say, keeping my tone firm.

"We need to discuss things now!"

"Can't."

The seminar has officially started. I finish gathering my things from the passenger seat.

"Did you know that boy wrote his name in ketchup across the white rug?" he adds snidely.

Shit! I forgot to clean that up. Zach was so proud to finally spell his name right. I didn't have the heart to scold him or the time to clean it up before I left. I was going to do it when I got back—wasn't expecting Stephan to come home so early.

"His name is Zach, Stephan. Not 'that boy.'"

"I know his damn name. It's all over the rug! Who's cleaning it? Not me. And definitely not Zionah. Oh, she's back on the computer, by the way."

Now I'm two minutes late. I get out of the car and start walking slowly towards the doors while juggling my briefcase, laptop, and notepad. I'm not feeling so empowered anymore.

"I'll do it when I get home. And I'll write the letters, *okay*?"

"It's not just for me. It's for both of us. It's your company, too."

He says it like he's confessing something. It's nice to finally hear him say it, but it would have been better if I had heard that before the company went belly up.

"Yeah, I know. I gotta go. I'm late."

"What are you doing?" He almost sounds disgusted with me.

"I already told you. I'll see you later."

"I need an exact time."

"Two o'clock."

"Two?! I was hoping to file this lawsuit today."

"I gotta go, Stephan."

Now I'm five minutes late.

As I rush towards the door, my phone rings again. I almost ignore it, but it's Zach's school. His teacher says he's come down with some virus, been throwing up, and I need to come get him now. She doesn't sound too sympathetic about it either. So, I tell her I'm on the way.

Damn! I miss the seminar.

What a life I have. Or do I even have one?

10
SAHARA
"The Old Me"

John's cross-examining me like he's a prosecutor and I'm on trial for murder. I wish he didn't have to come and pick me up the other day, but one of the officers recognized me and called him. I didn't even make it to booking. No cuffs. No cell. Just me sitting in the sergeant's office, sipping coffee and awkwardly making small talk until John showed up. He was the last person I wanted to see, and just the sight of him triggered round two of my breakdown. But this time, I held it together. Took deep breaths instead of beating his ass like I wanted to.

Now he's pacing the kitchen with his hand on his narrow chin. Every so often, he stops, looks up at the ceiling, and sighs, shaking his head as if I'm the most despicable person alive.

"So you just get out of the car and start kicking, and then you blank out." He snaps his fingers. "Lights out, and you remember nothing?"

I nod and rub my head. It's still throbbing from when the officer struck me like I'd stolen something. I don't have time for this shit. We shouldn't be talking about my outburst. We should be talking about how he's fucking that white bitch and him mentioning divorcing me.

"Okay," he huffs. "So…you…darn. I don't even know what to say to you, Sahara." He has that same condescending look he gives the kids when they've messed up.

"Maybe none of this would've happened if you weren't such an asshole to me."

He looks stunned—like he forgot I can talk. I don't blame him. I haven't said a word to him since he picked me up. He's even more shocked by my calmness—like nothing ever happened. I guess he wanted to see me fall apart with his own eyes so he could forgive me for what I did. But I don't need his forgiveness. He needs mine.

"So you're back to that ignorant cursing, huh? What's next, Sahara? Gonna hold up a liquor store with your fiend of a sister-in-law? Or maybe you'll streak across the stage during one of my campaign speeches and do the chicken dance. Or maybe—"

"Maybe you should shut the fuck up and tell me about the bitch you're fucking. Then we can talk divorce."

He's speechless, standing there with his mouth wide open. He definitely didn't train me to talk back to him like this.

"I can't believe you," he mutters before taking a seat at the breakfast bar.

He gives me a severe look, then slumps over and starts massaging his temples like *he's* the victim. He's got some damn nerve. I'm the one who just had a breakdown—because of *him*.

As I stand up to grab a bottle of water from the cooler, he jumps like I'm pulling a knife on him.

"What are you doing?" He throws his hands up as if he's surrendering. "Can I trust you, Sahara?"

"No. The question is, can I trust *you*, John?"

"I told you not to worry about that. Just a dumb brain fart. You didn't have to ruin my reputation or jeopardize this campaign. You know how important this is to me. Are you doing this on purpose?

Are you jealous? Do you know what this will do to me if it gets out? Darn it, Sahara!"

He slams his fist on the granite countertop.

"You know the car you don't remember kicking?" He doesn't wait for me to answer. "Well, it belonged to Wilson Hodge, an investment banker and someone who was going to be a major campaign donor. That's over now."

He slices the air with his hand and starts pacing again while mumbling something under his breath. I sip my water slowly, burning a hole in his back with my eyes. The more I look at him, the more I hate him.

"I've never been so humiliated in my life. Not even when we had dinner with Judge Lawson and his wife, and you asked what kind of steak we were eating—when it was lamb."

He'll never let that go. I knew it was lamb. Just misspoke.

"This is going to ruin me—and you wonder why I brought up divorce!"

"A divorce, huh? So you think you're better than me? You can say it. I already know you do, with your white-washed ass."

He grimaces at me, screwing up his face like I'm something dirty.

"You sound ignorant. White-washed? Because I speak proper English, get along with white people, and chase real opportunities? Would you rather I be like your brothers? Drug-dealing, garbage-rummaging, ball-throwing, wife-beating thugs!"

He begins mocking urban Black men, swaying his head from side to side, walking with an exaggerated limp, and sagging his pants. He looks comically ridiculous.

"Yeah, girl, I'll be your homeboy, and we just gonna be chilling," he says in a silly voice and making a stupid face like Buckwheat.

"You don't know shit about my brothers."

He lets out a sinister laugh while pulling his pants back up.

"Oh, I know more than I care to, but this isn't about them. It's about you. Your behavior. It's unacceptable, and my children shouldn't have to suffer because of it. Neither should I—or my campaign."

Ah. There it is. The campaign.

"So what are you trying to say?"

"I'm saying I might reconsider what I said earlier."

"About the divorce? Go right ahead."

"Maybe I will. Becca would never behave like this. She gets it. She understands the discretion I need as a state senator."

"Becca. So that's your prized white woman's name?"

"Why's it always 'white woman' with you? Why not just a woman who understands me? Maybe she can teach you a few things."

I've kept my temper in check long enough. I jump up from the barstool and hurl my water bottle at his head. It misses, but his shocked expression says it all.

"Oh, I've seen this type of ghetto behavior before—in *Baby Boy*, right? I guess now you want me to choke you or slap you, huh?" He laughs snidely.

"No. I want you to *get the fuck out!*"

"You can be so classless at times."

"I'm serious, John! Go be with your precious great white hope, *Becca!*"

"I'm not going anywhere." He stands up straight, folding his arms against his wimpy chest.

"That's for the judge to decide," I respond.

He laughs so hard that he bends over.

"Are you serious? You really want to go this route with me, Sahara? I know every judge in this city. I golf with more than half of them. You know what that means?" He raises his eyebrows.

I don't respond. I know exactly what it means.

"I think you get my drift." He steps closer. "I'm concerned about my safety and my children's safety. That incident the other day? It's going to look real bad in court. You might be seen as unfit."

"You trying to take my kids from me? Is that what this is? If that's what you think is going to happen, you better think again, buddy!"

"Hmm," is all he says before turning to walk away, but it says plenty.

"John, I swear! Don't fuck with me!" I yell at his back.

"Yeah, okay, Sahara," he says, smug as ever. "Tread lightly."

The front door slams, and I wait for the sound of his car leaving the garage before I collapse on the floor, sobbing like a child. I feel defeated. Sacrificing so much only to end up with nothing is heartbreaking. The reality turns sour in my stomach. If we get divorced, what happens? I'll become a single mother, and that's if I even get custody of my children. John is connected enough to ruin me. This isn't fair.

Unbeknownst to anyone, I just finished my last class for my law degree, but there will be no celebration. No graduation ceremony. No cap. No gown. No walking across the stage to accept my degree while supporters cheer. I hate that. Now I'm supposed to be studying for the bar exam, but with everything that's going on, I can't even concentrate for three minutes, let alone the hours I'll need to pass. What the hell am I going to do?

Becca. He said her name as if she were some jewel, claiming she could teach me a few things. After all the years I've stood by him—cooking, caring for him and the children, showing up at every boring event, laughing at his corny jokes, throwing elaborate parties to make him look good. I even got a perm to please him, and my hair has been falling out ever since. I've gotten too damn skinny. I used to have curves—now I'm rail-thin. I look in the mirror and feel repulsed by the image staring back.

I'm tired of tiptoeing through conversations, researching social media and political topics, and memorizing vocabulary words just to blend in with his pretentious friends. I'm sick of it and this nigga. I hate using that word, but that's what John is—a nigga! A weak, phony-ass, can't-fuck-for-shit nigga! And he wants to tempt me with divorce? Fuck you, John.

I would leave him right now if I had somewhere to go. Maybe it's pride or materialism, but once you've lived a certain way, the thought of downgrading feels like death. Honestly, I feel washed up. Who would even want me now? I'm not ready to face a life of uncertainty. Just thinking about it makes me sob harder.

And then there's the humiliation. Divorce would bring a lot of judgment. My family would say, *I told you so*. And what about Mama? Without income, how am I supposed to keep supporting her—or anyone else? Maybe I should rethink all of this. Maybe now isn't the right time for divorce. I need to pass the bar at least before making any major moves. Quick decisions can wreck your life. Hell, it might be smarter to wait until John officially announces his candidacy. No way he'd go through a messy divorce during campaign season. If there's one thing Republicans protect, it's their family image. Yeah...I'll wait. That way, the ball stays in my court.

Feeling a little better, I get up from the floor, wipe my face, take two deep breaths, and recenter myself. It's all becoming clearer. You don't divorce a man like John without a plan. I'll play the role. Submit to his arrogant, self-hating tyranny for a while longer. I've been doing it for years. A few more won't kill me. I'll play the doting wife, even if it means becoming the ultimate Stepford wife there is. If John tells me to jump, I'm going to ask him how high. And he can screw that Becca bitch as much as he wants. I won't flinch. Hell, he can bring her home for dinner. Whatever it takes. Because he's not just after what's left of my life—he's after my children. And if there's one thing you don't do to a Black woman, it's threaten to take her kids.

There is no way I'm letting him and Becca raise my babies, filling their heads with shame. One day, one of the twins asked me why so many Black people are stupid. The other wanted to know why her hair won't lay down straight like Angie's at school. But that's my fault.

I let John get to them. I allowed him to make them think they shouldn't be proud of their race. But I'll be damn if John and his whore finishes them off. They'll learn—just like I did—that Black is beautiful, bold, and worthy. And while I hide who I am to outplay this man, I'm going to rediscover myself. The real Sahara is coming. And when she does, she's going to prowl this world like a hungry, fearless lioness.

My little plan excites me. If John thinks his dream life is going to come true without my say, he's got another thing coming. By the time all of this is over, he'll resent marrying me as much as I resent marrying him. I'm going to ruin him. He's not going to become Senator if I have anything to do with it. He says I'm shaming him? Please. He ain't seen nothing yet. When I'm finished, his little white friends and judge buddies won't want shit to do with him. Then, I'll get the house I deserve and be free to raise my children the way I want. I just need to make it through the announcement. That's all.

Suddenly, I feel like celebrating. From tears to triumphant in under ten minutes. I'm so proud of myself. Damn, I forgot how powerful I am. I wonder what else I'll remember about the old me.

I head to the wine cellar and grab the first bottle I see—don't even care if it's red or white. I pop the cork, take a long swig straight from the bottle, and wipe my lips with the back of my hand. It's red— and strong enough to give me an instant buzz. Feeling unstoppable, I walk over to the fridge and search it for something indulgent. That's when I see the apple crumb pie I bought for the kids the other night. Perfect. I only allowed myself a forkful then—what a joke. This pie crunches when you bite it, floods your mouth with cinnamon, brown sugar, and nutmeg, then melts into gooey sweetness down your throat. I don't bother cutting a piece—I grab the whole damn pie. Then I grab the vanilla ice cream out of the freezer, which I plan to eat straight from the carton. I take my first bite of pie and chase it down with ice cream and then a sip of wine. Pie, ice cream, wine.

Rinse and repeat. Best solo party I've thrown myself in a while.

Mid-snack, I reach for a napkin to wipe the sticky mess from my lips and come across a pizza coupon. Large mushroom and spinach with extra cheese? Sounds like a plan. I head to the phone, wine bottle in hand. But before I can dial, the phone rings. I know it's not John because he never calls on the house phone. I take another swig and answer, feeling carefree as ever. No deep breath. No fake articulation. Just a simple *hello*.

"Uh, yes, I'm calling for Sahara Smith."

It's my brother, Kwame—and he sounds all dignified. Even my family can't stand to be themselves around us.

"Kwame, this *is* Sahara."

"Oh. You sound different."

"Well, I *feel* different. What's up?"

"You okay?" he asks, sounding concerned.

"Better than ever."

"Okay...well, are you sitting down? I hope so. Because what I'm about to tell you is sure to ruin your mood," he says, his tone heavy.

"What are you talking about?"

"Turn on the news. Channel 5, Channel 2—doesn't matter. It's playing on all the stations."

My heart drops. I put the bottle of wine on the island next to my pie and now melting ice cream and go to the family room in search of the remote. I already know what I'm about to see. My meltdown. Me wildin' out on the side of the road like some psycho. If that's what it is, I'm sure John won't wait forty-eight hours before taking the kids, filing for divorce, and moving that bitch Becca in my house. I'll lose everything.

"Sahara, don't cry," he says softly. "It's gonna be okay."

I don't even notice I'm crying until I hear his voice and feel a tear slide down my cheek until it reaches my bottom lip, where it hangs before evaporating into the thin air. His voice is peaceful. Honest.

No judgment. I want to believe him.

But when I turn on Channel 5, it's not *me* on the screen. It's Ebony. My sister's been arrested for attempted murder.

Shit! I break down again.

"It's alright," Kwame says gently. We gonna get through this. All of us."

11
EBONY
"I Can't Do Nothing Right"

I'm in jail, and I've never felt more at home—but I still feel like a failure. First, I failed as a mother. Then, I failed at a suicide attempt. Now, I've failed as a murderer. I can't do nothing right. Just my piss-poor luck the gun jammed, and I couldn't finish the job like I planned. Damn. What a life.

I've only seen that kind of thing happen in movies. I didn't know it could happen in real life until it did. I pulled the trigger over a dozen times. Nothing. I tapped the handle, thumped the barrel, and squeezed again and again—still nothing. At least I shot off the bastard's dick—or half of it. Same difference to me. *Ha!* I heard it on the news, and it gave me great joy knowing his ass will never be able to fuck again—legally or illegally. But it's really torturing me to know he almost died from that shot. If that nosey-ass receptionist hadn't dialed 911, he would've bled out. That bitch. I got half a mind to go back there and slap her meddling ass, but I can't. I'm probably locked up for good.

After I shot Kenton and had seen enough of him squirming, moaning, and groaning, I took a seat on one of the cushioned lobby chairs and waited for the police to come and get me. I was sitting so calmly that they ran right past me until that damn receptionist pointed me out like I was Hitler. I stood up and held out my wrists for them to cuff me—just like my father did the day they arrested him. He was ready because he believed in what he did. So do I.

Jail ain't like it is in the movies. No metal bars—just big steel doors with automatic locks and a small square window. The holding cell is no bigger than my living and dining rooms combined, but they got about thirty of us packed in here like sardines. It's hot, stuffy, and smells like hot breath. There's a tiny window too high to see out of, and it doesn't open. The cell reeks of piss, and there are no walls or doors for privacy. We're already paying for our crimes by being stuck in this funky-ass room. Why humiliate us further by making us piss and shit in front of strangers? And when we're not the one pissing or shitting, we have to deal with the smell of someone else doing it.

Some of these women look like axe-murdering cannibals, but I try not to judge. They might be just like me. The hard life they've lived is worn around their eyes—dark circles, sagging bags, yellowing whites streaked with red veins. None of them smiles. Maybe they ain't got nothing to smile about. I do, though. I really fucked Kenton up.

This place kind of reminds me of the middle school lunchroom. Some women form cliques, others pair off, and then there are loners like me—sitting quiet, trapped in our thoughts, and not wanting to be bothered. The loners get watched a lot. Some women stare at you hard, hoping you give them a funny look back just to have a reason to start something.

There's this frail little girl, no bigger than a broomstick, who got bitch-slapped by this burly woman I call Big Bertha. I felt sorry for her. Big Bertha kept mean-mugging the girl, rolling her eyes, sucking her teeth, and circling her like she was prey. The girl was so scared that she was literally trembling. When she finally made eye contact, Big Bertha hauled off, slapped her, and yelled, "Why you sweating me, ho?" Like that made her the Alpha female not to be fucked with in here. Hmph. She ain't tried me yet. I got nothing to lose and would love to take my frustration out on someone. When Big Bertha slapped the girl, the thin girl hit the floor face-first, and everybody laughed while she cried. Wrong move. She made herself a target without even knowing it—a punching bag for their boredom and pain.

This place is fucked up—but it's home now. Yeah, I may be stuck with a bunch of funky, rough-ass women, but Kenton's somewhere dickless, hooked up to tubes and aching in pain and shame. The thought alone makes me exhale. *Fucking rapist bastard!*

My legs are starting to feel numb, so I stand to walk around to circulate the blood. It's the first time I've been off this bench since I got here the other day except to use the community toilet. As I'm stretching, I notice Big Bertha looking in my direction. She rolls her eyes at me and whispers something to her little clique of five flunkies. They all start eyeballing me, but I ignore them. I'll be glad when they process me. At least then, I'll only have one cellmate to deal with and a cot to lie on instead of these wooden benches they have bolted to the concrete walls. There ain't enough room for everybody to sit, so some women are sitting on the nasty floor. I'd rather stand.

The TV's on, but nobody is watching it. Tiny 19-screen hanging in the corner of the cell with the news playing on mute with captions. I wonder if most of these women even know how to read. Some look like they can't spell their own names, let alone read *Jack and Jill.* I keep my eyes on the screen. I wasn't expecting media coverage this fast. When they show my mugshot, I almost think it's the wrong person––until I look a little harder. The unkempt, deranged-looking woman is really me.

Then they interview Kenton's receptionist. She's frantic while giving her encounter with me in the lobby. If I didn't know myself, I would've thought I was Freddy Krueger the way she's describing me. She looks so shaken. I know my Black ass is screwed for traumatizing the pretty white woman. I wonder if he was fucking her. I'm sure he wouldn't dare touch her daughter...if she has one. He knows better.

I know it's only a matter of time before they flash my father's mugshot to compare us. That's not fair. He ain't have nothing to do with this. He wasn't a murderer. But the media don't care. They'll mold him into whatever fits the story. They're like Dr. Frankenstein when it comes to publicity, good or bad. Eventually, the reporters will dig a little deeper. That's when they're gonna find out the truth about Kenton and what he did to Zena. That's what I really want—to see the truth exposed. I ain't looking for nobody's sympathy either. Just understanding.

The broomstick girl walks over with tears still in her eyes and stands next to me like she needs my protection. She's so frail. I feel like if I breathe too hard the air from my nostrils might knock her over. Looking at her forces me to think about Zena. Don't get me wrong—I did what I did with Zena in mind. But I don't want to think about how my actions will affect her now. I'm sure the media circus will bring her all kinds of unwanted attention—especially once the molestation comes out. I just pray she finds comfort in my family. I trust them—all of them. This is the last place I ever want my daughter to end up. Maybe, just maybe, by being here, I'm breaking the curse Kenton put on her life.

Up close, the girl looks about Zena's age, and I wonder how she ended up in here.

"What you doing in a place like this?" I finally ask, unable to fight my curiosity any longer.

She shrugs. "My baby daddy had some stuff in the trunk of his car and gave me the keys without letting me know."

She didn't have to tell me what the "stuff" was.

"Did you call him to let him know you in here?"

She nods.

"He ain't gonna tell the truth to help you?"

She shakes her head no.

"He acted like he didn't even know who I was when I called him. Said he don't know anybody named Tweety. Didn't even accept my collect call," she says, then sniffs up the tears that are threatening to fall.

So her name is Tweety. I ain't got to guess why they call her that.

"Your baby daddy sounds like a real asshole. How old are you?"

"I just turned eighteen."

"And how old is your baby?"

"Six months."

Damn! Now I'm thinking about shooting her worthless-ass baby daddy. I'm really feeling for this girl.

"Who got the baby?"

She shrugs again.

"I left her with my next-door neighbor when I used his car to go and pick him up from the park. I don't know who got her now. Told her I'd be right back. She probably don't even know I'm in here."

Of course, she ain't have to tell me what he was doing at the park. I already know his type.

"Why don't you call your family?"

"We only get one call," she says, holding up a shaky finger. "And I really ain't got no family to speak of."

"How long you been with this baby daddy?" I push the words through my lips like they're venomous.

"A year."

"Hmm. How old is he?"

"Thirty."

"Thirty?" I repeat, shocked.

She sees the look on my face and knows what I'm thinking. What's a grown-ass man want with a girl barely eighteen? I already know the answer.

Before my father got locked up, he was doing work to protect girls like Tweety. Society writes them off after they get pregnant, like the damage has already been done. But what they don't know is that without help and the right guidance, the damage is only beginning. Without support, the cycle repeats with the children. The mama, who became a single parent at a young age, turns her back on the child. The child ends up on the streets and falls into the arms of some sorry-ass man who becomes her baby daddy, only to keep repeating the same cycle. I was lucky. My mama encouraged me and let me know my life wasn't over––just starting a little early. My heart goes out to this young girl. Her baby has probably been picked up by social services by now. I feel for them both.

"Next time they give you a phone call, try to get in contact with the person who got your baby—and a lawyer."

"I ain't got no money for no lawyer. They say they're gonna give me one."

As soon as she says it, I already know how this will end for her. A public *pretender,* a guilty plea, and a win for the local police department. Poor thing. I wish I could help her, but I can't even help myself.

I start pacing, and when I look over my shoulder, I see her following me. I pretend not to notice. I just keep walking. When I stop by the slit of a window, letting the sunlight hit my shoulders, she's right beside me. Then I see Big Bertha and her dingy little squad walking our way.

"Oh shit," Tweety mutters.

I straighten up and stare Big Bertha right in her eyes. No blinking. Tweety's so afraid that she's just about melted into my side.

"You know me?" she asks, her voice slick with attitude.

That's a funny-ass question coming from somebody I've never seen a day in my life. I can tell she's just testing me—looking for even a flicker of fear so she can feel good about making her move. But she's gonna be looking for a while. Any fear I have has nothing to do with her.

"No," I say, locking eyes with her.

"You tryna get an attitude wit' me?"

Now she's all up in my face. Her breath is funky as hell—smells like raw pussy. Gross.

I don't say a word. Just give her a hard stare look and step in closer. So close she's forced to step back. We stand there, locked in silence. I'm calling her bluff. And if she calls mine, she's gonna get her ass beat today.

"Whatever, bitch!" she scoffs, rolling her eyes before turning to walk away. Her little clique copies her, rolling their eyes like loyal lapdogs.

She takes a few steps, then turns back, eyeing Tweety—who's standing so close to me, she might as well be holding my hand.

"What you say?" Big Bertha barks at her.

I blame folks like Tweety for fueling bullies like Big Bertha. Bullies only stay big when people let 'em. Big Bertha ain't nothing but one good ass whooping away from leaving everybody alone, and I'll be just the one to give it to her. My mother raised me not to fear nobody—no matter how big, what color, or what kind of power they think they got. And she clearly don't know how crazy I am. The more I stand in front of her, the more that crazy rises. Especially when I glance over my shoulder and see my damn mugshot on the TV screen again. They need to stop showing that and show the truth. Show how Kenton raped and molested my daughter. Now, I'm fuming.

"Bitch, whatever you want with her, deal with me!" I pound my fist against my chest.

I shove Tweety behind me and square up with Big Bertha, fists clenched, my eye twitching—something that happens when I get too angry to contain it. Big Bertha sees it. She sees my rage ain't performative like hers. This ain't no tough-girl act. This is real.

"Stop fucking with people, or you gonna get fucked up!" I say, jabbing my finger into her shoulder like it's a knife.

She blinks, shocked I touched her first—but still don't swing.

"People in here got enough damn problems. They ain't come to deal with your big, stank ass!" I step closer. "Don't fuck with me." I point to myself. "And don't fuck with her." I point behind me at Tweety.

I life my hand towards her head and she ducks like I'm gonna hit her, but I don't hit her. I just catch a handful of air above her head and squeeze it into my fist. A few people in her clique and a few others in the cell gasp. Big Bertha ain't used to this kind of energy. She's so thrown off, she's speechless.

She backs down, turning around and walking off with her tail between her legs. Her little crowd of minions trail behind her.

I look over at Tweety. She's still staring at Big Bertha, nerves rattled, until she looks up at me. I give her a slight nod that says, *You're good now.*

"Thanks," she says, her heavy Southern accent trembling through the word.

She takes a few deep breaths, trying to collect herself.

"You can't let people mess with you like that," I tell her. "People like me ain't always gonna be around to save your ass."

"But...that girl looks crazy."

"Looks are deceiving," I say, leaning down to scratch inside the cast on my leg.

"You seen how hard she hit me over there," she says, nodding toward the spot where Big Bertha assaulted her.

"Winning a fight ain't about who hits the hardest or the most. It's about not letting people treat you like shit. If it takes getting your ass beat a million times to understand that, then just sit there and get your ass beat."

She nods slowly, almost like she's getting empowered, but I know what I said ain't easy to live by. It takes a lifetime to learn that kind of lesson, but she's young enough to start learning. I don't know if she's strong enough, though.

Tweety nudges me on the shoulder, jerking her head toward something behind me. "They coming back over here," she whispers, voice tight with fear.

I turn and see Big Bertha and her crew heading back our way. Fine. I guess I'm gonna have to fight this bitch. Honestly, I don't mind. I could use the cardio. My nerves are wound tight now.

I don't wait. I walk right up to her. Tweety doesn't follow this time.

"What?" I bark, bucking at her.

But to my surprise, she throws up her hands like she's surrendering. Then she points to the TV screen.

"That you on the TV?"

I look up—and there it is again. That awful mugshot. Now everybody is looking at the screen.

"Yeah…why?"

"You really shot that man's dick off?"

"Yep," I say, thinking of Kenton's muffled screams.

"Damn! What he do? Cheat on you?" she asks, grinning like this is some joke.

I don't respond.

"He ain't cheat on her," a woman from her group says, her eyes glued to the screen.

Finally, the story I've been waiting for breaks. An investigator is talking about the child molestation and rape charges that were brought against Kenton years ago.

"He fucked her daughter, and she fucked *him* up!" the girl says with pride. "Turn it up!"

One girl rushes to the TV and gets down on all fours. Another climbs on her back and un-mutes the volume. Big Bertha silences the entire cell with a wave of her hand. For the first time today, you could hear a mouse pissin' on cotton.

Tweety is back behind me now, eyes wide and locked on the screen. They listen as the reporter explains that my motive came from the *alleged* sexual abuse Kenton inflicted on my thirteen-year-old daughter. They also said it is *alleged* that Kenton had been forcing her to perform sexual acts on him since she was nine. The reporter reveals everything I wanted her to reveal—and I feel at peace.

I lean against wall, needing a second to take it all in. By the time the commercial comes on, the whole cell erupts into clapping and cheering. They treat me like I'm some kind of hero. Then the confessions start. More than half the women in the cell—including Big Bertha—share their stories. They say the same thing happened to them when they were young. They smile at me. Not with pity— but respect. Respect for doing what their mothers or fathers never did.

A tear falls from my eye. I didn't expect this. Now I know—there was a reason for it all.

When the commotion finally dies down, Tweety leans in and tells me *"Thank You"* again. But this time, I can tell she ain't just thanking me for defending her against Big Bertha.

I smile at her, letting her know without saying a word—*You're welcome.*

12
KWAME
"Off the Couch"

I'm throwing up again. I don't know if it's because of the news about Ebony or that pastrami sandwich and fries Tammy made. Either way, I'm hunched over the toilet, throwing up so hard it feels like my stomach's about to launch itself out of my mouth. My head's so deep in the bowl I can smell the sewer.

Now my knees are starting to ache as I kneel on this tile. The pressure of the extra sixty pounds I've gained doesn't help, but I can't move. Every time I try to get up, my stomach churns, and I'm back down again. This makes the seventh time I've thrown up this month. The shit is weird, but I still ain't going to no damn doctor. Why? Just so they can pin an expensive disease on me because they got bills to pay—especially since I check all the boxes for every illness they say Black folks are prone to?

But this time feels different. My neck and the side of my face start to itch. When I scratch, I feel tiny bumps pushing through my skin like a rash. Maybe it's an allergic reaction. I ain't been doing nothing different, though—still on the same couch all day, still eating the same stuff. Maybe Tammy switched the detergent.

I hurl one last time, and this time it feels like it's really over. The wave of heat and sweating passes. My body temperature is back to normal, and the squeezing sensation in my stomach is gone, along with the rising lump in my throat. I use the toilet seat to push myself up from the floor. My knee pops as I stand, and my back is stiff. After stretching out the tension, I rinse my mouth with water and mouthwash, then splash my face. Although I'm black as tar, I notice the rash spreading across my skin like wildfire. It's still itchy, but it seemed to itch more while I was throwing up. I grab a face towel, wet it with warm water, dab some soap, and gently wipe at the rash. I don't know if it'll help. It just feels like something I should do.

"You okay, Daddy?" I hear behind me.

It's Levi. The boy I'm raising as my son, if that's what you want to call my limited interaction with him. He's seven and always sounds scared when he talks to me, but that never stops him from asking me if I'm okay. He's the only one who ever asks how I'm doing, and I'm starting to appreciate him for that. I start to feel bad for how I treat him. It ain't his fault his mama is conniving and trifling.

"Where your mama?" I ask, wiping my mouth with the same towel.

"She on your couch in the living room," he whispers like he's telling me a secret. "She watching Aunt Ebony on TV."

Tammy's really trying me. She loves doing that it. I told her ass I didn't want to see no more of that shit. It's making me sick. Just the thought of my sister locked in some jail cell is too much. One parent in prison was enough—now my sister, too? I've seen women snap and kill their husbands on the show *Snapped*. Usually, it's cheating or abusive men. I always thought Tammy might be the one to snap. But Ebony? Naw. She was the strongest one out of all of us. She has a sharp mind and is unshakable. I never liked that Kenton dude, though. Bum lived off her success.

When she dumped him, I thought she was finally freeing herself. But she never got over him. Still, I never thought of her as being the type to go crazy and attempt to kill her ex just because he moved on.

I heard he just got married, his business is booming, and he has a baby. Damn, Ebony. Why couldn't you just let him be? You could've had any man you wanted. It's funny how women with the strongest minds often have the weakest hearts.

I walk towards the living room, and Levi follows behind me. When I get there, I see Tammy sunk deep into my couch like the permanent dent made in the cushions from the weight of my body is swallowing her whole. She's sitting on the pillow I use to lay my head on, and my furry throw blanket is crumpled under her feet on the floor. The TV is blasting. What is she? Deaf? It's so loud that she doesn't even hear when I come into the room. She's got the remote, squinting at the closed captions, her shiny new nails tapping the buttons. I notice her hair is different. Instead of the bone-straight weave she had falling way past the middle of her back, she's sporting a short, curly hairdo.

Her cell phone has been nonstop with her gossiping girlfriends looking for the scoop. They act like this devastating news regarding my sister is an episode of reality TV. Once again, her phone buzzes, and she pulls it out of her bra.

"Hello…yeah. I'm watching it now. I'll call you back later."

She hangs up and still doesn't notice me. Levi runs over and curls up beside her, watching the news station like it's his favorite cartoon.

I barely glance at the TV. I've had enough. This ain't just some news story about a random person—it's my sister! I only found out by accident while flipping channels and ending up on Channel 5. That's when I saw her mugshot on the screen. I almost didn't recognize her, but there was something familiar about her eyes that caught my attention. When I looked closer, I knew it was her. Then the reporter confirmed it: *Ebony Sedah*. That's when I ran to the toilet and threw up. Once I finished my business in the bathroom, I forced myself to watch the rest of the report, then called Sahara. Balanah and Malichai didn't answer. I didn't bother wasting my time calling

Essence since she hates me now. Sahara assigned me to break the news to Mama. Mama don't watch TV, and I know she'd rather hear it from one of us instead of some nosy neighbor banging on her front door to tell her.

Tammy flips to another news station when a commercial comes on. Her phone beeps with a text. She quickly checks it and starts replying without even looking down—keeping her eyes glued to the TV. I've had enough. I grab her forearm and yank her ass up so fast her phone hits the floor, and Levi slides off her lap with the remote. He picks it up and mutes the TV, trying to calm the situation. Tammy looks shocked. So does Levi. But I don't hit her. I never hit her in front of Levi. No point messing up two lives.

"Damn, Kwame. What I do now?" she whines.

"I told you I didn't want to see no more of this shit!"

She rubs her arm while searching for her phone. When she spots it, she picks it up. It hit the wood floor so hard that the battery popped out. Her eyes dart back and forth between the phone and the TV as she's putting it back together.

"This is your sister. Don't you even want to know what's going on?"

"I already know. And your ass is sitting here gossiping with your nosey-ass friends."

"They ain't nosey. They're concerned."

"Bullshit!"

"People are starting to rally outside the jail. I'm going," she says, matter-of-factly. "You should, too."

She'll do anything to be in the limelight.

"You ain't going nowhere."

I remember the rally outside of the jail when my dad got arrested—hundreds of angry people chanting his name like he was Mandela. But this ain't that. Ebony shot a man because he left her. She doesn't deserve a rally.

Levi picks up the remote and hands it to me like a peace offering or a silent plea to lay off his mama. I take it and change the channel, but Tammy grabs it from me.

"Girl, are you crazy?" I snap, raising my hand.

She flinches like I hit her. Levi's wide eyes stop me from following through.

"Do you even know why your sister got arrested?" Tammy asks, rolling her neck so hard that her weave is swaying from side to side.

"Of course. She tried to kill her ex."

"But do you know why?"

I say nothing.

"Watch the damn news, Kwame." She throws the remote at me, and I catch it. "Another story broke. Ebony tried to kill that sorry bastard because he raped your niece when she was ten."

Her words hit me like a slap to the face.

Tammy grabs Levi by the hand, and as she storms out of the room, she yells over her shoulder, "I'm going down there!"

What the fuck?! I turn the volume up and listen. She was right.

I flop down on my couch. My body goes numb. Why didn't Ebony tell us? She's been walking around holding all this in for years. This explains a lot—her breakdown, quitting work, Zena's behavior. I've been so caught up in my own pathetic world, I missed all of the signs that something extreme was going on in their lives. It's time to wake up and get my ass off this damn couch.

I stand, but only because my stomach is churning again. I rush to the bathroom, barely making it. Between gags, I hear Tammy and Levi walk out the front door. If she's really going down there to support Ebony—and not just for show—I might actually be starting to respect her.

I start itching again.

Before I leave the house, I call Mama and tell her I'm coming to see her. Right away, she knows something's wrong. I don't tell her what, just that I'll be there in thirty minutes. Then she asks if everyone's alive and healthy. I tell her they are so she'll at least be relieved to know that.

I ain't been outside in months. The dull sunlight blinds me like I'm a damn vampire, but the fresh air feels good—renewing. I feel healthier already. I jump into my Escalade, and the new car smell is still lingering. I forgot what a joy it was to drive such a beautiful piece of machinery. After she growls in response to me revving the engine, I head down I-20 toward the West Side of Atlanta.

It feels like I'm waking up from a coma. It's sad it took something this heavy to snap me out of the dormant state my mind has been stuck in. But at least I know I ain't numb anymore. I used to feel helpless, but that ain't an option now. Ebony needs me. Helpless people aren't much help.

She don't deserve the sentence they gonna give her—not after what Kenton did to my niece. I almost want to go to the hospital and finish the job she started, but that wouldn't fix anything. Besides, that man's got to live with the foul-ass things he did—and now the world knows. Plus, his dick ain't never gonna be bigger than the size of a peanut again.

Damn, Ebony, that was some smart thinking.

When I pull off the exit and hit Joseph E. Lowery Boulevard, I feel like I'm home. There ain't a street corner in the West End that doesn't remind me of my father. His essence is in the air, in the people—strong, proud, Black. Everywhere you look, you'll see locs, natural hair, Malcolm X tees, kente cloth, and Bob Marley hoodies. The air smells like sandalwood, patchouli, and frankincense. I roll down the window to get a better whiff, and I feel powerful again.

Everybody on the street is hustling—not that phony, easy kind that comes from selling drugs, but real hustles that uplift people instead of dragging them down. Some are set up at makeshift kiosks, selling handmade jewelry and culturally graphic tees. Others are pounding the pavement, showcasing their goods. Everybody is smiling, greeting each other with daps, and enduringly calling one another "sister" and "brother" like family. Young, ambitious college students are in the mix, bringing a different kind of energy—maybe it's the hope that comes with an educated Black mind. Being here makes me wonder why I ever left.

I pass the West End Mall and come to a red light. That's when I see this tall brother dressed so sharp he looks like African royalty. He's wearing all purple, which brings out the silver shimmer in the locs that are pulled back in a ponytail. He seems very charismatic the way he greets the people walking by, and clearly, everyone already knows him.

He's posted at the corner by the light, holding what look like custom wooden clocks shaped like Africa. He holds them with such pride, it pulls me in. They're beautiful—each one unique. One has a collage and gold lettering that reads, *Remember the Love, Remember the Black Family*. There are magazine clippings of the Obama family, Dr. Martin Luther King with his kids, and other smiling Black families. Thinking about my own, I'm moved. I motion him over.

"Shalom," he says in a deep, confident voice.

"Shalom," I reply. "How much for that one?" I point to the clock in his hand.

"One-fifty," he says, knowing it's worth every penny. His tone makes it clear he's not open to haggling—and honestly, I don't want to. It's a real piece of art.

"You make these yourself?"

"Yes. My hands, heart, and love for my family help me. Family is love." He holds up the clock, admiring it like he doesn't want to part ways with it. He points to a photo, likely his own family. "I have six yeladim," he adds with a proud smile. Then he quickly clarifies, "Children," before I have a chance to ask him what yeladim means.

"Whoa. My mom and dad have six themselves," I say, feeling connected to him.

"Blessings to them," he says, giving me a fist bump and head nod.

"I'll take it." I pull out two hundred dollars from my wallet.

"I don't have change," he says with an innocent smirk, letting me know it's okay to tip him.

"No problem."

"Thank you, brother. Be blessed. Come back and see me. They call me Clock-Man."

"Alright, Clock-Man," I say, hitting the gas before the light can turn red again.

Five minutes later, I pull into Mama's complex. I never noticed how shabby it's gotten. It used to be a diamond in the rough. Now, after years of neglect, that diamond looks more like a cubic zirconia. The siding is rotting, the patched roofs are sagging, and the grounds are littered with branches, brown leaves, and trash. Yet, the Homeowners Association still harasses her about paying condo fees when they obviously don't do a damn thing for the money.

Looking around, I start to feel guilty. I made enough money back in the day to set her up in a nice house, mortgage-free. If I'd done that, maybe Malichai and his family wouldn't be nomads. He could've moved back into the place he bought for her. I should've thought like that when it mattered. But I was too caught up in my own problems to notice the suffering of those around me.

I pull into Mama's parking space, and there she is—standing on her porch, waiting on me. She's got a nervous smile, but I can see the worry in her eyes. I step up onto the wobbly wooden porch, and she wraps me in a tight embrace. I feel five years old again. That hug feels like healing. Like home. She hugs me like she ain't seen me in years, and that's partially true. I don't come around much.

"Hey, Mama," I say, kissing her cheek.

"Hey," she says back, then nods before leading me inside.

Inside of Mama's condo is totally different from the outside. She keeps it so clean that you can eat off the floor, and her creativity shines in her homemade décor—deep colors, positive energy, a palace designed on pennies. As soon as I make it inside the living room, she immediately takes a seat on the couch and gives me that look: *Spit it out.* She shifts, crosses and uncrosses her legs, leans back, adjusts a pillow in her lap, and taps her foot. She's waiting.

"Boy, will you sit your ass down! You driving me crazy. What's going on, Kwame? You trying to give me a stroke?"

I sigh and sit down next to her, giving her a guarded look. She starts squirming again. I hate being the bearer of bad news, but Sahara couldn't come—she's freaking out too bad. She'd just rile Mama up worse.

"If ain't nobody hurt, this must be about your wife. She's okay, ain't she?" she asks, sounding suspicious.

Her tone makes me assume she thinks I hurt my wife. Then I start to wonder if she knows I hit Tammy. Now, I'm feeling embarrassed, totally losing focus. The only person I confided in was Balanah, and usually, she's pretty good at keeping secrets.

"Tammy is fine, Mama."

I scratch that worry off her list, and she exhales.

"What about Levi? Did she…tell you something about that boy?"

Now she's eyeing me. I know what she means. Everybody knows Levi ain't mine, but they think I don't know that. When I don't respond right away, she assumes that's why I'm here.

"Look, you been in his life so long, you his daddy regardless. It don't take a man's seed to be a father," she says, patting my knee.

She stands up and sighs like she's relieved, thinking the worst is over.

"You hungry?"

"Mama…Ebony's in jail," I blurt out.

"What you say?" She turns around so fast I hear her neck crack.

I don't repeat it. I just get up and walk towards her. She starts panting like she's about to hyperventilate.

"Calm down, Mama." I try to hug her, but she pushes me back and stares at me like she misheard.

"Say that again. And this time, slowly." As she waits for me to respond, she takes several deep breaths and slightly closes her eyes like she's praying.

"She shot Kenton. He's in the hospital. Almost died. They're charging her with attempted murder."

"Oh Lord," she gasps, clutching her chest. She collapses, but I catch her. "Jesus!"

She's already freaking out, and I ain't even told her the worst part yet—the *why*.

"Who told you such foolishness?" she asks, like I'm making it up.

"It's all over the news, Mama. I wouldn't just say something like this."

"The news? Oh Lord. You mean them vultures with cameras done started already?"

She's horrified. I know she's having flashbacks to when Daddy got arrested. How fast the story changed, how the press flipped the narrative.

"Did they mention anything about your daddy?" she asks.

"Not yet," I reply.

However, I know it's only a matter of time before he's mentioned in the news—and probably me and Sahara's husband, too.

"What's wrong with that girl? Why would she do something so stupid? Why couldn't she let that man be? He wasn't no good for her anyway. She makes us all look bad. I can just imagine the things they're gonna say about your daddy because of this. His legacy ruined—over this!"

Mama slowly walks back to the couch like her legs are made of lead. She still has her hand over her chest, and her head is lowered, swaying from side to side in disbelief and grief.

"They gonna lock her up forever. What about Zena? What's she gonna do without her mama? Did she even think about Zena at all?" she yells, breathing hard again.

I run to the kitchen and pour her a glass of water. She barely takes a sip, but swallows hard like the pain is stuck in her throat. She sets the glass down and starts wiping at her eyes.

"Where did I go wrong with that girl? I thought I loved her enough. I thought I taught her better. I don't know what happened with her. Yes, I do." She pauses and looks up like she's talking to God, then down like she's blaming the devil. "When I went away for those two years, I messed up y'all's lives."

"That's not true, Mama." I sit next to her and wrap my arm around her shoulders. "Why would you say that? You did a great job with all of us. This ain't your fault."

"I'm her mama. No matter how grown y'all get, I'm still responsible for the crazy shit y'all do. I raised you into the adults you are."

"Don't blame yourself. Blame Kenton. He's one fucked-up nigga!"

"Boy, you know better than to use that word in my house," she say, referring to me using the N-word.

"Well, that's what he is! A nasty, filthy nigga who deserved every bit of what he got!"

I'm so heated that I don't realize I'm standing now with my fists clenched. Mama looks up at me with wide, bewildered eyes. Then something shifts in her.

"That motherfucker!" she screams.

She punches one of the pillows on her couch, then picks up the glass of water and throws it down on the floor, shattering it.

"Where's my baby? Where is she?!" she yells, referring to Ebony.

"Fulton County. People are out there protesting—supporting her, Mama. Just like they did for Daddy."

Her posture straightens, and she inhales deeply, collecting herself. She's starting to regain her power.

"Take me to my baby!" she demands.

I nod and head for the door—but not before rushing to the bathroom to throw up one more time.

13

ESSENCE
"The Batmobile"

Free at last! My so-called marriage to Resident McCall is officially annulled. Kicked his ass to the curb—legally—and crossed it off my to-do list. Not that anything was stopping me before, but it feels good to free up space—mentally and literally.

I had to threaten a restraining order just to get him to stop calling and harassing me. When he wasn't insulting everything from my dark skin to who my father is, he was begging me to come back. He even cried. Pathetic. But when I mentioned calling the police, I think he remembered my sexy officer friend roughing him up and finally backed off. See? Moving on isn't that hard after all. You just put one foot in front of the other and fucking step. Piece of cake.

All in all, I've had a pretty productive week. I showed three properties to a client with enough money to cover my bills this month, stuck to my five-day workout plan, and nearly finished my business plan—it's practically a wrap. And I saw Marco almost three times this week. That sexy, renegade cop is already eating out of my hand, and I'm not gonna lie, I'm eating out of his, too. The man is fine! Just thinking about him makes me melt. So, when he called me a few minutes ago and asked me to meet him for lunch, I almost did a cartwheel.

I adjusted a showing to fit him in. Hey, you make time for what matters. I told Marco I only had an hour when he suggested we meet for lunch at Lenox Mall. He said that was enough. I'm in Decatur— on the other side of the tracks, literally. The trendy side, with its boutiques and booming businesses, where property still holds value even in this trash market. Back in the day, it was mostly white, but like the majority of Atlanta, Black folks are taking over. My client is dead set on buying an overpriced house here, and I'm not talking him out of it. Up with the people, up with my bank account.

I told Marco to meet me in the area. Usually, I don't let a man— or anyone—mess with my money, but how could I say no to someone as sexy as him? I doubt he even hears that word often, and I'm not about to be the chick that introduces him to it.

I'm waiting in the Chick-fil-A parking lot. Marco said he was about ten minutes away. I got antsy, so I went inside to order myself a large lemonade. I love Chick-fil-A's lemonade. It has the perfect balance of sweet and tart, just like me. As I'm sipping on the lemonade, my phone rings. Since breaking it off with Resident McCall, I programmed Beyonce's "To the Left, To the Left" as the ringtone for him and my sister, Sahara. Just something to give me a heads-up about who's calling without having to look at the caller ID.

I hope it's not the broke resident. Then again, I hope it's not Sahara either. If she's calling, that means Balanah must've told her that I dropped her husband's boring little friend. I pull my phone from my bra. Sahara. I sigh and send her to voicemail before getting back in the car. I'm not letting her ruin my vibe before my lunch date. Not even a minute later, she calls again. This lets me know that she knows I'm ignoring her call. Once more, I send her to voicemail. She can wait. I'll deal with her after my date...or after my showing, or my workout, or dinner. Or maybe I'll just call her tomorrow.

I'm a quarter through my lemonade when Marco's black Ford pulls up beside me. He made it in five minutes. He hops out the car.

He damn sure doesn't look like nobody's cop in his black wife beater that's hugging his broad chest, revealing his bulging arms. It's forty-five degrees, but I guess when you're that fine, cold doesn't matter. He's got a police cap turned backwards, military-style pants, and boots laced up tight like he's ready for combat. I watch as he walks around and opens my door with authority like he's about to frisk me. I lift my arms playfully as I step out.

"What's up?" he says, giving me a serious look and raising his chin.

"*You*," I reply.

He doesn't flinch. Never does. He spreads his legs slightly and pulls me into a hug. His chest feels like a brick wall of velvet. I don't want to let go, but he does—like he timed it. Such a tease.

"Let's roll," he says, gesturing to his car.

"I told you I only had an hour. Shouldn't I just follow you?" I say in a stern yet flirty voice.

"Naw, you should ride with me. I'll get you back in time. Didn't I tell you that?"

I nod without saying a word. I can't help but respect authority—especially when it looks like that. I grab my lemonade, lock my door, and hop in his Ford. Last time I saw him, he was in a police cruiser. The car that I'm in now is unmarked—definitely giving detective or something higher up. I never heard of a detective responding to domestic calls. Maybe he got promoted. I don't know. It's got all kinds of gadgets—like the Batmobile. I'm almost afraid to move, scared that I might accidentally press a button and cause the car to self-destruct.

"So...you're a detective?" I ask, looking around the car.

It's crime scene clean. The seats are black leather and too comfortable for him to be transporting cuffed criminals.

"Something like that. I work for a special unit."

"Since when do special unit officers answer house calls?"

He shoots me a look like I'm asking too many questions. I flash him an innocent smile.

"I was filling in for a friend."

"Oh," I simply reply and take a sip of my lemonade.

"You couldn't wait on me?" he asks, eyeing my cup.

"I had this earlier," I lie, and he looks at me like he knows I'm lying.

"What's your day looking like?"

"Nothing much. Just showing a house to a rich couple."

"How you know they're rich?"

"Because they're buying a half-million-dollar house in an area where the property tax is equal to the mortgage."

"So...buying an expensive house makes a person rich? Sounds backwards to me."

I'm not sure what he's getting at, so I shrug and shift the topic.

"You don't look like a cop."

"Maybe I'm not." He gives me a weird look. I mirror it, not knowing what else to say.

He stays focused, scanning the streets and every passing car like his eyes are radars. Every so often, he shifts his eyes from looking out the windshield to glancing in his rearview mirror. I don't know what or who he's looking for. Everybody must be a suspect to him. He has one hand on the steering wheel, and his biceps flex as he squeezes it. He's so fine that I don't care what he is. I like the mystery. Beats all those boring, predictable jerks from my past, including the one I recently divorced. Still, I pry.

"You must have cool friends to let you borrow a cop car. What, you living out a childhood fantasy?" I chuckle, but he doesn't laugh.

"Not really," he says, eyes still on the road.

"Come on," I whine. "Why'd you become a cop? I want to know. It interests me."

"It interests you, huh?"

He finally glances at me, brow lowered. He looks at me as though he's trying to figure something out, but I don't know what.

I nod.

"You ever hear the saying, 'If you can't beat 'em, join 'em'?"

"Yeah..."

"Well, alright then," is all he says.

I kind of get it, but then again, I kind of don't. But I just let it go.

As we approach a yellow light, Marco speeds up instead of slowing down.

"You said you got about an hour, right?" he asks.

When I nod, he pushes a button in his Batmobile. The lights start to flash, and the siren wails.

"Buckle up."

And then he guns it. We hit 120 mph, weaving through traffic like a tornado and blowing through red lights like they're green. I've always wanted to do this. I try to hide how excited I am, but he knows he's getting me going. I can tell by the way he's cutting his eyes at me.

Fifteen minutes later, we're in Buckhead as if we arrived in a jet. Normally, it would take about thirty to forty minutes to get there. He spins into a space in front of a Greek pizzeria spot and throws the car in park so fast, I get whiplash. I was expecting a restaurant more fancy than foreign takeout, but I guess he really ain't the type. I don't mind that, though. I've already had the "five-star restaurant" kind of men, and I've had enough of them.

"You cool?" he asks, looking at me. I almost see a hint of concern in his eyes.

"As a summer breeze." I smile at him, but of course, he doesn't smile back.

"Cool. Let's bounce."

We get out and head towards the doors. As we're walking, he puts his arm around my waist like I'm a prize. Inside, a bushy-eyebrowed olive-skinned man greets him in Greek. To my surprise, Marco smiles and greets him back in the same language. The man then points to me and says something I don't understand. Marco *finally* smiles at me, nods his head, and looks me up and down. Not in a lustful way. More like he was...assessing.

"Hello," the man says to me in English. "I make you great pizza today?"

"Naw," Marco cuts in. "Give her a falafel, and do it up nice for her."

I love how he takes charge. I pretend to be excited, though Mama has been cooking international foods for as long as I can remember. I've eaten the dish before, which consists of cucumber cream sauce, a cabbage mix, feta cheese, and a parmesan cheese spread, all folded into pita bread. But Marco doesn't need to know that.

He leads me to a small table by the window with a clear view of his Batmobile.

"Wait here," he says, then disappears into the back with the Greek guy. *That's weird.*

This place isn't fancy, but it's charming. Worn green walls, orange tile floors, pictures of Greece, and the smell of spices in the air. It doesn't look like much, but at least it smells good. My eyes wander to the assortment of desserts they have on display behind a glass counter. Everything looks sticky, crunchy, and chewy. That gyro meat spinning on the machine looks so good that it almost makes me change my order—but I don't. I want Marco to feel in control.

I take the last sip of my lemonade, and when I get up to toss my cup in the trash, I spot Marco and the Greek guy in the back. Marco's arms are folded, chest puffed out. The other guy is waving his arms in the air like he's pleading. I don't watch for too long; it's none of my business what's going on between those two.

I sit back down. A second later, Marco comes from the back. The Greek guy returns behind the counter, trying to save face by giving me a nervous smile and a wave.

"One minute before you'll be licking your fingers," he calls out to me in a shaky voice.

Marco drops into the chair across from me, scanning his car and the area like he's looking for something. Then he sets his sights on me. He looks at me like it's his first time seeing me today. Reaching out his hand, he tugs one of the twists hanging down my shoulder.

"I like your hair," he says.

I got it braided up the sides like a Mohawk—or should I say fro-hawk—and the rest is twisted. I smile, trying not to look too caught off guard by his comment. He keeps staring—no smile, no blink. It's too intense, so I look away. But when I look back, he's still staring. Then he smirks, like he's thinking something private, and glances away toward the Greek guy.

"This your favorite restaurant?"

He smiles. He knows I'm prying again.

"One of them."

"Oh, so you got a few?"

"You ask a lot of questions. You should've been a lawyer."

"Nah. My sister is a lawyer, though."

"Oh yeah?"

"Sort of."

He doesn't press me on what "sort of" means, so I let Sahara's business be. He pulls out his phone and checks the time.

"Hey, man!" he yells. "Hurry up. I told you, I ain't got all day."

His tone is threatening enough to make the Greek guy scramble.

"Just one more minute," he says, holding up a trembling finger.

Marco rolls his eyes and grabs my hand. I nearly jump out of my skin.

"Your hands are soft. I like that."

"You like that, eh? What else do you like?"

He doesn't answer. Just looks at me, and I start to feel dumb. *Damn. How many hooks do I gotta throw before this man bites?* Then my phone rings. When I see it's Kwame calling, I react right away, forgetting I'm on a date. Still pissed, I answer the phone.

"You must have the wrong number," I snap, then hang up before he can say a word.

When I said I wasn't talking to him, I meant it. He calls right back. I suck my teeth and send it straight to voicemail. A second later, I get a text message. I don't bother to look at it. I know it's him.

Marco is watching me closely now with a suspicious look.

"That Urkel?" he asks.

I'm confused.

"Urkel?" I say back.

"Ole boy I had to shake down for you during that *house call.*"

Ah. Resident McCall. I chuckle. That's actually a perfect nickname. Before I have time to respond, the Greek guy approaches with our tray of food. Marco gets up and almost snatches the tray from his hands.

"What you want to drink?" he asks.

"Water," I respond.

While holding the tray in one hand, Marco steps behind the counter like he owns the place, grabs two bottled waters from the beverage cooler, then places my food in front of me along with my water.

After we finish eating, Marco goes behind the counter a second time, grabs another water, and then leans over, analyzing the odd-looking desserts.

"Hey, give us something good. Nothing too damn weird."

"Of course," the Greek guy says, eager to please.

He picks a few pastries, puts them on a paper plate, and hands the plate to Marco, who brings them back to the table. He looks down at the selection of desserts like he's iffy about them.

"Here, try one of these," he says, like I'm the guinea pig.

I take a sip of water to cleanse my palate, wipe my mouth, and choose something that looks like a brownie, drizzled with honey and sprinkled with brown sugar.

I take a bite. Marco watches me chew, waiting for me to swallow.

"What's that taste like?"

"A fancy granola bar. It's pretty good," I say, going in for another bite.

Marco tries it, too.

"It's alright." He doesn't finish it. "What you got planned for the weekend?"

"I need to work on my business plan and a few other things. Why?"

"Maybe I wanted to take you to a party."

"Is one of your cop friends throwing it?" I pry.

"Does it matter?"

I shrug.

"So you're a businesswoman with a plan, eh?" Now he's prying.

"That surprise you?"

He shrugs.

"What you trying to do?" He takes a small bite of another dessert.

"I want to open a real estate investment firm. A place where new and seasoned investors can get first dibs on Atlanta's prime properties. Maybe even financing."

"Sounds cool. Expensive to start, though."

"Yeah. If things pick up for me, maybe I can start saving and launch in about three years."

"Three years is a long time to wait on a good idea."

"Well, nobody's trying to give me a loan."

"You mean the bank?"

"Who else?"

"There's other ways."

"None that I know."

"Maybe I know some." He winks.

I just stare at him, dumbfounded.

"I got a business on the side, too. Nice little backup plan," he says, then takes a long sip of his water and stares out the window.

"What kind of business?"

"A little security company. I help people keep their money safe. Nothing big like your real estate investing firm."

"So, by day, you protect people, and on the side, you protect their money. Sounds cool."

"Yep. Got a small loan to start it and didn't have to go to no bank. Just gotta pay interest in favors from time to time, so I got a pretty sweet deal. I know how those racist-ass banks are about giving Black folks loans. That's why I don't mind helping you. You seem smart. Hell, if I help you, maybe one day you'll be able to help me."

"Ain't that the way it goes?" I say, unsure how serious he is.

Being able to start my business this year would be a dream come true—but talk is cheap.

"You 'bout ready?" He checks his watch for the time.

I nod, and a few minutes later, we're back in the Batmobile. Before leaving, though, I noticed he didn't pay the Greek. *Hmmm.* As long as I didn't have to pay, I'm not going to concern myself with their business.

Marco pushes that magic button, activating the sirens and flashing blue lights, and we're out in lightning speed.

Marco drops me off at my car in record time. Even faster than when we arrived at our lunch destination. Being a gentleman, he walks me to my car.

"Shit," I mutter when I see a parking ticket on my windshield. Signs everywhere indicate that parking is reserved for dine-in customers only. Downtown Decatur is like a circus when it comes to parking, but I should've known better and parked in a nearby garage. Marco grabs the ticket before I can reach out my hand to remove it from my vehicle.

"I got this," he says, folding it up and sticking it into his back pocket.

I want to ask him if he's sure, but I don't. Something tells me to just trust him.

"Wow…you're handy," I say, stepping close to hug him goodbye.

"You have no idea."

Finally! He flirts.

"Maybe I can see you tonight," he says, squeezing me tight while resting his chin on my head.

"Maybe," I reply, finally getting the chance to play hard to get.

I blow him a kiss, but he doesn't stay long enough to catch it. He's already gone.

Once in traffic, I check the voice message from Kwame. Maybe he's begging for my forgiveness. I could forgive him…maybe in a few weeks. Just to teach him a lesson. I press the button to play the message:

I know you're mad with me, but there's bigger stuff going on in the family right now than your anger. If you don't wanna talk to me, call Balanah or Sahara. They can tell you what's going on. It's important. We got a family meeting at Mama's tonight at 9. Nobody's heard from Malichai. So, if you talk to him, let him know. I love you, even if you can't stand me. And I'm sorry I didn't use you as my real estate agent. Just forgive me already, will you? Hell, I'll give you the commission money from my savings if that will make things better between us? I miss you, Ess. Damn. Give a brother a break.

That damn Kwame. I knew hearing him through a voice message would make me instantly forgive him. You can't stay mad at someone so calm and loving forever. He makes me sick. Still, I wonder what the hell is going on, though. I wish he had just said it in the message he left.

I don't call Kwame back. I'll just deal with him at Mama's. Damn. I was planning to text Marco and have an overnight visit with him tonight. What the hell is this family meeting about anyway? I have a feeling it involves money. Last time, it was about helping Malichai get back on his feet, and nobody really followed through. I couldn't commit to it then, and apparently, I wasn't alone because he's still in the same rut. I'm not in the mood for nobody begging me for money or asking me to do them a favor. I've got too much going on right now.

I call Balanah, but she doesn't answer. I don't bother calling Sahara; I don't need her bringing up the resident and killing my vibe. I call Ebony—she doesn't answer either. I'm low-key relieved because I've already decided I can't make it tonight. One of them can fill me in later regarding the reason for the meeting.

I send a quick text to Marco: *Meet me at my place at 9.*

Then I turn my phone off. I have other plans for tonight—and they don't include family. I'm ready to get to know this mysterious cop in a whole new way.

14

MALICHAI

"Super-Mal"

I'm cracking my knuckles, but it doesn't stop my fingers from aching. At this time of year, the cold weather always makes them feel arthritic. I detailed three cars today—made a hundred and twenty dollars with tips—and yesterday's cans and scrap brought in another hundred and seventy-five. That still ain't enough to pay Rauel, though. So, it looks like we getting put out.

Trying to avoid Rauel, I take the back stairs to my room. But just my luck, I literally run straight into him. The impact of our shoulders colliding catches us both off guard, and we almost fall backward. I keep walking like I don't notice him, but Rauel can smell when somebody owes him money. He ain't got to see them.

"Malichai!" he calls in that foreign accent of his.

Caught, I turn around. "I'm gonna have your money," I say, holding out my aching hands.

"There will be no more chances for you, my friend! I need money now!"

He's looking at me like he's ready to chop off my hands. Maybe that's how they handle debts in the country where he's from. I can't blame the man, though. He needs his money. Unfortunately, I just ain't got it.

"You gave me until the end of the week, remember? Come on. I ain't got it right now."

"Yes…you say same thing every week. No more extensions. Give me something or you must go now!"

"I don't have anything," I lie.

"No…no…no!" He waves his finger. "Then you leave today, my friend."

"Damn, Rauel!"

I dig in my pocket, trying to pull out two bills, but end up with four twenties instead. *Damn! I hate new bills—always sticking together.* I don't want him to know how much I have. Sure, it's not enough to cover what I owe, but I'm sure that won't keep him from taking it.

"This is all I got, man. My whole week's pay. I guess I'll just starve."

Rauel shrugs, licks his fingers, and separates the bills. He seems satisfied.

"You starving…that's not my problem," he says, stuffing the money in his shoe. "Today is Monday. You must be out by Thursday."

"Thursday?! Come on, you said Friday!"

"Thursday…Friday…no difference. You still not pay!" He points at me, shaking his head.

One day makes a big difference. Even though I probably won't have it by then, I owe $670 now. Rauel keeps adding late fees, so by Friday, it'll probably be a grand. He just wants me gone.

"Alright, man," I say and walk off.

I can feel him burning a hole in my back. The broker you are, the less people understand. And respect? That shit don't exist when you're broke. I jam my hands in my pockets as a cold wind swirls around me, jet up one more flight of stairs, and reach the fourth floor. I just want to sleep. To tell you the truth, I don't even feel like waking up tomorrow. I'm too tired. Feels like I'm never gonna catch myself. Never.

Before I can get to my door, Donna, my next-door neighbor, swings hers open like she's been waiting for me. She always "just happens" to hear me coming in. Normally, she flatters me with compliments about how sexy I am—even though I know she's lying—but today, I'm not in the mood. I don't want to talk; I want to smoke. I spin around before she can stick her head out and jog back down the stairs to the bottom floor to buy a dime bag from my man, Crunch.

Crunch is already outside, sitting in a folding chair in front of his door, with his burly pit bull, Coco, lounging at his feet. The thick cloud of smoke swirling around him almost makes him look mystical. His eyes are bloodshot red, his muscles look relaxed, and he's taking it easy. Coco knows me, but that don't stop her mean ass from getting up and giving me a growl.

"Sit yo' ass down," Crunch tells her, and she obeys.

"What's up, man?" I say, giving him dap. I think about patting Coco, but decide against it.

"Nothing but the money and the bullshit," Crunch replies in a southern drawl, revealing his gold fronts.

He takes a hit from his fat-ass Bob Marley blunt before generously passing it to me. I take a puff, and it goes straight to the head. My hands don't ache so bad anymore. I take another puff, hold it in a while, and then exhale slowly. Now, my thoughts don't feel so heavy. My burdens are floating lightly in my head like they're in outer space. I feel relieved.

"Yeah, this shit here is the truth," he says, holding up a bag of the greenest bud I've ever seen. "Just got this from ole boy today. It's that fire! Look at those big-ass nuggets—big as seedless grapes."

By the smell of it and the quick high, I already know I can't afford it. It's high-grade. I barely have enough for mid-grade.

"I can't do that today." I hand back the blunt. "Just give me the regular."

Crunch's mid-grade is decent—not full of seeds like most dudes in Decatur. Used to be Decatur was the best place to buy green, but it ain't like that no more. Crunch is the last stand-up dealer. He don't skimp you like the rest.

He pulls a bag from underneath the rug his folder chair is sitting on and tosses it to me.

"You been keeping your head up, my man?" he asks, giving me a strange look like he wants to say more but holds back. I guess he feels sorry for me. He knows how I used to make my bread back in the day, and he sees how I make it now.

"Trying to."

"I admire you, man. You walk around with the weight of the world on your shoulders but don't bend. That's cool," he says, handing the blunt back.

I just shrug and take another long puff. I bend—I just don't let anyone see it.

I toss him the twenty and try to give the blunt back that we barely put a dent in.

"Naw, man. That's you."

"Cool, man," I say with gratitude, but really, I'm shocked. Weed this good never comes free. *Hell, I guess I finally got a break.*

I tuck it behind my ear and give him dap before walking away.

"Keep your head up, man," he calls out.

I turn around, pound my fist against my chest, and throw up the peace sign. He lifts his chin, already rolling another fat one.

When I get back to my floor, Donna's sitting on the steps with her legs spread so wide I can see the red panties under her robe. I'm beginning to think the girl doesn't own any regular clothes. She's got on some matching house slippers, and the caked-on makeup makes her look like she's about to be buried.

"Hey, baby. Thought I heard you earlier."

She tries to hand me a cigarette; I wave it off. She knows I hate cigarettes, but that don't stop her from offering them to me.

"What's up, Donna?"

"Nothing but this good view in front of me," she says, rubbing her neck and giving me a hungry look.

I force a smile but still ain't in the mood. I just want to go in my room and finish off this blunt.

"You need a good woman to rub you down after a long day," she adds, spreading her legs wider.

Donna's sexy but trashy—thick thighs, ass shaped like a rump roast, and maybe the prettiest natural breasts I've seen. But she's a whore. Some lonely nights, I admit, the woman is hard to resist. Looking at her, I can tell she's almost Mama's age, but this hard life hasn't dimmed her beauty. Somehow, she manages to keep it up. She still wears too much makeup, though.

"That sounds nice," I say, walking past her.

"You know where I live."

"Yep," I mutter, fiddling with my keys.

"I don't want no money from you, you know."

"Oh, yeah?" I turn to see her squirming like she's trying to put out a fire between her legs. "Why is that?"

"'Cause it would be my honor. I done fucked a lot boys, but never a man. And you, Malichai, are a man. Sexy, smart, and hard-working. I hope that girl in there knows what she got," she says, gesturing with her head towards my door.

"You seen Meka today?"

"Yeah. She in there, waiting on something I crave every day." She licks her lips and smiles.

I stick my key in the lock and try to open the door as fast as I can.

"Oh, your sister B...B...B something came by here the other day," she says before I can walk in the room.

"Balanah?"

"Yeah, that's her. Said to call her. It's about your son."

"Thanks for looking out, Donna."

"Anytime," she purrs.

Inside, I see Meka standing in the kitchen, stirring a pot, and I feel like I can finally breathe.

"Mal!" she squeals, leaping into my arms and planting kisses all over my face and neck.

I close the door behind me and carry her over to the bed, where I set her down. The room smells like she's making my favorite dinner—chicken alfredo. I do a quick scan of her body with my eyes like I'm inspecting her for damage. All in all, she looks good. Her short hair is slicked back, and she's wearing the same clothes she was wearing the last time I saw her—short jean skirt, black tights, snug sweater, knee-high boots—but she's clean.

Meka jumps up and kisses me hard.

"I missed you," she says, arms wrapped tight around me.

I squeeze her back, relieved she's alive. Then I pull away.

"Where the hell you been?" I demand.

She sighs, then walks back over to the steaming pots while shaking her head and smiling like she's been on vacation.

"You won't even believe it." She waves a hand in the air like it's too much to explain. "I'm making your favorite—chicken alfredo— but with bow tie pasta instead of spaghetti noodles. The store was out. Can you believe that? Oh...and garlic bread." She opens the oven and pulls out a pan of bread. "I also got a salad in the fridge with your cheddar ranch dressing, and for dessert..." She winds her narrow hips. "...Meka Surprise."

She rushes over and jumps into my arms again, kissing me. My blunt falls from my ear. She picks it up, looks at me, and smiles before handing it over.

"Where you been, Meka?" I say firmly. She gets my point.

She sits down on the bed and sighs. "Okay, here's what happened."

Excited, she jumps back up and faces me like she's about to share her favorite story. There ain't no telling what kind of wild two-week adventure she's about to tell me, but knowing how convincing she can be, I'm sure I'll believe every word.

"So, me and Wavy were chilling at Dudley's, like we do every Thursday and Friday night. And her new man comes strolling in the club—the one she been bragging about like he King Tut or something," Meka says, sucking her teeth. "He's buying us drinks and shit, and we partying, dancing, and whatnot. You know how we do. Then we go out back to cop one."

She means smoke some crack.

"That's when he asks us to make a run with him. The bar was closing, and I was about to come home to you and Zach. But Wavy begged me to ride with her. So, I said what the hell?" She shrugs. "We go to his friend's house, where we party some more. I don't know how long we was there." She looks up at the ceiling like she's trying to think. "Maybe a few hours. Anyway, I'm thinking we're done, and I'm ready to come home to my man, right?"

She says it like she's waiting on me to agree with her.

"I'm so through—" Meaning she was high and drunk off her ass. "—that I pass out in the backseat and start dreaming I'm being chased by a fucking cow." She starts laughing, her arms flailing about. "Mooing at me and shit. When I wake my ass up from that nightmare, guess…the fuck…what?"

She waits for me to guess, but I just shrug my shoulders. She's starting to get on my nerves with her damn theatrics.

"We were on a fucking cow farm! The sun was out, roosters crowing and shit!"

She's bent over from laughing so hard. Then she notices the pot of noodles boiling over.

"Shit! Hold on, baby."

She holds up one finger and rushes to the stove to strain the noodles, glaze them with butter, stir the cream sauce, and lower the heat.

"What was I saying?" she asks, turning around to face me. "Oh, yeah—we were on a damn farm!" Her eyes widen with excitement.

"A farm?" I ask, confused. "Where the fuck is there a farm on the West Side?"

Her outrageous story is pissing me off.

"That's the thing," she says, smiling bigger. "We wasn't on the West Side!"

"Then where the fuck were y'all?!" I ask, standing up.

My anger is rising, but she's too caught up in her story to notice.

"Our black asses were in fucking Alabama! Me and Wavy slept the whole ride, and when we woke up, the car was in a pasture with a flat tire—ten feet from the fence he had crashed through. And that nigga was gone! He left us there to get eaten by them damn cows!"

I shake my head, but she's still grinning like it was fun.

"I was so mad 'cause I knew you was gonna be pissed. That bitch didn't tell me the run was in Alabama. She still claims she ain't know. I didn't know what he had in that car, so I got my skinny ass out before some redneck came to hang our asses or call the police. We hitched a ride to town, but we were broke and stuck like Chuck."

"So how'd you get money to survive?" I press.

"I didn't have to do shit. I told that bitch she got me in the mess, she was gonna have to get me out." She starts shifting, her eyes darting from me to the floor. "We found a truck stop, and she tried to hustle up bus money."

"Just her?" I ask, suspicious.

"Yeah, Mal! You know I don't lie to you. I sold some of my food stamps, though."

"Oh, your food stamps worked out there?"

"Boy, government money is accepted anywhere. But let me finish," she says, quieting me with a wave of her hand. "It was taking

Wavy too long to hustle up the money. I mean, she's only got one pussy," she laughs. "Plus, what little she made, we had to spend on food and rooms. So, we hitched a ride with a trucker to some city where they be betting on dog and horse racing. He thought Wavy could make some more money there. Cool dude."

She walks back to the stove and turns it off.

"That's where I sold my food stamps. Three hundred bucks' worth for a hundred and fifty dollars. Enough to get us home—but I started feeling lucky. It was bizarre enough that we ended up in Alabama, so I took a chance."

"What you talking about?"

"I put all that money on a black horse!"

"You foolish," I say, shaking my head.

"Uh-uh," she beams. "That black ass horse ran like he was running for his life. And guess what his name was?"

"Blackie? Shit, I don't know," I grunted.

"Super Mile! But when they said his name over the PA system, it sounded like 'Super Mal'! I knew that shit was more than a coincidence. So, I bet on you, baby—and I won!"

She jumps up and down screaming like she hit the lottery. Now she has my attention. I stand up, cautious but hopeful. I don't want to get too happy for nothing.

"How much you win, girl?"

"Five hundred!" she says, holding up five fingers.

I started thinking about the rent. Maybe we won't get evicted after all. I can easily pull the rest together to give Rauel this week. Hell, I was sitting here worried about Meka and getting evicted, and she comes back home with five hundred dollars in her pocket. I grab her face and kiss her. She squeals.

"You know how bad we needed that, baby?! We were 'bout to be put out of here on Friday."

I lean in to kiss her again, but she steps away and looks down.

Shit! I already know. She don't got the money no more.

"Damn, Meka!"

"I'm sorry, baby. I tried to get home with it. I wanted you to be proud of me. But after tickets, hotel stays, and…"

She doesn't finish the rest of the sentence. I know she blew it partying it up with Wavy in Alabama instead of bringing her ass home while I was here worried sick about her, the bills, and every other fucking thing I got to worry about.

She tries to kiss me, but I push her away, flop on the bed, and fire up my blunt. I don't say shit to her 'cause I ain't got shit to say—I'm too tired. She doesn't take nothing seriously. Not being a mother, not these bills, not her addiction. Life's just one big escapade to Meka. It used to thrill me, but now it just fucking drains me.

I hear her clanking dishes and silverware as she fixes my plate, but I ain't hungry. I take a slow drag of the blunt. I hear her talking, but I'm tuning her out.

Meka comes handing me the plate of food like it makes up for the five hundred dollars she burned. I take the plate and set it on the nightstand. She looks like her feelings are hurt. Her eyes are sad, and her chin is lowered to the ground.

"I'm sorry, Mal. I missed you so bad. I really was trying to get back to you, but shit just got fucked up. That's why I said the least I could do is use the last of my food stamps to make your favorite meal. I wanted us to have a romantic night, but I'm always fucking shit up."

She starts crying, and I get up to kiss her on the cheek. It's my way of saying, *Don't worry about it.* Then I lay back down and continue puffing my blunt.

"You too good for me, Mal. I know it. Even your family knows it. Why do you put up with me? You're like your dad. I'm like my mom. We don't mix," she says, lowering her head.

Meka's mother was a junkie who died from an overdose.

"You're a hero, and I'm nothing but a damsel in distress."

"First of all," I lean in, "I couldn't be a hero without the damsel." I stroke her cheek, and she brightens up a bit. "Second, you walk through fire when you love somebody." I pull her down beside me on the bed. "And lastly, I love you, girl. I told you I got your back. You're my son's mother."

She looks around the room and notices Zach ain't around for the first time. She must've thought he was out with me when she came back and didn't see us there waiting for her.

"Where is he?"

"With Balanah."

"Oh." She kisses my forehead. "I'm sorry, Mal. I'll get better one day. I promise."

"I know you will, but come Thursday, we ain't got nowhere to live."

She sighs. It isn't her burden, though. It's mine. And as a man, I'll carry it on my own.

"You know, Wavy's Section 8 voucher is getting her a five-bedroom house in a pretty decent neighborhood. Since her kids stay with her mama, she's gonna rent out all those rooms. She said we can get the master bedroom for a hundred and forty bucks a month— way less than we pay here."

"Hell no," I say, pulling on my blunt. "I ain't staying with no fucking Wavy."

"What you got against Wavy? You didn't mind her before, remember?" she says, hinting at the times I was balling, and Wavy used to partake in threesomes with us. But back then, it was just fun—I wasn't living with the bitch.

"Everything," I say flatly.

"Well, maybe we can stay with one of your sisters? You know how much they love me," she says, being sarcastic.

She stares at me, waiting for me to validate whether my sisters like her or not. I don't do either. When I say nothing, she climbs on top of me, straddling my waist.

"I don't care where we stay, Mal—even if we have to sleep in the Chevy. As long as I'm with you, I don't give a damn," she says, then kisses my forehead again.

I know she means it. Meka may be reckless, but she's down for me.

She starts grinding on me. I put my hands on her tiny waist and slide them up to her breasts. They used to feel like juicy mangos; now they're flat. I don't make her feel bad, though. I tell her she's sexy, and she trusts me enough to believe it. Her moans get louder, her grinding faster.

"I missed you so much, Mal," she whispers, licking my neck, then chest, and moving lower.

I pull her back up into a kiss. As I reach to grab a condom out of the drawer, she gives me a look. She already knows why I use them with her. I don't know what Meka be out there doing when she's under the influence, and I got to protect myself. I have two condoms left. I take one.

"We don't need that today," she says while kissing me, then sits upright to remove her sweater and bra. "I don't want nothing between us."

"You know better than that." I tear open the wrapper with my teeth.

"Why?" she asks.

She knows the answer. Still, I lie. Well, sort of.

"Because we don't need another kid right now. That's why."

I guess my reason isn't good enough because she tries to snatch the condom from my hand. That's when I see her arms. Red and brown needle marks. My stomach drops. I grab her wrists tightly.

"Ouch, Mal, you're hurting me!"

She looks down at the tracks, almost like she forgot they were there.

"What the fuck is this?!" I shout.

"Nothing!" she says, yanking away.

"It don't look like nothing! You shooting up now?"

"It was just one time in Alabama. I didn't even like it. I ain't gonna try that shit again."

"Oh yeah?" I say sarcastically, remembering her saying the same thing the first time she snorted powder. "Who gave it to you? That bitch Wavy?"

"I'm grown. Don't blame Wavy for the shit I do."

She jumps off me, snatches her bra from the floor, and puts it back on before slipping into her sweater.

"What you're doing is bad enough. Now you add heroin to the mix. That's some shit you don't want to play around with, girl. You got a death wish or something?"

"I said I wasn't gonna do it no more! Lay off me! I don't give you grief about smoking your weed!"

"Don't compare weed to heroin and crack!"

"Oh, so you're better than me because of how you choose to get high? A high is a high, Malichai!" she argues while looking for her boots.

"You playing with fire, girl. You need help."

"When I'm ready for it, I'll get it," she says, pulling on her boots.

"Where you going now?"

"I need some fresh air."

"Then open a fucking window, 'cause you ain't going nowhere!"

"I'm just going to the corner store for a soda. I'll be back."

She's standing in front of me, glaring like she's pissed off. I don't care.

"Alright," I say, knowing I can't stop her from leaving.

"I need some money," she says in a low, humiliated voice while holding out her hand like a child waiting for lunch money from their parent.

"Food stamps work in Alabama but can't buy soda here?"

"I told you—I sold most of them and used the rest on this dinner."

"Well, I ain't got it."

She looks at me like she don't believe me, then starts rummaging through the nightstand drawers. She's having one of her fits; she needs to get high. She starts to have fits whenever she gets upset. That's why I try not to piss her off too often, but I can't help it this time. Now she's shooting up? I don't know how far I can ride with her on that kind of horse. Crack is one thing, but heroin is another type of fire. It don't just burn you; it bleeds you.

"Ain't no damn money in there! What? You going to shoot up?!"

She grabs something from the drawer and stuffs it in her pocket.

"Fuck you, Mal!" she yells before storming out the door.

I shake my head. *What the fuck can I do?* My answer? Spark my joint. Then I see the box of condoms on the floor. I pick the box up. It's empty. *Shit!* I almost chase after her, but I don't. I'm too tired. Instead, I smoke the rest of my blunt and then fall asleep, thinking, *Fuck the world.*

15

KWAME
"The Dramatic Shades"

I've contacted everybody about Ebony except Malichai and Essence. Hopefully, Essence called Balanah or Sahara and got the news. I called a family meeting today at Mama's. We need each other now more than ever—and Ebony needs us most. That's why I'm driving to Decatur to pick up Malichai. I just hope he's home. As for Mama, I don't know how she's really handling this. One minute she's crying, the next she's ready to tear down the jail in protest. She'll never show us her true feelings because she don't want us worrying about her.

I was shocked by the number of people who protested outside the jail. Women's groups of all backgrounds came out to support Ebony, demanding her release and stronger laws against child molesters. They argued that the system discourages victims like Zena from speaking up, leaving molesters unpunished. The statistics on their signs were heartbreaking, showing how many girls are sexually abused but never report it, or the case just gets dropped.

Ebony's fans were there, too, holding up her artwork to show who she really is. I know seeing all those people fighting for Ebony gave Mama strength and made the situation feel less hopeless. I even saw signs with Daddy's face. His supporters came out, reminding everyone of his legacy fighting the kind of abuse my niece endured. When people spotted Mama, they surrounded her like a queen, cheering her on. She walked tall and proud, and I was right by her side, feeling more alive than I had in years.

The press swarmed us like paparazzi, desperate for a word from the wife of the great Akimbo "Black-Man" Sedah, but she didn't speak. When they turned to me, I looked at her, and she gave me a look that said, *Not yet.* And I obeyed. Mama wasn't there to protest or answer questions—she just wanted to see her daughter. I guided her through the thick crowd, shielding her from the reporters and cameras. It took nearly an hour to get inside.

At the counter, Mama demanded—not asked—to see Ebony. The clerk told her visiting hours were over, and she couldn't see Ebony without being a lawyer. Mama didn't take no for an answer. She held out her hands and told them to arrest her. The heavy bass in her voice turned heads. Just when it looked like things might get ugly, a tall Black woman came over and whispered something into the white guy's ear. He looked at Mama like she was a celebrity before walking away humbly. The woman told Mama that she would let her see Ebony, but only her—no one else. That was fine with me; I just wanted Mama to see her daughter.

Before leading Mama to the back, she grabbed Mama's hand, gave it a gentle squeeze, and expressed her gratitude for my dad saving her family's life a long time ago. Honored, Mama smiled as if to say, *You're welcome.* Mama then followed the woman, taking confident strides while everyone stared at her like she was a living legend. I watched until she disappeared around a corner.

Mama returned to the lobby almost an hour later with tears in her eyes. When she saw me, she ducked into the bathroom and came out looking strong again, like she'd cried out her pain in private. Once she reached me, she wanted to leave immediately. I wanted to ask about Ebony, but something told me to lay off it for a while. I guided Mama back through the crowd, again shielding her with my body the best I could.

Once in my truck, she let out a heavy sigh that echoed her pain, then turned to me and said we have to find Zena. I promised her that we would. As I pulled off, she stared out the window and mumbled in a low voice about having to go see my father. I knew she was just thinking out loud, but she had my full attention at the mention of visiting my father. Her husband. The man we hadn't seen or heard from in years.

I offered to drive her to see him, but she quickly shook her head no. When I tried to ask again, she yelled that she wanted to go alone. She'd never yelled at me before. I wanted to tell her she shouldn't go alone, that she was too emotional right now, but Mama knows best. So, I let it go.

Before I dropped Mama back off at home, she made me promise that I wouldn't tell my brother or sisters. I gave her my word—after all, there wasn't much else I could do to help this situation be any less painful for her.

* * * * *

It's a quarter past six, and I pull up to the motel where Malichai is staying. When I see his Chevy parked in the lot, I know he's home. I need my big brother to help me look for Zena. We're the only two men left in the family, and it helps to share the weight of protecting our sisters and nieces. It's painful knowing we failed Zena. I feel like a grim messenger; I've been giving bad news all day.

I walk up the stairs to the second floor, trying not to get distracted by the filth. I'd offered Malichai and his family to come and stay with me until they get back on their feet, but he turned me down— probably because he don't want to be in that house. I'm gonna extend the offer again tonight, even though I know he's gonna turn me down. It's just the right thing to do.

Before I can reach his door, a half-dressed woman steps into my path, sticking her breasts in my face and flashing a money-making smile. I already know what that's about. Ignoring her, I proceed to go around her and knock on Malichai's door. I hear some rummaging inside before he finally raises the blinds. He stands there for several seconds, rubbing the sleep from his eyes and just staring at me like he's seeing a ghost. I guess I can't blame him for being surprised by my pop-up visit since I don't leave the house. Then, the locks click, and he swings open the door.

"Kwame? What's going on, man?" he asks, looking concerned.

He steps aside for me to come inside his room, which smells like hot cream cheese and strong-ass weed. I almost get a buzz just sniffing the cloudy air.

"Hey, man." I sigh as he hugs me.

He clears space on a worn chair for me to sit. My brother looks like he's been to war. He looks exhausted, his face sagging, like life had drained him. He works harder than I ever worked, and if anybody deserves to spend a lifetime on the couch, it's him and not me.

"Where's Zach?" I ask, looking around for my nephew.

"Oh, he's with Balanah. I gotta get his bad ass before he drives her crazy," he chuckles with a guilty look.

"He probably having a good time," I say, trying to make him feel better. "Balanah complains, but she's the best when it comes to kids."

Suddenly, my stomach is starting to churn again.

"I'm gonna use your bathroom," I say, jumping up and rushing towards the only room that can be the bathroom.

I fall to my knees in front of the toilet and let 'er rip, getting it all out of my system—whatever *it* is. When I return, Malichai is giving me a strange look.

"What's up with you, man? You pregnant?" he jokes.

"I don't know. Maybe I'm coming down with something," I reply, avoiding his gaze.

He studies me, then pulls out two cigars from his nightstand and tosses one to me. He splits it open with his fingernails and opens a small sack of green.

"You lost weight, man?" he asks, concerned.

"I don't know."

I noticed my pants had been fitting a little looser, but throwing up almost daily for four weeks will do that.

"I think so," he says, stuffing the cigar with weed. "How long you had this little…bug?"

I shrug. I'm not here to talk about me.

"Look, man. Should I tell you the reason for my visit after we light up or now?"

He stops rolling the blunt but doesn't set it down. Instead, he lowers it to his lap and gives me a suspicious look. He knows something's wrong.

"Shit, man! Is everybody okay? Is it Mama?"

"Everybody's alive and healthy."

"Is it you? You sick?"

"Ebony's in jail," I say bluntly.

"What?" He jumps up.

I nod, then motion for him to toss me the sack of weed, which he does. I haven't smoked in years and can't think of a better time than now.

"It's all over the news. People are protesting—it's a circus, man. That's why I'm here. We're having a family meeting tonight at Mama's."

"What the hell did she do?"

I sigh. "She tried to kill Kenton."

"What?! What the hell is wrong that girl? She crazy as hell! Why in the fuck would she do some dumb-ass shit like that?"

I let him vent, rolling the blunt while he curses Ebony. I hate this next part of the conversation. It makes everything more real and makes my burdens heavier each time. When he finally stops ranting, he stares at me. I motion for the light; he hesitates at first, then tosses it.

My stomach is starting to churn again. I squirm in my seat, trying to settle it, but give up and rush to the bathroom. I lower my head to the toilet, gagging. Malichai stands outside the door watching until I lean up and shut it in his face. When I return ten minutes later, he's already lit the blunt, and the one he rolled is sitting on the nightstand. He gives me another concerned look.

"You need to take your ass to the doctor. Throwing up twice in thirty minutes ain't normal for anyone, not even a pregnant woman."

I wipe my mouth and wave him off.

"You want me to go with you? We'll go tomorrow," he insists.

"We ain't got time for that. There's too much going on. I'm fine. I told you I'm just coming down with something."

He hands me the blunt, and I take a few puffs before passing it back to him. The smoke calms my stomach and my nerves.

"So what happened? She just shot him after being broken up for years? I thought she was over that man."

"I wish it was that simple. But does that sound like Ebony?"

"No," he says, handing the blunt back.

I sigh before puffing again, then pass it to him. I wait until he exhales so he don't choke because of what I'm about to say.

"She shot him because he raped Zena. He started when she was nine."

Malichai freezes. He has the blunt raised to his mouth, the ashes dropping to the floor. Finally, he squints, puts it out, and sits heavily on the edge of his bed. Hunched over, he rests his elbows on his knees and rubs his face while shaking his head in disbelief. When he looks at me, he has tears in his eyes. So do I. Zena was our first niece, the one who made us uncles and aunts, made Mama a grandmother.

"He...went all the way?" Malichai whispers.

"Yeah. For years."

He buries his face in his hands like he's trying to fight off a bad image.

"We should've been the ones to kill him! Us!" He pounds his chest, then stands up and starts pacing. "I'm gonna finish him! How's he still alive? Did she miss? Ebony don't know shit about shooting no gun. How'd she think she was gonna kill him? She should've told us!"

I smirk, trying to lighten his mood a little. "She didn't miss. She shot his dick off. Clean. I heard the bastard only got one nut, too. No dick and one ball."

Malichai chuckles. "She shot him in the dick!"

"She tried to shoot him again, but the gun jammed."

"Damn!" he squeals. "Ain't that a bitch."

"To be honest with you, I'd rather he live the rest of his life in the misery she caused him. What's a man without a dick?"

"A bitch!" he says.

We both laugh, then take a few moments to process the pain.

"You think they gonna convict her?" he asks me, breaking the silence.

I shrug. "She's got a lot of people behind her. When I took Mama to see her this morning, there were more protestors than we ever saw for Daddy."

"Damn, Ebony," he mutters with a sad chuckle. "Why you think she ain't tell us, man?"

"You know her—always holding things in, turning her pain into art."

"I hate that I couldn't see what was going on," Malichai says, voice breaking.

"Imagine how she feels. It happened under her roof for years."

He drops his head. "How can a man do that to a child? This shit gonna stay with her forever. As men, we're made stronger to protect women and children, not hurt them. Rapists and molesters are worse than fucking Hitler. They're sick!" He spit the words out like his thoughts were leaving a bad taste in his mouth.

I nod while lighting up the second blunt and taking a slow drag.

"Now I understand what Daddy was doing all those years," I say. "That case got dropped because Zena wouldn't talk. Nobody cared enough to protect her, to just believe her. No, they wanted to humiliate her further by wanting her to take the stand in court. Girls don't lie about something like that. Think about how many girls are going through this shit right now, and their assaulter knows the system really don't give a fuck. The system gives them the freedom to be rapists. Remember that little girl found raped and dead in that old building Daddy blew up?"

Malichai nods.

"Now I see why he did it. He was the only one who cared. No one stepped up after him, and now look. Generations are being ruined by the very evil he tried to vanquish. It's ironic and sad."

"Hmm," Malichai murmurs. He never has much to say about Daddy.

"Mama's going to see him," I blurt, despite promising to keep it to myself.

"What? When? Why?" Malichai looks upset.

"What you mean, man? I think it's a good idea."

"I don't. It ain't gonna do nothing but make her feel worse. What can he do from prison? Save Ebony a spot at the cafeteria table?" He shakes his head. "He can't even write us, let alone do something about this shit. We here, and we gonna handle it."

"Look, don't tell Mama I told you. She don't want nobody to know."

"Whatever, man." He waves it off. "Where's Zena at now?"

"Nobody knows. That's why I'm here. Mama wants us to find her and bring her to the meeting."

"You sure it ain't best for Balanah or Sahara to handle that. You think she wants to see us?"

"She needs to know she has men in her life who love her and will protect her. She needs that type of reassurance if she's ever going to heal and have a normal life."

"You right, man. I just…"

He lowers his head and starts sobbing like I've never seen him cry before. I get up and put my arm around his shoulders.

"I feel responsible. She ain't have no father, no grandfather—but she had an uncle. And I was too caught up in my own shit to know she needed me."

"Zena has two uncles. I can say the same, Mal. My eyes have been shut for a long time. I've been just as caught up in my own shit as you—we all have. But this is our wake-up call. We can't stay in our own little worlds anymore. Family comes first. Family is love, man," I say, thinking about the clock I got in my car. "It's our first love, the most important love."

Malichai sucks up his tears in one masculine sniff and then stands up tall, looking like Daddy. He acts like Daddy, too. Strong and sensitive.

"Let's go find our little girl, man," he says and starts putting on his boots.

While we are waiting at a stoplight, we spot Meka climbing into a white work van. I ask Malichai if he wants me to stop, but he tells me to keep going. He keeps his eyes fixed on the van until it becomes a white blur. Then, he sighs heavily. I feel for my brother. I know he's already dealing with a lot. Now, he's dealing with even more. He's strong enough to handle it, though. We all are.

"You, Meka, and Zach can still come stay with me," I offer. "You'd have the basement to yourselves, and we won't bother y'all none."

"I know, man…I know," he says, rejecting my invitation in his own little way.

16
BALANAH
"See Ya"

I've been crying all day. You'd think Stephan could handle dinner for the day, but *no*—I had to cook. You'd think Zionah would stop being a spoiled-ass brat and look out for her two younger siblings, but *no*—I had to help them with their homework and keep them entertained while she locked herself in her room. It's like I'm the only one who notices my tears. Am I imagining the moisture glazing my eyes like tiny ponds? Do the bags under my eyes and the dried tear streaks on my cheeks exist? Maybe not—because no one else seems to see them. Maybe I'm imagining everything: my sister in jail, my niece being raped. It must all be in my head.

When Stephan first heard the news, his idea of offering empathy was rambling for an hour about how emotionally distraught he was when his uncle went to jail for two years for a DUI. Then he patted me on the shoulder and dismissed the entire situation like he'd done enough. Zionah only cares if she'll be on TV. She says she doesn't want to be *embarrassed* at school. Meanwhile, I can't stop thinking about the horror my niece went through for years and what my sister is suffering. I need to be with my family. I'm getting ready to leave now. The family meeting is at nine, but I want to get there a little early to comfort Mama. I can imagine she's blaming herself, tearing herself apart, and worrying about what this will do to Daddy's image.

I locked Zach in the room with Zionah while I showered. The girls are fed, have finished their homework, and are in front of the TV. When Stephan sees me stepping out of the shower, he looks surprised that I'm leaving.

"You going somewhere, honey?"

"We've got a family meeting," I sigh.

It's the third time I've told him today. It just goes to show that he doesn't listen to me.

He sighs, annoyed. "Oh…today?"

"Yes, Stephan. Today."

"I thought you'd have time to finish those letters. I planned to go to the courthouse tomorrow morning."

"I'll finish them tonight," I quickly say.

My heart is pounding at his insensitivity. His business is the last thing on my mind.

"You sure you'll have time?"

"What did I say?" I snap.

"Why are you so hostile? If things don't go right, you'll have more to worry about than your sister's mess."

"Fuck you, Stephan!"

"That's how you treat me? You don't think I'm going through things, too? I just had to close down my business that I've busted my ass to keep running for the last seven years!"

Now it's *his* business again.

"My sister is in jail. My niece was sexually assaulted. How do you think I feel, Stephan? You think I'm in the mood to talk about failed contracts?"

He sits on the bed, watching me get dressed. I hate when he does that. I can't have a second of privacy. The worst is when he talks to me from the bathroom door when I'm on the toilet.

Everything I've said goes over his head.

"You act like this just happened yesterday. I saw the news. I know what's going on—and it happened years ago."

When I glare at him, he tries to backtrack, only because he hates looking bad. "I'm not saying that what happened to her isn't horrible—it is. But…it happened years ago."

He shrugs and gives me a look like he's trying to talk some sense into me. I just shake my head. I have no more words. The more he talks, the less I like him. I see him for what he is: selfish, self–absorbed, and self-centered. He is incapable of empathy unless it directly affects him. I'm done. When he sees the look on my face, he starts catching on.

"Balanah, please…I don't want you thinking I don't care about what happened, but you have to understand the stress I'm under. I need you, too."

"Yeah, Stephan, I know," I say sarcastically.

I pull on a t-shirt and jeans. They look wrinkled, so I heat up the iron to give them a quick press. Stephan stands behind me, staring a hole in my back.

"I'm not being insensitive, right? Tell me what to do. You want me to come with you?"

He rubs my back, and the touch of his hand feels like fire.

"No," I say quickly, stepping away.

"What could I do then?"

"Well, let's see." I face him, arms folded across my chest. "You could make dinner—oh wait, I already did that. You could help the girls with their homework—no, I already did that, too. You could clean the kitchen—nope, did that, as well." I roll my eyes at him.

Stephan stares at me, not out of guilt but searching for a defense for himself. In his mind, he's never wrong.

"I thought you wanted to cook to keep your mind off things. And the girls don't need help with their homework. I told you to let them figure things out for themselves sometimes. And why can't Zionah clean the kitchen? She does nothing around here."

"You asked, Stephan."

He breathes heavily. "We're both under a lot of stress, but if we don't come together, we could lose everything. Do you want that?"

"Do I want what?" I challenge.

"To lose it all—our house, our cars..." He's counting on his fingers. "...the lights, gas, food—everything."

"Oh...so to you, everything is just material."

"It's more than that! It's shelter for my wife and children," he snaps.

"What about the insurance payout from closing the business? We can survive off that. Plus, the rental properties, stocks, and—"

"That's *just-in-case* money. It won't last. We need income again—fast."

"Fine, I'll open a business then. We can use some of the insurance money. It's my turn anyway, right?"

He looks dumbfounded—the same way he always looks when I talk about starting a business. He's trying to think his way out of this one. The plan was always to open another business once we got the first one off the ground. That was supposed to make things equal.

Stephan sucks his teeth and sighs like he's annoyed with the conversation. This tells me that he doesn't have a compelling reason yet as to why starting another business would be a bad idea now. He turns and walks out of our bedroom. *Such an asshole.* He always walks away when he loses control of the conversation.

I start ironing my jeans, pressing harder than needed. I have too much on my mind. I hate the taste resentment leaves in my mouth. It's bitter, just like poison. If only he knew my thoughts about him lately. He's worried about losing it all—but I guess I'm not part of his *all*.

After pressing my jeans, I put them on and start tackling my afro, spraying it with a leave-in conditioner, water, and oil mixture. I hear

Stephan's footsteps returning, and my heart races. I don't want to see him, but he's back in the room. He stands behind me in the mirror, holding a bottle of water.

"You have nice hair. You're such a pretty woman, Balanah," he says while patting me on the back.

Is that supposed to make me feel better? He sighs when I move away.

"Why do you have to be so competitive?" he asks, opening his water.

I stop picking my hair and glare at him through the mirror. *Competing with him?*

"What the hell are you talking about?"

"Whenever you're upset, you start with that nonsense about your own business and whose turn it is for this or that. I didn't know we were taking turns. I thought we were a team. Besides, you don't even know what you want to do. You have a million different businesses you want to start. It's impossible and risky."

Risky? All businesses are a risk at first. He makes me sound incompetent and delusional for wanting to branch off and do my own thing.

"Not anymore, Stephan." I give him a hard look. "If you can't take regard to what I'm saying, then fuck it. I'll do it myself. You do your thing; I'll do mine. And you know what else? Write your own damn letters. I'm done with *Superior Property Management.* I'm officially off your invisible clock that never…ever…pays."

He rolls his eyes and snickers like it's a joke. He's not taking me seriously. He expects me to keep helping, but I'm done. I fluff my hair into a puff, then turn to face him.

"You know…I had a way to save the company. If you had consulted with me, you wouldn't have had to close it," I say matter-of-factly.

His eyes widen—he knows I'm telling the truth. He trusts my skills, but won't respect them.

"You could've offered your advice anytime if you thought it would help," he says casually.

"No, Stephan. I *knew* my advice would help, but that's beside the point. I'm done." I slice the air with my hands.

He looks like he's realizing what me being done with the business could mean. I walk out of the bathroom, go across the hall to Zionah's room, and tap on the door to tell her I'm leaving and to do as she's told. When I open the door, I see her room is still a mess. She's lying across her bed on her stomach, feet swinging in the air, and hunched over her laptop...probably on Facebook. She's giggling, but when she sees me, she rolls her eyes and frowns.

"I thought your dad said no computer!"

"Alright," she sighs, slamming the laptop shut. "Are you leaving?"

"Yes."

"Can I go?"

"No."

"Please. He'll just yell at me the whole time you're gone and make me clean the whole house by myself, even though he knows I have homework. He wants me to fail so he can have a reason to punish me."

"Zionah, please," I sigh heavily. I don't have the energy for this.

"Please, Mommy. Let me come. I want to see Grandma."

"This isn't that kind of visit. We'll be discussing serious things."

"I already know everything. It's on the news and online."

"You know everything, huh?"

"I can read," she snaps, arms folded across her chest, eyes rolling.

"If you know everything that's going on, why are you acting so insensitive? Don't you care about what happens to your Aunt Ebony and how Zena must be feeling?"

"Yes, but there's nothing I can do, so what's the point of getting upset?" she says like she's giving me wisdom.

"You *can* do something."

"Like what, Mommy? I'd protest, but I know you're not gonna let me."

"You can start by respecting me—do what you're told and help me out around here."

"What about him?" she says.

She's talking about her dad but hasn't been referring to him by that title lately.

"Why doesn't he help you around the house? I'm only a kid!"

I'm two seconds from strangling her when Stephan calls my name.

"What?!" I yell over the catwalk.

"Come see what Zach did!"

Shit! That's when I notice Zach isn't in Zionah's room.

"I thought I told you to look after him? I just needed time to shower. Damn, Zionah."

"He kept grabbing my computer and almost dropped my phone in water—"

I cut her off with a dismissive wave and roll my eyes. Stephan calls my name again, like the house is on fire. I rush downstairs and peek in the family room. The girls' eyes are still glued to the TV. He calls my name for a third time, and I follow his voice to our home office. When I walk inside, I find Zach surrounded by shredded papers. Stephan's briefcase is open. *Shit!* He must've seen me shredding documents earlier and copied me.

"Look at this!" Stephan gestures wildly with his arm. "Do you know how many important papers I had inside this briefcase? Original signed contracts of all the clients who bailed! How are we going to win in court without them?!" he yells.

Startled, Zach jumps up and hides behind my leg.

"I have copies. We don't need the originals."

"Yes, we do!" he yells.

"No, we don't!" I snap back.

"Well, how am I supposed to get those copies?"

"I'll give them to you," I say, annoyed.

"I thought you were done with this business. Isn't that what you said?"

I don't respond. Instead, I kneel and hug Zach to let him know everything is all right.

"Oh, yeah…reward him with a hug," Stephan sneers.

"What do you want me to do? You know he didn't mean it. He's a child."

"Yeah, right," Stephan mutters as he picks up the shredded papers and tries to piece them back together like a puzzle. "Is your brother going to be at this *family meeting*?" he asks cynically.

"I guess."

"Hmm," he says, clearly wanting Zach gone.

"So you're taking Zach with you?"

"Yes," I reply sharply.

"Wasn't Zionah supposed to be watching him? She didn't, huh? She does whatever she wants around here. I wouldn't be surprised if she handed him the papers and showed him how to use the shredder!"

I grab Zach's hand and lead him to the living room to put on his shoes. He's rubbing his eyes like he wants to cry, but I kiss his cheek, and he smiles before settling in front of the TV with the girls to watch *SpongeBob*. I look around for his shoes, finding one under the couch. I put it on his foot, but the whereabouts of the other is a mystery to me.

Stephan went back upstairs, stomping like Zionah does when she's mad. Before I leave the living room to look for the missing shoe, I tell the girls to keep an eye on Zach. They nod, eyes still glued to the screen. I check the office, bathroom, and kitchen—nothing. I just want to find this damn shoe so I can get out the door and get some much-needed fresh air.

I wasn't planning on taking Zach with me, but the tension is already too high in this house. Maybe Mama can keep him for a few days. I'm sure it will help take her mind off things. The last time I talked to Kwame, he told me he was going to pick up Malichai for the meeting. I hate the idea of Zach back in that environment, but it's not up to me. I finally find the shoe in Zionah's room, and as I'm returning to the living room, I hear the girls whining and screaming my name.

"Mommy! Zach took the remote! He's changing the channel and won't give it back!"

I sigh heavily and rush to the living room. Zach is giggling and pressing the buttons like it's the most he's been amused in weeks.

"Zach, give me the remote," I say, holding out my hand and giving him a stern look.

He shakes his head no. When I reach for it, he pushes another button and dives away from me.

Suddenly, the girls scream, "Mama, it's Aunt Ebony! She's on TV!"

I hadn't told the girls what was going on. They're too young. And I haven't watched TV since Kwame broke the news to me this morning. Seeing it makes me want to cry. My sister's wild-eyed mugshot flashes on the screen, and my eyes get misty. Then, they show a picture of Zena from her younger days. I wonder how they got that. I answer my own question when I see Kwame's wife on TV, rolling her neck and talking a mile a minute.

Before I can cry, Zionah and Stephan's shouting rattles the house. They storm down the steps so fast it sounds like an avalanche. I don't even bother leaving the living room to go see what's going on. I keep my eyes on the TV, studying my niece's photo for signs of Kenton's abuse hidden behind her smile. Tears spill down my cheeks.

"Mommy, he broke my laptop charger!" Zionah cries. "He ripped it out of the wall, and he dropped my phone when he snatched it out of my hands!"

Stephan is standing behind her, holding Zionah's laptop and phone like trophies.

"She didn't clean her room. She doesn't listen…" He's counting on his fingers again.

"I was going to clean it!" she yells at him.

"She's on punishment! If you won't do it, I will!"

My tears flow as I look from them to the TV, but they still don't see them.

"Being in the house with you is punishment enough!" Zionah quips.

"Did you hear what she said to me? That's another week. Keep going. You won't see this phone or laptop for two months!"

"Fine! Take them! I'll buy my own!"

"Oh, yeah? With what money?"

"I'm going to get a job since you quit yours!" she fires back, rolling her neck.

"Do you hear what she's saying?" Stephan shouts.

I turn back to the TV. Ebony's face fills the screen again. One of the girls tackles Zach for the remote, and he kicks her in the knee.

"Mommy! Zach kicked me!" she cries.

He takes the remote and changes the channel again.

"Mommy! He has the remote again!" the other one screams.

Stephan yells, "Do something about this girl! Take her with you—she doesn't listen!"

"Please, Mommy!" Zionah pleads. "Take me with you. He doesn't want me here anyway!"

Zach flips the channel, and there's Zena's face again. That's when I start to scream.

I scream—loud, raw, chest hurting. My invisible tears are drowning my face. I'm almost choking on them. I don't know what I'm saying, but I know what I'm thinking: *I need to get the fuck out—and I'm never coming back!*

Everybody is now quiet. Even Zach freezes. They stare at me, wide-eyed, like statues. I don't care. I bolt upstairs, still screaming, grab my packed suitcase out of the closet, run back downstairs, and yank Zach by the hand with so much force he falls. I drag him out of the house, one shoe on, the other left behind. I don't hear anything. My screams drown out their words; my tears blind me. I don't know or care what they are thinking.

Two minutes later, I'm in my car. I crank it up, throw it in reverse, and floor the gas—but I forget to open the garage door. I bust right through it. The loud crash makes Zach laugh. I see Stephan standing in the garage, mouth hanging open. Zionah and the girls watch from the window, faces streaked with tears. I almost give all of them my middle finger as I make my exit, but I don't. My packed bags say it all. I speed out of the driveway, tires screeching. I'm *so* fucking out of here it's not even funny! *See ya!*

17
THE MAMA
"The Family Meeting"

I wish I could trade places with my daughter, take all her pain and bear the consequences of another man's evil, but I can't—at least not in the way I want to.

Ebony, my Ebony. My artist. My secret keeper. My child with the shielding smile. I knew she was keeping secrets, hiding her pain behind her paint and canvas. I felt something was wrong, but she wouldn't let me in. Ebony is stingy with her pain, sharing it with no one. Without Zena or her art, she'd be a lonely, tortured soul. I think she finally released what's been trapped inside of her for years when she shot Kenton. When I visited her in jail, she broke down like never before, melting into my arms as if she'd longed to be there all along. I held her tight and wiped her tears while holding back my own. I told her it was okay to be weak, that I was there to carry her load. I kissed her cheeks, looked her in the eyes, and told her how brave and strong she was for enduring all that she had. Then she crumbled again, saying she wasn't brave or strong, but rather scared and weak. I told her that was nonsense—just fear talking. I reminded her to always trust her instincts, and if shooting the man who defiled her daughter was what they told her to do, I wasn't backing away from that. I told her I would've done the same thing.

She looked at me like she expected judgment, like I'd blame her for not knowing what Kenton had done to Zena. It hurt me that she thought I would be so critical of her during such a hard time in her life. Am I too hard on my children? Do I expect so much from them that it makes them feel like failures? I assured her that I, nor any of her siblings, blamed her in the least. Some things are simply too unimaginable for a mother to see coming—like monsters under a child's bed. Monsters who wear masks of kindness, who give you a false sense of security so you never suspect what's happening just down the hall. Monsters like Kenton. When she asked how she'd ever see through such masks, I told her sometimes you need a mask of your own—two faces, two pair of eyes, two minds—to look at things from every angle.

Ebony collapsed in my arms again. She knew she was safe there. I kissed the top of her head and rubbed her back just as I had when she was five and fell off her bike, and I whispered for her to get back up and keep riding. I told her that soon her stride would be unbreakable, and she'd never fall again. When she was ready, she confessed what she'd been holding back from me for years. Suddenly, it all made sense—why her smile seemed forced, why she never wanted to look me in the eyes for fear that I would see right through her. The truth is, I did, but I didn't know what I was looking at until now. She told me Zena was a lesbian, and she cried like she was mourning her daughter's freedom to choose the alternative lifestyle instead of being forced into it. She knew what Kenton had done destroyed Zena's trust in men.

Then came the secret of all secrets. She told me that Zena's real father wasn't some random neighborhood boy but that vile Sir Zion. She assured me he hadn't raped her like Kenton did Zena, but I disagreed—he coerced a naïve girl who was longing for a father to lay with him. He disgusts me. Her words burned inside me like heartburn. They burned even more when she admitted to me that she thought she was in love with him for years—and maybe still was. I said nothing in response. Just held my child again, silently apologizing for exposing her to such slime. I prayed she heard my unspoken words: that it wasn't love she felt, just the longing for a father, and that Sir Zion loved no one—not her, not Zena, not Black people, not even himself.

When the guard told us that our time was up, Ebony didn't want to let go, and neither did I. I'm still holding her now, even though she's not with me. She asked me to find Zena, and I promised I would. I told her I'd hold Zena until the hurt was gone. She looked at me and knew I was telling the truth. She sighed in relief, wiped her tears, and was escorted back to her cell, shackles on her feet, chains on her heart. As I watched her walk away, I noticed her stride was different—stronger. She had her power back, plus a little of mine. My mission was accomplished, but my work was far from done.

The kids will be here soon. I've finished cooking and set the pots on warm. I want them to have a good, comforting meal to ease their burdens before we grieve about Ebony and Zena. My best China is out, the floor cushions are arranged, patchouli-scented incense is burning heavily, candles are flickering, and soft music is playing. We're dining like royalty today, just like when my king was still around.

I decided to make a meatless meal today—enough flesh has been sacrificed already. My Indian-spiced chickpea stew is simmering with purple onions, spinach, and roasted peppers, seasoned with coriander, curry, masala, celery powder, and a few other spices. Seasoned brown rice, steamed vegetables, fried bread, and their favorite apple crumble pie complete the spread. Everything smells wonderful. I can't wait for them to get here, to feel my love in every bite. I want them to know that, even in crisis, I'll do anything for them. They are my children—the spawn of my king.

To calm my nerves, I read Psalm 103 while praying to my newfound Savior, Jesus Christ. His invisible embrace gives me comfort I didn't know I could feel. I know He got His arms around me and my babies, including Zena. Being in the shelter of His arms is soothing and gives me hope. Me and my king were never religious folks, but we were spiritual—believing in the power of love and the good in people. We breathed in air, felt the wind against our faces, and gazed up at the stars, knowing there was something out there greater than Mother Earth, but we never acknowledged its power as we should have. My king distrusted organized religion, especially Christianity, seeing it as the faith of our oppressors. He called it a slave religion. But I had an experience that made me feel the opposite of a slave. I felt free.

One Sunday, I went with Sahara to church, worried about how she was changing after marrying John. I started seeing less of her despite how often I physically saw her—noticing that she was straying far away from who we raised her to be. I went into that service expecting to leave amused by people praising a white God that looks like a slave master, but I came out inspired, color-blind, and filled with a love so overwhelming I cried for weeks. I knew the power I felt was real.

That was three years ago, and the warmth of that day is still with me. When I feel it fading, I just call out "*Jesus*," and it returns like it never left me. I joined a church the next Sunday—my own, not Sahara's. I needed to know this was real—without the distraction of the love I feel for my daughter confusing me—and it was. I often wonder what my king would think about my new religious findings. I remind myself that he's an open-minded man, that he loves what I love, and I dream of us sharing this faith together, rebuilding everything we learned with a new purpose.

It's 5:15 now. I know my children so well that I know the exact order they will arrive in. Balanah will come first, worried about me despite what she's going through internally. She'll watch my every move, ready to fill my void, then do the same for her siblings. About thirty minutes later, Sahara will come in, ready to give orders, demand answers, and devise a plan to resolve this. Kwame will arrive quiet, humble, and reserved——until an argument erupts and he plays mediator. Then Malichai will come tall and strong like a peaceful warrior, ready to do whatever needs to be done. And if Essence comes at all, she'll be ready to fight, to rage for her sister. Having them all together will be like having my king in the flesh. I can't wait to see them—can't wait to see my king in action again.

This morning, I was thinking out loud when I told Kwame that I was going to visit his father. That's something I didn't want the kids to know. So much is going on right now, and I don't know how they'll feel about it. His absence has been hard on them, and I know they miss him. They sometimes feel left behind by the sacrifices he made for others. They don't see that by helping others, he helped them, too. He led by example on what to do, and although they haven't spoken to him in years, his essence is deeply ingrained in their subconscious. I haven't seen or heard from him either, but it's time to make that journey. This is something he needs to know. I need his guidance, as well. But I'm still afraid. He left his children and legacy in my hands. Sometimes, I feel like I've failed him. Have I done right by our children? I often wonder if he would be disappointed by the choices I've made pertaining to raising them. Are they strong, positive, confident? What we are about to endure now will be the ultimate test to find out.

I'm about to pour myself a glass of wine when I hear the door unlock. Balanah rushes in with Zach like the house is on fire or she's expecting to find me lying on the floor unconscious. I'm watching her from the kitchen, but she doesn't see me. Zach is following behind her, mimicking her every move. When she looks to the left, he looks to the left. When she throws her hands on her hips, he does the same. She pauses, inhaling the rich aromas, and smiles when she sees the dining room set up. I know she's channeling up good memories of me and her father. So, I give her a moment to reminisce.

"Mama?" she calls out.

"Hello, beautiful," I say, coming out of the kitchen with outstretched arms to give her a welcoming hug.

"You did all this?" she asks, looking at the beautiful spread.

"Yes. I want us all to relax today. Wine?"

"Uh…yeah?" She stumbles into the kitchen like she's confused. "Mama, are you sure you're okay?"

"I'm fine. What about you?" I hand her a goblet of wine.

"I'm making it," she whispers, holding the gold-rimmed wine glass like it's an accessory.

I know she's lying. I can see that Balanah is two seconds away from a nervous breakdown, and Ebony being in jail is only a fragment of her pain. I don't say anything, though. Tonight is about peace, not pain.

"Drink your wine," I say, holding up my glass.

She takes a small sip. Zach starts flipping over my pillows and has his eyes on my China. I gently pull him away.

"No, Zach. Don't touch that, baby. Those are Grandma's nice things."

Balanah looks at Zach like she's exhausted with him, but she tries to hide it.

"I'll get him, Mama. You just relax," she says, gesturing with her head towards the couch and then leading Zach upstairs to the sitting room so he can watch TV.

I take a seat on my couch and listen as the sound of cartoons drifts down, bringing back memories of when my kids were that small. Minutes later, Balanah rushes down the stairs like I'm on the brink of collapse.

"Can I get you anything, Mama? Need me to run to the store?"

I shake my head no and pat the couch for her to sit down beside me.

"It smells amazing, Mama? Is it your chickpea stew?" Her eyes light up.

I nod, and she shrieks with excitement.

"Did you make fried bread, too?"

Another nod, and she beams.

"Mama, you too much. You didn't have to do all this. We should be cooking for you."

"Am I not the mother?" I tease, flashing a smile.

She laughs, then glances at the pillows arranged in a circle–one for each of my children, including a spot for Zena, but none for her father. A brief sadness crosses her face before she looks back at me, still trying to find any hidden emotions behind my shielding smile. She'll never find them.

"So did you see her?" she asks like she couldn't wait any longer.

I nod.

"How is she?" Her voice cracks. She takes another sip of wine.

"She's…" I look up, searching for the right words. "She's being the strong one."

I can see by the look on her face that it gives her some comfort.

Just then, Sahara storms in. Balanah must have forgotten to lock the door. She's carrying a legal notepad in one hand and a laptop in the other. She looks like she's ready to go to work.

"When did you get here?" she asks Balanah, like she assumed she'd be the first one to arrive.

"Not too long ago," Balanah replies in a guarded voice.

I can tell she's holding back resentful emotions. Something in Sahara's tone upset her, but she'd never say it outright, and Sahara, oblivious as always, would never know she upset her.

Sahara sets her laptop and notepad down on my coffee table. Her quick movements tell me she's hiding something, putting on a good show. When she hears Zach jumping around upstairs, she looks confused.

"Who's upstairs?"

"Zach," I tell her.

"You're still watching him?" she asks Balanah, who nods. "I should've brought my kids. They might need to spend the night with you. I've got so much to do with this...Ebony situation," Sahara says, like it's her burden alone to carry.

Balanah has that resentful look on her face again.

"I can't watch them," she says, and I'm proud of her for saying no.

Sahara seems surprised by her sister's response.

"Why? Is everything okay? What's going on?" She fires questions at her like a machine gun, not giving Balanah time to answer.

"Nothing's wrong. I've just got things to do, too."

Sahara looks confused, and Balanah looks on the verge of anger, burying it with a swallow of wine.

"What do you have to do?" Sarah demands, but before Balanah can answer, Sahara's attention is drawn to the dining room. "Mama, this is beautiful," she says, admiring the spread. "Mmm...it smells divine in here." She finally leans over to kiss me. "You okay? How you holding up?"

"I'm fine, honey. Don't worry about me. Ebony needs all the attention right now."

She scans the room again. "Where's Essence?" she asks, annoyed.

"I tried calling, but her phone's off," Balanah says. "I don't even think she knows what's going on."

"The girl knows! She's got a TV the size of a theater in her house. She knows!" Sarah snaps.

"Maybe she'll make it," I say hopefully, though I don't cross my fingers.

Sahara rolls her eyes.

"Kwame told me he took you to see her. What's going on?" She grabs her legal pad and pen, preparing to take notes. "Does she have an attorney? Did she make a statement yet? I hope she's not talking to the press. None of us should." Sahara cuts her eyes at Balanah and then at me.

"Baby, put that up." I point to her legal pad. "We not discussing any of that right now. Right now, we just gonna wait for your brothers to get here with Zena and eat dinner as a family."

"*Zena?*" they both say in unison. I nod. They exchange worried looks.

"She needs to stay with one of us until this blows over. When things really get going, it's all going to be too much for her. Balanah, maybe she can go home with you tonight."

Balanah's eyes narrow, but she doesn't protest. She'd never turn down Zena or any of us, no matter how much she's juggling. Sahara shifts her weight on the couch like that arrangement is set in stone, and she scratches it off her mental to-do list.

"Mother," she says slowly, like I can't keep up, "I know you're upset, but we really need to discuss these things. We'll have dinner, but right after, we have to talk. Okay?"

She nods like she's agreeing for me. I just smile. She means well, even if she's feisty with her delivery.

It's half past nine, and the boys still aren't here. Neither is Essence. We tried calling, but her phone is going straight to voicemail. All three of us left her voicemail messages. If she doesn't know what's going on, she will when she checks them. Sahara is getting anxious, Balanah is in a daze, and thank goodness, Zach is fast asleep. I try to lighten the mood by showing them my new fabric and how I redecorated my bedroom with paisley curtains and matching pillows. They ooh and ahh, but I can tell their minds are somewhere else. I can't blame them. Mine is, too.

We're in my bedroom when the front door opens. It's 10 p.m. I know Balanah and Sahara are as nervous as I am to see Zena. We all feel guilty for missing the signs and fear she will resent us for not protecting her. We rush down the stairs as if we were in a relay race, ready to smother Zena with love, but when we reach the bottom, Malichai and Kwame are standing there alone, eyes downcast.

"Mama said y'all had Zena." Balanah looks over their shoulders, hoping Zena will walk through the door.

Malichai shakes his head. Kwame meets my eyes with a silent apology. I sigh, then inhale resolve.

"It's okay," I say, kissing both sons on the forehead. "You'll find her. Just bring her here when you do."

They nod, still looking defeated.

"Let's eat," I say in high spirits, clapping my hands as I lead them to the dining room. "Sit," I instruct before rushing to the kitchen to get my pots.

"I'll help you, Mama," Balanah says from behind me.

She helped me prepare everyone's plate and set them in front of her siblings. When Sahara asks for more rice, she swallows her pride and adheres to her request. Malichai looks over the spread, nodding his head in approval. My son is strong, but I can see the strain from the weight of the world he carries on his shoulders. I wonder how long he can hold it all together.

Everybody's making a fuss over how elaborate my meal is and engaging in small chatter. Everybody except Kwame. He's just enjoying hearing the conversation. He looks at me several times to make sure I'm enjoying it, as well. Suddenly, he gets up and rushes to the bathroom. I catch Malichai's concerned glance following him. When Kwame returns, he has a sour look on his face that he quickly straightens when he sees me watching him. Malichai gives him a look like he's asking him if he's okay, and Kwame nods.

"Where's Essence?" Malichai asks, like he's just noticing her absence.

198

"Of course, she didn't come!" Sahara snaps.

"Maybe she doesn't know. I couldn't reach her on the phone. She's still mad at me," Kwame says, sounding hurt.

"She's got no reason to be mad at you. She just got a taste of her own medicine," Balanah says.

I try to bring peace to the situation. "Be patient with your sister."

"So…you guys couldn't find Zena anywhere?" Sahara asks, changing the subject. She's spooning my chickpea stew onto the fried bread.

Everybody gets silent, waiting to hear his response.

"Not yet," he says with a mouth full of food.

He glares at her as if to say, *Don't start with me*, but Sahara pays his look no mind.

"Are you sure you looked everywhere?" Sahara asks.

Malichai positions himself to yell, but Kwame speaks before he does.

"We're sure. We have all day tomorrow. She's probably at a friend's. It was late, so we couldn't ask around like we wanted."

"I'm just saying finding her has to be our top priority," Sahara insists.

"Why wouldn't it be?!" Malichai explodes.

"Well…for one thing, you two are stoned. I smell it. You can't see past your own self when you smoke that shit. How the hell you gonna see Zena?" she fires back.

Balanah silently agrees with a nod while nibbling her bread. Kwame looks guilty. Malichai looks like he's ready to erupt.

"You really are a piece of work, Ms. Perfect. Nothing's ever good enough for you! We been looking for Zena for three fucking hours!" Malichai yells.

"Do you have to talk like that in my mama's house?" Sahara snaps in an icy, harsh tone.

"I know it's Mama's house. You seem to forget I bought it!"

Malichai reminds everyone.

"Yeah, one transaction from you!" She holds up a finger. "But I'm the one who's been keeping it up for years! Get over yourself, Malichai, and get yourself together for crying out loud!"

"He really is doing the best he can, Sahara," Balanah says softly, surprising Malichai.

"Everybody, calm down. We losing focus," Kwame pleads, drawing their eyes to me.

I ain't surprised they're fighting. Everybody is so stressed that it can't be avoided.

"Sahara, we gonna find her," Kwame says, then turns to Malichai. "You do work hard, man. I respect that."

Sahara rolls her eyes but mumbles, "I'm sorry, Malichai," like it pains her. "We need a plan," she continues. "Everybody needs tasks."

Malichai leans forward. "Before we get into that—I just want to say I don't think Mama should go see Daddy," he says firmly.

Everyone gasps and turns their heads towards me so fast that I hear their necks crack. Well, everyone except for Kwame, who's avoiding eye contact with me. I don't hold it against him, though. I knew he couldn't keep this secret, and I'm tired of secrets anyway.

"Daddy?" Balanah says, stunned. "Mama, is this true?"

I don't answer.

"She told Kwame today," Malichai says, his voice low.

They now turn their heads to him for details, but he stays silent. He knows he's said enough.

"That's a good idea," Sahara says.

"You're crazy!" Balanah shoots back. "That's not gonna do nothing but cause more heartache."

"I agree," Malichai says firmly.

"If anybody knows how to handle this situation, it's Daddy," Sahara adds.

Malichai sucks his teeth. Balanah rolls her eyes. Kwame stays quiet. I watch them, amused that they think it's their decision. It hurts me to hear the resentment in Malichai and Balanah's voices, but they're the oldest and have the most memories of their dad. They don't understand why he refuses to see, write, or call us. To be honest, neither do I, but I trust his decision as I always have in the past.

I decide to put an end to this debate before it starts.

"Look," I say, voice steady, "he's your father and my husband. That means that even in his absence, he is still the head of this household, and you will respect him as such. Understood?"

They lower their heads and nod.

"This is my decision, not yours. And I don't want to hear of it again. Understood?" I repeat, and again, they nod.

They sit in silence for a while, picking at their food and talking to each other with their eyes. Kwame breaks the silence when he mentions the apple crumb pie he smells. Their eyes light up like it's Christmas morning. I go to the kitchen to get it. Balanah tries to follow, but I tell her to stay seated. I need a minute to collect my thoughts. Once in the kitchen, all of the emotions I've tried to keep buried are starting to rise up. I don't release them, though. I breathe deep, pushing them back down, and dry my tears before they can fall. I return smiling, pie in hand.

After dessert, we move to the den. We hear Zach whimpering upstairs, and everybody looks to Balanah to go check on him. Naturally, she gets up, but Malichai stops her.

"I got him," he says, returning a few minutes later with a sleepy Zach in his arms.

Zach is resting his head on Malichai's broad shoulder. When Malichai sits down, Zach spots Balanah and reaches for her. She takes him from Malichai and kisses him on the cheek, maternally. He dozes off in her arms. She's so good with that boy. He really needs a mother, and Meka is far from that. Malichai looks at Zach curled up in Balanah's arms like he's thinking the same thing.

The fireplace burns as we sip on wine. I stand up to call this family meeting to order. Taking the lead as the existing head of the family, I try to plan things and assign tasks fairly and precisely—just as my king would.

We must control the press before it turns on Ebony. The only way I know how to do that is to get the right people on her side. We need support from a few esteemed feminist leaders, activists, and groups of women against rape and child molestation. We must show Ebony as the beautiful, talented, charitable artist that she is—not the angry mugshot they keep flashing on the television. After that, we need to get her some good representation—I mean a lawyer who's Johnny Cochran good. And most of all, we got to get Zena to talk. I know that's going to be the hardest part, but she can't be the victim anymore. She's been the victim long enough. It's time for her to rise above that label by using her voice to turn pain into power. She can be a muse to others who have been in—or are still dealing with—the same situation she endured for years. The people need her to speak so they can understand her pain, and hopefully, in that understanding, they'll understand why Ebony did what she did.

I assign Balanah to rally women's organizations, and maybe reach out to Kenton's wife. It might be a long shot, but she might hold truths that could help. Sahara's job is to find a lawyer through her husband's connections, though the uneasy look she gave me when I assigned her the task worries me. I'm not sure what that look was about, but I pray she comes through for us. Malichai and Kwame will find Zena, protect her, and remind her of good men. It's important for her to see that there are still men out there whose love isn't hurtful or corrupt. I also told them that they are responsible for our safety. Things might get ugly, and we may need protection. They both looked at each other and nodded like they were way ahead of me. Essence—whenever she finally decides to show up—can raise funds that we'll need for legal fees. She knows a lot of people, has a big mouth, and doesn't take no for an answer. With those two qualities combined, I trust she'll be able to raise enough money for us to afford good representation for Ebony. We'll also need funds to pay a couple of prominent speakers so they can have the motivation to say something good about my child on camera. As for me, my role is to keep everybody strong—to hug them, kiss them, tell them I love them, and let them know I believe in them. I need to be the glue to hold everything together.

When they leave, they seem lighter—a little less stressed and a lot more loved. I'm shocked when Malichai grabs Zach, who is still sleeping, from Balanah's arms and takes him home with him. Although Balanah looks relieved, I can sense she's hesitant to give Zach back to him. I wait outside my doorway until the last car disappears into the night, feeling my mission has been accomplished for one day.

18

ESSENCE

"A Squirt of Pee"

Marco's working out on my zebra-print rug that's in the middle of my living room, using his own body to stay fit instead of weights. He's doing one-handed push-ups. I'm not sure if this is part of his regular workout routine or if he's showing off. Whichever, he sure looks sexy doing it. One arm is anchored deep in my rug, and the other is tucked behind his back. His toes balance his lean, muscular frame, his head is level with the ground, and his biceps bulge with every rep. I figure he's keeping count in his head since he hasn't uttered a word. The only thing I hear is his slow, controlled breathing. I'm counting for him, though. Forty so far. I bet he'll hit fifty, just like his leg curls earlier. Yep, I counted those, too. I've got nothing better to do than watch him lustfully.

Our Friday night hangout turned into a weekend-long slumber party. It's Sunday, and we haven't been out of my loft once. No TV, no phones, no work—just us. My place has become our personal love cave, and Marco is a wild caveman in more than just the bedroom. He's pleasured me in the living room, shower, on the dining room table, kitchen floor, outside on the balcony, and even in the closet.

We can't keep our hands off each other. This man is strong, powerful, and shockingly well-endowed. He should've been a porn star with all that schlong he's packing in his pants. When I first saw it, I was terrified—then excited. Marco flipped, bent, lifted, and rode me like a rodeo horse. His energy was relentless. I felt tackled, pounced on, and clobbered—all in a good way. You would think I'd be exhausted, but my body is still craving him.

This wasn't tender lovemaking—it was raw fucking. And I liked it. I've had enough of weak-ass, boring-sex brothers like Resident McCall, who pretend they know how to fuck because of something they've seen in a movie. Those types couldn't find my clit with a GPS, and they didn't know the first thing about turning me on. Marco knew, though. Our sex was intense, passionate, and animalistic—no sweet nothings needed. I did all the moaning while he stayed silent, eyes heavy with pleasure, tossing me around like a rag doll. Every time I thought he was done, he was right back on me again.

We're supposed to be going to some party one of his friends is having in a few hours, but honestly, I don't feel like going anywhere. We got a good thing going here, and I don't want to break the flow of things. Hell, I missed an appointment with a client yesterday—didn't even bother canceling, which isn't like me. But shit…what can I say? I'm trying something different. Being spontaneous for a change. I'm probably going to be fired, but Marco thinks he can get me a loan to start my business. He sounded serious about it. Marco has me feeling so optimistic that I'm believing anything is possible. Hell, I just might win the lottery. Who knows?

When Marco finishes his sit-ups—yep, he hit fifty—he catches me ogling him and winks. Then he flips onto his back to start doing crunches. He's been working out for almost thirty minutes, just like yesterday morning and Friday night before we had sex. I hope he's warming up for another round in bed before we leave.

I lick my lips, wearing nothing but a zebra-print satin robe that's tied tight around my small waist. I bend over and pick up one of my red throw pillows that fell off the couch, flashing him my bare ass and hoping he gets the hint. He doesn't look, though. He's too focused on his workout.

"You hungry?" I ask, but he doesn't answer. He's deep in concentration.

I head to the kitchen. The fridge is almost empty: three eggs, half a turkey sausage link, a couple of tablespoons of shredded cheese, one English muffin, and a few swallows of orange juice. I didn't get to do my grocery shopping on Friday like I usually do, and we've been ordering takeout like it's room service. I rummage the vegetable drawer: a quarter of an onion, a green bell pepper that's a few hours away from being spoiled, and a handful of spinach about to wilt. There isn't enough for both of us, but I don't mind going without breakfast. So, I make him an omelet. It's the least I can do for him after all the pleasure he's given me these past three days.

I brown the sausage and dice it into tiny pieces. Then I beat the eggs, add both the sausage and veggies to the mixture, sprinkle a dash of salt and pepper, and pour the mixture into a hot non-stick skillet. Once my egg starts to fry, I get excited. My omelet looks like something from an IHOP ad, golden and perfect. I plate it on my nicest black-and-red square plate. The dish set reminds me of something you see in upscale Asian restaurants.

Marco's done working out now, stretching his muscles to loosen up any knots. My kitchen smells wonderful, and because he has a nose, I assume he can smell it, too. But he still hasn't looked this way yet. *Whatever—I'll bring it to him.* I sashay over with the plate, putting an extra twirl in my hips, feeling like Dorothy Dandridge.

"I made you breakfast," I announce, smiling while handing him the food. "It's an omelet with spinach, bell pepper, onion, turkey sausage, and cheddar."

He raises an eyebrow, looks down at the omelet, then at me, then over his shoulder like he's expecting someone else. He grabs the plate out of my hand so quick that it's almost like he snatched it. I let that go, thinking maybe the food looks so good to him that he can't wait to dig in. He brings the plate up to his nose and sniffs it, then looks at me again. His brow is still lifted, and I'm still smiling like a fool.

"I don't eat spinach. And I don't eat eggs with yolk," he says flatly, setting the plate on the coffee table. "I'm not hungry, either."

"Oh…" I hear my voice trail off.

My cheeks start to droop. But before my disappointment sets in, he lifts me up, throws me over his shoulder, and carries me to the bedroom, where he tosses me on the bed, rips off my robe, and buries his face between my legs.

"Maybe I am a little hungry," he says with a wink before diving back in.

Forget that damn omelet. He doesn't eat yolks, but he sure devours me. I clutch my sheets from the immense pleasure he's giving me. I sure hope he's an overeater.

* * * * *

"These are some cool people," Marco says while speeding down I-85, heading towards Midtown with sirens blaring and lights flashing. I'm beginning to think this is the only way he travels.

I'm dressed in black tights, knee-high brown leather boots, a fitted cream V-neck sweater showing just enough cleavage, and a leopard-print belt to accentuate the curve of my waist. Marco didn't say I looked good, but his wide eyes and nod when I stepped out of the bathroom told me enough.

"I'm gonna talk to the guy I mentioned—the one who can hook you up with the loan."

"Are you serious?" I ask.

"I'm always serious," Marco says, shooting me a serious look.

"He must really trust you if he'll give a stranger a loan."

"He trusts me—and the people I vouch for. Do you want the loan or not?" he snaps.

"Yeah, but—"

"But what? Take the money, do your thing, and pay him back when it's due. You might have to do my man a little favor, though."

"Favor?" I ask, alarmed. "What type of favor, Marco?"

He shrugs. "I don't know. Depends on the situation."

"Is this legal?"

"What is illegal about some rich dude giving a loan to a businesswoman?" Marco scoffs.

He got me there. Maybe I'm overthinking. Besides, if I get fired for missing my last appointment, this might be my only shot.

"How much do you think he'll give me?"

"How much you need? Didn't you say you need about fifty grand?"

"Yeah. Will he give me all that at once? Do I need to submit a business plan or give a presentation? Do I need a lawyer to look over the documents?"

Marco gives me an annoyed look and shakes his head.

"This is an unconventional loan. No lawyer, no bullshit-ass presentation needed. Matter of fact, I'll do all the talking for you. He likes to stay private. So, you don't need to see him," Marco says with a wave of his hand, dismissing me.

It's weird that somebody would give me fifty grand without meeting me or asking how I'll repay it. But I ain't no fool—I'm taking the money if I get it. Maybe I can even get a little extra to cover my bills until the business gets up and running. Hell, if fifty is a drop in the bucket, why not seventy since he's so generous?

"You think he'll give me seventy?"

Marco just looks at me. I don't know what he's thinking because the expression on his face never changes, and of course, he doesn't respond to my question to let me know what he's thinking. But he does wink—that no-telling, expressionless wink. My mind races with possibilities: quitting my job, opening my dream office downtown, decorating it with trendy furniture, maybe even getting fancy gold signage with my name. I wonder how much that cost. Considering all that I want to do, maybe he can just make it an even hundred thousand. I can do a whole lot more with that.

When Marco cuts the sirens and lights and slows down, I assume we're there, but I don't see any houses. We're on a bridge in the dark. The only light comes from our taillights and the lights from the cars driving on the highway below us. Marco squints in the direction of a man walking on the bridge.

"Do you know him?" I ask, squinting too, but of course, Marco ignores me.

There's just enough light for me to see that he's wearing a black hoodie, jeans, a skullcap, and white Nikes, and he's scratching a lottery ticket.

Marco turns off the engine. "Stay here," he orders.

Where am I going to go? Then, I wonder where he's going. He cracks his knuckles, kisses them, and gets out. I watch Marco slowly approach the man, who's too busy with his scratch-off ticket to notice him. When Marco says, "Aye," the man freezes like a deer caught in headlights and then looks like he's debating if he should run, but Marco's already within arm's reach. The guy raises his hands like he's surrendering. I wonder if he's a prisoner or an escaped convict who has to be hauled back to jail. That will be cool to witness, if so.

Marco grabs him by the collar, and the man drops his ticket, which floats toward the windshield. I wonder if it was a winning ticket. Without thinking, I open the door to catch it. Marco shoots me a murderous glare, and I quickly get back inside the car, shut the door, and stuff the ticket in my purse, hoping it's one that'll make me a millionaire. Then I won't need the loan.

Marco lifts the guy off the ground, bending him backward over the railing, dangling him over the highway. *What the fuck?!* Marco is saying something to him, but I can't hear him over the man's frantic pleas and screams. Horns blare below. My heart is pounding. *Oh my God! What the hell is he doing?* I'm so nervous that I feel like I'm about to pee on myself. I cross my legs and squirm in my seat to try to hold it in. Hell, if I pee in his precious Batmobile, I might be next to go dangling over the railing.

I close my eyes, praying it's a bad nightmare. When I open them again, Marco pulls back up, tosses him to the ground, yanks him up by his forearm, says something I can't hear over the man's sobs, then punches him so hard the man collapses again. Marco returns to the car, silent, offering neither an explanation nor an apology. He just turns on the sirens and flashing lights and speeds off as if nothing had happened. I look down at my feet like I didn't see or hear anything, still having to pee.

"Um...I need a bathroom," I hesitantly tell him after about ten minutes of driving.

He smirks before making a violent U-turn into a gas station, almost causing a collision between an SUV and a tractor-trailer. I sprinted inside, barely making it to the restroom. A squirt of pee hits my panties, but at least I didn't soak myself.

* * * * *

When we get to the party, I'm shocked. First of all, it's more like a small get-together than a party. There are no more than twenty people, and in a house this big, it feels like even less. None of these people looks like I'd expect Marco's friends to look. Most are in their fifties, and half are white. Yet, they all seem to know and respect Marco, greeting him with handshakes and whispered words, a few slipping him money like I wouldn't notice. Marco keeps his arm around me possessively, guiding me through the house. The men barely glance at me—I feel like a piece of jewelry more than a person. Oh well, they're not my friends, although I wouldn't mind networking. Judging by their suits and watches, these men are big spenders—dirty money, but money all the same. I know dirty money when I see it, but I accept all kinds of it. As long as I work for it, I'll make it clean.

The person who owns this house paid at least a million dollars for it. Marble floors, thick wood columns and paneling, towering ceilings with matching tall windows. There are a few women scattered among the men, but they all look like bitter old hags with bad plastic surgery. I know their type–they'll resent me for my youth, scorn my natural beauty, and look down their nose at me because I'm not wearing the ridiculously expensive brands of clothing they're wearing. Those kinds of women tend to run in cliques and don't easily let newcomers into their exclusive, close-knit circle. Fine by me.

I take the first drink somebody offers me: vodka and cranberry. My nerves are still shot. Marco's arm feels more like a leash than comfort. When he leans over and kisses me on the cheek, I almost choke on my cocktail. It didn't feel sweet—just wet.

Marco leads me across the massive foyer into a den twice the size of my living room and bedroom put together. It's the room where the women are sitting. I realize he's dropping me off here. *Damn. I'm not in the mood for this.*

"Chill out. You wit' cool people," he says like he knows I'm uncomfortable. "I gotta do business," he adds, and I perk up, thinking he's working on my loan.

Maybe these women can be potential clients. I mean, I am about to be large—so large that they might beg for me to join their circle. I step into the den like I'm diving into shark-infested water. They look at me like they're bored and hungry. When one whispers in another's ear and they giggle, I know I'm tonight's entertainment.

"Hello, darling. I'm Amber Anterior. This is my home," says a tall blonde woman with Anna Nicole Smith lips and a maybe-fake British accent. "Come join the rest of the girls."

She introduces the other women, but I don't bother to memorize their names. They all look like victims of botched surgeries—crooked noses, oversized lips, funny jawbones, and giant boobs on stick-thin bodies. Some are holding tiny dogs that look like rats. Then I watch in shock as they start snorting powder from a silver tray. These same women think they're better than me? Please. I take a seat on the sectional next to the only three Black women in the room. You would've thought I had a disease the way they shifted to the left away from me. *Fuck them!*

"What's your name?" one of them—I believe her name is Victoria—asks me.

Her nose job is obvious; it's awkwardly narrow on her chubby face. Her face is saturated with makeup, but it was flawlessly done. She's dripping diamonds and petting a rat-like dog. When it's her turn to sniff, she does it smoothly and hands the tray to the other Black lady with leathery skin and a bad weave. Then she looks back at me, waiting for my response.

"Essence Sedah," I say, like she should know the name.

She raises her brow and exchanges a look with the others. They giggle under their breath.

"Oh...how...ethnic," Victoria says. "It's cute. Did you change your name?"

"No," I reply. Trying to keep my composure, I take another sip from my cocktail.

"What do you do?" another woman asked.

"I'm a realtor."

"Oh, poor you."

I know what she means. Since the housing market crashed, I've been getting sympathy from a lot of strangers.

"No, not really. I'm actually about to start my own investment firm," I add confidently.

"Oh, really?" Victoria perks up.

Now I have their attention. I know I have the upper hand with these women, because if it is one thing they are not, it's businesswomen. They probably never worked a day in their lives. I explain to them the nature of the business I was going to start, laying it on thick and tossing around big words—some I don't even know myself, but they can't tell. By the time I finish, they're looking at me like I'm young Oprah. Victoria even offers me the tray of coke, which I decline. That makes them admire me even more.

"I would kill to have that youthful figure. Get up, honey. Twirl around."

I show off—something I love to do. They go on and on about my curves and even compliment my natural hair. It's pathetic—if they didn't have money from their crooked husbands, they'd be nobodies.

"I remember when my breasts sat that high naturally," Amber jokes.

"She reminds me of the girl fucking my husband now," another says. "He loves curvy Black women. Maybe I should get a butt implant."

She gets up and sticks out what she can of her flat ass. They all laugh. At least they are being entertained; I'm bored as hell and ready to go.

I endure an hour of their babbling about who their husbands are screwing, who's getting divorced, who's getting more work done and on what. Blah…blah…blah. Then they start talking about some crazy mess they saw on TV—something about a woman shooting off a man's dick.

"The way people are out there protesting for that woman makes me wonder if I should shoot my husband's dick off. You girls will have my back, won't you?" Amber jokes.

"Amber, I don't think there's a gun small enough to shoot your husband's dick off. I noticed that the last time we fucked," another woman says with a wink.

The women laugh.

"Ladies, this is serious. You shouldn't be joking about it," the Black woman sitting next to Victoria says in a serious tone. "They say she shot him because he tried to fool around with her young daughter or something like that. That bastard got what he deserved."

"That's awful," Amber joins in, turning up her nose. "Too bad she's going to get the book thrown at her. Can't just go around shooting off dicks because someone betrayed you—or we'd have no dicks left to fuck!"

They all cackle.

I'm relieved when Marco returns. Hopefully, we can leave. As soon as he steps into the den, all the women blush and stand to their feet, hungry for his attention.

"I've missed you, Marco," one coos.

"Me, too," Victoria adds.

"Me three," another chimes in.

"We all miss him," Amber says, and the women giggle.

"You ready?" he asks me.

"So sexy!" Victoria sighs.

"They don't make them like him anymore," Amber purrs, licking her lips.

Ignoring them, Marco wraps his arm around my shoulders and escorts me out. Just as we reach the foyer, somebody else arrives: Sir Zion. He looks me dead in the eye like he knew I would be here. Not wanting Marco to know I knew him, I try to ignore him, but Sir Zion isn't about to let that happen.

"Essence!" he exclaims, his arms out. "Baby, is that you?"

What a phony. As usual, he's dressed outlandishly, wearing a bright orange smock, matching pants, and carrying what looks like a tribal stick. His locks are almost dusting the floor now. There are three men standing behind him, guarding him from whom I don't know.

I don't hug him. I just look at him like he's crazy. Marco looks at us both.

"You know this man?" he asks.

"Sort of," I reply.

Sir Zion laughs. "Come on. It's more than sort of. I held her as a baby."

"So did the doctor," I mutter, trying to push on, but Marco's arm hooks me back.

"Marco, don't forget our meeting," Sir Zion says, then looks back at me. "Oh, I just talked to the press about your sister. Tell your mother..." He smirks. "Tell her...I told her so." He laughs darkly. "Your father would be ashamed."

"What the hell are you talking about?" I snap.

"You know," he insists, smiling. "I'm happy to see you handling this tragic time so well."

I give him a weird look. That's when his expression gets serious.

"You really don't know, do you?"

My silence lets him know that I don't.

He turns to Marco. "Tell her. Remember that call a few days ago?"

Marco's face changes.

"Go on, tell her. It was her sister," Sir Zion says, then walks away while laughing, his minions following close behind him. "Don't forget our meeting," he yells over his shoulder.

When we get back to his Batmobile, I'm anxious for Marco to explain, but he doesn't. He drives in silence for the first ten minutes. Finally, I force myself to ask:

"Well?"

"Well, what?" he responds coldly, keeping his eyes on the road.

"What was Sir Zion talking about? What did he want you to tell me?"

"How you know him?" Marco shoots back.

"What?"

"How do you know Sir Zion?" he asks again.

"He was my father's partner. Now, what did he want you to tell me? Is it about my sister?"

"So that *is* your sister, huh?" he says casually.

"Who?" I demand, growing frustrated.

"Ebony Sedah. The crazy bitch who shot that nigga in the dick," he chuckles.

My stomach drops. Ebony? Shot someone? Shit! Was she the woman those women were talking about?

"Crazy bitch?" I snap.

"Yeah. What else do you call a woman who shoots a man's dick off? Even if he was fucking her daughter—she let it happen."

"What?!" I yell, hitting the seat with my fist. "What the fuck are you talking about?"

"I just told you," Marco says flatly.

"Are you telling me that my sister shot somebody? For molesting her daughter?"

"Yep."

"Is she in jail? Where's my niece? Is she okay?"

"Yes, your sister's in jail, and I don't know shit about your niece," he says cold.

"Fuck you!" I scream.

He slams on the brakes so hard that I nearly get whiplash.

"What'd you say?" he growls.

Remembering what he did to the man on the bridge, I go quiet.

"You better calm your ass down with all that emotional shit. It's annoying as hell."

I try my best to conceal the tears that are falling down my face, wiping them soon after they fall from my eyes. I realize the family meeting I missed must've been about this. I'm scared for Ebony, and I feel sick thinking that Zena got raped. When did it happen? Who was the man? Wait a minute…Marco said she knew about it. So, it couldn't be some random person. I'm so confused. I just want to get home.

Marco breaks the silence. "So, if that girl is your sister, you must be Akimbo 'Black-Man' Sedah's daughter." He says my father's name like it's poison.

I don't respond.

"I knew your dad. He fucked up my father's business." Marco gives me a mean look.

I'm even more nervous now. I knew my father had enemies, but I wasn't prepared to face them. I clench my legs, trying to hold in the sudden urge to pee, and stay quiet for the remainder of the ride home. So does Marco. When he pulls into my parking lot, I barely close his door before he speeds off. I don't care. I sprint inside to call Mama— and to finally pee.

19

EBONY

"Thinking About It"

"**M**a'am, you got two more trying to see you," one of the guards tells me, peeking her head inside my tiny cell.

It's visiting hours. I shake my head no, like I did the last three times today. I know it's only reporters, and I'm not in the mood to talk to the press yet.

"You sure, ma'am?" she asks, smiling.

She's about Mama's age but looks much older. Twenty years working in this place, like she told me, must've aged her. But she's nice—to me, at least. Everybody here treats me like a hero or some type of celebrity behind these bars. The guards refer to me as *ma'am* instead of my last name, and when speaking to me, they ask instead of demand. The inmates treat me like their muse, offering me cigarettes or the fruits and vegetables off their trays—things they'd never give up under any other circumstances.

"I'm sure," I tell the guard, and she leaves me alone.

I finally have a little quiet time to myself. After the chaotic weekend, they finally processed me and assigned me a cell that I somehow ended up sharing with Tweety. The bed I'm laying on feels more like a cot with a blanket on top than an actual mattress. It's so short and narrow that my feet almost dangle off the end, and I swear my hips are wider than it. But it beats sitting on the steel bench or resting my back against the cold brick wall like I did in holding.

Tweety has come out of her shell—or maybe my newfound fame and her connection with me broke her out of it. I liked the girl better when she was a shy, quiet mess. Now she talks me half to death. You'd think I'm a shrink or priest the way these girls confess their life stories to me. During lunch or recreation, they surround me, hounding me with questions or begging me to give them advice. It's starting to annoy me, but Mama always said when you're blessed with strength, others feed off it—and you can't keep it all to yourself. She said that was Daddy's sacrifice: sharing his strength. I try my best to enlighten these women, but my mind is on one thing only: Zena.

With my face all over the news, Zena has to know what's going on by now, and I'm worried about her. I keep hoping the guard will stick her head inside my cell and tell me that my daughter is here to see me, but she hasn't yet. To be honest, I want to see Zena, but I don't want her to see me like this. Now, I understand why Daddy didn't want us visiting him in prison. This is no place for a reunion. But I still want to see my baby, if only to know she's okay. I'm driving myself crazy wondering if she knows I did this for her, and if she feels safer now that justice has been served, even if it was outside the law. Maybe now she can have a normal life without the fear of Kenton walking free and unbothered. I made sure that wouldn't happen when I shot his dick off. Last I heard, he was still in critical condition, possibly facing a life where he'll never function normally again. He can't pee normally, can't walk normally, and he'll for sure never be able to fuck normally again. I guess I didn't do too badly.

It felt good seeing Mama the other day. Something about her presence made me feel warm inside—hopeful even, like everything is going to be okay even if it's not. It felt good confessing everything to her, especially the heavy things like Zena being a lesbian and Sir Zion being Zena's father. I felt like a fifteen-year weight was lifted from my shoulders. Mama didn't judge or question me; she just understood. I felt her love in the way she embraced me for almost the full hour of our visit. I still smell her patchouli-scented oil on my skin. She promised she would find Zena, and I believe her. I just hope she finds her before the press does. Zena doesn't need the media treating her like a spectacle.

Zena is such a private person; she'd never handle having her photo flashed on the news, labeling her a victim. That kind of exposure would feel like emotional rape—an invasion of her deepest, darkest secrets. But it's more than that. It also exposes how fucked up and insensitive the system is about protecting women or children. It's a wake-up call about monsters like Kenton Jones—and a warning to others like him. There are more women out there like me, and if there aren't, I hope I paved the way for them to fight back. I'd even buy the gun and bullets if they need me to.

I feel myself dozing off. I haven't slept much since I shot Kenton—not out of guilt, but because of all the chaos around me. I'm sure if I had a moment of peace, I'd sleep like a baby. But that ain't about to happen now because I hear Tweety being escorted back by the guard. She's benefiting from my celebrity benefits, getting treated nicely just for being my cellmate. I don't mind—she looked like she needed kindness.

I sit up on my cot, knowing she's going to be extra chatty after her second meeting with her court-appointed lawyer. I wanted to slap that man—though I've never laid eyes on him—when she told me he advised her to plead guilty to a crime she didn't commit. Thank goodness I was here to tell her not to do that. I told her she needs to make his lazy, slimy-ass work for all those taxpayer dollars he's getting to represent her. I also suggested she give up that snake-ass baby daddy of hers, but that didn't seem like an option she wanted to explore.

It's funny how innocent hearts cling to the people who hurt them, like loyal dogs abused by their owners. They sit, stay, and protect even when they're mistreated. Just like Tweety—still worried about a man who ain't concerned one bit about her or their child. I want to shake some sense into this girl, but I ain't trying to frighten her. Women like her need to take baby steps toward their independence because if pushed too hard, they'll only relapse into the arms of another abuser.

I prop myself against the wall, then pull my blanket over my ice-cold feet and up to my chin. I guess they don't believe in heat around here. I start combing through the kinks of my matted afro. In its best form, my afro is big and fluffy like Angela Davis's, but now my hair is so tangled that my fingers keep getting stuck in it. I yank them free, and strands of dry hair fall from between my fingers. I count Tweety's quick footsteps—by the tenth step, she burst into our cell, grinning so big you would've thought she'd just had a visit with Jesus. I'm glad to see her smile; I hadn't realized how pretty she is until she smiled.

"You were right, Ms. Ebony!" she says before she's fully inside.

I told that girl a million times to drop the "Ms.," but she never does. It makes me feel old.

"Right about what?" I ask, twirling a coil of hair.

"When you said everything was going to work out with my baby! She's alright, and social services ain't got her! I just saw her pretty face!" Tweety jumps up and down, clapping.

"She's with her father?"

Her smile fades, and she lowers her eyes.

"Naw," she replies, shaking her head, and scratches the back of her neck.

"Well, who? I thought you said you ain't have much family."

"I don't. She's still with my neighbor."

She smiles as though relieved and sits down at the foot of my bed. The bed is so weak that it nearly collapses under us. Her bed is literally an arm's reach away, yet she always wants to sit on mine when we talk. I pull the blanket up closer to my chest. When she sat down, she accidentally shifted it, exposing my ice-cold, ashy feet.

"That's good, Tweety."

"Yeah! My neighbor said she knew something was wrong when I didn't come back to get her. She knows it wasn't like me to just up and leave my baby." She shakes her head. "She heard I got arrested from some neighborhood folks and came here as soon as she could."

"Any word on your baby daddy? He been back to your apartment?"

"I don't know," she answers quickly, like she don't want to talk about him.

Tweety goes over and climbs into her own bed, thank goodness, propping herself against the wall like me.

"You need to find out where he is so the police can get his ass, girl," I tell her.

"My main concern is my baby."

"That's good, but if you don't get yourself out of this mess, your baby ain't gonna have a mama for a while. Your neighbor can't keep your child forever. She doesn't have any children of her own?" I ask.

"Naw. She loves babies—says she can't have any, though. I guess that's why she's always volunteering to watch the kids in the neighborhood. I can tell she likes my baby the most. She calls herself her *play mama*."

"Watching a baby ain't the same as raising one, play mama or not," I say, pulling my hands from my hair and filing my rigid fingernails down with my teeth.

"I know," Tweety says, sounding defeated.

"But it'll work out," I add to lift her spirits.

"I was thinking about what you told me about my lawyer. I think I'm gonna tell him I ain't pleading guilty."

"Now you thinking smart. But you know if you clear yourself, you'll have to turn in your baby daddy."

She shrugs, rolling her eyes.

"Tweety, I wouldn't tell you anything I wouldn't tell my own daughter."

Her face lights up at my words. This girl has probably been looking for a mama her whole life. And if I can help it, her baby won't have to grow up searching for a mother in strangers.

"Let me ask you something."

She nods for me to go on.

I swing my legs over the bed, feet against the cold concrete, and give Tweety some serious eye contact. "If you, your baby daddy, and your baby were stranded in the desert with only a few drops of water, who would you give it to?"

"My baby," she answers without hesitation.

"If your baby and your baby daddy were trapped in a burning building and you could only save one, who would it be?"

She laughs like it was a dumb question. "My baby. Duh!" she says sarcastically.

"Okay, would you give your baby the last bite of food from your plate, or would you make her share it with your baby daddy?"

"My last is her last. Of course, I'd give it to her. What you think I am, Ms. Ebony—one of them mamas who don't give a fuck about their child? Like my own mama?"

"I know you ain't. But you need to really see that. Your baby has to be your last drop of water, your last bite of food, and the one you save from the fire. Because if you won't be that for her, who will? Think of this cell you're in—and turning in your baby daddy—as the last drop of water in a blazing-hot desert, the last bite of food in your baby's hungry belly, and saving her from a blazing fire. Forget your baby daddy, Tweety! It's you and your baby against the world—and only the strong survive. Will that be you and your daughter?"

She doesn't answer at first. I don't expect her to. It's just food for thought. Maybe thinking will help her stop talking so much.

Sometimes people use constant chatter to avoid thinking. Sometimes you just need to shut up and reflect.

"He ain't perfect, but he was there for me when I needed him," Tweety blurts out after a long silence.

"Well, he sure ain't consistent," I say.

"You don't understand, Ms. Ebony. He already got two strikes. If he gets another, he's gone for life."

"With the amount of drugs you told me were in that trunk, you're only looking at one strike." I hold up a finger.

"My mama put me out when I threatened to tell the police about her boyfriend raping me. I ain't have nowhere to go. Nowhere! Nobody cared—not my aunt, not my grandmother, nobody. But he did. He let me stay with him, paid the bills, bought groceries, and didn't put me out when I got pregnant, like Mama said he would. Now I'm supposed to thank him by turning him in?"

"You don't owe him your life, Tweety, and if he was such an honorable man, he wouldn't let you sit in jail a single second. Look at the Atlanta rapper and his wife who got in trouble recently."

"Young T?"

Tweety reminds me of the name and I nod.

"When police found drugs in her purse, he took the fall because he was a real man. He wasn't gonna let the mother of his children rot in jail. If your baby daddy loved you like that, he'd take the rap. You didn't have anything to do with the two strikes he got before you met him, did you?"

She shakes her head.

"He could at least get you a lawyer, act concerned about your daughter, and come visit you. Hell, he hasn't even written you a letter or taken a phone call."

"He just scared. Going to jail is one of his biggest fears. His granddaddy, father, uncles, and brothers are all in jail."

"Well, he should feel right at home then. He'll have his own welcoming committee—a fucking family reunion. Do what you want, but I hope you're smart about it. Years from now, when you see your baby go to prom, graduate from college, and walk down the aisle to get married, you'll be glad you made the right choice. She's small now, but babies grow up—and they need their mama. You should know that better than anybody."

Tweety starts crying. I hear her whimpering, wiping her eyes. My maternal urge is to get up and wrap my arms around her to console her, but I don't. She needs to feel this. Maybe when she cries out her fears and guilt, she'll be left with sound reasoning—and turn in her worthless baby daddy. After a few minutes, she curls up on the bed in a fetal position, face buried in her blanket. I can tell she's still crying by the way her shoulders shake, but I leave her alone. At least I got a moment of silence—until the guard sticks her head in again.

"Got another visitor. This time it's family."

"Is it my daughter?" I jump off the bed.

"I don't know. The people up front just said family. You wanna see 'em?"

"Yeah," I say.

Before I walk out of the cell, I look over my shoulder at Tweety's cot. She's peeking at me from behind her blanket, eyes still wet. I wink at her, and she smiles.

* * * * *

On the walk to the visiting room, I pray it's Zena, but I know that's probably wishful thinking. She's still punishing me for what Kenton did to her and ain't gonna let me off the hook that easily. Doesn't matter that I shot him—or where I shot him. When she's ready, she'll come around. If it ain't Zena, maybe it's Mama. I hope so. I'd love to see her. And if it ain't Mama, then it's probably Kwame. I wouldn't mind seeing him either. His calming energy

226

would be a blessing right now. But I'm shocked when I walk into the small, stuffy room and see Sahara sitting at one of the round wooden tables. She can be here for a lot of reasons. The reason that would annoy me the most is if she's only here to talk about how my arrest affects her and John—or how it could benefit them.

I stop and stare at her. She stands like she can hear my thoughts and is offended. Then she smiles, and I know her smile is telling me that she loves me. I smile back, letting her know I love her too, even though I know she's about to annoy the shit out of me. She sits back down when I start walking towards the table.

Before I can even get my butt in the seat good, Sahara starts with her questions, demands, and plans.

"You haven't talked to the press, right? Do you have an attorney yet?" she asks, pen in hand.

"Calm down, Sahara. Damn. You worse than the press. Let me just take a deep breath."

"That's a good idea." She puts down her pen, closes her eyes like she's meditating, and takes a deep breath in and out. When she opens her eyes, she looks refreshed and ready to go with her questioning again. But she gives me a minute.

"I was thinking of a way for you and me to get together, and then it came to me—I'll just shook Kenton in the dick, and she'll come. If I shoot him, she'll come," I say in an animated voice.

She tries not to laugh but can't help it. I'm only joking to keep her from crying because I can see the tears forming.

"You would crack a joke at a time like this. How are you doing, Ebony?"

Her voice sounds like she's on the verge of tears.

"I'm gonna slap your ass if you cry. I got a reputation to keep in here, and if you start crying, I'm gonna start crying. Then Big Bertha and her crew will eat me alive."

She laughs a bit, sucking back her tears with another deep breath.

She's such a drama queen. I love her.

"You sure you're not one of the Big Berthas?" she jokes.

I laugh and flip her off.

"Let me ask you something, Sahara. Did you see me that time you and John were at that fancy restaurant downtown?"

The guilty look in her eyes tells me everything. She swallows hard and clears her throat before nodding.

"That's all I wanted to know," I say.

"I'm so sorry—" she starts.

"Whatever." I wave off her apology and lean back in my chair. "So, you here to tell me what to do?"

"Yep." Sahara picks up her pen.

"Y'all find Zena yet?" I ask, hopeful.

"Not yet, but Malichai and Kwame are looking. Got any leads?"

"Maybe a few." I pause as she gets ready to write. "She hangs out at Little Five Points and sometimes Five Points train station. Her band practices at a bar called Rave. It's somewhere in Edgewood. Her closest friends are Lena, Tracy, and Brian. I don't know their addresses, but Lena lives next door to us in that ugly pink stucco house. She can point you to Tracy and Brian."

"Okay, we'll find her. But in the meantime, what about your lawyer?"

"I don't want one."

"What do you mean?" She sounds exasperated. "You can't represent yourself."

"Why not?"

"Because if you do, you're screwed. You need good representation."

"You know I can't stand y'all lawyers. Y'all just manipulate innocent folks' minds."

"Come on, Ebony," she sighs. "Let me get you a good lawyer. With the right representation, the right press, and Zena's testimony, you might walk away from this."

"Leave Zena out of it. She's been through enough."

"She's important, Ebony. She's the key to your freedom. You can't help it if you went insane and shot Kenton."

"I didn't go crazy. I was clear-headed and planned the shit out."

"Ebony! Do you want to spend the rest of your life in jail, rotting like Daddy?"

"I don't care. I have a newfound respect for Daddy. He stood up for what he believed in, no matter the consequences. I'm gonna do the same."

"You need a lawyer. This isn't the time to be stubborn, Ebony. Please!"

She's crying now, tears streaming down her cheeks. I fight back my own.

"I'll think about it. Just find my baby, okay? This ain't about me no more—it's all about her."

"If this is about her, then you have to fight for your freedom. She needs you, and you can't help her behind bars. Think about that," she says.

Her words hit me hard. I start thinking about them right away—and about what I told Tweety.

"I said I'll think about it!" I tell her, getting up to leave before she can say another word.

I don't look back, but I know Sahara is wiping her tears while watching me walk down the long hallway until I'm gone. I'm still thinking about what she said. Maybe I do need a lawyer. Zena needs me, just like Tweety's baby needs her.

Damn it! Sahara makes me sick, but she's right. She's always right.

20

SAHARA
"Ambush"

After I got back from seeing Ebony, stepping into my house felt like walking into a damn ambush.

When I pulled into the driveway, I noticed a red Mercedes parked in the turnaround, facing our front door. I figured John called a last-minute babysitter since he got pissed when I told him I had to go out and he'd have to watch the kids for a few hours. I didn't tell him I was going to visit Ebony, but he probably suspected it. He sulked like the kids weren't even his.

Upon closer inspection of the vehicle, I noticed a Republican emblem on the back bumper. Babysitter? Probably not. Then again, knowing John, being a white Republican was probably his top babysitter requirement.

I walked into the house and found John, Essence's husband, Lawrence, and his mother, Mrs. McCall, all sitting in the guest den. As soon as they saw me, they turned their noses up in unison—John included. Lawrence looked flushed, his foot anxiously tapping the floor like he was about to explode. Mrs. McCall sat rigid on the edge of the other leather chair, as if our furniture would give her the cooties. She wore so much blush on her sagging cheeks that she looked like a clown, plus a giant Sunday hat—even though it was Tuesday—and enough diamond rings and bangles to rival Liberace. She might as well have worn a t-shirt that said, *I'm rich and you're not.* The tight, frozen look on her face could've been anger or an indication that it was time for another Botox treatment.

I walked in smiling and looking around for Essence. Why would her husband and mother-in-law be here without her? I prayed their visit wasn't about Ebony.

"Hello, everyone. What a surprise. Where's Essence?" I ask.

"Lord knows," Mrs. McCall responds snidely.

I ignore her. This visit has to be about Essence, not Ebony.

"Can I get you something to drink?"

"No, we won't be here long," she hisses, glaring at me like I was the help.

John validates her look by shooing me out of the den.

"Honey, go fix the kids something to eat. I'm sure they're hungry."

"What's going on?" I ask, looking at Lawrence.

"Your sister's a con artist!" John yells.

"Excuse me?"

Essence can be a lot of things, but a con artist isn't one of them. She's more shamelessly honest than anyone I know.

"Your *sister* annulled her marriage, causing immense embarrassment to the McCall family—and us, might I add."

"Annulled? Well, what happened?" I ask.

"You want to know what happened?" Mrs. McCall sneers. "Your sister abandoned my generous son on their honeymoon, took all the wedding gifts, and probably pawned them. How tacky can she be!"

So that's what Essence meant when she said not to be mad at her. It's probably the reason she's been dodging my calls.

"Calm down, Mrs. McCall. We'll get to the bottom of this," John says, fawning over her like she's royalty.

"When I heard who your father was, I knew my son was making

a mistake," Mrs. McCall continued. "We're humiliated! We let that nappy-headed hussy in our house, around our children and loved ones. We've been seen in public with her for crying out loud!"

"Mrs. McCall, please…," John says, trying to calm her down.

This bitch is testing every nerve I have—and John kissing her toes is making it worse. I'm not mad at Essence and can learn from her. I should've left John on our honeymoon night and cashed in on the wedding gifts. At least, I would've gotten something out of this botched marriage. Essence has some real balls. If she weren't so stingy, I'd ask to borrow them.

"I really trusted you, John!" Lawrence said, shaking his head.

"I know you did. What can I do to make it right?" John pleads.

"You're darn right he did," Mrs. McCall snaps, scooting so close t the chair's edge that she's one scoot from falling off…if I didn't push her first.

"Is this the kind of senator you're going to be?" she seethes. "One with in-laws who are thieves, con artists, attempted murderers, jailbird fathers, drug-dealing brothers, and—"

"That's enough! You don't speak about my family that way. Not in my house!" I scream.

"John? Whose house is this?" Lawrence asks.

John looks at me like he wants to strangle me.

"This is my house, and you're welcome here," he says to Lawrence. Then he turns to me, voice low and threatening: "Sahara, go see to the children. If you can't show sensitivity to the shame your family brought on the McCalls, you don't need to be here."

I take a deep breath and try to stay composed.

"I'm glad she annulled the marriage," Mrs. McCall continues. "Otherwise, my son could be the one lying in a hospital bed, missing his member. What kind of family are *you* people?"

"Mother, it's okay," Lawrence says, trying to calm her down.

"I want our family emblem back. Then it'll be okay. She probably sold it to some drug dealer by now. Just imagine all the filthy hands that's been on that jewel by now—a jewel passed down five generations. Oh, the shame!" She covers her eyes like she's trying to block out the sun.

"I'll get it back for you. I promise," John vows, rushing to her side and patting her on the back. He sounds like a lying politician already. "Sahara…leave."

I don't know if he's telling me to leave the house or the room. So, I just walk out of the room. If I'd stayed, I would've planted my foot up Mrs. McCall's ass. As I walk down the hall toward the kitchen, I pass our family room. Peeping inside, I see the twins, Lauren and Ashley, sitting in front of the TV. When they spot me, they jump up to hug me.

"Mommy!" they squeal.

"Where's your brother?" I ask, referring to my toddler son, Michael.

"He's still sleeping. He's tired from the park. Daddy had to carry him in the house from the car," Ashley says.

"Your dad took you guys to the park?" I ask, surprised. That isn't like John to do.

I start walking towards the kitchen to get dinner started. The twins follow behind me.

"No, he dropped us off," Lauren blurted.

Ashley shot her a look like she'd just told a secret.

"Dropped you off? With who?" I ask as I pull some chicken breasts out of the freezer to make teriyaki stir-fry.

"Becca," Lauren answers quietly.

I'm confused. "Becca? Is she a new babysitter?"

"No. She's daddy's new assistant," Ashley chirps.

"Oh, really?"

"Yeah, and she's so pretty, Mommy. She has red hair all the way down to here." Ashley points to her butt. "And red freckles and green eyes! I wish my hair was long like that and my eyes blue. Is my hair going to get that long?"

"Why does it matter? Your hair is beautiful the way it is, and your eyes are perfect," I tell her.

"But all the girls at school have long hair and blue eyes. Except us," she says, looking up at Lauren.

All the girls at her school are white, but I don't think she has noticed that yet. I don't even think she notices that she's Black.

"We can get you braids if you want long hair."

"Braids?" Lauren scoffed. "Daddy said braids are ghetto and only poor people wear them. We don't want to look ghetto like those other Black people."

"Excuse me?" I stop rinsing the vegetables to give Lauren a serious look. "What did I tell you about using the word ghetto to describe Black people?"

She drops her head, knowing she said something wrong.

"But Daddy said it. He told me to never wear braids because they will make me look ghetto and poor."

"Well, your daddy is wrong!"

They stare at me, shocked. I've never defied anything their father told them. I feel sick realizing how much he has already brainwashed our children.

"I'm sorry," Lauren whispers.

"Becca doesn't wear braids. She's lucky," Ashley sighs.

"Mommy, you should see her. She reminds me of Princess Belle from *Beauty and the Beast*," Lauren says, referring to her favorite Disney movie. "And she talks funny."

"She sounds like Ms. Blanch," Ashley adds. "The old lady who always wants to invite us to have tea."

She's talking about the British woman who lives around the corner from us. So, I now know this Becca woman is European.

"Becca said she used to be a famous ballet dancer," Lauren says.

"Um…who did you say she was again? Your dad's new assistant?"

I ask, becoming more curious about this Becca character.

"That's what Daddy said. But she told us that her and Daddy are good friends, so that means we are her good friends, too. I like her."

I don't know which one of them was talking. I was too busy trying to figure this Becca thing out to notice.

"Daddy met her at the park?" I ask.

"No. Daddy took us to her house," Lauren answers. "She gave us some lemonade, and we sat in the living room playing with her cat, Mr. Mittens. Daddy said they were going in the back to have a meeting. Then they came out, and we went to the park. He said he'd be right back—that he had an important meeting and was going to pick us back up when he got finished."

"When daddy came back, he played with us at the park for a while," Ashley says, picking up where Lauren left off. "He pushed Becca on the swing and pushed us, too. Then we had ice cream. After we took Becca home, we waited in the car while Daddy went inside. When he came back out, he asked us if we had fun and if we liked Becca. We both said yeah."

"She gave him a good luck kiss on the forehead before his meeting, too," Lauren blurts out, and I catch Ashley giving her another weird look.

They didn't have to say any more. I knew who this Becca bitch was. She was John's mistress—the woman he was preparing to leave me for. And he had the nerve to have her white ass around my children! He's gone too far.

"Did she ask you anything about me?" I say, trying not to sound pissed off.

"No. She just asked us about school and other stuff, like what types of games we like to play, our favorite movies, and the kinds of books we enjoy reading. She's really nice. I think you'll like her, Mommy," Lauren says sweetly, sounding so innocent and naïve.

"What about Michael?" I ask.

"She held him most of the time. Said he's cute as a button. Michael didn't cry, so he must like her, too."

I don't realize how angry I am until I nick my finger chopping the vegetables. The girls scream at the sight of blood. Luckily, the cut isn't bad, so it won't require stitches. I assure the girls that I'm fine and send them back to the family room to watch TV. Then I rinse off my finger and put the chopped vegetables and seasoned chunks of chicken breast in the wok.

When the front door opens and closes, I know the McCalls have finally left. John's footsteps start echoing down the hall towards the kitchen, and my pulse spikes. I don't want to see his ass. Then I hear that ticking sound in my head again. I take several deep breaths. I can't afford to snap—not yet. I told myself before that I have to play it smart if I want to make it out of this marriage still standing and with my children. And now that Ebony is in her predicament, it's not just about me anymore. I have a role to play, and I need to stick to it. I can't let my emotions get the best of me and ruin my entire plan— whatever it is.

My back is turned to the entry of the kitchen, and I'm standing over the stove when I hear John's angry footsteps come to a halt. I don't bother turning around to face him.

"You know they asked me for their portion of the wedding money back—and the family emblem?! Who knows where your ghetto sister pawned it!" John barks.

His words sting. He's never openly called my family names before. Yes, he would often allude to his feelings about my family through his cynical behavior and sarcastic innuendos. But it was always indirect. Now his contempt is out in the open.

"How do you think I'm going to pay them back or find that damn jewel? Huh?!"

I stir the food in the pot, my back still turned to him.

"I've had it up to my nose hairs with you and your broken family.

I tried my best to make them respectable, but it was pointless," John says, shaking his head like the words left a bad taste in his mouth.

Tick...tick...tick.

"If it wasn't for me, they wouldn't be half the citizens they are now—if you can call them that."

Tick...tick...tick.

"I introduced your sister to a man of status—somebody to clean that dirty last name of hers—and she humiliates me by abandoning him! Steals wedding gifts and vanishes like a thief in the night!"

Tick...tick...tick.

"And your crazy sister—whose career I helped build—she goes around shooting people!"

I finally turn to face him. Now he's going too far. He didn't bother to mention my niece, Zena, and the reason for Ebony shooting Kenton.

"Come on, John. That's not fair." I respond so calmly that he looks stunned by my composure. "Most of your friends spent thousands on her artwork. Her art speaks for itself."

"They only bought it because of me. Her paintings are colorful craziness. And now she proves her insanity by shooting a man."

I turn back to the stove, gripping the spoon tightly. The sight of him makes me want to bury a knife in his chest. He'd better keep his distance.

"Oh my God, I'm running for fucking office here! This is my lifelong dream we're talking about! I can't be connected to this chaos! I deserve better!"

"We'll work it out, John. I promise," I say, forcing a smile.

He looks confused, then smug.

"If this is going to work, it's going to be on my terms. You're gonna stay the hell away from that damaged family of yours. Don't think I'm going to ask for a favor from any of my pals to represent your psycho sister or use the organization to help her. And you need

238

to call Essence and get that jewel back. Oh, and she needs to pay me back my half of the money for that botched wedding—or else I'm going to sue her little narrow ass! Is that understood!"

"Yes, John," I say through gritted teeth.

"With everything going on, I'm moving up my candidacy announcement. I can't wait until Christmas. By that time, the press will be all over me about your sister. So, I'll announce in three weeks. Can you handle that?"

"Yes, John," I answer robotically.

Perfect. In three weeks, he's going to announce his candidacy and will need me to play the role of a loving wife for his campaign. He will have to save face for his constituents by pretending to be a devoted father—not a self-hating asshole who is having an affair and threatening to kick his wife of ten years to the curb with nothing. Fucking bastard! Soon after the announcement, I'm going to expose him and publicly humiliate him. I'm going to make it so bad for him that he'll have to move to another city and start over—and he can take his precious Becca with him. But he better leave my children with me, or Ebony and I will hunt him down like a dynamic duo. Asshole! He's pushed me too far for too long. Now it's my turn.

Tick...tick...tick.

21
MALICHAI
"Three Minutes"

"**Y**ou remember what I told you, right?" I ask Meka. Her hair is sticking up on top of her head like a messy Mohawk as she sits on the mattress on the floor, rummaging through a black garbage bag filled with her clothes. One skinny, ashy leg bounces nervously.

"Yeah," she says, quickly smoothing her hair like she's late for a job interview.

"What'd I tell you then?"

"Zach's bus comes around the corner by the big tree at ten minutes after seven, and he's home by one-thirty. Same as yesterday and the day before. I got it, Mal! Damn, I ain't got amnesia!" she whines. "You seen my sweats?"

She jumps up, digging through my stuff now.

I don't respond. It was 6:15 a.m. Meka's only up because Wavy knocked fifteen minutes ago, telling Meka to get her Wheaties before she missed out.

We moved in with Wavy on Friday. It's only Wednesday, and I'm already sick of this place. But I didn't have nowhere else for us to go, and what she's charging for rent is dirt cheap. Raul wasn't going to give me no more chances, and I've burned every motel bridge. So, this is home for now.

The house is nice, but it's packed wall-to-wall with desperate, strung-out folks. It's like a halfway house for functioning crackheads, and Meka acts like she's in a Hyatt suite. She's like a kid in a candy store. Wavy's always got dudes coming by with party favors that she shares with Meka. Meka's barely been in our room since we got here—she's always in the living room, basement, or on the back patio smoking or shooting up—sometimes both.

I keep to myself. Too many people under one roof. Every room of the five-bedroom house is occupied, and some even sleep in the basement. We're the only ones with a kid. The TV or music blasts all night, and the front door never stops opening and closing with strangers coming and going. At least we have the master bedroom at the end of the narrow hallway with a private bath.

The first thing I did when we moved in was install two bolt locks on our bedroom door. I ain't no fool. Living with dopeheads, I got to watch our backs constantly. I don't need nobody trying to steal what I already don't have. I hate leaving my car full of scrap metal out front; the fiends eyeball it, knowing its worth in cash. The worst part about being here is that some of these folks are old customers who can't accept I'm out of the game. One kept tapping my door all night, trying to cop something from me until Meka finally convinced him I had nothing.

"Keep this door locked, Meka."

She gives up on trying to find her pants, slipping into a pair of my oversized sweats. She looks ridiculous, but I don't say anything. She's in a hurry to base up. The veins in her arms look worse every day from the puncture marks—red, purple, or scarred brown.

"I know, Mal! I ain't stupid. I keep the key in my bra. Nobody's finding it there but you." She winks.

I give her a look that says, *Are you sure?* She forces an uneasy smile.

Wavy taps on the door again. Damn, she's relentless. It's not enough for her to be a fiend; she's determined to keep Meka strung out, too. I've never seen anyone as giving with their hits like Wavy.

"Meka, hurry up before Toya wakes up and beats you to the punch. I already owe the bitch from last week."

"I'm coming! Hide in the basement. Don't give it to her. I'm just looking for my shoes."

"Three minutes, girl. I ain't waiting," Wavy says, then taps the door again. "Morning, Mal," she adds flirtatiously.

"Horny bitch, my man ain't thinking about you," Meka mutters while flipping bags and blankets, even lifting the edge of the mattress. "Mal! My shoes! Where are they?"

"How should I know where you left your damn shoes? Probably in that drab-ass basement you love so much."

"You mean the party cave?" She grins. "You should come chill with us sometimes. You drink beer, right? Wavy sells beer down there, but I know she'd give you yours free."

"I don't need Wavy or nobody else in this house giving me shit for free!"

"Calm down, Mal," she says, finding one slipper under a bag. "Why don't you loosen up? Folks think you're stuck up since you never leave this room. Relax. Being here is better than being at that stank-ass motel."

"Better for who? You?"

"For all of us. Zach's got a yard to play in and burn off some of that energy he always has. There ain't no whores huddling around outside the front door. It's a nice place—mostly older folks. Damn, where's my other shoe?"

"Why don't you get on Section 8? Then we can get our own place."

"It ain't that easy. They ain't taking no more new people. And even if they were, there's a long waiting list for this area. We would have to live way out somewhere for a year or two before we could move back up this way. Not unless I find somebody to switch vouchers with me, and I don't know anybody willing to stay way out in the boonies."

"That wouldn't be so bad."

She gives me a weird look. "Yeah? And how you gonna get to work? You know how much gas money it would take to drive into the city each day to collect cans to recycle and scrap metal?"

"I got a new job working for Darrel, and it pays well. Once I sell what's in my car, I'm done scrapping."

"Work for him? I thought he worked for you," she scoffs.

"Don't matter. We're making good money, and it's his contact."

Zach's on the bed, knocked out. She'll have to wake him soon for school, so I don't know why she's rushing down to the basement. Tuesday, she was too high to get him to school, and he had to stay home. When I got back, Zach was locked in the room. He tore our room to pieces and had pissed on himself. I could've killed Meka, but she was so high, she wouldn't have noticed.

She rummages near Zach, careful not to wake him, looking for her other pink house slipper.

"What's good money?" Meka asks.

"Good enough to get us the hell out of here soon."

She pauses and gives me a worried look.

"What's the rush? Didn't you pay Wavy two months upfront? We'll be here at least that long, ain't we?"

"I hope not. We need our own space."

"I know you ain't making enough to afford regular rent somewhere else. Where we gonna go—another cheap-ass motel? We're banned from half already."

"I'll figure something out. Just don't get too comfortable."

She rolls her eyes. "Fuck it," she says, leaving with only one slipper on.

"Don't forget Zach's gotta get up soon. He can't miss no more school. I'm serious, girl."

"I know, baby!" she yells from the hallway.

And keep the damn door locked!"

"Got you, baby," she says, her voice trailing off as she rushes to the basement.

I know Meka won't be back in enough time to get Zach dressed and on the bus, so I wake him up myself. I've got a few minutes to burn before meeting Darrel.

"Wake up, little man," I say, nudging him.

He pops his eyes open instantly, always ready to be awake and not wanting to miss out on anything.

I would've left him with Balanah a few more weeks, but when I saw her at Mama's the other day, she looked exhausted. I know Zach misses her; he cries for her all the time. I tell him she needs a break, but he doesn't understand. He misses the stable home she gave him—three meals a day, hugs, consistency—things me and Meka don't provide. Sometimes I think Meka forgets he exists. When she does notice him, she treats him like a nuisance. She wants him quiet and locked away. Part of it is her addiction, but then I think it goes deeper than that. I know seeing him reminds her that she's to blame for how he turned out. Looking at him makes her feel too guilty. Maybe if he was normal, she would respond to him better— maybe a lot of people would, even me. It takes a very patient and loving person to deal with a special needs child—a person like Balanah, but he's not her responsibility.

I carry Zach to the bathroom. Mornings are when he's calmest. He doesn't move around too much and pays closer attention to what I'm saying. He almost seems normal.

I tell him to lift his arms and pull off his nightshirt. He removes his pants himself—one of many things that Balanah has taught him. He spells his name now, picks up after himself, and eats with a fork instead of his hands. I'm grateful to her. It gives me hope that with help, Zach can function better. His school don't teach him a damn thing. All they do is drug him up and let him run wild with the other special needs kids while the staff watches soap operas. It's the area. These schools are broke, low-performing. If we had stayed in our old neighborhood, Zach would've gotten real help.

I run a bath for Zach, and he jumps in on his own and starts washing himself. After I pull him from the tub and wrap him in an oversized towel, he points to the sink, gesturing for me to help him brush his teeth. After helping him with that, I get him dressed and then give him a juice box and a donut for breakfast.

"Mommy will be here soon, little man. Then you're going to school. Learn something smart today, okay?"

He nods, and I kiss him on the forehead. I hate leaving him locked in the room alone, but I ain't have a choice. I have to make money.

I lock all three locks behind me, then place my ear up to the door to listen to what Zach is doing. It's quiet. He's probably sitting in the same spot on the bed where I left him, eyes sad and empty. Instead of feeling guilty, I promise myself I'm going to make it better for him.

Before I leave, I head to the basement to remind Meka about Zach. The house already reeks from what's happening below. The carpet on the stairs is so worn that the plywood shows, and the handrail wobbles under my grip. Voices mix with the sound of the morning radio. When I reach the bottom step, a cold draft hits me and sends a chill up my spine. There's only one bulb casting a weak light. It's one of those old-fashioned lights that didn't have a cover, exposing a single bulb sticking out of the ceiling and a string you have to tug to turn it on. Wavy's makeshift bar of cheap beer and vodka sits in a corner, cobwebs hovering over it. In the darkest part of the basement, I see Meka's other pink slipper lying beside a king-sized mattress. I don't even want to imagine how it got there.

On a worn couch in the other dark corner, Meka, Wavy, and two other dudes are huddled around a lopsided coffee table littered with drugs, empty beer bottles used as ashtrays, a stack of playing cards, and an opened box of condoms. One man tightens a belt around Meka's outstretched arm. Wavy and the others look half-dead—their bodies slumped back into the couch cushion and heads lowered to the side. Just when the guy is getting ready to shoot the contents of the needle into a very anxious Meka, I call out her name.

"Meka!" I call, startling them.

"Mal," she says, jumping up from embarrassment—or so I assume.

The dude gives me a weird look that I return.

"I thought you left for work, baby. Did you forget something?" she asks me while loosening the belt from around her arm.

"He forgot to give you your kiss," Wavy slurs.

Wavy shifted her weight on the couch, trying to focus. Her beauty's long gone, though I don't think she was ever pretty, just sexy. She's tall, with curves and a wavy wig down her back, but years of drugs have worn her down.

I give Meka a disapproving look; she drops her head.

"Get your other shoe. You gonna get sick down here," I say.

She shoots me a guilty look, slips on her slipper, pulls up my baggy pants, and walks back over towards the couch.

"You sure you can't wait? Zach's bus is gonna be here soon," I say, eyeing the impatient man with the needle.

"Um…yeah. It don't matter," she replies, looking over her shoulder at him, too.

"Girl, don't get mad when Toya takes your spot," Wavy warns.

"Yeah, and I ain't waiting on you," the guy snaps, glaring at me.

Meka hesitates, glancing between me and the drugs.

"Go tend to our son!" I demand. "You got all day to shoot the breeze."

"Not without no money," she whines. "This is a party favor from Wavy."

"Yep. I figure I owe her, considering how generous y'all used to treat me back in the day—back when Mal used to have fun."

I ignore Wavy and wait for Meka's response. When she doesn't answer fast enough, I grab her by the arm and yank her away from the crack couch.

"Take it easy, Mal. Damn!" Meka whines.

"Yeah, man, why don't you take it easy?" the guy chimes in, standing up.

"Is this your business, man?" I shove Meka to the side and step up to him.

When he sees the look in my eyes and how I tower over him, he backs down.

"I guess not," he mutters, taking Meka's place on the couch. "Give me my tie rope!" he yells to her.

As I'm taking it off her arm myself, she tugs away from me.

"Hold on, Mal! Just give me a minute. Zach's bus doesn't come for another thirty minutes. This will only take a few minutes. What you want me to do, stare at him until then?"

"Be a mother!"

"That was low, Mal. Meka do the best she can wit' that boy," Wavy says.

"Wavy, mind your fucking business."

She laughs. "I'll do whatever you say, Mal. Whatever, whenever, however."

Meka rolls her eyes at Wavy's flirting.

"I'll be three minutes," she tells me and walks back over to the couch.

"Three minutes, huh? Then what?"

"Then I'm gonna get our son off to school like I did yesterday."

"If I find out he ain't been to school today…"

I shake my head at her. I don't have to finish; she knows what I mean. She'd be in for it.

"Give the girl three minutes. She needs her coffee, then she gonna be up and about. I'll make sure she gets him on the bus—just for you, Mal."

"Bitch, shut up!" Meka snaps at Wavy, who only laughs in response.

I run back up the steps and out to my car to go and meet Darrel. Now, I'm running late.

* * * * *

I started working with Darrel on Monday. It seemed too easy to be true. All we do is hit vacant houses, rip out the walls, and pull out the copper and metal wiring. Sometimes, they still have appliances inside. Just in the last two days, we've split the cash from a stove, dishwasher, water heater, and the golden prize: an air conditioning unit. Those sold like hotcakes. Since Monday, I've already made fifteen hundred dollars doing half the work I used to. It wasn't exactly honest, but it was quick money—and like Darrel said, the banks had insurance. Honestly, I don't think they give a damn about those houses. The yards look like jungles, property values tank, and some they can't even give away. So, we take what we can for them.

There are no nosy neighbors snooping around to ask us questions because most of the other houses in the area are already foreclosed. The only problem is competition. This isn't a new hustle, and everybody is catching on. Sometimes, we'll get to a house too late and find the copper and units already gone.

I pull into The Home Depot parking lot three minutes late. Darrel is leaning on his truck, scanning the traffic for me. When he sees my car, he looks relieved and hops in his truck. Time is money. If we don't get in and out of all the houses, someone else will beat us to it—messing up our money. I jump from my car into Darrel's truck.

"Man, we gotta start leaving earlier. Somebody can be at the houses already digging for gold."

"I know, man. My bad." I give him dap. "Meka, Zach, and fucking Wavy!"

I shake my head. I don't have to say anything else. He already knows the deal.

"You gotta get your phone back on, man. You got the money for it."

"I know. I'm just scared to spend it."

"I know how you feel, but we need to be able to communicate, man. We got five houses on the list today. If we hit them all, that's about five grand split between us."

"Damn." I shake my head at the thought of making that kind of money in one day without having to sell dope. "You wasn't lying about this money."

"I told you. Pretty soon, we gonna be riding in your truck. I still see you got all that junk in your car. When you gonna sell it?"

"I got to find time to do it. I got a lot going on."

Darrel knows about Ebony being locked up and what happened to Zena. I really respect that he doesn't bring it up. He just waits for me to talk about it.

I hope we can get to all five houses, but I don't know if I'll have the time to pull an eight-hour shift today because I'm meeting with Kwame so we can continue our search for Zena. So far, it feels like a wild goose chase. Sahara gave us some leads she got from Ebony, but nobody told us anything solid. Kwame said Mama has been calling him every hour for updates. She's probably a little upset I'm working instead of looking for Zena all day, but I have to work—even if they don't consider what I'm doing "real" work. Kwame told me to handle my business; he looks for her during the day. But I really need my phone back on—mine and Meka's—so I can check on things while I'm out and keep in touch with my family for updates on Ebony. Sahara went to see her the other day, and Kwame is supposed to go visit her this weekend. He asked if I wanted to come. I told him I'd think about it. I hate to see my sister like that, especially when I can't tell her shit about where her daughter is. I don't know if Balanah has seen her yet or if Essence knows what's going on.

Meka's been too busy getting high to know anything about Ebony or Zena, and I'm gonna keep it that way. There isn't anything she can do, and she will only feel burdened by the bad news, which might give her even more of a reason to overdose on that liquid death she's shooting in her arm. She's too sensitive. She cares too much about everybody else but never herself. I wish she would show herself the same compassion.

"You know if there's anything you need me to do, I got you, right?" Darrel says.

I nod. I know he means that.

We pull up to the first house—a brick bungalow off Glenwood Road with boarded-up windows and grass as tall as trees. I grab my tools and jump out of the car, eager to work. Sometimes the doors are unlocked; other times, they are boarded or just locked. If it's boarded, I use my hammer to pry the plywood off a back window. If the window is locked, we break the glass.

The A.C. unit is gone, but we get all the copper and a refrigerator. The small house only takes an hour. The next few houses are nearby, except one across town off Flakes Mill Road, where the newer houses are. So far, we've copped two units, all the copper, three water heaters, and a dishwasher. Darrel's old truck has a long bed, and we managed to get everything inside, but I'm not sure we can fit anything else back there—although we are hoping this next house has a unit we can take. I don't know where we gonna fit it all.

It's going on five o'clock, and I know we should call it a day. I told Kwame I would meet him at his place around seven, but I don't want to walk away from money. We've hit our goal. However, there's about another fifteen hundred on the table if we get this last house.

"I'm not sure these newer houses have copper—mostly PVC,"

Darrel says as we pull into the subdivision.

It's a nice neighborhood, with modern brick homes, manicured yards, and clean streets. I could see me, Meka, and Zach living somewhere like this. Many houses are vacant, with winterized notices plastered on their doors. I get the crazy idea to become a squatter in one, but I dismiss it—too risky.

"This neighborhood ain't like the others. We gonna have to watch our backs out here," I say, noticing a big neighborhood watch sign.

"If anybody asks, we were hired by the bank to clean up," Darrel suggests.

"Well, we got to be in and out of this one quick. If they don't got no copper, we should skip the electrical wiring and just take the units and go."

Pulling copper from wiring is tedious—breaking through drywall, cutting through thin wires—but copper plumbing is easier. But I don't think this house has those kinds of pipes.

"If they ain't got no units, we'll take the fixtures," Darrel says. "These new houses be having nice cabinets, countertops, light fixtures, and whatnot. You know what some of them investors would pay us for a full kitchen of new cabinets? Shit, at least three hundred dollars."

I look over my shoulder at his overloaded truck bed. "We can't get greedy, man. In this kind of neighborhood, we need a plan. Let's grab units if they got them, maybe a few fixtures, but we ain't got time to be breaking apart an entire kitchen. Not today."

"You right, man," he agrees, pulling into the driveway of our last house for the day.

The house looks like the others in the neighborhood—red brick, big bay windows. I cross my fingers and hope the units are still there.

We walk around the side and spot two units right away. Darrel smiles at me, his eyes twinkling with dollar signs. As he runs back to his vehicle for the hand truck, I watch my surroundings. Then I hear a sweet voice call my name. It's not Darrel. It's coming from the neighbor's house.

It's Natasha Sanders. We went to high school together before I dropped out and started selling dope. She was a good girl, and when I was good, she had a little thing for me. Back then, I thought she was boring because she didn't put out like the other girls. Now, I know better. The exciting girls led me here, but Natasha...she looks like real peace.

"What's up, girl?" I say, trying to hide my nerves. After all, this good girl could end up calling the cops on me.

"Give me a hug, boy!" she says, rushing over to me.

She smells like coconut and oatmeal lotion, and her curvy body feels warm and welcoming. There is something healing about her embrace. I almost don't want to let go. When she steps back, her big brown eyes are bright and sincere, her full pink lips curling into a smile that reveals perfect teeth. Her micro-braids are tied back in a bun, making her look even more youthful, and her smooth, caramel-colored skin glows. She's more beautiful than ever.

"How have you been?" she asks in a peppy voice like she's hoping I'll tell her something good.

"I can't complain. It's been a minute."

"Yeah, about ten years."

"Damn, I'm getting old."

"No, you're not." Natasha playfully pushes my shoulder. "You're getting wiser," she adds, flashing another pretty smile.

We stand silent, just looking at each other. She looks at me like I'm the Malichai she remembers—the promising young man who could've been somebody. For the first time in years, I feel a sense of hope. If she can still see him, he must still be there.

Darrel comes rushing down the hill with the hand truck, but when he sees Natasha, he stops dead in his tracks, looking guilty.

Natasha folds her arms over her snug-fitting cashmere sweater like she caught a chill. Then she does a little wiggle, twirling her shapely hips in a non-sexual way, gesturing a shiver.

"It's cold," she says, steam coming from her mouth. "I saw you from my window and just wanted to say hi."

She waves at me and at Darrel, smiling kindly. He nods at her as if to say, *Hello.*

"It was good seeing you, Natasha."

"Tell your mom I said hello. I'm sorry about…everything," she says, eyes down.

"Yeah, we getting through it."

"I run a program for at-risk girls. If Zena wants…" She shrugs like she doesn't know if she's asking the right thing in the right way. "…she's welcome to come to our center. We have good counselors in a positive environment where they discuss this kind of thing candidly. It's a real safe space."

"Thanks…I'll keep that in mind," I say honestly. The fact that she is involved in such a selfless program makes her even more beautiful to me. "Right now, I just need to find her."

"She'll turn up. I bet she's just hiding out with all the media attention. It's got to be really hard being in her shoes right now. I'll keep my eyes open," she says, patting my arm.

Damn, what is it about this woman's touch? Even the slightest touch from her is filling a void that's been empty in me for years.

"I appreciate that."

I smile at her, and she smiles back, almost blushing.

At me? She can't be. I'm nothing to blush at.

"Oh…" She tilts her head, giving me a sincere look. "How's Meka and Zach?"

Natasha and Balanah were in the same class. They used to be close before she got clocked up. Although I hadn't seen her in ten years, I'm sure Balanah keeps her updated about me from time to time. That's how she knows I have a son with Meka. Meka was in my class but dropped out in ninth grade. She was so popular everybody knew her name. They still do. She's always going to be a legend. It's just how she shines.

I feel bad because being in her presence is the first time I didn't think about them. I hate to admit it, but it was a nice mental break. Still, the reality is, they are my family, and I shouldn't stop thinking about them. Not even for a second.

"Zach's good, and Meka…you know Meka."

"Yeah," she says uneasily. "I saw her walking down Glenwood the other day." She lowers her eyes like she doesn't want me to see what she's thinking, but I already know. "The center I work with has other programs, too. You should check them out."

I like the discretion she used in front of Darrel, although he already knows the deal.

"When she's ready, we will."

"There's no time like the present." She smiles again. "You're just like your dad—committed to your family. Meka's blessed to have you. You know, my dad's life changed because of yours. Your dad helped him get into rehab, and it saved our family. My parents are still married today. I appreciate that so much and just want to thank you for it."

"It wasn't me," I say, not wanting to accept a morsel of my father's honor.

"Not directly, but I'm sure you and your siblings inspired him. It was good seeing you."

She leans in and hugs me again, then waves goodbye to Darrel, wiggling two dainty fingers at him before disappearing back into the house.

"We got three minutes, man, then we gotta jet," Darrel says, reminding me of what I told him about being in and out.

"Three minutes," I repeat, watching Natasha until she's gone, her scent lingering in the cold air.

22

BALANAH
"Being Heard"

I never realized how much time there is in a day. Twenty-four hours seems to stretch on for days now that I'm out of the crazy house I used to call home. And the silence? Wow! I've seen that saying on library walls: *Silence is golden.* But I hadn't been able to fully grasp that concept until I left Mama's house after the family meeting and checked into a hotel. Silence really is golden. More than that, it renews my thoughts. I'm having ideas I haven't had in a long while, and the peace is so deep and steady, I might get used to being alone.

I feel productive, full of energy, and ambitious, like I could conquer the world. But I don't need the whole world—just to take back control of the little space of Earth I've occupied these last thirty-something years of my life. I thought I would be able to work on my business plan, but my priorities have shifted. My business now is setting up a campaign for Ebony and Zena to share their story with the world. I've been busting my ass, but it's going well. I'm proud of myself, and that's a nice feeling. Pride in yourself—who knew it could feel so powerful? I visited Ebony, too. That girl is a trip. Seeing how strong and brave she is lets me know I don't have to worry;

everything will be okay. She was excited when I told her about what I was doing for her, and that makes me want to work even harder.

I'm in East Point, at a nonprofit organization called The Survivor's House, getting ready to leave another meeting with the director, Teresa Leslie. She's a real character.

"Thanks so much, Ms. Leslie," I say to the thin woman with a stern face staring back at me.

Teresa is so moved by Ebony's story that she unknowingly motivates me to keep going. Before we even got down to business, she eagerly took me on a tour of The Survivor's House. The building is modest, made of gray concrete blocks, but there's a colorful mural of children of all colors running into the sunset across one wall. Most people probably walk past the building every day without realizing the power inside.

Inside, the modest structure bustles with the energy of love, hope, and the safety net Teresa and the volunteers provide. She pointed out each room with pride: the confession room, where girls can talk about their abuse; the overcomer's room, where survivors and guest speakers inspire each other; the writing room, where girls process their painful emotions through journaling; and the newcomer's room, where recent victims take small steps into recovery. The walls are painted in soft, calming colors. The place is amazing!

"Honey," she waves her hand, "just call me Teresa, and I'm honored to help. Your sister has the balls my mother had—and the balls I didn't." Her voice lowers, eyes drifting to what I assume is a bad memory. "Whatever The Survivor's House can do, we'll do it."

I smile in relief. Teresa Leslie runs a powerful outreach program for women and children who've survived incest, rape, and molestation. She agrees to help in whatever way I need her to: talk to the media on Ebony's behalf, protest if needed—whatever it takes. She wants this story heard as much as I do. I like how real she is, how brave. Even though she's skinny, she has a tough aura like she'd knock Mike Tyson out if he got in her way. I guess she had to learn to be that way after all she'd been through. As an openly confessed incest survivor, whose daughter was also abused at the same age as Ebony, Teresa lobbies hard for survivors. She hates the word "victim," saying it traps people in hopelessness and shame that belongs to their abusers. I remember seeing her on *Oprah* years ago talking about sexual abuse, and she's received several local awards for her community service work. Ebony needs someone like her by her side.

"I can give you a few other contacts, too."

"That'd be great!" I say, excited.

"I can probably even get you airtime on a local TV station. I know the director down at the Atlanta station and a few radio personalities. Just let me know when you're ready, and I'll open my big mouth so wide it'll take a hammer, a nail, and an entire army to close it!"

She laughs, but I know she's serious.

Other programs I reached out to either didn't have time or wanted a fee to speak or talk on Ebony's behalf. Some even turned their noses down at me when they realized I wasn't some fancy news reporter who could get their program video coverage. But Teresa isn't like that. Even after her *Oprah* appearance, she's down-to-earth, driven by change, and not chasing fame.

Teresa pulls out her Rolodex and starts jotting down numbers on a discarded envelope.

"I have to tell you…it's not easy getting people to sign on to this type of campaign. Maybe they worry about their funding. It's a touchy topic."

"Oh, touchy my ass," Teresa grunts. She glances up at me, shaking her head in disgust. "Some of us are here for the girls and women, and some are here for the awards, the interviews, and the fancy galas claiming to raise money for the cause but really just dressing up buildings instead of creating programs. We need more programs," she emphasizes, pounding her fist on top of the wobbly desk covered in papers. "When this happens to young women and girls, we lose them. And the *man's world* we live in doesn't get it. When we ask for funding for counseling and other services, they think we're just whining. Some dumb cops treat rape survivors like they've got PMS instead of real trauma." She folds her thin lips tight, sighing. "The real rape isn't just the act—it's the shame, guilt, and self-blame the abuser plants in your head. That's what destroys you. That's the real rape."

"Wow," I whisper.

I never thought of it that way before. Then again, I never really thought about it at all. My kids are safe, I'm safe—sexual abuse and rape just isn't something I've had to consider. But turning a blind eye to disturbing things doesn't help to change them. My eyes are wide open now, and I'm not closing them again. Hopefully, this campaign opens others' eyes, too—enough to evoke change. After all, sexual abuse doesn't just affect those abused. It affects entire families and can have a trickle-down effect if help is not obtained.

Teresa hands me the envelope with at least five leads scribbled on it. Then, she pushes her Rolodex aside and starts flipping through a worn composition book, licking the tips of her fingers to separate the pages. After a while, she sighs and pushes it aside, too.

"I guess that'll do for now. If I find more, I'll call you. Give me your number again, sugar."

I tell her, and she writes it carefully.

"This is a good start. I appreciate it."

"I've known these people for years. If anybody can help, they can. Tell them Teresa from The Survivor's House sent you."

"Will do," I say, smiling.

She watches as I gather my things and get up to leave.

"You sure you know what you're doing?"

"No. But I'm sticking with it."

"That's not what I mean. The media loves stories like your sister's, but when they move on, your sister's just another angry woman who shot a man the system didn't convict, and your niece becomes a charity case. Are you prepared to fight that? To talk about what some people don't want to hear, no matter how loudly you speak. You ready for everything that comes with it?"

"I have no choice. I have to be."

"Then you already have the right attitude. Listen to me," she says, stepping around her desk, eyes serious. "You make them listen. Even if you have to pry their hands from around their ears and scream at the top of an echoing mountain with a megaphone, you don't shut up until they hear you. You understand me?"

"Yes, ma'am."

"Let's open up this conversation so wide that people talk about it at dinner, at lunch, in bed with their spouses. Let's make them hear us once and for all!"

She smiles hopefully at me, and I leave, adding her to the list of people I don't want to let down—Mama, Ebony, and Zena.

Back in my car, I check the missed calls on both my phones. I purchased a prepaid cell phone just for campaign business and to avoid getting distracting calls from Stephan and Zionah. In the hour I'd been at The Survivor's House, I have five voice messages and seven missed calls on my personal phone: two from Zionah, four from Stephan, and one from Essence. I don't return any. I haven't spoken to Stephan or Zionah since I left them a few days ago, and I don't plan on talking to them until I'm ready. I didn't feel like talking to Essence either. I have too much to do. I did give Mama the number to my prepaid phone and to the hotel in case she needed me for anything.

I don't feel guilty for taking a much-needed break from my

family. The sad part is, they didn't notice I needed one. It would've been nice if this retreat had been planned by them, but it happened the way they forced it. Maybe now they'll see my worth. I hope they're worried sick about me, too. It serves them right. I spend every day worrying about them; now they can worry about me. When I return home, I hope to be well-rested, more respected, and a new person. There will also be a lot of changes if I'm going to stay. And I mean a whole lot.

Checking my prepaid phone, I see three missed calls and three voicemails. One is from Teresa, who was probably calling as I arrived at The Survivor's House. I'd gotten lost and tried to call her, but she wasn't available. By the time she called back, I had already found the building. The second is from another organization I reached out to: A Safe Place. Betty Peters, the director, is nearly impossible to get in contact with, but she has similar credentials to Teresa. But it's the third call that sends a surge of excitement up my spine. It's from Naja Ray Jones. Kenton's wife.

I've never met Naja before, but Ebony used to talk about her, saying she was rich and dumb for marrying a savage like Kenton. Back then, I didn't understand why she used such harsh insults when talking about Kenton, but now I get it. I conducted some research on my own after checking into the hotel. Naja runs Ray Jams and Affairs, a successful event-planning business that mostly caters to the hip-hop community. I couldn't find a direct number for her, so I left her a few messages at her office and sent a certified letter explaining who I am and why I needed to talk to her. After several calls went unreturned and my letter was confirmed as received, I figured it would be a while before she reached out—if at all. But she did, three days later, and I'm eager to hit play on her voicemail.

"Look," she said with an aggressive sigh.

The conversation was already off to a bad start. I knew all this publicity had to be horrible for her image and business, and if for no other reason than to protect herself, I assumed she would defend her husband.

"I don't know *why* you're so hell-bent on stalking me. I got your letter and your phone calls, and I don't want to be bothered. I already got the press hounding me, and I don't need you hounding me, too. So, just bug off. Please." She hung up.

By her voice, she sounded like she was from New York or somewhere up North. That didn't go as well as I'd hoped, but it's not over yet. I call Naja back. I've heard of women turning a blind eye to their husbands doing foul things like molesting a child. I never understood it, but it happens, and I have to face the reality that Naja might be one of those conveniently blind and deaf women. But I remember what Teresa said and prepare myself to make her hear me.

The receptionist answers, reciting the name of Naja's business with perfect diction. By now, she knows my voice and name.

"Naja Ray Jones, please."

"Hold," she says with an exaggerated sigh, not bothering to ask who was calling.

I don't know what I expect from Naja or how she can fit into my campaign, but I have to talk with her. Mama insisted. She and Kenton have only been married for three years. He met her a few years after Ebony kicked him to the curb, so I assume she has no idea he was ever accused of such a disgusting crime. It's kind of scary—how you can never really know a person. But like Mama always says, a funky dog is going to keep fleas, and maybe, just maybe, Kenton's fleas have already bitten her.

"Balanah?" Naja answers after a few moments.

She knew it was me, and the tone of her voice made it clear she thought I hadn't gotten her message to leave her alone.

"Naja, I just want to talk."

"About what?" she snaps, sucking her teeth.

"Can I meet you somewhere?"

"No! I'm not dumb, you know. This could be a setup. You trying to hurt me or something? I have nothing to do with what happened between Kenton and your niece or sister."

Her words let me know she isn't on Kenton's side. She knows he's guilty, but that makes me wonder why. I had to meet her.

"I'm not trying to hurt you or set you up or get the press involved. I just need to talk. Give me thirty minutes, and I promise I won't bother you again. It'll just be me."

She's been silent for so long that I almost think she hung up the phone.

"Hello? Naja?"

"I'm here!" she yells, exasperated. "My life is already a mess because of this. I had to move out of my house just to get away from the press. This is the most humiliating I've ever felt. You harassing me isn't helping!"

"I can only imagine what you're going through," I say sincerely. "But imagine the shambles my sister's and niece's lives have been in. Imagine the shame and humiliation they've carried for years."

"Like I said before, I don't have shit to do with that. I didn't know anything about it. That happened before I met him."

"I'm sure you didn't, but now you do—and it's haunting you. That's why your life feels like it's falling apart." She goes silent again. "You have a daughter, right? A baby girl?"

"Yes," she says dryly.

"I have three girls. The thing I love most about them is their innocence. Think about your baby's face and how innocent it is… then imagine someone stealing that from her, the way your husband stole it from my niece."

"Look, I filed for divorce as soon as the story broke, and in my mind, he's not my husband anymore, so please don't call him that. And if he'd done that to my daughter…" She pauses, taking a heavy, angry breath. "I'd have aimed for his head, not his dick."

She's on my side. She just doesn't know it yet.

"Meet me. Give me thirty minutes."

"I'll give you fifteen, and this better not be no bullshit."

"I promise it won't. Name the place, and I'll be there in less than fifteen minutes."

Twelve minutes later, I walk into a dark, half-empty bar without a name—just a sign that says "BAR" on the outside. I scan the dim room until I see a woman waving to me from the back. She's smoking, eyeing me guardedly. Her appearance surprises me. I don't know what I was expecting her to look like, but she sounded nothing like the roughness her voice portrayed. Up close, she looks biracial or maybe Puerto Rican. Her New York accent now makes sense.

She gestures for me to sit. She's smoking the cigarette like it's oxygen to her lungs instead of clogging them, and she has two shot glasses in front of her—one empty, the other half full. Tapping the table with her French-tipped nails, she stares at me impatiently. She downs the second shot, her face contorting like the liquor was battery acid. She then looks at me and tilts her head to the side.

"So, you want me to apologize for what he did? You think that'll make it better? Fine. I'm sorry the motherfucker was so foul." She looks at me seriously, then squints when the smoke stings her eyes. She takes another puff anyway.

"That helps," I admit honestly.

"But that's not all, is it? You want some dirt, right?"

I stay silent. I do, but the way she said it makes it sound dirty.

"I don't know shit about that man beyond what he told me—no family, no close friends, nothing." She puts out her cigarette. "What am I supposed to do?" She shrugs and leans back on the cushioned bench. "When he talked about your sister, he told me she was crazy, a drunk who did drugs."

"My sister wasn't a drunk and never touched drugs in her life. Not even weed."

"Is she crazy?" she asks with a smirk.

"She's emotional."

"Look, I'm not mad at the girl. I just hate being caught up in his mess. He always made her sound like some stalker who'd come stab us in our sleep or something. I didn't know he was lying to cover up his filth. I think he knew she'd do something like this one day. He talked about the woman too much—had me on night watch for her."

She pulls another cigarette from her clutch bag and lights it.

"Only went to see him once at the hospital, then I saw that shit on the news. It was a done deal for me then. I called my attorney that same day. I don't play that shit. Molesting a child?! Anyone who does that deserves a special spot in hell as far as I'm concerned."

I nod. "I agree."

"I'm just trying to run my business. That's it. Now all these reporters won't leave me alone."

"Why don't you talk?"

"Because I don't want shit to do with none of it. It's not my business."

"It's not that easy. They'll want you to say something—even if it's just that he should rot in hell."

She gives me a look.

"You mean that's what *you* want me to say."

"Do you think my sister should spend the rest of her life in jail?"

She hesitates. "Honestly? No. He should. He brought it on himself."

"Then yeah, that's what I want."

I tell her about my campaign, how I'm trying to spin the press and get the truth out. I mention all the people I'm working with, including Teresa, and when I say Teresa was on *Oprah*, she listens more closely. But when I tell her that I need her, too, she hesitates.

"What can I do?"

"You're worried about what your clients will think. But they already have their thoughts. I know I did. I blamed you at first, assumed you knew he was a predator but chose to ignore it."

"Well, that's not true. I'm not like that!"

"Then show it. This isn't going to disappear. The women you plan events for have children—some might've been abused themselves. You don't want them thinking you knew. Tell them you didn't. Tell them you don't blame my sister. You don't have to defend my sister, but defend your own honor."

She nods slowly, starting to get it. I continue, trying to reel in the fish I barely have hooked.

"Too many people hide from this. I'm doing this campaign not just for my sister and niece, but to make people stop hiding. It's time we face it."

Naja lets out a heavy sigh, her shoulders slumping. But her eyes show she knows what's right.

"What do you want me to do?" she asks quietly.

"I don't know yet, but I need to know you're with me."

"I'm in. You're right. Everything you said is right."

She looks at me and smiles like she's relieved by her decision.

"You know, when I was seventeen, some dude tried to grab me when I was getting on the subway in the Bronx. I had my pepper spray and lit his ass up. I was able to get away, but I always wonder what would've happened to me if I hadn't had it. I never told anybody what happened because I felt embarrassed, even though all he did was grab me from behind, squeeze one of my breasts, and then rub his hand over my crotch before I stabbed him with an elbow in the gut and sprayed his ass." She tells the story like his advances were nothing. "But I always think, would I be the success I am today if he had succeeded in what he was trying to do?" She shakes her head. "Probably not. And that wouldn't be fair—just like it wasn't fair what happened to your niece. How is she handling all this attention?"

I shrug. "We can't find her."

"She's hiding, huh? Like I was."

"She's been hiding for years."

"Maybe we'll find her." Naja puts her hand on mine, assuring me that she's on my team. "I'm not hiding anymore. As a matter of fact, I'm going home today. I miss my bed."

"Good for you," I say.

"Maybe you should hire a PI. I know a guy—he's like a gardener, digging up dirt on people's personal lives. One of my girlfriends, who is going through a divorce, hired him to find out shit about her husband. I'll get you his number when I get home."

I hadn't thought of that. She's already being helpful.

"Thanks," I say, grabbing up my bag to leave, but Naja isn't done. She has something else to say.

She leans in, her two large breasts sitting on top of the table like it's a serving tray.

"You know that same friend who hired the PI? I kept her little girl, Dolly, while she and her ex-husband worked out the madness of their divorce. Dolly is my goddaughter, and she's so bubbly. Always happy and friendly with people. I love her to death." Naja smiles, but it quickly fades. "One day, I left her with Kenton for one hour while I ran to the store. Just one hour!" She holds up her index finger. "When I came home, I thought it was weird because she wasn't so bubbly anymore." She looks up at me with tears in her eyes. "Something was so strangely different about her. She didn't talk, laugh, or smile the rest of the time she stayed with me. Kenton just said that she missed her mother and was sad about the divorce, but I knew that wasn't the case," she says, wiping the tears that are now falling down her cheeks. "It was something weird going on, but I never would allow myself to admit what it could be." She breathes heavily. "Then after I had my baby, I never wanted to leave her alone with him. Not even for a second. People thought I was just being an overprotective mom since it was my first child, but no." She shakes her head. "I knew it was deeper than that."

"That makes you a good mother."

"Yeah." She looks at me, almost thanking me for the reassurance. "My daughter does have a good mother—too bad she didn't have a good father."

"I hear you," I say, grabbing her hand and squeezing it. "Your daughter will be fine."

"What about Ebony's daughter?"

"Once she's heard, she'll be fine, too."

Naja nods her head in agreement.

23

ESSENCE
"Go Away!"

"I gotta call you back, Sahara!" I tell my persistent sister. "I know it's important, but something just came up. I'll call you back in a few minutes. Damn!" I hang up.

I look through the peephole. *Why does this man keep harassing me?* If I'm not answering his calls, what makes him think I'm going to answer my door? I can't believe Marco actually showed up at my house unannounced. I wish he'd just go away! I watch him through my peephole, knocking on my door like the police. Well, he is the police, but his ass ain't on duty—so he can stop banging on my door with his fist like he's trying to break it down. When he starts pressing buttons on his cell phone, I wait for mine to ring. Three seconds later, my phone vibrates.

I shake my head. This man really doesn't get it. I'm so done with him. His barbaric, insensitive ways just aren't cute anymore. Actually, they never were—just sexy. But I don't need that kind of sexy in my life.

And the people he hangs with are dirty money, overrated lowlifes! Seeing Sir Zion at that party, looking all smug, was the icing on the cake. I don't want to be affiliated with anyone who's associated with a life as low as his. And I know they're more than just acquainted because Sir Zion told him to call him. Why would he have his number? Oh, right... Marco's a crooked cop! And to top it off, he has a problem with my daddy. If you can't get with my family, you can't get with me. What a waste. I don't even know what I ever saw in him. Okay, okay...it was his sexy chocolate skin, the six-pack abs, and his bulging biceps, but even that gets boring. If I want to see that, I can flip through a *GQ Magazine*.

I haven't talked to him since he told me about my sister. After fifteen missed calls and unreturned messages, you would think the brute would get the message. He's starting to really irk me with all this calling, leaving casual messages as if we didn't have a minor altercation the other night. I have to keep ignoring him, though. I don't want him distracting me for one second. I've got too much going on, and right now, my primary concern is my sister and niece.

I tiptoe away from my door and look out the window at his Batmobile. He knows I'm home because my car is parked out front. *Okay, it's been like five minutes. Why is he still banging on my door like the building is on fire?* I have a mind to open the door and tell his ass to go to hell, but I'm scared he might arrest me or tackle me or something worse. I'll just keep ignoring him, even though my door is only a few bangs away from falling off its hinges. I would call the police, but they'd probably just tell me there's already an officer at my door.

I went to see Mama after I found out about Ebony's arrest. I'm surprised at how well she's taking it—probably just putting on a strong face like she always does in a crisis. She briefed me about the family meeting. I told her I was with a very important client all weekend, which is why I turned my phone off and therefore didn't know about Ebony. Sahara and Balanah aren't as forgiving, though. Balanah has been ignoring my calls, and she doesn't think I know it. I guess it's her way of saying I should've made the meeting. When I talked to Sahara a few minutes before the barbarian showed up at my door and interrupted our call, she was being cynical, acting like she couldn't trust me to handle a task to help Ebony. She said the family is worried that I wouldn't come through and that everything's under control. She made me so mad, I told her to kiss my ass. Then she told me to kiss hers before hanging up. But she called me back before the dial tone buzzed.

That's when she started talking about the Resident and his old hag of a mother coming over, talking about how they want back the money they spent on the pretentious wedding and that raggedy-ass family heirloom Lawrence gave me. It was a pin in the shape of an M, and it was hideous. I don't even know where that dusty piece of metal is. I almost laughed when he handed it to me like it was some sort of crown I should wear in honor. He must've been crazy to think I'd wear that cheap shit that represented his delusional, racist family. I had it appraised when I was selling my wedding gifts, and it wasn't even worth two hundred dollars. The McCalls are phony as hell. They are more than welcome to have it back if I ever find the damn thing.

I tiptoe back to the peephole to see what Marco's dumb ass is doing now. When I put my eye up to the tiny hole, I jump back because his eye is looking through it. What an idiot! Go away already! Then I look again. That's when I see the back of his head as he walks away. Finally. He tries calling me one more time, and I send him straight to voicemail.

My plan is to leave soon and head downtown to visit Ebony. I want to be one of the first on the list before it gets too long. All these distractions have slowed me down. I haven't even showered or made breakfast yet. I decide to go to the kitchen, start a pot of tea, and make myself an egg white omelet before I shower. Just prepping for my omelet pisses me off. Marco had the nerve to turn down my perfectly made omelet—the one I made from the last of my groceries. I must've been dizzy to do that, and he must've bumped his head to turn it down the way he did.

I try shaking off the negative thoughts as I turn on my skillet and flip through the stack of mail that I've neglected for three days. I didn't feel like seeing any bills, especially with my savings draining and no income. Since I'm not messing with Marco anymore, getting that loan is out of the question. I don't need his dirty money anyway. The Essence of Investments is going to get off the ground, but just not as fast as I thought. Nothing good comes that easy.

Just like I thought, it's mostly bills and junk mail. But I get curious about an envelope from Kwame. *What the hell does he want?* I open it, and a check falls out for ten thousand dollars—almost the amount I would have made in commission for the half-million-dollar house he bought without my assistance. He wrote on the check, *For my loving sister. Please forgive me. Sorry, and I love you.* Damn him. I could shake him and hug him at the same time. This check couldn't have come at a better time. He should've just used me in the first place, but no use crying over spilled milk when I can just wipe that shit up with the ten grand he gave me. I fold the check and stuff it in my purse, telling myself that I will call him today to say thanks.

My teapot starts whistling, and I rush to turn it off. As I'm turning down the burner underneath my skillet, my phone vibrates again. I know it's Marco. *I need to put an end to this.* I grab my phone from my purse, preparing to tell his ass to go to hell and stop calling me. But when I look at the caller ID, it's Sahara.

"I thought I told you I'd call you back!" I huff, carefully cracking my eggs.

"Well, you took too long! We've got important things to discuss."

"Look, when I find that raggedy ass pin, I'll give it back, but I ain't rushing. So, don't rush me," I tell her as I start chopping my veggies.

"John is pissed off!"

"I knew y'all would be," I say, not surprised.

"I said John, not me."

"What?" Now I'm surprised.

"Your mother-in-law is a real bitch, and I don't blame you for getting out while you can."

"Am I hearing right?"

"Did I stutter?" Sahara jokes.

"She ain't my mother-in-law, so please don't refer to her as such when speaking to me. Remember, I got an annulment. So, it's like the shit never happened."

"Tell that to John. He wants that money back."

"I don't have it, and even if I did, I wouldn't give it back. I didn't ask you guys to pay for the wedding. Are you forgetting you and your husband's ulterior motives?" I enlighten her. "Pimping me out for campaign money."

"It wasn't like that, Essence. I really thought we were introducing you to a nice guy. Besides, no one forced you to say 'I do'."

"I know that. I just made a mistake, but I didn't force y'all to pay for my wedding either."

Sahara sighs heavily.

"He's threatening to sue you," she whispers like it's a secret confession.

I laugh.

"Did the lawyer forget the law?" I reply, unmoved by John's threats. "I never signed a promissory note or made a verbal agreement with either of you. If he tries to sue me, I'm gonna call your ass to the witness stand to testify on my behalf, and you better not sell me out either."

"This isn't funny, Essence. He's serious. He wants the money back so he can give it to the McCalls."

"Maybe it's not funny, but it's definitely laughable. The McCalls and John need to learn how to take a loss. I'm not giving them shit. They'll be lucky to get that chipped-ass metal pin back. Family heirloom, my ass!"

"What should I tell him?" Sahara asks like she's all out of solutions.

"What you should've told his ass when he asked you to marry

him over decade ago: go to hell!" I chuckle, and to my surprise, she does, too.

I carefully pour my omelet into the skillet, hoping it comes out as perfect as the one I made for Marco's ungrateful ass.

"Why is John being so evil anyway?" I ask Sahara. "Usually, he only gets this way when he's fucking around. Is he fucking around again? 'Cause if he is, I can sharpen my keys and do a Picasso on that bitch's car like I did the other one. Or I can smack her ass down like the last one. Or I can just pull an Ebony on John for you."

"I can take care of myself," she tells me. "I didn't ask you to do those things. You only caused more trouble. Besides, it's not me you need to be concerned about helping—it's Ebony."

"I know. I tried to tell you that this morning. Mama told me about everybody's role, and I'm ready to handle mine."

"She didn't give you one, Essence. Nobody can trust that you'll take this seriously."

"You really gonna piss me off. Y'all act like I'm incompetent."

"It's not that. We're just worried that something more important will come up, and you'll ditch Ebony like you did by not coming to the family meeting."

"I told Mama I had clients."

"Yeah, right. Balanah told me about your new little boyfriend. Is that your client?"

"Look, if I knew what Ebony did, I would've been there. Besides, I'm here now, and Mama did give me a role."

"What does she want you to do?" she asks, sounding doubtful.

"Raise money to help Balanah with her campaign. How's she doing on that anyway? I thought you knew more important people than she did. You sure she can handle it?"

"I hope everybody can handle their task because I can't do everything. I tried reaching out to Balanah the other day just to touch base, but she's been ignoring my calls. I just pray she's on top of her game. If she needs help, I know she'll be too prideful to ask me. I stopped by her house this morning, and Stephan said she ain't been home in days."

"What?! What the hell is going on now? Y'all husbands are really trippin' with their trifling asses."

"Stephan ain't trifling, and I don't know what's going on. I just hope she's on her job. This isn't the time for a mini-drama. If Ebony's convicted, she could spend the rest of her life in jail. I can't live with that."

"None of us can. What about Mal and Kwame?"

"All they have to do is find Zena, and they haven't done that yet. They came over to Mama's house smelling like weed, talking about how they couldn't find her. Well, go figure!"

"I'd be surprised if Kwame made it off the couch for anything other than to smack Tammy across the head," I laugh.

"What are you talking about?" Sahara says, naïve.

"Girl, you can wear the blindfolds, but don't try to get me to put them on. That's not my style."

"Kwame doesn't hit that girl."

"Yes, he does, and she deserves it. You know Levi isn't his child. That boy doesn't look nothing like him or anyone else in the family. Shit, the way she be all jumpy around him should tell you enough. Last time I saw them together, he blinked hard, and she jumped like he was going to hit her."

"If Kwame's hitting Tammy, he needs help. Nobody deserves that kind of treatment. You should know better, Essence."

"Shit," I sigh.

"He made it off the couch and to the mailbox to give you that check. Why don't you use that money to raise funds? Balanah is probably paying for all the things she needs out of pocket. I know she and Stephan are struggling financially, especially with having to close their business. He told me all that when I saw him."

"Mind your business! I practically worked for that money. I showed Kwame three houses before he went with another realtor. I deserve that money, and it's for my bills! Raising funds means soliciting money, not giving it away. Why doesn't the great senator-to-be contribute? I know y'all have it."

"Actually, we don't," Sahara admits, then says, "I just hope you forgive Kwame now that he had to pay for your forgiveness. He's been upset that you haven't been returning his calls. You know how sensitive he is."

"Don't worry about my relationship with my brother," I snap.

"He's my brother, too. Just get it together, Essence. Mama is counting on you, and so is Ebony and Zena."

"I'm gonna do what I do. As a matter of fact, after I eat this omelet that you made me burn, I'm going to the jail to see Ebony."

Sahara sucks her teeth. She pisses me off doing that because I know what it means. She thinks I'll upset Ebony instead of relieving her grief.

"Just don't frustrate her. She's going through enough. She doesn't need to hear about how you think she should've killed Kenton instead of shooting him in the dick or that you knew something was up with him all along. She doesn't need to hear the 'I told you so' and—"

I cut her off. "Shut up!" Then I hang up before she says anything else.

I'm not a fool. I'm just going to show my love and support. That's all. I know the last thing Ebony needs to hear is that she was wrong. I don't believe in kicking someone when they're already down. Sahara needs to shut up. That's more her style anyway.

My phone rings again, and I already know it's her. I answer without looking at the caller ID.

"What now?" I yell.

"Did you see Sir Zion on TV?" she asks, like my hanging up on her was a dropped call.

"Worse...I saw his ass in person."

"What?! When? How? Where?" she asks in one aggressive breath.

"It's a long story I don't feel like talking about."

"Well, turn to Channel 5. He's on now. They've been replaying his two seconds of fame all day," Sahara says, disgusted.

"I don't want to see that man! I think I hate him more than Mama does."

"Nobody hates him more than Mama does," Sahara says truthfully. "The press is starting to change, which means Ebony's conviction is starting. He told the reporter she's been a troubled youth since Daddy went to jail for murder. Can you believe him? He called what Daddy did 'murder'! Like he wasn't right there supporting. He better be happy Daddy didn't turn his ass in. I wish he had. He would've done the world a huge favor. And this is the kind of garbage John wants to support his campaign. What an idiot!"

"John? I didn't know they were affiliated. Sir Zion doesn't seem like someone John would be acquainted with."

"They're both scumbags!"

"Whoa!" I laugh. "What the hell did John do to you?"

"Everything. John is using him to fund his campaign. He's standing at the top of the corporate and legal ladder, selling tickets to share his status with the highest bidder, no matter who they are. Hell, if Hitler was alive, I wouldn't be shocked if he solicited him for money."

"What a lowlife," I mutter. "I have to go. I need to eat what's left of my omelet and take a shower. See ya."

I hang up without saying goodbye, and she calls right back. I don't answer this time. Then she sends me a text: *Don't tell Ebony about Sir Zion's interview.* Duh! I knew that much.

Marco calls again before I get in the shower. I'm tempted to respond with a text telling him to go away! But I don't. I just ignore him.

24

KWAME

"The Last Hit"

Tammy is peeping through the blinds at the circus she brought to our front yard. She's dog shit, and they're the flies. I knew after she talked to the press some shit like this would happen. I don't want or need this attention right now.

The first van showed up early this morning, right after I dropped Levi off at school. Taking him to and from school every day is something I've committed myself to doing. I'm trying to bond with the boy, make peace. It's not his fault his mother's trifling or that I've been an abusive asshole these past two years. When I decided to stay with Tammy after learning Levi wasn't mine, I took on the responsibility of being his father. It's about time I start acting like it.

Tammy's loving all this attention. She's been in that damn window all morning like a kid watching snow fall, itching to go outside and play in it. The more I watch her, the more I pissed off I get. She never cared about Ebony or Zena, never mentioned them before. For Christmas parties at Sahara's or Thanksgiving dinner at Mama's, she always stayed home by choice. Levi and I would go alone. Now, suddenly, she wants to insert herself. I swear I'm trying to control my anger for this girl. Everything that went wrong in my life ain't her fault, but it feels easier to blame her. She makes it easy, too.

"Get out that damn window!" I yell like I'm scolding Levi.

She jumps, rolls her eyes at me, and keeps peeping.

"Did you hear me?" I warn her.

She sucks her teeth and shoos me away with a dismissive wave like I'm nothing. This ain't never happened before. I walk toward her slowly. She's standing in the living room—the room I've been avoiding since I found out the news about Ebony. I've kept myself busy, haven't touched the couch in days. Honestly, the thought of lying down makes me sick. I feel like I just woke up from a coma, bursting with energy I don't want to waste. I hate being in this living room, but her peeping out at the press ain't doing nothing but taunting them to stick around.

"Get...out...the...window!" I say, slow and stern.

"Kwame, go take a nap," she snaps, shooting me a sordid look.

"What you say?"

I don't even realize I'm walking towards her until I yank her by the elbow, spin her around, and smack her with an open hand. She drops to one knee, holding her face with one hand and bracing herself on the wall with the other. She blinks a few times, dazed, then looks up at me boldly.

"Go ahead and do it again. This time, smack the other cheek," she says, pointing to her face. "I've been asked to talk about this on the radio, and I'm going to do it. I don't give a fuck what you say," she hisses.

She crosses her arms defiantly, daring me to react. She shrugs as if to say, *What are you going to do?* Smacking her ass again would only deepen my guilt.

"I told you not to talk to the press. You hard of hearing?"

"Nope. I hear just fine. I'm just doing what the hell I want. You don't own me, Kwame."

"Why do you want to do this? Don't you understand what you

talking to the press could do? You don't even know my sister. She's facing a life sentence."

She shrugs like she couldn't give a fuck.

"Everybody saw me on TV the other day—even my mama. I ain't talked to her in years, and she called to tell me how pretty I looked. Everybody did."

"So that's it? You're using my family's pain to get famous."

"Pretty much," she says, rolling her neck and bulging her eyes at me.

I can't believe her boldness. At least she was being honest.

"You're worthless," I spit.

"And you're better?" she shoots back.

"Leave my family out of our issues. If you want fame, go get a talent agent. Don't gamble with my sister's life."

"Hell, I take opportunities when they come. Mama didn't raise no fool. I married your sorry ass, didn't I?"

That hit a nerve. The truth slaps me harder than I hit her. I knew this bitch was using me all along. Rage takes over, and I smack her again, harder. She spins around so fast she looks like the Tasmanian Devil, then falls, the side of her face slamming into the corner of the coffee table. She screams in pain, and I rush to her aid, lifting her from the ground. I know that shit hurt because I heard the thump, maybe a crack, before her teeth-grinding scream.

Shit! What the hell did I do?

"Get the fuck off me, Kwame!" she cries, cupping her swelling eye.

"I didn't mean…I'm sorry!"

I try to wrap my arms around her again, but she kicks me away.

"You're not sorry! You think you can control me, but not anymore," she growls, looking at me with one angry eye. "I'm going on that radio show and telling everything! When they ask me what happened to my face, I'm going to tell them you did it and that violence runs in your family! I don't give a fuck about your crazy-ass sister! When I leave that radio station, I'll have a reality show! You watch! Then me and my son are gone! We're gonna leave your miserable ass to rot on that couch!"

She pulls her hand from her eye and waves it angrily. When I see her face, I gasp. Her eye is purple and swollen, looking like a plum bulging through her bruised socket instead of an eyeball. If Tammy goes through with what she just said, I'll fail Ebony. My mistakes will become hers, hurting her case. And with all this press, Tammy could absolutely get a reality show. *Shit!* I don't know what to do. I look over my shoulder at the couch. I want to collapse on top of it and sleep this nightmare away—but I promised my family. I promised Mama. I can't back down now.

"You want a divorce? I'll sign the papers today. I'll give you and Levi what I've got left in my savings."

Her good eye widens almost to the size of her swollen eye at the mention of money. Now I have her attention. I'd give her everything to protect Ebony.

"How much?" she asks sharply.

I look up, thinking. "About…maybe two hundred grand, give or take."

"Two hundred thousand!" she blurts, spittle flying. A sly grin tugs at the corners of her mouth. "And I can have it all?"

"That's what I said. But you have to stop with the interviews, or the deal's off."

"You sure that's all you got?" she says with a sassy tilt of her head and her hands on her hips.

"That's everything. But I'm not giving it to you until all this shit with my sister blows over. I'll hold it like a security bond."

"What? No deal," she snaps.

"You think I'm stupid enough to just give you all my money and let you run free? I know you, Tammy. You love fame even more than money."

She doesn't dispute what I said. She crosses her arms over her chest and sucks in so much air that she whistles. Then she walks back to the window and takes another peek outside. She stares out like she's pondering my proposition.

"You'll put it in writing *and* get it notarized?" she asks finally.

"Whatever it takes."

She turns back to the window, weighing her options. It's a sweet deal. I don't know why it's taking her so long to make a decision.

"I don't know," she says.

"What? You don't trust me? I might not have been the best husband towards you or the best father for Levi, but I've always been a man of my word."

"It ain't that, Kwame."

She leaves the window and takes a seat on the couch, gingerly touching her swollen eye. Without her asking, I run to the kitchen, grab a few ice cubes from the freezer, wrap them in a clean dish towel, and hand it to her. She rolls her eyes but takes it, dabbing the bruise and flinching with each touch.

"What is it then? Isn't that what you always wanted—my money?"

"Yes," she admits coldly, "but my circumstances have changed. I always knew that one day I would be a star. I just felt it deep inside." She points to her chest. "When I married you, I came close, but not close enough. Now, with all this attention, it feels like my time."

"Come on, Tammy. Two hundred grand is a lot of money."

"It's nothing compared to what fame could bring me. You had your time in the spotlight, with your commercials, parties, and action figures that looked like you. All that time, nobody gave a shit who I was," Tammy hisses like she's been holding resentment against me for just as long as I've been holding it against her. "Now it's my time to shine!" she yells, standing to her feet.

I know there's nothing I can do or say. Her mind is made up.

"Do what you gotta do. Do what makes you happy."

"Like how you do when you hit me?" she sneers.

"No. That shit doesn't make me feel good—it makes me feel worse. I'm fucked up for doing it, and I ain't asking for your forgiveness because I don't deserve it. But mark my words," I look her dead in the eye, "today was the last time I'll ever lay hands on you or any woman again. Hitting a woman is the weakest shit a man can do, and I ain't weak. I come from good stock—I'm my father's son, my mother's pride, and a real Black man. To prove it to you, I'm moving out today. You and Levi can stay here."

I turn to leave. I don't know how smart it was to offer her my savings, but I have another account she doesn't know about. Also, I'm still receiving income from past endorsements. Two hundred grand is generous. A judge wouldn't even give her that amount in divorce court. But leaving is the smartest decision I've made. Our marriage has been purgatory, teetering on hell. I just pray my family doesn't suffer because of it.

"Wait!" Tammy yells at my back. "What are we going to do for money?"

I stop and turn to face her. "I'll pay the bills until you figure things out."

"But…what about money?" she asks, dumbfounded.

She's talking about her splurging money—the money she flaunts around her friends and throws around bars like she's some superstar.

"I'll pay the bills," I repeat sternly, heading upstairs.

"Wait, Kwame! We need to discuss this more!" she panics, following me.

From now on, I'm only giving Tammy money for what's necessary. If I'm not here abusing her, I'm not handing over guilt money. All of that is over.

"How long are you going to be gone?" she asks as I start packing my clothes.

"I told you—until you figure things out."

"What if I don't take the money or do the interviews?"

As bad as our relationship is, it's Tammy's comfort zone. She wants to be a star, but there's no guarantee it will happen, and even with the money I offered her, I know she's thinking about what she will do once it runs out. And with the way she spends money, it'll probably be gone in a year.

"I still need to leave. This ain't working. Look at your face. Look at me. I'm not the same man. I'm tired. You deserve better. Levi deserves better."

"But y'all were getting so close lately. You're just gonna up and leave him after all these years? He don't know you ain't his real daddy. Have you even thought about him?"

"Levi's better off without me."

"You're all he knows! He won't understand."

"Will he understand when you air our dirty laundry on the radio or a reality show?"

She goes quiet for a moment.

"So you want a divorce?"

"Don't you? Are you forgetting what you confessed to me? You just admitted you married me for fame and money."

"We can work it out!"

"No."

"I'm just upset. You always hit me and talk down to me. I just wanted to hurt you back. I ain't going on no radio show, Kwame. I don't know how to be anything but your wife. If that means I gotta be your punching bag, too, so be it."

What she said made me pity her even more.

"That's the saddest thing I've ever heard. That's why I need to go. It's not okay for me to do what I do to you, and it's fucked up that you're alright with it."

"I didn't say I was alright with it. I'm saying I do what it takes to keep my marriage. My mama, grandma, aunts—they ain't never been married. They all envy what I have. They've never been more than side chicks, but I got the honor of being a wife. And I'll do whatever it takes to keep that honor. I'm not like them."

"We both need help, Tammy. I thought it was just me, but we both need it."

I pull my white t-shirts, boxers, and socks from one of the drawers and toss them on the bed. Tammy rushes over, putting them back in the drawer.

"Please, Kwame!" she sobs. "Let's get help together. Just don't leave us."

When I turn to look at Tammy, she's whimpering so much that I start to feel sorry for her all over again. I feel that old pity—the same pity that made me stay when she told me Levi wasn't mine. And the same hero in me that wanted to save her then wants to save her now, but I don't know if I have the strength to save both of us. I surely don't have the strength to just up and leave her so easily, although I don't trust her. I saw the look in her eyes when she said all of those horrible things that I knew were true, and I know if she got the chance, she would do them. Yet, I still feel like I owe her something. Looking at her purple eye isn't making it better either.

"We can get through this, Kwame. Just don't leave your family," she pleads, hugging me from behind.

I can feel the weight of her head against my spine. Her hands are clutching my chest. *Damnit!* Maybe I'll give it one more try. But today was definitely the last time I hit her. I don't know what happens next, but that part of me is over. Today was the last hit.

25

EBONY
"A Mind is a Terrible Thing"

I just had a visit with Essence, so I've officially seen all my sisters. Balanah came by yesterday. I don't know when my brothers are going to show up—if at all—but I still feel the love. Funny how I never realized how much they supported me before. When they didn't come to my art shows or call to check on me, my mind would spin with all kinds of dark thoughts. The mind can play dirty tricks, making you believe things that ain't true—like Tweety thinking her baby daddy really loves her. It's a self-made weapon we use against ourselves.

If Essence can't do anything else, she sure can take your mind off your problems with her wit. She had me cracking up talking about how Sahara called John a scumbag. About time she noticed. I guess he ain't too keen on helping her find good representation for me. Not that it makes him a scumbag—there's a long list of other things that do. Then Essence told me she got her marriage annulled, calling that doctor guy she married a fraud because he was still in training. She's a mess. I was shocked when she promised to help raise money for Balanah's campaign on my behalf. I was even more shocked when Balanah told me that she met with Kenton's wife and all she had to say about his sorry ass.

My family is really trying, but I don't want them to get their hopes up. This could go exactly the way I expect, and I might spend the rest of my life behind bars. I'm prepared for that. I haven't let myself dream about getting out—I don't want to disappoint myself. I can tell they're all worried sick about me, so I let them think what they're doing might help, but it's a long shot. If Sahara can find a lawyer to get me off for a premeditated crime, that lawyer is better than Johnny Cochran. At best, their efforts might ease Mama's mind. She never gives up or loses hope, especially since she became a Christian. But when I saw Sir Zion on TV today calling me a troubled girl beyond help, I knew his statement marked the beginning of the end for me. The press is having a field day, and they'll spin me into a crazed, psychopathic attempted murderer if it will boost their ratings.

Nobody has heard a word from my baby. Maybe she's punishing me by staying hidden. Zena knows I'm worried sick about her. I thought my time in here would earn her forgiveness, but I guess I was wrong. By now, with Kwame and Mal asking around, she must know we're all looking for her. I almost want to tell everyone to call off the search—let her show up when she's ready.

Whenever she's ready to come, I'll be ready to tell her everything, including who her father is. That's another reason she spent so many years upset with me. I've kept it a secret because I know that knowing the truth won't do her any good. Sir Zion is trash. He never claimed her, even though she looks just like him. But if she wants to know, I'll tell her everything—how I felt when I found out what Kenton did to her, how she was my first and last thought when I pulled that trigger, how I would do it again for her if I had to, and how I will always have her back, even from behind these bars.

Speaking of these bars, a new girl arrived today, charged with killing her baby. Everybody is treating the girl like she's cursed, but not me. I don't know why. When she looks up at me, scared and sad,

I just smile at her. I don't talk to her, though. Most of the time, she roams around like a zombie. The girl is about as young as Tweety. I'm just relieved it ain't my mugshot flashing every minute across the TV anymore. They ain't treating this girl like she's famous, though––more like infamous. I heard some of the other women talking about hurting her, but I think they just feel sorry for her. Somebody tried to talk to her. They asked her why she would do something so stupid, and the girl just threw a fit, just like Zach does when he gets upset. Now everybody thinks she is not right in the head, but you have to be mentally ill to kill your own flesh and blood—or any child, for that matter. The news says she drowned the baby while giving her a bath, then put the body in a trash bag and left it by the curb for the garbage men to find. A real murderer wouldn't be that sloppy. There has to be more to this story, but I'm not sure I want to get to the bottom of it. I've got enough issues of my own to deal with, and now that Tweety and I are close, I've got her issues to deal with, too.

Tweety's been back and forth on the phone all day, trying to get in contact with the woman who got her baby. She hasn't heard from her since the girl brought her baby to visit. She's so worried that she's about to drive me crazy, asking me questions like I've got psychic powers that can give her answers. I told her to call social services, but they don't have any new infant cases. I'm starting to think this girl has more problems than Zena and me combined. Here she comes now, dragging her feet and wiping her tears.

"Did you find her?" I ask.

"No. It's weird because yesterday she wasn't answering the phone, and now today, the operator says her phone is disconnected."

"Oh Lord." I suck my teeth and sigh, startling a naïve Tweety with preconceived notion.

"What? You think she got locked up or evicted?"

I don't think she's serious until I see the dead-serious look in her eyes. I just shake my head. The mind really is a terrible thing.

"You don't want to know what I think. And it might not even be true, so it don't make any sense for me to tell you," I say.

"Tell me," she begs, sitting on the edge of my cot.

"How old did you say your neighbor was?"

"About twenty-six or twenty-seven. Why?"

"She got a boyfriend? Husband?"

Tweety shrugs and gives me a puzzled look. "Not that I know of. Why?"

"She cool with your baby daddy?"

"She buys weed from him, but so does everybody in the neighborhood. That's how he pays our bills," she says, almost proudly.

"Hmph," I grunt, but her look tells me she needs it spelled out.

Call me a skeptic, but it all sounds off. The woman willingly took her baby. Her baby daddy is ignoring Tweety. The woman can't have kids, ain't got no man, and probably been creeping with him all along. Tweety's just too young and naïve to see it. I bet anything that bitch got her baby—and her man. Why else would she change her number and disappear?

"What is it?" she taps my leg, annoying as always.

"I think your barren neighbor has got herself a ready-made family: your baby and your man."

"Naw!" She waves me off. "She wouldn't do that. She's always talking about him, telling me I can do better."

I could slap this girl for not giving a half-thought to what I say.

"Hmph," I grunt again. Now it makes even more sense. "What do you think happened?"

Tweety shrugs, then looks up at the ceiling like it's a magic ball.

"I just hope she ain't hurt, 'cause if she is, who's going to look after my baby while I'm in here? I gotta hurry up and get out of here."

"You ain't going nowhere if you don't tell the truth about whose shit that was. They don't really want you; they want him. But if you don't give him up, they'll settle for you."

She sucks her teeth and sighs. "Here we go again," she mutters, throwing her head back like Zena used to when she didn't want to hear what I had to say.

She stands up from my bed and crawls into her own.

"Tweety, I'm through with you," I snap.

"'Cause I don't agree with everything you say?" she shoots back.

"No, 'cause you don't think! Wake up! Look around! You're in jail, honey! The woman watching your baby done changed her number, and your so-called man acts like he don't know you when you call! Wake up!"

I don't realize I'm yelling until I see my dark shadow looming over her bed like a monster as she lays there shivering in fear. I take a deep breath to calm myself. Why am I so upset over someone else's daughter? Tweety ain't my blood or my business. I'm just lucky Zena don't think like that. As much as she hates me, I'd rather her keep hating me than ever be this naïve.

I leave my cell to get some fresh air—if you can call it that. I start pacing the narrow hall, trying to clear my head. Maybe this place is really taking a toll on me. It's not just my problems trapping me—it's everybody else's, too. And I can't seem to escape either. I stare at the scuffed linoleum floor like I'm searching for a hole to fall into. When I look up, I see the girl who killed her baby pacing, too—but much slower. Instead of being trapped in her problems, she looks tortured by them. She mumbles under her breath, eyes drowning in stuck tears that won't fall. I watch her for a moment before turning my attention back to the floor. Her pain's too much for me—I've got enough on my plate.

"Ms. Sedah," the nice guard calls from behind me.

I turn to see Officer Rachel waving me over with a smile like I ain't a criminal. I walk over to her slowly. I'm not in the mood to be bothered, but considering how kind she's been to me, I try to hide my annoyance.

"How you doing, Officer Rachel? Starting your shift?"

"Yeah. You getting some exercise?" She taps my shoulder.

"Uh-huh."

"Your cellie is driving you crazy, ain't she?"

She laughs so hard she bends over. I just smile.

"What about the new one?" She points at the girl.

"It's sad," I say.

"Yeah, it is. I feel sorry for her, then get mad at myself for feeling sorry. What makes someone kill their baby?"

I shrug.

"They've sent her to every counselor we have on staff, but no one can get through to her," she says, frowning.

"She'll talk when she's ready. She's probably still in shock."

"Maybe," she says, revealing her silver-capped tooth in a wide smile before giving me a strange look.

I feel what that look might mean—and I hope I'm wrong.

"I better keep moving," I say, trying to escape whatever she's about to ask. "Need the cardio after being cramped up in that cell."

"Hold on." She takes a deep breath like she's trying to gather her thoughts. "I was telling the counselors about you."

"Me?" I try to play dumb.

"Yeah." She taps my shoulder again. "You've been helping a lot of these girls. I see a big change in them since you came in—even that little Tweety girl. You get them thinking straight."

"Well…it ain't me. It's them," I say modestly, trying to slip out of the limelight.

"Naw, it's you. That new girl needs to talk. We need to know what's going on in her head. Otherwise, they'll really throw the book at her. I've seen it too many times."

"What's that got to do with me?" I let my tone show I'm not up for whatever she's thinking about asking me to do.

"A lot. These young counselors have expensive degrees and

textbook knowledge, but you got a gift some of these women can really use."

"I don't know, Officer Rachel," I sigh, shaking my head as I watch the girl pace past us, still mumbling and in a daze.

"Just call me Rachel. I done told you that before." She taps me again.

Nothing in this world is free—not even Officer Rachel's kindness. I guess it's time for me to pay up. Why won't people just leave me be? All I did was shoot a child-molesting rapist, and now I'm some Rosie the Riveter.

"What you want me to do?" I ask, like she's giving me my real sentence.

"Try to get her to open up. I'll switch her with Tweety. Let her spend a little time in your cell. I think you can reach her."

I want to stomp my feet and pout, but I don't. Instead, I force a smile and reply, "I'll try my best to get into her mind. A mind really can be a terrible thing."

"Don't I know it," Officer Rachel says, tapping my shoulder one last time.

I try to look on the bright side. At least she won't talk me to death like Tweety.

26

THE MAMA

"Stay on the Path"

"I'm Akimah Sedah, here to see my husband, Akimbo Sedah," I say with pride about ten minutes after walking into the prison. A guard points me toward a long line of visitors.

It's been a tiresome journey to get here, but I made it. If I were one of those superstitious people, I'd swear driving all the way to South Georgia to see my king wasn't a good idea. Too many bad omens.

First, a tractor-trailer forced me off the road. The driver veered into my lane like I wasn't even there. To avoid getting crushed in my beat-up Honda Civic, I swerved into the next lane, nearly hitting a PT Cruiser. Their furious honking and screeching tires shook me so much that I ended up off the road. I had to sit there for several minutes, trying to catch my breath. I could've died.

While sitting in my car, I thought about how ironic it would've been to die on my way to see a man who has practically made himself dead to me for years. I almost turned around to go back home, but a billboard caught my eye: *Stay on the Path*. Thinking about my own path, I decided to move forward with my visit. I stopped thinking about dying and started thinking about living, and finally got the nerve to get back on the highway.

About an hour into my drive, I ran out of gas. That wouldn't have happened if I'd fixed my gas gauge that's been broken for months. But it hasn't been a priority since I don't drive much. I had just passed the exit for the gas station, and the next one was almost five miles ahead. I didn't have the energy or the endurance to track it five miles up the highway. At that point, I just sat in my car and cried. I couldn't call any of my children because I was too far away for them to come help, and I didn't want them to know that today was the day I went to visit their father. They knew I planned to go, thanks to Kwame's big mouth, but not when. I didn't know myself. An hour before leaving, I just decided and got in the car.

Still, I'm nervous. It's been over fifteen years since I've last seen the love of my life, and I wonder if he's changed—or worse, if he'll see me as changed. I've held on to my memories of him for so long. Seeing someone different would shatter the hope I cling to for our children's and grandchildren's futures. Without that hope, I don't know who I'd become. Maybe the real me that hid behind his greatness will finally come out, and I will be seen as weaker than anyone ever thought.

Then there's everything I need to tell him. How do I explain Malichai playing with the same fire that his father sacrificed his life trying to put out? Or Sahara abandoning the culture he taught her to cherish? Essence is so caught up in her own world that the only sacrifices she makes are the ones that benefit her. And Kwame, being in such a state of depression, never leaves the house and is possibly beating his wife over a child that isn't his. What will he think about his firstborn daughter, Balanah, turning bitter and resentful? So resentful that she abandoned her own family. And Ebony, the child who inherited his creativity and talent—what will he think of what she's done? Will he be ashamed, or will he find it honorable? And Sir

Zion, his supposed loyal and trustful friend, betrayed him by sleeping not only with me, but also our daughter—impregnating her and abandoning our grandchild. Will he blame himself? Or will he blame me for it all? He trusted me with his children, his legacy. Will he still trust me? These questions terrify me, but the one that will be hardest for me to answer is *why*. Why did these things happen? I wish I had the answers for him, but I don't—just painful truths.

I hadn't cried in years—not since they gave my king a life sentence—but I found myself crying on that highway for more reasons than being stranded. What I didn't remember about crying was how healing it is. The tears I cried in my car seemed to wash my fear, frustrations, and uncertainties clean out of my psyche. I prayed to God for the strength to stay on my path and for His grace to light my way. Then, I prayed for help.

Moments later, a tractor-trailer pulled up behind me. It looked like the same one that ran me off the road. The driver, a rugged white man with a red face and long beard, stepped out. My fear spiked. I pictured him spitting hateful words or dragging me into the woods to lynch me. But he just smiled at me and offered his help. His kindness made me ashamed of my assumptions. He gave me some of the gas he kept in the trailer of his truck for emergencies and even inspected my back left tire, kicking it with his dusty boot, telling me that I needed to pull over as soon as I could to put some air in it. When I tried to hand him a crumbled ten-dollar bill to show my gratitude, he didn't accept it. He waved it away with a smile, told me to have a safe trip, and encouraged me to continue smiling during my travels.

I know God sent him—or maybe he was an angel. He helped me in more than one way, because afterwards, I had a sudden burst of joy that only God's good grace can give. I wasn't worried about seeing my king anymore. I just had a feeling that everything was going to work out.

About three exits from the prison, I started to fantasize of reuniting with my king: his arms around me, his lips on my forehead before finally resting on my lips, complimenting my dress, and praising my locks that I've grown since his sentencing—each strand symbolizing my faith, love and strength in him. My daydreams were such a pleasant distraction that I forgot to stop at the gas station to put air in my tire like the man had suggested, and it went flat. Stranded again.

This time, I didn't cry or pray. I had faith that my earlier prayer would cover this little setback. God sees things before we do, and I knew He would send help. So, I waited patiently, smiling like the kind man told me. But after twenty minutes, my smile started to fade, and my frustration boiled over. I punched the steering wheel five times, hitting it so hard that my horn honked loud enough to catch the attention of a passing police officer. He changed my tire, and I was back on the road again. I knew God had a way of working things out even in the very midst of my anger. I just had to have patience. Half an hour later, I finally walked into the prison lobby and exhaled. What a journey.

This place resembles Ebony's jail, but more permanent—gray walls, scuffed floors, and stale air. There's more order here: visiting lines are organized by the inmate's last name. I didn't call ahead. Like I said, once I decided to come, I hopped in my car and left. Luckily, I arrived during visiting hours. I just hope there aren't rules in place that might prevent me from seeing him, such as having to be added to the list by the inmate. If that's the case, I know I'm out of luck.

I tap my foot against the linoleum floor to keep my nerves calm. The room is beginning to fill with anxious visitors now. Around the corner, a Spanish woman hugs a man in an orange jumpsuit. That hug tells me they'll let me touch my king, and my smile grows so big nothing can wipe it away.

I'm next in line. I walk up to the window, still smiling. A tired-looking Black woman is sitting behind the desk with a clipboard.

"Name?" she says without looking up.

"Akimah Sedah, here to see Akimbo Sedah."

"Inmate number?" she asks dryly.

"I don't know it."

She finally looks up at me, annoyed. "Have you been here before?"

"No," I answer, hoping formality won't turn me away.

She sighs, pushes her weight back on a rolling chair, and grabs a stack of forms from a cabinet behind her. Then she slams them down in front of me and hands me a pen.

"Fill these out and then stand over there," she says, pointing to a much longer line.

It's five pages. You would think I was trying to see the president. Before stepping away from the counter, I quickly flip through them and see a section asking for the inmate number. I lean forward.

"Do I need the inmate number?"

She huffs and rolls her eyes.

"Name?!" she asks again.

"Akimbo Sedah."

She holds up her hand, stopping me from speaking, then hands me a pen and a sticky note.

"Write it down," she grunts.

When I hand her back the pen and sticky note, she rolls over to a computer behind her desk and starts punching the keys so fast I can tell she must've been doing this for years. Then she stops typing, looks down at the paper like she's double-checking the spelling, and starts again. She stops a second time, looking confused.

"You sure this is the spelling?"

"Yes. I'm his wife."

She sighs, stands with effort, and disappears into the back with my note. I start getting anxious; it feels like she's been gone for hours. I can feel the burning stares and hear the groans from the people behind me who are getting frustrated with me holding up the line. When the woman finally returns, shaking her head, she points me to a shorter line.

"Stand in that line."

Relieved, I thank the woman with a nod of my head and walk over to the appropriate line. Once it's my turn, I introduce myself again, but I didn't have to do that because the old white man behind the counter was already briefed on who I was and who I wanted to see.

"You're the wife of Akimbo Sedah?" he asks with a thick Southern accent.

I nod. "Yes."

"Okay, well…it's nice to meet you. Never met a fella like him before. I knew your husband back when I worked inside as a prison guard. I did that for twenty years. Now I'm up for retirement and spending the rest of my time up front, taking it easy."

I'm not here for small talk. I'm more concerned with why I keep getting shifted around in lines, and more importantly, why he's speaking about my husband in the past tense, saying he *knew* him.

"Is something wrong, sir?" I ask.

I feel a little scared, but since he's still smiling, I figure it's nothing bad.

"Well…he ain't here no more, ma'am?"

"What?" I'm stunned.

"They moved him ten years ago to a South Carolina penitentiary. He didn't write and tell you?"

"Why?" I ask, ignoring his question.

The disappointment inside me is already swelling my aching heart.

"He wasn't safe here. Some of the inmates in here didn't like him much. They kept at him until he had to go to protective custody. Even then, he wasn't safe, so he chose solitary. Was he some kind of big-time gang leader or something?"

I'm too offended to even respond to the man's ignorance about

302

my husband's character.

"Can you give me some information on the prison?"

"Sure, I'll write it all down for you."

As he scribbles it down, he shares how my husband had many enemies there, saying that my husband spent more time in the infirmary than in his cell.

"These cons wanted him dead. What'd he do to piss them off so?" he asks, handing me the paper with the prison info on it.

"He had honor," I say firmly, snatching the paper from his hand before leaving.

Back in my car, I feel numb. Now I understand why he didn't want us to see him. When they sentenced him to jail, they didn't care that they were sending him to a place that housed his enemies—the same crooks and criminals he boldly helped put there. I never thought his life would be in danger. I never imagined he would face daily attacks on his life, and that the prison would be a jungle where he fought to survive. Just imagining what he went through day after day makes my eyes fill with tears.

During the drive back home, the tears fall slowly down my cheeks. I don't even try to wipe them away. When I pass by the billboard again that reads *Stay on the Path*, I sniff and remember my purpose. Things didn't go as planned, but I won't give up now. Today proved my strength. Despite every setback, God made a way. I see this day as a test of my faith and loyalty, and a sign that my king needs to see me just as much as I need to see him. I'm staying on my path—even if it leads all the way to South Carolina.

27

SAHARA
"Desperate"

Ebony is a trip. A person in her situation should be grateful for any help that's offered, but she acts as if she has options and demands unrealistic things. She refuses to plead insanity, which is her best bet and not entirely unfounded. Besides that, she is threatening to plead guilty and forego the trial or represent herself if I don't find her jail friend—some girl named Tweety—a good lawyer first. What she doesn't get is if I can't find her a good attorney, I sure as hell can't find one for Tweety.

Finding Ebony a solid defense attorney is damn near impossible. I knew it would be, even before Mama assigned me the mission-impossible task. Without John on my side, my options are limited. The high-powered, esteemed attorneys like the ones John knows don't take cases like Ebony's. They've got the pull to get her off before trial, but this case? It's beneath them. It's messy. Attempted murder trials aren't considered classy crimes like the white-collar criminals they very selectively choose to represent. Ebony being Black makes it even harder. She's not likely to receive the same sympathy a white woman would get in a similar circumstance. Then, the case deals with sexual abuse of a minor. This is the kind of case that can ruin reputations, not build them.

Then there's the celebrity-driven attorneys. The ones who wanted to become Hollywood stars but settled for being lawyers when they didn't make the cut. They are too beguiling—just actors with law degrees who are more concerned about their image than the outcome. They want screen time, not justice. These attorneys wouldn't care if Ebony wins or loses. She would be just another headline.

After that, there are the fresh-out-of-law-school types—those young, ambitious, and inexperienced attorneys who just passed the bar. Maybe if this case didn't have so much media attention, one of them might've stood a chance. But this case? They would get eaten alive in the courtroom by the prosecutor and eaten alive outside the courtroom by the press. It would be like throwing a kitten into a cage of pit bulls.

That's why I've decided to represent her myself.

I don't have time to study for the bar. That would take weeks—time Ebony doesn't have. I've already registered, and the test is in a few days. I should be nervous, but I'm not giving fear a chance. Ebony needs me. I know her better than anyone, and I'll be damned if I let them throw the book at my little sister.

Lately, I've been brooding, especially with all the shit going on in my life. The kids told me they saw Becca again, and John's becoming more of an asshole every day. Between that and Ebony's case, my faith is teetering to the point of disbelief in God. So, I attended a Wednesday night Bible service at World Changers Church. Pastor Creflo Dollar couldn't have been more on point—preaching about faith without works, and how it's impossible to please God without it. He reminded us that faith isn't what you see; it's what you believe. He drew real-life analogies, comparing them to David, an overlooked shepherd boy who slew the evil giant Goliath. I could relate to that one a lot because I had two Goliaths in my life: one being the divorce with John, and the other being my sister's possible life sentence.

Next, Pastor Dollar preached about Moses raising his staff—turning something ordinary into something powerful just by believing in God. That's when I had an epiphany: my "staff" is my law degree, and I would use it to slay both the Goliaths in my life. I told myself I don't need to be perfect: I just need to believe. I signed up for the bar the minute I got home—before doubt could creep in. I'm going to hold onto that mustard seed of faith the pastor talked about and give it my best shot. I'll take the test and give Ebony the best defense I can.

Now I'm sitting in the Chocolate Bar in downtown Decatur, waiting to meet Balanah for lunch. She finally called back and sounded eager to update me about what progress she has made. I don't know what she'll think about me representing Ebony, but I'm her best shot at winning— whatever winning her case would turn out to mean. Maybe I'll convince the jury she's innocent, or at least get her probation or house arrest instead of a life sentence.

Balanah's almost five minutes late, which isn't like her. I wonder if she'll bring up leaving Stephan and the kids. I'm sure not going to mention it. I've got enough of my own secrets. Nobody knows about the divorce, and I don't want my family to think they can't count on me when they need me the most. John hasn't mentioned it again, but the way he's parading his white mistress around, it's sure to happen. My family thinks I live for John. And maybe I used to—but not anymore. I've found myself again. The woman I was before he controlled me.

This place is more of a dessert spot than a lunch joint. The menu primarily features chocolate and wine. But it's where Balanah wanted to meet. I'm not even a big fan of chocolate, but the sweet aroma is tempting. The waiter has been beckoning me to order something since I took a seat, so I ordered a bottle of red wine and two dark chocolate-covered strawberries to get him off my back.

Before the waiter could return with the wine, Balanah walks in, spots me instantly, and heads over with her hands full—a sleek briefcase, folders, papers, and her laptop.

"Sorry," she says with a sigh when she reaches the table.

Before she can sit down, one of her phones rings at least three times. She sent all three calls straight to voicemail. With the little secret I know about her and Stephan, I was expecting her to be in a sour mood, but she never looked better. She was dressed in a pair of fitted black slacks and a matching blazer, and confidence radiated from her like a CEO of a Fortune 500 company.

She snaps her fingers at the waiter.

"A bottle of red wine," she says once he approaches our table, and he looks at me.

"I already ordered it," I tell her.

"Oh," she replies, already pulling papers from her briefcase.

Her phone rings again, and she sighs before powering it off.

"If I didn't know any better, I'd think you were working for the White House."

She rolls her eyes at me like I was trying to be sarcastic, but I actually meant it as a compliment.

"I'm taking what I'm doing for my sister more seriously than the White House."

"I know," I say, softening.

The waiter returns with our bottle of wine, two wine glasses, and the strawberries. I take one and hand the other to Balanah.

"Thanks," she says and takes a small bite, then smiles. "Stephan always gets me these from here. They're cheaper at Publix, but he likes the fancy box."

"That's sweet," I reply, though we both know the truth behind that sweetness.

I liked Stephan. He wasn't perfect, but he was a good man. John never did stuff like that for me. I wonder if he does those kinds of things for Becca.

"Okay," she says, setting her wine down. "I can't tell you everything because I don't have much time. I have to meet with the video editor today, and afterwards, Teresa from the Survivor's House is doing a radio interview."

"What video editor? Who's Teresa? What radio station?"

The questions fly out of my mouth like bullets.

Instead of answering my question, she slides a flyer across the table––bold red and black colors, a touching image of a little girl mending the broken heart of an adult woman. Across the top of the flyer, it reads: **Save the Child. Save the Woman. Save Ebony Sedah**. Below is Ebony's story, beautifully written and heartbreaking. I almost cried myself. In the center, a photo of young Ebony holding Zena as a baby. The picture shows both their beauty and innocence; the story paints the truth behind Ebony's crime of passion. Balanah did a fabulous job.

"Wow. How many of these do you have?" I ask.

"Tons. The designer gave me a deal. I've got posters, yard signs, and this same design is going on our YouTube video and website tonight, right after Teresa's interview on V-103."

"You made a video, too?"

She takes a bite of her strawberry and a sip of wine before answering.

"It's not a video like what you think. It's more like a montage—pictures of Ebony, her work, children, the Survivor's House. It sends a good message. And you'll never guess who we got to endorse the video, singing a never-before-heard song for this occasion in the background!" she shrieks and then waits for me to throw some names out, but I'm stumped.

I shrug. "Who?"

She grins before saying, "Fancy Brown! You know, the new hot singer who lives right here in Atlanta and sings 'Faithfully' and 'Just Because'. She recorded a new song for us: 'Save the Child'. It's beautiful, Sahara. Wait until you hear it."

"No way! How'd you get her?" I'm shocked.

"Naja."

"Kenton's wife?" I take a sip of wine, even more surprised.

"Yep." Balanah nods proudly. "She planned Fancy's album release party. They're tight. Fancy has a daughter, too."

"Damn, girl. Keep this up, and we're gonna own that jury. But how are you paying for all of this?"

"Mostly trade. We promote their names on flyers and the site. The web designer did it for free because of the song. With all the downloads, he's making his money in exposure. Plus, people can give us donations on the site."

I'm so proud of Balanah and feel bad for ever doubting her.

"When this airs, the press is going to want more interviews, and the ball is going to be back in our court. How are you doing on the attorney part?" she asks, pouring herself another glass of wine. "We're going to need him or her to speak on Ebony's behalf soon."

"She'll be ready next week," I say, quickly sipping my wine before she asks more questions.

I have to admit I'm starting to feel intimidated—like I'm not coming through on my end. Balanah has celebrities and local public officials backing us, whereas I have nobody but myself, and I'm inexperienced to boot.

"Perfect. I'll schedule a TV interview for the attorney with one of the reporters for the Friday after next," she says, jotting down a note.

"Wait…let me confirm that first."

She gives me a look. "Why?"

"I just need to talk to…him," I say, referring to the attorney that doesn't exist.

"I thought you said the attorney was a her?"

Balanah catches my slip and reads the panic on my face.

"What's going on, Sahara?"

Before I can answer, John and Becca walk in—hand in hand, looking like newlyweds. Balanah sees the look of contempt in my bulging eyes, turns around in her chair, and spots them. Then she quickly looks at me and shifts gears. She's no longer a CEO but my big sister who is ready to whoop a white bitch's ass and the dumb Black fool she's with.

"What's going on?" she hisses.

"That's Becca. John's mistress," I say.

I can't stop staring. I know it's Becca because the woman has the red hair that my twins went on and on about. Her hair isn't so hot in my opinion. It actually makes her pale white skin look even more like snow. She does have a graceful walk, though. I'll give her that. She doesn't seem much younger than me, and she's no beauty queen for sure. But John is looking at her like she's gold. I've never seen him smile like that, not even when our children were born.

"Maybe we should say hi," Balanah huffs, pushing back from the table.

"No. Let them enjoy their lunch. Let's finish our meeting."

"You serious? That's your husband with another woman! That bitch looks like a redheaded ghost!"

I laugh. I'm glad it's her here and not Essence. Essence would've flipped, and all hell would've broken loose. Then John would have used it against me in court to try to get custody of the kids.

I lean in. "Read my lips: I…don't…give…a…fuck."

We both glance back. John has his hand on top of hers and is whispering something in her ear. She giggles and kisses him on the lips. They look like teenagers in love.

"How long has this been going on?" Balanah asks, turning away in disgust.

I shrug and turn away, too.

Looking up at the ceiling, I reply, "Anywhere from four weeks to four years. Who knows?"

I casually take another sip of my wine.

"And you're just...okay with it?"

"No, but I can't just up and leave."

"Yes, you can," Balanah says matter-of-factly.

"It's not that simple. He knows too many people, and...there was a little incident a few weeks ago."

"What little incident?"

I tell her about the breakdown, the arrest, the cop. Everything. Including John's threat to take the kids from me.

"The hell he will! And a nervous breakdown? You got arrested and didn't tell anybody? Damn, Sahara. You know it's okay not to be perfect all the damn time, right? How could you be going through so much and keep it all to yourself? What is it with this family and secrets?" she sighs.

"I have a plan."

"Let's hear it," Balanah says.

"I don't feel like getting into that right now."

"I've got time."

"You didn't two minutes ago," I say, reminding her that she has to meet somebody soon.

"Well, I do now. They can wait. This comes first." She stabs the table with her finger.

"I don't want to talk about it. If I wanted to talk about husbands, I would've asked *you* why *you* left yours."

I had to go there. It was my only defense, and it shut her up.

Balanah leans back in her seat and looks at me like she'd just been defeated.

"It's only temporary," she says.

"I hope so. Stephan's a good guy."

She gets silent. She knows I'm telling the truth.

"Yeah, but he doesn't support me. And I'm tired of all the

bickering between him and Zionah. It's driving me crazy. They're both brats."

"Zionah's just hormonal. It's a phase and will pass. And Stephan makes good money. What do you mean he doesn't support you?"

"I'm not talking about material stuff. I mean emotionally. Professionally. None of y'all do. I have a degree, but everyone acts like I'm incompetent because I haven't landed the perfect job. I'm smart, Sahara. I just never believed it because no one confirmed it."

She's right. I did overlook her. But not anymore.

"You are smart. And I'm sorry. I believe in you, Balanah. Starting today, I'm going to show it."

Her eyes get misty, and she nods like I told her just what she needed to hear. Then, being her usual selfless self, she refocuses on me.

"I'll watch the girls while you finish school. Bring them anytime," she says, then rolls her eyes towards John and Becca.

"You don't have to. I've already finished my classes and am taking the bar next week. I'm going to represent Ebony myself."

She gasps, then claps her hands.

"You little heffa! Why didn't you tell anybody? We could've watched you accept your degree and then celebrated." She threw the last bit of her strawberry at me playfully.

I shrug. Not once did she question me taking the bar so soon without preparing first. The way she is looking at me tells me that she believes in me more than I believe in myself.

"I always thought you'd be the best lawyer for the job," she says with a smile and head nod.

And just like that, I feel hope again.

"I'm glad you think so. I'm just happy I have your help before you blow up. After this campaign takes off, you're going to be in high demand. You finally crossed over from 'potential' to 'real'. Your marketing firm's gonna be hot."

Balanah grins wider than I've ever seen. She's glowing with the same hope I feel.

"We'll see."

We're still smiling until we look back over at John and Becca—just in time to watch them greet a third guest: Sir Zion. Balanah and I look at each other and shake our heads.

"Birds of a feather," Balanah mutters.

Becca stands to hug Sir Zion like she's known him forever. He kisses her hand and slightly bows his head like she's the Queen of England. She giggles, takes her seat next to John, and scoots over, making room for Sir Zion to sit. He shakes John's hand, and John smiles at him like a crooked politician.

"They're getting real acquainted."

"You've seen them together before?" Balanah asks, surprised.

"Oh yeah."

"Hmm." She taps her wine glass like she's conjuring up a scheme in her head. "Did I tell you I hired a P.I. to dig up dirt on Kenton?"

"No," I say, leaning in closer to her.

"Naja hooked me up. The guy's good—and fast. He already has a report on Kenton that he's sending over tonight. They say he's good at investigating things and uncovering skeletons. You want his number?"

"Definitely," I reply.

She scribbles it on a napkin and slides it over.

"I hate digging into people's lives, but in the moment of desperation, you do what you have to do. Let's go say hi before we leave," Balanah says and winks at me.

I drop some money on the table and follow behind my big sister. She walks right up to their table with confident strides and a pretentious smile. I stand beside her, giving them the same look.

"Hello," she says, locking eyes with Sir Zion.

They all look up as if we've just caught them in the act of

committing a crime. John gives me that smug smirk of his, and Becca avoids giving me eye contact. I didn't think her white skin could get any paler, but it does. She lowers her eyes to the table, scooting away from John like I don't know what was going on.

"Hi, honey," I say to John, all sugar. "Sir Zion. I always thought you two would make great friends."

"Well, if it isn't two of Black-Man's kids," Sir Zion sneers.

We ignore him. He's not worth the words.

"Hello, Becca. I'm John's wife." I hold out my hand for her to shake.

She stares at my hand like I'm holding a gun, then gives me the world's most awkward handshake.

"Thanks so much for being nice to my children."

John's eyes widen.

"And my husband," I add with a giggle.

Balanah giggles, too, agreeing with me.

"That's so important—to show kindness to someone else's spouse. She's a good woman," Balanah says, turning to me.

Becca's face turns redder than her hair. She's trembling.

"Are you two here to make a scene?" John asks, voice low and hostile.

"No, we've *seen* enough," I say. "Enjoy your lunch. I'll see you at home for dinner. Don't eat too much."

I laugh and walk away. Balanah waves goodbye and trails behind me. Out of the corner of my eye, I see a desperate look in John's eyes. He knows I have a one-up on him. He stands like he wants to follow.

"Sahara, wait a minute," he calls out, using the voice he used to seduce me years ago—the slick one that sounds like a used car salesman.

I ignore him and keep walking. Balanah wouldn't have had it any other way anyway. She grabs my arm, guiding me out the door. Now it's his turn to be desperate. And oh, how fun that's going to be—

watching him squirm, watching how far he'll go to keep me quiet about his little meeting. Tables turned. Finally.

And I don't care what the twins said—Becca is ugly as hell. Just like John.

28
MALICHAI
"Time for a Change"

"I'm going back to the house this weekend. Since you paid Wavy two months in advance, we might as well get our money's worth. We wasted too much leaving like we did," Meka pouts.

I knew she wouldn't be thrilled about us moving out of that crack house, but it's the best move for us. Yeah, I lost a few dollars leaving early, but it was worth it. This side of town is clean, quiet—hell, even the air feels better. But Meka hates it. Not because it's not nice, but because it's too far from where she likes to party and get high. Can't score crack out here, can't find nothing to shoot up her arm. This side of town ain't her, but I was hoping I could change that.

"You ain't going nowhere," I say firm enough to let her know it was the end of the discussion.

"Why?!" she screams, stomping.

She's already fidgety—pushing her sleeves up and pulling them back down again like she can't be still. Pacing back and forth. Walking in circles.

"Because it's time to chill out with all that shit. That's why I moved us here—for change. You don't like the house?"

Meka glances around. I know she likes it, just not the location. If this house was in Wavy's backyard, she'd be thrilled.

We stayed at Wavy's for a week, and that was even too long for me. Since I started working with Darrel, I've been making decent money and thinking differently. All them nice abandoned houses we stripped down to nothing got me wondering: what if I just moved into one? Nobody cares when we gut them. So why not stay in one for a few months before moving on to the next one? Less chance of getting caught. And if I do, I'll play dumb and say I rented it from a guy advertising it on a street sign. Maybe they'll feel bad for evicting a family with a special needs son and offer help. Not that I'd need it––living rent-free saves money—but I wouldn't turn down anything offered to me. I even created a fake lease and printed it off at Office Depot to get the utilities on. Too easy. And this house? Too sweet.

I chose this neighborhood after running into Natasha here last week. The house has four bedrooms, a dining room, a spacious kitchen, a catwalk overlooking the family room, and a fully finished basement. We kept it empty—just brought our mattress and mini fridge. Coming from the cramped living quarters we used to live in, it was nice to have all the extra rooms. Now Zach can run all around the house without disturbing anyone or bumping into walls.

The house feels good. I feel normal. Like I'm finally getting a taste of the life I always wanted. The only problem is that now that I've tasted it, I'm not gonna want to go back. I'm tired, and something's got to change. I feel a change in the air now more than I ever did before. Something is brewing in the universe for me. I just wish Meka could feel it, too.

"I don't even know what bus comes out here!" Meka complains.

"You act like we moved to another state. We didn't even leave the city, for crying out loud! This house is a blessing—not full of crack heads and whores."

"Oh, so now you judging my friends? The same people you used to hang with ain't good enough now that you call yourself going clean? You're a hypocrite, Malichai. You went from selling drugs to stealing houses!"

"Just like now...everything I did then, I did for my family."

"Well, I don't want to be here!" she yells before running into the bathroom and slamming the door so hard it startles Zach, who starts screaming at the top of his lungs.

I rush over and pick him up as he kicks and flails. One foot hits me in the gut, and I fight the urge to drop him. Instead, I hug him tight.

"Calm down, little man."

His tiny fists were balled up, punching the air. I know this kind of fit, and if it doesn't stop soon, it'll go all night. He used to act like this when Meka disappeared for hours, days, or weeks. Staying with Balanah calmed him, but we're back to this again.

"You wanna go for a walk? Ride on my back?" I try to kiss his forehead to seal the deal, but he's moving his head around so much that my lips catch his chin instead.

"No...no..." he whines, working himself up even more.

"You see what you've done to your son?" I yell at the door.

Meka doesn't say anything, so I walk up to it and kick it with my foot while still holding a screaming Zach.

"Leave me alone. I ain't feeling good, Mal," she sobs.

Damn.

"Zach, straighten up!"

"Stop yelling at that boy!" she yells from behind the door.

"Oh, so now you want to act like a caring mother? You want to come out of that bathroom long enough to help me raise him? That would be nice, Meka. I can't do this shit by myself anymore. Something's gotta change, or I'm gonna..."

I catch myself before saying too much.

"You're gonna what?" she challenges, swinging open the bathroom door and facing me with her arms folded across her chest.

I can't tell if she's scared, angry, or daring me.

I cradle Zach, rocking him like a baby. I look at Meka, but the words don't come. The truth is, I'm tired. I'm tired of dragging us all uphill while she pulls us back down with her drug addiction. I feel like I'm at a crossroads. If something doesn't change soon, things are going to get permanently worse, and I can't deal with that. All this love I have for her could turn into resentment, and it'll spill onto Zach, who doesn't deserve it.

If she won't get help, I may need to let her go. Just thinking that makes me feel lighter and guiltier at the same time. Maybe I'm more of an enabler than a savior for her. She doesn't want to change because she knows she doesn't have to. She knows I'll carry the load, so she never even tries.

"I'm taking Zach for a walk," I say.

He's stopped crying, so I put him on his feet. He clings to my leg and wipes his nose on my jeans.

"When you coming back?"

"In a few."

"I need some money," she says with a guilty look.

"I ain't giving you no more money, Meka."

"What?! How am I supposed to get around?"

She's talking about having bus fare to get to Wavy's to buy drugs.

"I don't know," I say and grab Zach's hand to head out.

"Mal!" she screams like she's ready to stab me in the back. "I'm sick! I need money!"

Being dramatic, she starts gagging like she's going to throw up.

"If you're really sick, I'll take you to the hospital. Maybe they can help."

Last time I took her to the hospital, they forced her into rehab. The way Meka talked about how horrible that experience was, you would've thought that the doctors and nurses were exorcists instead of medical professionals. She made it sound like torture.

"Why are you doing this to me?" she whines. "You're so hateful!"

I stop and turn around to face her. Hateful? After everything I've done for her? After sticking by her side through the worst times? That's the word she uses to describe me? I'm ready to go off on her, but when I see how she's sweating bullets and trembling, I know it's the drugs talking.

"It's just time for a change, baby. I'll be back."

"Mal!" she yells, but I don't look back.

As soon as Zach steps outside, he dries his last tear. Now he's smiling and bouncing with energy. I swear his moods mirror our home life. He feels our stress deeper than we do, and that's why he throws those fits. Something about the air out here makes him come alive. The last time I saw him this happy was at Balanah's.

"Let's go," I say, leading him down the tree-lined sidewalk.

I remember seeing a playground the last time Darrel and I were in this area doing a job. I figure I'll let Zach burn off some energy so he can eat and go straight to sleep when we get back home. I know Meka is going to be fuming, and I don't need her getting Zach all upset again—me either. She's affecting the good spirits that this neighborhood is bringing me.

People here are friendly. One car honks and waves. Another driver smiles. Everybody's yard is manicured and clear of debris, and women jog the streets peacefully. It's a perfect place to raise a kid. Zach is so happy he's humming, which lifts my spirit.

He spots the playground before I do and yells, "Yay," while jumping up and down. It's behind the clubhouse.

"Okay, we're going," I tell him, and he smiles even bigger.

I can't remember the last time I took him to a playground— maybe never. *Damn.* Yeah, I definitely need to make some changes. Chasing Meka down on the streets and keeping a roof over our heads has really gotten in the way of me raising my son. It takes more than paying the bills to be a father. You have to spend time with your kids. Get to know them like you know yourself.

When we get close to the playground, Zach lets go of my hand and takes off running towards the slides to play with the other kids. I sit on a yellow bench nearby. The sun's shining, and it's almost seventy degrees, which ain't bad for the end of November. I watch Zach and the other kids laugh and play so innocently, and it almost makes me feel innocent again. There's something about a child's laughter that evokes jubilation. I giggle when Zach slides down backwards and lands in the mulch headfirst. He starts laughing as if he fell into a pool of toys. A little girl helps him up, and they head back to the stairs together. Zach seems happy to have a playmate.

I stretch out my legs and yawn. Sometimes I go nonstop and don't realize how tired I really am. My motto's always been, "Sleep when you're dead." But damn, I could use a break.

"Mal?" a familiar voice calls from behind me, and it ain't Meka. That perfect diction and sweet tone—it's Natasha.

I turn around and see her dog before I see her—a spotted Cocker Spaniel. She looks good in a winter blue jogging suit and white Nikes. Her micro braids fall down to her shoulders and are slightly curled at the ends.

"What's up, girl?" I stand to hug her.

She still smells like coconuts and feels so warm that I don't want to let her go. I hold her a second longer than I should. She takes a seat on the bench next to me.

I've been trying to fool myself into thinking I didn't want to run into her again and only chose the neighborhood because I liked the location. But the truth is—I did.

"What you doing here?" she asks with a smile.

"Giving Zach a little time to run around." I point at Zach, who's on his way back down the slide again.

She squints, shielding her eyes from the sun. "Oh my goodness.

He looks just like you."

I'm not sure if that's a compliment or not, but I nod in thanks. I'm just glad I got a fresh cut and am wearing new clothes. I look ten times better than I did the last time she saw me—and she looks even better than I remembered.

"Who is this?" I ask, eyeballing her dog.

"Milo," she chuckles.

"Milo?" I laugh. "What's up, Milo?"

The dog's too busy sniffing around to care.

"You stay over here?"

"Yeah. Just a few blocks away." I point down the road.

"Wow. Okay. It's nice to finally know someone in the neighborhood," she says, smiling.

She glances around. "Where's Meka?"

"She's out," I lie. I don't even know why.

"Okay. Well, you two have to stop by sometime. Bring Zach, too."

"You married yet?" I ask, even though I don't want the answer. A woman as fine as her has to have a husband, right?

"Nope. No kids either." She shakes her head like it's something to be embarrassed about.

"What you waiting for?"

"For the right timing, right man, right situation. I'm not in a rush."

"Good," I say, meaning it in more than one way.

"So what have you been up to, Mal? I know you've got a lot going on, but how are you holding up?" she asks, playfully pushing my shoulder.

"Me?" I'm not used to people genuinely asking me how I'm doing and don't even know how to answer the question, so I just keep it generic. "I'm cool. Surviving, you know."

"Surviving, huh? Aren't we all. You've always been a survivor, though."

"How you figure?"

"You've been through so much in such a little time you've been alive, and you're still smiling. Even now, with all the stuff going on with your sister, you still find time to take your son to the park. That's a real survivor."

She looks at me like she sees something worth admiring. Imagine that.

"I ain't all that," I say modestly.

"Give yourself a break," she says, nudging me again.

A soft breeze blows her scent right to me. I inhale and hold it in my lungs like hope.

"Oh…I almost forgot to tell you. Your sister, Balanah, came by our center the other day. She's working with our director on a campaign for your sister, Ebony. It's really great. She has tons of awesome ideas and is putting out a really powerful message. I told her that I had just seen you. Isn't that wild?"

"Yeah," I answer, pretending like I know everything that's going on.

Truth is, I haven't talked to my sisters or mother since the family meeting. Kwame and I agreed not to contact anyone until we found Zena. So far, nothing. She don't want to be found— that's how it feels.

"You're probably helping Balanah with the campaign, huh?" she asks.

"Naw, that's all her. You know she has a degree in marketing. I never finished high school, remember?"

"Yeah, I remember, but that doesn't mean you're not capable. College isn't for everybody, and some of the most successful businesspeople only have a GED."

"Well, they got more than me. I ain't even got that," I admit.

"You can always get it. It's never too late. You're smart, Mal. You can do anything."

I look at her sideways, trying to figure out if she really means that or if she's just trying to sell me a dream. I appreciate the support, but it's almost too much.

"Easier said than done."

"Yeah, but it still can be *done*. If it's too easy, it probably ain't worth doing. You should know that."

I know what she's talking about. The easiest and hardest thing I've ever done was sell dope.

"Mal?" she says, catching my eye again. "If you could start any business or get your dream job tomorrow, what would it be? I'm just curious."

She shrugs and tugs on her dog's leash for him to sit.

That question hit harder than I expected. I've spent so long just trying to survive, I never really thought about thriving.

I shake my head. "I don't even know."

"Well, what do you enjoy doing?"

I'm stumped again. I enjoy having a roof over my family's head and a little change in my pocket to move around, but how do you make that a business?

"Washing cars," I finally say, the thought coming to me as an epiphany.

"Okay. That's good."

"Yeah, if I had a little grip, I'd lease or buy one of them car wash buildings and specialize in detailing. I'd have my own formula for getting rims shining and carpets spotless. Maybe even add a little chill spot inside—pool table, free Wi-Fi. Something to keep folks relaxed while they wait. Yeah, that'd be cool," I say, smiling at the idea.

"That's a great idea. Car washes have low overhead and steady profits if done right. And there's tons of grant money out there that never gets used because people just don't know about it."

"Grants?" I say, looking clueless.

"Free money. It's like a loan, but you don't have to pay it back. I started my organization with grants. I did all the grant writing myself."

"Word?"

"Yeah, and I don't mind helping you either. You might need to get your GED first, but that's the easy part. It'd be fun to plan this out—get your mind off things. Write down your ideas, research locations, and draft a business plan. The library has books on it. I mean...it don't cost a thing to dream."

She's making a lot of sense. And for once, my dream doesn't feel so far-fetched.

"You'd really help me with that?"

"Of course," she says, sounding offended. "Why wouldn't I? We go way back. We're friends, right?"

I nod, smiling. "Yeah, we are."

She pats me on the knee, then wraps Milo's leash around her wrist and stands up.

"Whenever you're ready for that change, you know where I stay."

She smiles, and I get this urge to jump up and kiss her—not in a sexual way, but like I'm grateful. Like she just gave me something I didn't know I needed.

"I'm gonna give Zach a quick hello and goodbye hug," she says, asking with her eyes.

I nod to let her know it's okay, then watch as she walks over to Zach with her dog. She wraps her arms around him and hugs him like he's her own child. Zach melts into her hug like her touch was the touch he'd been waiting for. Then, he pets Milo while she guides his hand gently. She kisses him on the forehead, waves at me, and walks off. I didn't want her to leave, but she did anyway.

* * * * *

Just as I get to the door, my phone rings. It's Kwame. He says he has a solid lead on where Zena's staying, and he's on his way to get me. I give him my new address and head inside.

Meka's gone, but I'm not surprised. I'm not jumping in my car to go look for her either. I'm done with that. It's time I stopped chasing her and started finding myself. I'm ready for a change. A real one.

29

BALANAH
"Turbulence"

Teresa's radio interview went perfectly. Her voice was powerful and compassionate. She spoke with a perfect balance of sharing Ebony's story and highlighting the message about sexual abuse among young Black girls. I even said a few words on my sister's behalf, but the show wasn't about me; it was about Ebony and sexual abuse.

Many callers phoned in to share their secret stories and to support Ebony. Afterwards, they called Fancy Brown for a quick interview before her song aired. She talked about the sexual abuse her grandmother endured for years, and how that, along with Ebony's story, inspired the lyrics of her new song. After the song aired, the callers went crazy. The disc jockey provided everyone with the website where they could listen to the song again, watch the video, and make donations. When I checked the website hits, I nearly exploded with excitement. There were so many zeros under the visitors' tab that I didn't even bother reading the exact number, and the YouTube video was already getting comments and people liking it on their Facebook page. Everything was going smoother than I expected, and I could just imagine how many donations we would receive.

I just got off the phone with the private investigator I hired to look into Kenton's background, and he told me to watch for an email with his detailed report.

"This is some fella," he had grunted, hinting that he found something on Kenton.

Now that I have Ebony's justice in route, it's time to work on Zena's. Hopefully, Sahara can do something with this info. Maybe even get them to reopen the case. I know that if the report is as thorough as I think it'll be, I'll have to try to contact some of the girls. That's going to be hard to do, though. Usually, like Zena, girls who've been abused just want to forget about it, but maybe Teresa can give me a hand with that. She's good at it. I'm sure they can relate to her more than they can to me.

When the PI texts me to let me know the email has been sent, I rush over to my laptop. However, before I can log in to my Gmail account, both my regular cell phone and my temporary one start buzzing. I know it's Stephan calling on my regular phone because he's already called me about ten times in a row. I figure he heard me over the radio and the song and wanted to take credit for my good deeds. I don't know how he plans to do that, but knowing him, he'll figure out a way. I'm already busy and don't want him to distract me, causing unnecessary trouble. So, I send his call straight to voicemail before turning my phone off. Then I pick up my prepaid phone. Not recognizing the number, I think it's just reporters and PR staff from TV and radio stations trying to get interviews. They've been calling me nonstop since the Fancy Brown song aired and Teresa spoke. I have to stave them off a little longer. Right now, I am focusing on Zena.

I open the PI's email. In the subject line, it read *Kenton Jones Report*, and in the body, he wrote, *This is one sick bastard. Let me know if you need more help pinning the tail on this donkey. I'll do whatever I can at no extra cost.* I'm glad he's on my side, but I'm scared of what's in that report. He sent the document as a PDF. So, I have to download it to my hard drive and wait for the download to finish. As slow as my computer is, that'll give me time to go to the minibar and fix myself a quick cocktail. Something tells me I'm going to need a drink to cope with this.

I pull out a miniature bottle of Grey Goose vodka and mix it with a half-empty can of Red Bull that I'd been drinking earlier to keep me energized. I've been working so tirelessly that I need all the energy I can get. Sometimes, I can't believe I'm actually doing all this. I try not to think about it too long because my fears of failure will rise to the surface and distract me from the good progress I'm making, but I'm doing it. I spent so many years convincing myself—while cleaning the house, cooking dinner, and washing clothes—that even with my degree, all I would ever be good at was being a housewife and mother. It took my sister's love and a whole lot of frustration to break me out of my comfort zone and do something that truly makes a difference—something I can say I did on my own, without Stephan soaking up all the limelight.

This isn't about fame for me. It's about succeeding and not failing my sister. I've made so many contacts since I started doing this that I have to remind myself not to get upset about not trying something like this sooner. Many organizations are asking for my help to market their campaigns, and some have even offered me jobs. Why did it take Ebony getting arrested for me to step out of my shell and actually believe in myself? The surprising part is that all those years I thought I lacked something, I actually had it in me all along. These aggressive, tenacious qualities that keep surprising me are flowing out of me effortlessly. Fear combined with low self-confidence can be tricky and dangerous. It can fool you into seeing and accepting false versions of yourself. One thing I know for sure is that after all of this is over, I won't be fooled by fear again.

I take a slow sip of my vodka and Red Bull cocktail. The vodka is bitter, and it burns my chest when I swallow, no matter how much Red Bull I've added. It's been so long since I had a stiff drink—or any alcoholic beverage for that matter—that I'm like a virgin to it. When I sit back down in front of my laptop, the file has finished downloading. I open it and start reading it like it's the Bible. The report is almost twenty pages long. After I get through the first page, which mostly contains minutiae about Kenton's place and date of birth, I move on to page two and wonder if I have the stomach to read the remaining pages.

Apparently, Kenton grew up dirt poor in some gutter butt town in Maryland right outside of Baltimore. He was a product of a teenage mom who abused his paltry ass so often he had to go live in foster homes for a few years until she, so-called, got saved and sent for his sorry ass. He really doesn't have my sympathy for that. She started a daycare center and an after-school program, where she cared for children aged two to ten.

Kenton's first victim was a five-year-old girl. There was a report that said he fondled her when he was sixteen years old. Somehow, it got thrown out. Then, two years later, he did it again. This time, he made a little girl put her mouth on his penis. This girl was eight, but that was thrown out, as well. The PI had it highlighted that Kenton's sanctified, hypocritical, pious mother had a pastor who was tight with a bunch of city officials, and that might've helped him get off the way he did. *Asshole!*

Then he moved to Ohio, where he went to a community college. He moved in with a girl who had a seven-year-old daughter, who alleged that Kenton went all the way with her. The mother, whom I assume was afraid of getting convicted herself for allowing it to happen, took the girl and fled before the case even went to trial, and Kenton's ass got off yet again.

This bastard has been getting away with this shit for years.

The last girl, before Zena, wasn't a victim but a witness, and she lives right here in Atlanta. Her name is Rene Tolson, and she's probably about Zena's age right now. She reported that she found Kenton naked and in bed with a ten-year-old girl who lived next door to him in an apartment complex. The girl's mother was on drugs and obviously didn't give a damn about her nine-year-old daughter falling victim to disgusting predators like Kenton. Apparently, she didn't cooperate with the police and didn't bring her daughter in for questioning, and Rene Tolson moved shortly after filing the report. So, there was no solid case.

The rest of the report includes more detailed accounts of the incidents. Some of them have contact information for the parents, but it's been so long that I'm not sure if the details are still current. I need to get in touch with my PI again. By now, all of the girls Kenton assaulted are adults and probably have a clearer understanding and stronger memories of what happened. I need to talk to these girls. I email the PI and tell him I'm ready to take him up on his offer. I ask for contact information for all five girls involved with Kenton's abusive behavior, including Rene Tolson. Since she lives in town, I figure she'll be the easiest to find. I send the email and hope he replies quickly.

I take another sip of my cocktail, this time longer. How can someone get away with the same wrongdoings for years? It's a shame we are governed by a judicial system that turns innocent people like my sister into murderers because of flaws and the endless loopholes that allow criminals like Kenton to walk free. Thanks to Ebony, his ass isn't going anywhere anytime soon. Ebony isn't a criminal but a freaking hero! Somebody had to put an end to Kenton's madness, and it didn't seem like the law was going to do it. So, Ebony was the next best person to step up, and unlike the law, she didn't fail.

No matter how much I sip on this cocktail, I'm still disturbed by all this information. I can't help but think about my own daughters, and with that, I have to appreciate Stephan more. He and Zionah fight like cats and dogs, but at the end of the day, Zionah is safe. He would never lay a finger on her to hurt her. Zionah has much more than other children her age. She has peace of mind and a good night's sleep without worrying about some man sneaking in her bedroom door at night like a thief, stealing the best parts of her. But she doesn't understand that. That's something I never appreciated before, either. Don't get me wrong—Stephan doesn't deserve a trophy for not being a child molester, but he does deserve respect for keeping my daughter safe and not harming more than her pride.

I don't even realize I'm crying until I swallow a salty tear with my vodka. I miss my family, and the stuff I just read makes me miss them even more. I want to go home, hug all three of my girls, and make love to my husband. A real man. But I'm afraid that if I do, the best part of me, which I found inside these secluded hotel walls, will be lost. They won't understand or support the new me, and I'll fall back into old patterns, letting them walk all over me and always putting myself last. I can't go home yet. Not until I'm sure I'll be respected and have a solid, unshakeable position in this campaign. I love them, but I can't let them ruin this for me now, not when I'm so close.

I pick up my regular cell phone and turn it back on. I decide to listen to the messages Stephan and Zionah left. My heart races with all the worry I feel behind the phone—all the bickering, insensitivity, and complaining. I don't want to be distracted any more than I want to fall back in line and continue playing the role they've assigned me. Mother, referee, secretary, counselor, chef, doctor, lawyer, maid, babysitter, sex toy, and floor mat—everything but Balanah, the college graduate. The creative, career-driven, ambitious young businesswoman in the making, who also has family at home that she would walk through fire for.

I take a deep breath and press the button to play my messages. I have fifteen voicemail messages. Fifteen. Lord. Here we go.

To my surprise, the first one is Zionah. I was sure it was going to be Stephan. She's still arguing about her dad and her so-called miserable little perfect life. What a brat she can be. Then she makes me feel bad. She called herself an orphan because her real father is dead and her mother abandoned her. That kind of talk goes on for a few messages. The fifth message is from Stephan. I guess he was staving off calling me just to prove a point. He probably was trying to tell me that he didn't need me and didn't care that I left. I knew then that he was missing the point of my absence.

The first few messages he mentioned talk of a divorce, something he often did to try to win an argument. His silly idle threats that I've called his bluff on several times before, winning against him each time. To my surprise, the last few messages were apologetic. I'll admit it, I was sappy. He missed me. He's sorry. He wants to work things out. He loves me and Zionah and wants to go to counseling. He understands how much I'm going through right now, and he's been a jerk for being insensitive to my feelings. Then came the excuses. But he's going through a lot, too. But I have to see his side, too. But he's only looking out for Zionah because he loves her. Blah, blah, blah. I almost want to hang up the phone, but I have three more messages.

The next one is from Zionah. It was from two days ago. She said if I didn't come back home within the next hour, she could live with me wherever I am. She's so dramatic. Then she said she was leaving forever and that Stephan and I wouldn't have to deal with her again. Zionah really knows how to be crafty to get her way. I don't pay her demanding threats any attention. Instead, I listen to the last two messages. They were from today and both from Stephan, but what he said this time really caught my attention. Zionah had run away! She really did it. He sounded frantic and scared. He told me he called the police, but she'd been gone for two days now. Where the hell is she?! All I could think about was her running into somebody like Kenton!

My heart races with fear, and I start to cry heavily.

I jump off the bed, staggering to the floor and dropping my cocktail from my hand. As I hurry to throw on my shoes and coat, I dial Zionah's number, but her phone goes straight to voicemail. I leave her a message, begging her to call me back. I pray she hears my tears and returns my call right away, but she doesn't. I call again and again. Still, no answer. So, I keep calling. I call as I'm leaving my hotel room and getting on the elevator. I call while passing the front desk and again when I get out to the parking lot and crank up my car. She answers none of my calls. A million thoughts race through my mind. I wouldn't be so worried if she'd only been missing for half a day or even a full day, but two days? That isn't normal or like Zionah. And for her not to answer her phone? Anything could have happened to her. She could've been snatched off the streets by some sex-crazed maniac or sold into human trafficking by now.

Oh, my baby. Lord…keep my child safe.

I try calling her again, but still no luck. I drive 90 mph all the way home, one hand on the steering wheel and the other on my cell phone, dialing Zionah's number.

As soon as I open the garage to park my car, Stephan must've heard me pull in, because a few seconds later, he's standing in the garage. I jump out of the car, and he runs to hug me.

"Where is she?" I wail.

"I'm sorry. I'm so sorry. This is all my fault. I know it is. I…I…I should be the one to leave. I forced her out of here. I know I did."

I've never seen Stephan so frantic. He usually holds himself together during the worst of times.

"It's not your fault. Where are the little ones?"

"They're asleep," he says.

I walk into the house. He follows behind me. I don't know why the first place I run to is Zionah's room. I burst through her door like I'm going to find her laying on her stomach, fiddling with her phone, surfing the net. But she's not there, and I start to cry.

"Balanah, please…I'm sorry. Don't cry. I promise I'm going to find her."

Stephan tries to console me, but I run to my younger girls' rooms.

I peek inside. They are both fast asleep. With me being gone and now their big sister—who they idolized—being gone, too, I know they've been having it hard. I kiss them on the cheeks and hug them without waking them.

What in the world have I done? What possessed me to leave my family?

I feel like a worthless woman. I feel Stephan's hands on my shoulders. He squeezes them, then lifts me from the corner of one of the girls' beds and leads me out of the room.

"What happened?" I ask as we walk down the hall towards our bedroom, stopping at the door.

"We had a big fight—the biggest one yet—and she just left."

He shrugs, trying to keep the tears that are floating in his eyes from falling down his cheeks.

"Fight about what?"

"I don't even remember. That's how stupid it was. We both were upset and blaming each other for you leaving."

I sigh, thinking that Stephan is childish for going tit-for-tat with a thirteen-year-old girl. It's not right for her to blame him for me leaving, but it's stupid for him to blame her. She's just a child.

"You blamed her?" I say to him like he's despicable.

"Not in those exact words, but I think she kind of got the impression that I was blaming her. I take full responsibility for this, Balanah?"

He raises his hands like he's surrendering to a fight before it gets started.

I sniff up my tears and shake my head at him. Once my eyes are dry, I notice what a wreck the house is. Dirty laundry in the hallway and up the staircase. When I walk down the steps to look at the kitchen,

I'm even more disgusted. Stephan follows behind me like a puppy who is about to get in trouble for shitting on the carpet. The kitchen and the entire house look like it hasn't been cleaned since I left. The floor is so dirty that I can't even remember what color my tiles are. Pots, pans, plates, cups, bowls, and pieces of silverware with dried-up food on them are scattered about the countertops. The garbage hasn't been taken out in God knows how long and is busting through the bag, most of it falling onto the floor.

I walk to the bathroom and am surprised to see wet towels on the floor and hanging over the shower curtain rod, dried-up toothpaste stains all over the mirror and sink, and dirty clothes piled high on the floor. The house has an odor so severe that I almost gag. It smells like day-old dirty dishwater and trash. All I could do was look at Stephan and shake my head. This is what I was missing? The house is a wreck, and my daughter is gone. I'm so upset that my body is shaking. But I still fall in line, like a patriotic wounded soldier.

I bend over and start picking up dirty clothes, trash, and whatever else is lying around. I'm doing the job they left for me. With the way the house looks, it's going to take me hours to clean up, but that will keep me busy enough so I don't have to look at or talk to Stephan. He follows behind me from room to room, watching me clean in silence without even considering lifting one finger. I hear him sniffing and know he's crying, but I refuse to turn around to give him any attention.

"Are you going to divorce me?" he asks me, his voice trembling.

The way I'm feeling right now, he ought not be putting good ideas in my head.

"I heard you on the radio the other day and saw that website you started."

He says that like it's the reason he asked if I was going to divorce him. He didn't say anything else about the website or that I did a good job. Just that he saw it.

"You are, aren't you? You're gonna divorce me. I really did it this time, huh? You're already under so much stress, and I've gone and made it worse. You left us, and now you're here, but you're still not here. I've never seen you like this before, Balanah. Are you going to do it? Huh?"

I want to continue ignoring him, but I know that will only prompt him to continue making himself out to be the victim in all of this.

I turn to him and give him a serious look. "Right now, the only thing I'm sure I'm going to do is clean this house, then go look for my child. That's it for now."

"Is there anything I can do?"

I roll my eyes at his stupid question. There's plenty he could do. The first would be to get the fuck away from me. The second would be to go find my child. Instead of telling him this, just go back to ignoring him. While I continue to pick up items from off the floor and separate trash from dirty clothes and household items, he continues to watch me from behind, saying nothing and doing nothing.

"Maybe I should leave. You can come back home, and I'll get a hotel. I think that's fair. You obviously need some time away from me."

I could have turned around and hit him with the broom. Him leaving would be just the vacation he didn't deserve. Everything will fall on me. As usual. Between dropping off and picking the girls up from school, cooking dinner, helping with homework, cleaning the house, and dealing with Zionah and all her mini dramas, I wouldn't have enough time to continue with the campaign. He knows what I'm doing and how important it is to me, but he still doesn't get it. He still isn't trying to see it.

"I'll be out of here in the morning," he says, patting me on top of my back as I bend over, picking up toys and dirty clothes.

He walks up the steps like the decision he just made was mature and right. He almost looked proud of himself. I guess my time for smooth sailing is over. The turbulence is officially here.

30
KWAME
"Long Enough"

I'm doing something I haven't done in a long time—surfing the net. I've got about an hour and a half before I pick up Levi from school, so I'm killing time online. I checked out the website Balanah made for Ebony, and it's fire. It's running slow, probably due to all the traffic. The video with that Fancy Brown girl singing is amazing. I can't stop watching it. It would've been dope if Zena was in the background on drums, especially since her band is on the come-up.

Yesterday, one of Zena's bandmates, this white boy named Brian, called and said he might know where she is. Told me to meet him at a bar called The Rave. I didn't even know Zena was in a rock band. When this all settles, I need to take time to really get to know my niece. All of them.

I called Malichai, and we headed to the bar. We'd been there twice before, chasing leads that Ebony gave to Sahara, but nobody talked. I don't know what made Brian change his mind. He did mention that Zena had threatened to leave the state and that he was worried about her because she didn't have any money or contacts outside of Atlanta. He gave me his number and promised to text me as soon as he sees her. The band has practice coming up in a few days, and he assured us that Zena never misses practices. Brian said practicing is the only thing that mellows her out. I could tell this Brian kid really cares about Zena by the way he talked about her. Malichai and I appreciated his help.

We have to find Zena before she skips town. Where would she go? How would she support herself? If Zena fled the state before we got to her, Mama would freak out, and Ebony's situation could get even worse.

Once I locate Zena, I'm going to take that trip to visit my sister. I wrote Ebony a few short letters, letting her know I'm on the job, that I've got her and Zena's back. She never wrote back. From what I hear from everybody else, she's doing okay, considering. That's Ebony—always strong. Essence still hasn't called me, but I know she got the check because I checked my account and saw that she cashed it. I'm done chasing her. When she's ready to talk, I'll be here.

Things at home are stable, I guess. Just like I promised, I haven't hit Tammy again, and I even signed myself up for anger management— basically wife-beaters anonymous. It starts next week. One class a week for six weeks. After that, I plan to get more help. I've been searching online for counselors. Admitting I need help feels almost as good as being healed. But I'm not naive. Saying I need help isn't enough—it's just the first step.

Tammy's eye is healing slow. I hate looking at it. Seeing her swollen, blue-black eye is like staring at the evil side of myself that I've been trying to hide from everybody. She don't even try to cover it. Sometimes I wonder if she's dragging out the healing process on purpose—like that black eye is her meal ticket. But I shouldn't think that way. She used to talk to me more when I was hurting her. Now, we barely speak. I sleep in the guest room, avoiding her and the couch as much as I can. But living together means crossing paths: in the kitchen, on the stairs, in the shared bathrooms—even with four of them in this ridiculously large house.

I got her attention when I met with a realtor and put a "For Sale" sign in the yard. She's pissed off at me, but she's also more scared since her future is tied to mine. I'm sure once Essence gets wind of this, Tammy ain't going to be the only person mad at me. I tried calling to offer her the job of selling the house, but she won't speak to me. So, what can I do? I need to downsize. I thought this house was a step down, but it's still too much—too big, too expensive. With what I pay in taxes, utilities, and mortgage, I could have enough money to buy three homes outright: one for Mama, one for Malichai, one for myself. And I plan to. Mama deserves a nice house after all the stress she's endured. Then Malichai can move back into the condo and get his family out of that foreclosed house before they get caught and thrown out on the street.

After making a list of potential counselors to call, I hop online and start looking for houses. I find about five properties that I think are suitable for Mama. All have a minimum of four bedrooms, big kitchens with plenty of counter space, and one even has a big yard for the grandkids. I check other cities in case I can convince Mama to move from the West End. If I find the right house at the right price, she might be open to it. My main concern is that she's in a safe neighborhood. I jot down more listings.

I still have an hour before it's time to pick up Levi, so I keep surfing. This time, I Google myself. It's my first time ever doing this. I click the images—old photos from endorsement deals, football highlights, parties with Tammy. I looked good back then. My skin was smooth, my body was in tip-top shape, and I actually looked happy when I smiled.

Then I scroll through the latest news about me. Right away, pictures of me and Ebony side by side pop up. Gossip blogs are speculating that I had something to do with Ebony shooting Kenton. Ridiculous. There's also a picture of my father's mugshot, Ebony's, and a photo of me in the middle. The tagline reads: **Trouble in the Sedah World**. I scroll down even further on Google and see Tammy's name. So, I click to open the page. There's a recent picture of her wearing her best designer brands and those oversized Marilyn Monroe shades I can't stand. The article states that she has just signed a deal for her own reality show, set to air next fall. What the hell?!

I wish I had started anger management sooner. That way, I'd know what to do to curb the rage that's swarming in my chest, causing my fists to ball up and my vision to blur. This is the feeling I usually get before I strike Tammy, and I don't know what to do to stop it. So, I just do the generic thing and breathe in deep. I have to keep my promise to myself. I have to. I breathe again a few times, and my fists loosen. After a while, I feel a little better, but I still want to knock her ass out. I fight the urge to confront and instead, Google her name.

More articles pop up. One headline: *Tammy Sedah Fears for Her Life,* with a photo of her black eye. Another: *She Saw It Coming: Tammy Sedah Tried to Stop the Shooting.* Then: *The Horror of Bearing the Sedah Name—Tammy Sedah Tells All.* A few more sites report the same thing about her reality show deal, as well as a tell-all book that exposes her marriage to me and her ties to my family.

I've seen enough. If I read any more, I'm going to break my promise. I call Tammy into the office and am surprised when she appears from the hallway seconds later like she's been standing there all along.

"What the fuck is this?" I point to the computer. "A reality show? A book? You airing our shit on these trifling-ass gossip sites?"

She shifts her weight, glancing at the screen and smiling at her photo like she's in love with herself.

"What you want me to say? Some of that shit ain't even true. You know how they do—just make shit up for clickbait."

"What about the reality show? The book?"

She shrugs. "Nothing's official yet. Producers are still pitching it. As for the book...I don't know. We'll have to see. If I get the show, I'll write the book. That way, I'm sure it won't flop," she says casually, like what she's trying to do doesn't affect me.

"I thought we had an understanding. You weren't gonna drag my family into this shit."

"I told you I wouldn't go on the radio," she says, hand on her hip. "And I'm still considering your deal to give me two hundred grand to keep quiet."

"Well, fuck that deal! I ain't giving you shit!"

I jump up, and she jumps back.

"See! That's why I'm doing all this—to secure me and Levi's future."

"You ain't thinking about Levi. You're thinking about yourself," I say, shaking my head in disgust. "If I have to, I'll get a lawyer to keep you from ever speaking my name or anything pertaining to my family. Sahara knows plenty of lawyers. I'll sue the hell out of you. You think you're gonna be rich? Naw! You're just gonna be infamous and broke."

She gasps, processing what I just said.

"Why are you so mad? They don't even know how they want to spin the story yet. Ever since Fancy Brown sang that song and that video aired, everything changed," she mutters, resentful.

"Yeah, it changed. I was ready to give us another shot the other day. But now? I need to cut all ties. Me and you—we've always been headed in different directions. We just used each other for comfort. I'm done with that shit!"

"That was your plan all along!" she whines. "That's why you're selling the house. You're planning on putting me and Levi out on the street, ain't you?"

"No! I ain't that damn cruel. But you ain't getting no two hundred grand from me. Not now! Not ever!"

I turn to walk past her, and she backs up slowly until she hits the wall. She flinches when I pass. Then she starts following behind me like she's daring me to hit her—damn near begging for it. I breathe deep, stretching my hands wide to stop them from balling into fists.

"I hate you!" she spits. "Always have! You ain't shit but a has-been. Without football, you're just a fat slob my friends laugh about. They don't know why I stayed with you. I could've been with any baller, but I settled for your stupid ass because you were the easiest. I done had plenty of niggas—before you, after you. Hell, you even paid some of their bills."

I stop walking but don't turn around. If I look at her, I might strangle her ass. I continue walking around the house, trying to catch my breath and control my anger.

"You a sap, Kwame. Always have been. I don't know how such a pussy like you ended up playing a contact sport like football. Probably cried every time you had to tackle one of them dudes—unless you liked it," she adds, taunting me with an animated voice.

My vision blurs, and I think I black out for a second. Everything goes dark, and I lose my balance, crashing shoulder-first into the wall.

"What? You gonna puke again? You're so disgusted by your own life, you can't stand yourself. That's why you keep throwing up all the time! I'm gonna be something, Kwame. And if it takes dragging your pathetic name to get me there, then so be it!"

I feel dizzy. I push off the wall and head toward the bathroom, my stomach churning. I haven't thrown up in a few days, but it's back. I wonder if it was that smoothie Levi brought me last night—said his mom helped him make it. I'm worth more to Tammy dead than alive, but she's too ignorant to pull something like that off. Maybe it's just stress eating me alive.

I sprint to the bathroom. Tammy's still behind me, yelling, egging me on to hit her. That's what she wants—to sell the next bruise to the blogs to fuel her reality show dreams. But I'm not giving her that. I reach the bathroom and try to close the door behind me, but she blocks it with her foot and barges in. I drop to my knees and vomit. She laughs while watching over my shoulder.

"You're so damn pathetic," she sneers. "Look at you, Kwame. I was the best thing that ever happened to you, and now you gonna fuck that up. You really think you gonna find another woman who looks like me? Ha! You look like a fucking gorilla. No woman in her right mind wants a gorilla."

I vomit again—harder. Maybe it's the sickness. Maybe I'm reacting to what she's saying. I gag, emptying what feels like my entire insides. Then the itching sensation starts again—around my neck, behind my ears.

I stand and lean over the sink to rinse out my mouth. Tammy's behind me, smirking at me through the mirror. She really thinks she's got it all figured out. I almost feel sorry for her. She doesn't realize she won't be getting that reality show. No producer in their right mind is going to use her to smear Ebony—not while Balanah's campaign is working its magic. Tammy's playing herself.

I turn and look at her before wiping my mouth with my hand.

"I'm sorry you see me as all those things and that you felt stuck with me. I really am. But I'm gonna make this better for both of us."

I check my watch. Time to get Levi. I grab my keys, but Tammy snatches them from me.

"Where are you going?"

"To pick up Levi."

She gives me an incredulous look, then tosses the keys back.

"What you mean by you gonna make it better? What's that supposed to mean? Is that a threat? There ain't nothing you can do to make it better, boo boo, or change the fact that I'm getting that show."

"I can leave. File for divorce in the morning. You can have your stardom. I'll pay child support for Levi, and hopefully, you'll let me see him sometimes. If not, I'll still pay the support until he turns eighteen."

"We don't need shit from you, Kwame. You know how much money I'm going to be making when I blow up? Your endorsement checks ain't gonna last forever. Then what? You're too fat and sloppy to get a job as an announcer. What the hell are you going to do? People don't even remember you anymore. Hell, this reality show might be the best thing that ever happened to you. Maybe it'll remind folks you still exist and aren't dead like everybody seems to think."

"Maybe," I say and walk out the door.

She's still screaming when I reach the car, but I ignore her. I'm proud of myself. She said the nastiest shit, and I didn't lay a hand on her. Can't even be mad. If that's how she feels about me, then that's how she feels. After I pick up Levi, I'm going to pack my stuff and move in with Mama in the morning. Then, I'm going to file for divorce. This bullshit between me and Tammy has gone on for long enough. I'm done pretending we're salvageable.

I arrive at Levi's school fifteen minutes early. There's nothing left between me and Tammy—if there ever was. Staying together only turned us into monsters, and I'm tired of being one.

I turn on the radio to clear my mind. Fancy Brown's "Save the Child" is playing. It's acoustic, her sultry voice gliding over soft guitar strokes and rich background harmonies. Beautiful. I close my eyes, trying to escape.

In my mind, I see Ebony painting, and Zena smiling big and beating on some drums. My father is hugging Mama and nodding at me like he's proud. Malichai is with his family, living in a big house, and Meka is clean. Balanah realizes her true potential and is no longer afraid to utilize it. Sahara is returning to her beautiful self, the one she was groomed to be. And I see Essence, wrapping her arms around me and whispering in my ear that she forgives me.

I see Tammy, too—happy. Her and Levi both, happier than they've ever been.

Then I see myself. I'm running for a touchdown, knocking down every negative obstacle that ever tried to tackle me. But I'm not holding a football. I'm holding my life. And I make it. I cross the line. I make that touchdown, and finally, I feel fulfilled.

When the song ends, I try to open my eyes, but I can't.

I can't move.

I'm not even sure I closed my eyes to begin with. Everything's just dark. A darkness so deep, it's beautiful. I can't feel anything either. Then I hear music again—softer and sweeter than the song that played before. It lights up the dark. It fills me. I almost feel like I *am* the music.

I want to get out of the car, wrap Levi in a hug, tell him I'm sorry and that I truly love him—even if he's not really mine. But I can't. I want to call Mama and tell her I love her, but I can't. For some reason, everything feels too late. I feel like I've run out of time.

I hear somebody tapping on the window. I think it's Levi, but they're screaming *Sir*, not *Dad*. Then I hear somebody yell, *"Call the ambulance! I don't think he's breathing!"*

Who are they calling the ambulance for?

Who's not breathing?

I still can't move.

Then...nothing. No music. No voices. The only thing that's keeping me company is the darkness, and I'm not afraid.

31
ZENA
"When?"

The only reason I'm coming out of hiding is to meet Zionah. She texted me about an hour ago and said she had run away from home and wasn't going back. I got scared. Knowing what kind of evil lurks on the streets and not wanting her to fall victim to the same trap I fell into, I convinced her to meet me at the Five Points train station downtown. Once I talk her into returning home, I'm probably going to leave the state. I'm tired of seeing my pain broadcast on TV for the world to analyze. It brings up too many buried memories and too many avoided questions.

When did it start? It's the first question everybody seems to want to ask. Mama, the social services lady, the police officers, the medical examiners, the judge, and now my friends—all of them want to know when. But they wouldn't understand if I told them. Nobody can really understand. They can only feel for me, and that ain't enough. They want to know when, but I want to know why. Why me?

When? The answer is that it began with a lingering smile that fell somewhere between kindness and sneaky. The kindness is what allowed my innocent childhood heart to let him in so quickly, and the sneakiness is what fooled me into letting him come in even closer, assuming it was all real. And in between the kindness and sneakiness lay what helped me fill a void that was so hollow I could feel it echoing inside me, affecting the future development of the woman I was supposed to become. The void of a little girl without a daddy.

His smile was ever-changing. The single curve of his sneering lips could transform into something different in the blink of an eye without him moving his mouth, holding so many obscure meanings all in a moment's time. The first second of his smile always said hello— nothing too alarming and brief enough to fool the average person into thinking it was just a simple gesture of genuine concern about how I was doing. But it wasn't real. Then the seconds that followed, the seconds no one else seemed to notice but me, revealed a reaction to a dirty secret he was hiding from the world. A secret that he was slowly pacing himself to share with me. A secret that, once revealed, would force me into the same arena of seclusion and shame that he lived in. His misery really loved my company.

I used to think I was happy. I was starting to feel normal with Kenton around. But the normal I knew was based on a child's view. Back then, normal to me was having a mother who wasn't much younger than all my school friends' mothers and a father who lived under the same roof with me and my mother, co-parenting and loving me together. It was like the cheesy TV shows I watched, where the mom baked cookies and tucked the child in at night, and the dad worked all day and kept his family safe. As I got older, I realized that wasn't real, and that true normal didn't exist in any form. But by then, it was too late. The damage had already been done.

Kenton fooled me into thinking he cared about me. He showered me with compliments. Don't get me wrong. My mother complimented me, too. She told me I was beautiful, talented, and smart, but hearing all of that from a man's voice took on a whole new meaning for me. It almost validated my mother's compliments, and the compliment didn't just seem like something my mother was saying to make me feel better; it felt real. If Kenton thought I was beautiful, then maybe I really was. If he said I was smart, then maybe I truly was. The words took on a whole other meaning when delivered through his deep, masculine voice—a voice with a bass I wasn't used to hearing that gave me a sense of comfort and security I'd never felt before. He could have told me anything, and I would have believed it. There was something about a man's voice back then that spoke life to me. Even in the casual hello and goodbye of strangers, the sound of a man's voice warmed my heart and filled a void, but it wasn't a lasting fill.

I have uncles, but I didn't see them often enough to feel fulfilled. The only grandfather I had is serving a life sentence. I had heard great stories about him, but not being able to put a real face to the stories made him seem more like a figment of my imagination than anything else. When Mama told stories about him, it was almost like she was telling me a fairy tale.

I don't know who my real father is to this day. That's Mama's best-kept secret. She told me it wouldn't matter if I knew because he wouldn't come around anyway, but it would've mattered to me. She doesn't understand. Not knowing who he is makes me feel displaced in this world. When I was little, I used to search the aisles of the grocery store, inside the cars zooming by us on the highway, and study the faces of random people walking the streets, wondering if one of them was my father. Sometimes, just to make myself feel better and to fill that terrible void inside, I'd point out a stranger and tell myself he was my dad. The only thing is, that only worked until the next day. Before Kenton came around, I had claimed a hundred strangers as my dad. By the time Mama brought Kenton home, he became imaginary Dad 101, and after him, there was no 102.

By the time Kenton finished with me, the emptiness of not knowing who my father was—or any man—ended. I felt betrayed by myself all those years, wanting to know who my real father was. If a man could do what Kenton did to me, I didn't want to know any man.

After his suggestive smiles, it progressed into suggestive hugs. His hugs lasted longer than anybody else's. He would pull me into his chest, wrap his arms around me, and keep them there almost as if he was counting backward from one hundred. Then the heavy breathing started. The muffled moans and pleasure-filled panting rang in my ears. In those hugs, I felt everything but love. I felt deceit, shame, and a bulge in my stomach that seemed to grow with every second he squeezed me in his arms. I was smart enough to know what that bulge was, but not smart enough to run. I understood what was happening, but I dissociated myself from it so much that it was almost like it wasn't happening at all. It was like an out-of-body experience.

The hugs started with both of us standing up, and then we moved to lying down. I will never forget the day he hugged me and then guided me toward my bed, where he laid my back down on the mattress and fell on top of me. We kept our clothes on, and for some strange reason, that made everything seem okay to me. The bulge I felt on my stomach then moved to between my legs, pressing against my blue jeans, while his moaning and panting grew louder, always ending with a shudder and a long sigh. Then, he rolled off me, flashed me that dirty smile of his, and walked out of my room awkwardly, as if he'd just peed his pants.

That went on for about a year. The next year, he added to it all. Then, he became the puppet master, using my hands to his advantage—placing them where he wanted them and making them do things I'd never dream of doing. He stuck my hands in his pants, and I closed my eyes tight and pretended not to feel the hard, sticky, sweaty, smelly thing I was touching. *Squeeze,* he would say, and I'd do it. *Not too hard,* he told me, and I would ease up. *A little harder than that*, he'd whisper, and I would adjust the grip of my fingers. He'd grab my wrist and force it up and down...then faster...then slower...and then all of a sudden, my hand was covered in filthy off-white grime that made me feel so disgusting I'd much rather chop it off than wash it. I felt so tainted by the puss that spurted out of him that I stopped using my hands altogether. I barely ate. I didn't want to use them to comb my hair, and I stopped drawing. Drawing was a gift I held so dear because I'd inherited it from my mother, who inherited it from her father, but it just didn't feel the same. My hands couldn't work the way they used to. No matter how much I washed them, they always felt sticky and dirty. How could I draw beautiful pictures with dirty hands?

Soon after that, things began to evolve. He didn't need to use my hands to venture for him anymore. Instead, he used his own hands. Or maybe I should say his fingers. They felt like knives when he used them to poke between my legs. Then they felt like icicles when he used them to rub across my underdeveloped chest and my backside. But I didn't know then that the worst was yet to come.

The first time he went all the way with me, I was only thirteen. I was so confused; I really didn't know what was going on, and the pain. Lord, the pain was almost unbearable. I wondered how something that felt so awful to me could bring him so much breathtaking pleasure. I was just confused. I detached myself from the situation just as I did during the early stages of the molestation. I put myself somewhere else mentally.

Mentally, I traveled the world for those few short minutes he spent gyrating on top of my little body. Sometimes, my mind traveled to Disney World or Six Flags. Other times, I never left town. My mind would just take me to places I felt most comfortable—to my grandmother's house where I would lay across the bed while she read to me, or running through Aunt Balanah's yard trying to catch lightning bugs in the night. But, when I got too hot, I'd get deported from whatever region of the world my mind ventured off to because I couldn't breathe.

He almost smothered me, and sometimes I wished he would just end my misery. I couldn't breathe when he was on top of me, pushing up and down like he was exercising. His chest hairs scratched against my face so hard I felt like I had rug burn. His large arms towering on each side of me, closing in with each push, made me feel claustrophobic. I felt like I was in a coffin enclosed by his sweaty body. That's exactly what it felt like—a stiff coffin made of his body.

Why didn't you tell me? Mama asked me almost like she was trying to clear whatever accusations her conscience was starting to fester in her mind. I just shrugged my shoulders and said I didn't know because I really didn't know why. At least not then. Kenton had been raping me for two years, and after those years, it took only one look for Mama to finally catch a clue to what was going on. She was living in her own world then. The fancy, esteemed rebel artist didn't draw pictures unless they was perfect. And that just translated into how she dealt with her personal life. She had the house, the child, the talent, and the man. Everything was perfect to her. I always say that if she saw the pain in my eyes, then she saw it all along, but she just didn't want to face the truth. It would disturb the perfect world she was living in. So, she ignored it. And I did, too.

Kenton never threatened to kill me or Mama if I told on him. In fact, he never told me what he was doing. He just did it to me like it was his rite of passage. I knew what he was doing was wrong, but admitting it would make it too real, and I wasn't ready to accept all the stigma that was associated with a molested child. If what he was doing to me wasn't real, I felt like I had a chance at a normal life, like I could still have the same experiences as other girls. So, I buried what he was doing to me—buried it so deep I couldn't find it anymore. That's why I was shocked that day when Mama took one look at me and saw what was happening. She'd found it. But then I resented her for it, telling myself she saw it all along.

I was more scared of what the exposure of what he did to me would do to my character. I can't handle the shame of it all. I can't handle people looking at me like Mama, the social workers, and the police officers—like I'm ruined. Damaged goods. Doomed. Mostly because I already felt like all those things. Now, I have to avoid the damn press, my uncles, my aunts, my grandmother, and my mama. I know she's behind bars, waiting for me to see her, but I just can't. Not yet. I wasn't planning on seeing any of them anytime soon. But then Zionah calls, and my plans get diverted.

I decided to leave the state after Mama did what she did. She really thought she was making things better, but she only made them worse. I don't want my dirty laundry aired in public for everyone to see and comment on. I think what Mama did was foolish, but ironically, I've thought about doing the same thing in exactly the same way so many times that I've rocked myself to sleep at night with that fantasy. I guess we really are made of the same cloth.

She asked me if I blamed her for what happened to me, and I told her yes. I did blame her because blaming her was better than blaming myself. At thirteen, I couldn't handle all of that being my fault. That blame ate her up inside to the point where she became somebody else, but I still wasn't satisfied with that. I needed to see more regret. More remorse. More sorrow from her. Anybody can walk around the house all day, eating what they want and drowning their pain in liquor. So, I told her that Kenton made me a lesbian.

When I told her I was gay, her whole body looked as if it had frozen in time. I knew that kind of news would really rock her world, but what I didn't expect was to see her lying on the floor underneath a broken banister with a drop cord tied around her neck. I caught a glimpse of her from the foyer window, and when I saw her body lying across the floor, kicking the ground like she'd just committed a mission impossible, I had seen too much and I saw enough. I didn't go inside. Instead, I ran and am still running. I hadn't seen her since then, and I had no idea she was going to conjure up a second plan of death, all over a simple lie. I wasn't a lesbian because of Kenton. It was just the way I was born.

For years, I feared the judgment and conviction that would come with coming out of the closet, so I took the easy way out and caused my mother more pain. Back then, I saw it as killing two birds with one stone. But ironically, there were no birds. Only my mother. I just wanted to make her feel more guilty about what happened to me. Kenton wasn't guilty for what he did to me. So, I figured she was the next best thing. But I didn't mean to drive her mad. I didn't mean for her to try to kill herself and then throw away her own life. Now, I'm the one who feels guilty.

I know my uncles are looking for me. I wish they were looking for me back when I was easier to find—back when Kenton was fucking me—but they didn't seem to care then. I'd been hiding out at different friends' houses. I was at one of the houses, crouched down behind the couch, when they knocked on the door and she told them she hadn't seen me. I just don't feel like answering all the questions and dealing with the pity—all the *I'm sorrys* and belated *I love yous*. I avoided all that when I was thirteen and Mama called the police to our house, and I'm going to avoid it now.

I didn't cooperate with the police and refused to take the medical exam. Because they had no proof of what he had done, he got off. But the pain I carried wasn't limited to the intangible emotions that burdened me inside. The real proof was in the blood-soaked panties he soiled the first time he forced his way inside me, not even bothering to pull off my underwear. I kept them in a shoebox in my room. Why? I hope nobody asks me that because I really don't know why I kept them. Maybe it's a matter of physical memory to go along with the mental one. Or maybe it was just a souvenir for all the pain I'm carrying—a physical reminder to never let anyone hurt me again.

After Mama put Kenton out, I felt a little freer. Still trapped in my pain, but free. Now, I'm back in hiding. I'm in public now, disguised just enough so I won't get pointed out by a random person in the crowd or hounded by the press. I'm wearing big sunglasses even though there isn't a ray of sun in sight. I have on my skull cap, a scarf, and a big overcoat. I'm disguised so well that I know I'll have to look for Zionah before she looks for me because she won't recognize me in this costume.

Zionah seems like she doesn't have a reason to run away, but if anybody knows that nothing ain't what it seems, it's me. The curse Kenton put on my life gave birth to a warped gift. I can take one look at a person and see the pain I have in common with them. I can point out a sexual abuse victim from miles away, and they seem to be able to pick me out, too. We see each other in public and try to pretend not to see the secrets that haunt our eyes. I'm gonna look in Zionah's eyes for the same secrets. It's the least I can do for my little cousin. I want her to know she can count on me, and it feels good to be something for somebody that nobody could be for you. I want to know why she's running away. Stephan's not her real father, but he's raised her, and just like I got the gift to be able to tell if a child is getting sexually abused, I can tell an abuser. I see them walk the streets freely every day without a care in the world, but I have never seen that in my Uncle Stephan. Never. But I could be wrong. After all, I'm not perfect.

As soon as I get off the train, I see Zionah sitting on a bench outside with her eyes glued to her phone. She looks like she's texting. She's all dressed in the latest styles—designer sneakers, designer shirts, and expensive jeans. She seems to have no real cares in the world. Just as I thought, she doesn't notice me, not even when I sit next to her.

"Zionah," I call her name.

When she sees me, she jumps like she's seen a ghost, then smiles at me all excited. She leans over to hug me. I look right into her eyes, so serious that she starts to look nervous.

"Why are you looking at me like that? What's wrong?"

That's when I know nothing's wrong. She's just being spoiled. Just as I expected.

"Why you leave home? These streets ain't no place for you."

"I hate him!" she pouts.

"Who? Your dad?"

"Stephan?" she says sarcastically.

"You mean your dad," I say again.

We both never met our birth fathers, but we have nothing in common. Zionah's father died when she was still a baby, and Stephan stepped right up to fill that void. I thought Kenton was going to be the Stephan in my life, but I was painfully wrong. Zionah really doesn't know how good she's got it. Sometimes, I envy her seemingly perfect childhood, and it annoys me when she's always complaining about nothing. She has the family I always wanted: a supportive mother, siblings, and a father figure who would never hurt her.

"Why do you hate him?"

"He fusses too much. Blames me for everything, and Mama left us. She left me there with *him*!"

I sigh.

You really scared me, Zionah. When you called, I thought something serious had happened to you.

"Like what?" she asks naively, unable to fathom the horrific things a child who has been molested might.

I decide to give it to her straight and to the point.

"I'm sure you heard the news."

As soon as I say that, she looks away from me like I'm plagued. I know she's getting uncomfortable. I was bursting the bubble around her perfect and safe world.

"I watched the news," she says in a low voice.

"Well, I hate the man who did that to me."

"Me, too," she said quickly.

Maybe you don't understand what hate really is. Because if you hate your dad just for being a dad, that's not true hate. Now, if he was doing all the things Kenton did to me, then I'd get why you'd use that word, but he's not. Kenton never took care of me. He never bought me nice things, nor did he care how I did in school or whether my room was clean. With me, he only wanted one thing, and he didn't have to ask for it; he just took it from me. Something I can never get back. Does your dad do you like that?

She shrugs. I can tell she's starting to feel guilty.

"I just feel left out of the family sometimes. I feel like he hates me because I'm not his real *daughter*."

"You feel like he hates you because he makes you clean your room, wash dishes, and do a little work for all the nice things he buys you. He may be a little stricter than your mom, but I think he treats you just like he treats the other girls, if not better. They don't have expensive phones and laptops and fancy clothes."

"They're younger."

"So? But what I'm really trying to say is that there are some men out there who deserve to be hated. Some can really hurt you, and Stephan ain't one of them. Kenton hated me, and he didn't treat me even half as good as Stephan treats you. You have to learn how to appreciate the good in people, Zionah, because if you don't do that, you won't be able to see the bad in some people, and you can easily get misled."

Now she's quiet. She doesn't want to hear what I'm saying.

"I know your mom and dad are looking for you and are worried sick about you. That's not fair. It's not fair that you make them suffer like that when you know they love you so much."

"But you're doing it. Grandma is worried sick about you, and everybody is looking for you, and you don't care."

Now I'm quiet.

"That's different, Zionah."

"How?"

She has me stumped because I couldn't figure out how it was different. Suffering was suffering, regardless of what caused it. I made my mother suffer so much that she tried to end her life and then tried to end someone else's. Now she's still suffering because I haven't gone to see her. There's been enough suffering in my life. I'm tired of it all, especially my own.

"I don't know. It just seems different," I tell her.

"I'll go home if you go home," she bargains with me.

She has me thinking. Maybe it's time I face the fire and go home—just get it all over with so I can truly move on with my life. Kenton did enough damage to me that it crossed over to my mother, and now my entire family is feeling the effects of it. A lot of it, I allowed him to do without saying a word. Maybe it's time for that to change. Mama did her part and shot him, but I have a part to play, as well. I'm just not sure what it is yet, but maybe going home and coming out of hiding will help me figure it out.

"Maybe I will?" I mutter.

"Really," Zionah says, clapping like she's done something good.

"Yeah, really."

"When?" she asks.

I pause for a moment. I can't go right away. I need at least a few hours to get my mind right.

"Maybe after we get some lunch."

"Can I just hang with you for a few days?"

"I don't know, Zionah. Like I said, your mom and dad are probably worried sick."

"People are worried sick about you, too."

"We'll see," I sigh.

"Okay," she says, then looks at me with that look I'm afraid of getting from people.

I know what's coming next, and before I can get up to avoid it, she says it.

"I'm sorry for what happened to you, Zena. You didn't deserve that."

She spoke in the softest, most genuine voice. A voice so genuine, it's almost healing and makes me question why I ever ran from the empathy in the first place.

"Me, too. I'll be okay, though," I say, then stand and wave her up with my hand.

She doesn't move, though. She just looks up at me like she's curious about something.

"When?" she asks again, and I shrug, hoping that it's sometime this century.

32

ESSENCE

"Too Late"

I've decided I've made Kwame suffer long enough. I'm on my way to see him now. I tried calling earlier to tell him I accept his apology, but he's not answering. And no, I'm not just calling because he left me a message about selling his house. In fact, if he offers me the listing, I might not take it just to prove a point. Or maybe I will. I could sell that place for half a mil easy. His side of town is the only area that hasn't been affected by the housing market crash. He also mentioned something about finding a house for Mama. Kwame's too sweet. I really did overreact when he went with another realtor. I miss my brother. He's the only one who listens to me whine and complain without calling me spoiled—at least not to my face. He never judges me for feeling the way I feel. Kwame is an angel.

Before I surprise him, I'm going to stop by Malichai's motel and give him the present I have for him. I have to pass by that raunchy place to get to Kwame's anyway. Malichai's going to love what I have for him, considering it's something he collects. I don't know why he collects scratch-off lottery tickets, old and new, but whatever keeps his spirits up, because I know it's hard out there for him. It's not money, but it's thoughtful. I just hope he doesn't ask for any money, because I'll have to say no. Then he'll get mad at me. And I'm not in the mood for that.

I didn't exactly buy the ticket—I found it, or rather, it blew out of the hands of some guy Marco's crazy ass was trying to kill. I'm just glad that fool finally got the message and stopped calling me. What a waste of my time he was.

I thought about swinging by Mama's house, but I don't know where she is. Knowing her, she's probably marching into every politician and police commissioner's office in the city, demanding the immediate release of Ebony. Mama thinks it's still the sixties. Protests only go so far nowadays. If they didn't let Daddy out, they're not releasing Ebony—at least not without a trial. I just pray she gets off. If she ends up with life, it'll change all of our lives.

I'm a few miles from Malichai's exit. I turn up the radio when I hear Fancy Brown's "Save the Child" playing. This song has been playing on every station all day. Everyone's requesting it in support of Ebony. That makes it sound even sweeter. I don't know how Balanah pulled off getting a celebrity on board, but like I said—she's surprising the hell out of me.

As I take the exit, Malichai calls me.

"Damn, you must've felt me coming. And I hope you don't smell money, 'cause I'm only stopping by for a few seconds," I joke, laughing so he doesn't take it personal. But when he doesn't respond right away, I already know he's taking it personal.

Whoever said women are emotional creatures got it all wrong. Men are worse—like postpartum women on their period.

"I work, Essence. I don't need your money," he says to me curtly. "What you coming to see me for anyway?"

"I have a present for you. And when did you get a new job, or are you doing the same thing?"

"Why does it matter to you?"

"Damn, you got a nasty attitude. Keep that up, and I'll just turn around. I'm right by your motel."

"I don't stay there anymore. If you called me more often, you'd know that. But I guess you're too scared I'll ask you for money."

"Whatever, Mal. So, where you stay now? That other motel down the street?"

"No."

"Well… you gonna tell me where or not?"

"What's the present?" he grunts like he doesn't believe me.

"Don't get excited. I just found something I thought you might like. If you want it, tell me where you're at. Otherwise, I'll continue 'bout my business."

He gives me the address, which is on a different side of town. I plug it into my GPS.

Since when can he afford to live over there? I hope he's not selling drugs again.

Fifteen minutes later, I pull into his new neighborhood—and I'm shocked. Clean houses, manicured lawns, landscaped sidewalks. No way he's affording this without dealing. And with the way Meka's been getting on, I doubt he's making much money at all. She's probably smoking up the supply. And God help us if he gets her ass pregnant again. One Zach is more than enough, and he can barely handle him.

I call Malichai to let him know I'm in the neighborhood. That's when he tells me he sees my car and waves me down the street where he's walking. I guess he doesn't want me to see his house—trying to keep it a secret. I bet it's decked out with flat-screens, leather couches, and fancy art just like his last place. I don't have to see the house to know it's posh. But the neighborhood already told on him, and I'm so disappointed.

When I see him, I'm stunned. I haven't seen Malichai look this good in years—clean-cut, bathed, wearing new clothes. *Yep. He's slinging again.* But what really catches me off guard is the woman's he's with. Definitely not Meka. This girl looks decent—something Meka never was. And she's holding Zach's hand. Meka hardly *looks* at that boy, let alone hold his hand. What the hell is going on over here?

I roll down my window as Malichai walks up. But I'm still watching the girl with Zach. She stands away from my car, like she's trying to mind her business. Malichai sees me looking and shoots me that "please don't" look. But how can I not? I've been praying for years that he'd leave that crackhead. If this is what I think it is, I'm proud of him—even if he *is* back in the game.

"Who's that?" I ask, peering over his shoulder.

"Where's my present?" he says, ignoring my question.

"Mal? Did you hear me?" I look at him.

"Stop being nosey. You ain't here for all that."

"I want to see your house."

"Maybe another time. I'm busy right now."

"Don't I know it," I say, teasing him.

I dig in my purse and pull out the ticket.

"Here." I hand it to him, but yank it back when he reaches for it. "Wait." I give him a playful look, and he sighs, annoyed. "One question first—You ain't selling drugs again, are you? Because if you are—"

"Girl, get the hell on!" he snaps, walking off.

"Wait, Mal! Don't take it personal. It's just a question. Damn. Come get your ticket. I risked my life to pick this up for you. Here."

I wave the ticket out the window, and he snatches it from me.

"No, I ain't selling no drugs. Not now, not ever again!" he says, tight-jawed.

"Good for you, Mal!" I clap and grin big. He chuckles.

"You something else, girl. Where you coming from?" He eyes the ticket. "If I win, you gonna sue me for half?"

"Nope. Just gonna say congratulations." I wink, then look back over his shoulder at the girl and Zach.

She's standing there looking nervous and even a little guilty. Little homewrecking floozy. She's cute, though. Definitely an upgrade from Meka's funky ass.

"I'm gonna say hi to my nephew. That okay?"

Without waiting for permission, I get out and walk over. The girl smiles at me like she's in a pageant. She looks real sweet. I give her that.

"Hello," I say, holding my hand out for her to shake. "I'm Essence—Malichai's little sister."

"Hi, Essence," she says, chipper. "I'm Natasha. You probably don't remember me, but our families used to stay in the same neighborhood. My family knew your dad."

Oh, Lord. Another one of Daddy's disciples. I try not to roll my eyes.

"Okay. Well…nice to meet you."

I squat and grab Zach into a hug, lifting him off the ground and kissing his forehead.

"What's up, boy?"

"Aunt Balanah!" he squeals.

Ouch. That stings. But that's on me for not spending enough time with him. Malichai laughs, knowing my pride just took a hit.

"No, baby. Aunt Balanah *wishes* she looked this good," I joke. "Say Aunt Essence."

He doesn't. Just keeps calling me Balanah. So, I just leave it alone. I look at Natasha, who's still smiling while twirling one of her micro braids around her finger.

"So y'all staying together?" I blurt out, and she nearly faints.

"Girl, you something else. You know that?"

"Of course, I am," I say, flashing a grin.

"No, Mal and I are just friends. I live around the corner from him and Meka."

"Meka?" I sigh. "Oh. That's too bad," I mutter, and she blushes. Malichai does, too. Slick bastard. "Well, I'll see y'all. Bye, baby,"

I wave at Zach, and he waves back.

"Wait—I almost forgot why I called you."

"What now?" I groan.

"You talk to Kwame? I know you're the last person I should be asking, but no one's heard from him. I got a text from this kid with a lead on Zena. He texted Kwame, too, but he didn't respond."

"Maybe he's knocked out on that couch."

"Naw, he's been putting in work these past few days looking for Zena. Give him a break, will you? And stop ignoring his calls. He feels awful that you've been dodging him."

"I know," I say, a little defensive. "I'm heading to see him now. I'll tell him to call you. So y'all found Zena?"

"We will tonight."

"Good," I sigh, relieved. "Let me know once y'all have her."

"Alright."

"See ya," I say, waving once more.

As soon as I crank my car, that song is playing again. I don't mind, though. I'm obsessed with it like everyone else. I bob my head to the soft melody as I hit I-20, then merge onto I-85 North. I try calling Kwame one last time to give him a heads-up that I'm coming, but he still doesn't answer. This time, I leave a message.

"I hope you're not trying to beat me at my own game, Kwame— because you'll never win," I joke. "Anyway, I've been meaning to call you. Thanks for the money. I forgave you even before that. I just hadn't said it yet. I love you, Kwame. Can't wait to see you. Oh, and guess what? Malichai's got a new girlfriend. I'll tell you all about it. See you soon."

I toss my cell phone on the passenger's seat and turn the radio back up. My thoughts drift to Malichai and that girl. It would be nice if he finally dropped Meka, but that ain't his style. He'll never turn his back on that girl, no matter how much she drags him down. And that Natasha girl? He's just gonna end up hurting her feelings. She's already sprung. I can tell by the way she was looking at him. Poor thing. She's about to get her heart broken.

Then there's Kwame. I don't know why he wants to list that house. He got a steal when he bought it, and with the minor renovations he did—new paint, floors, landscaping—he could easily walk away with a ten-thousand-dollar profit if he markets it right. The man keeps downgrading, though. The last place looked like a damn mini mall. I could understand leaving that, but this current house suits him. Kwame was made for the simple life. He doesn't care if he lives in a box or drives a garbage truck. He's not flashy at all. I wish I were that content.

As I'm merging onto I-85 towards Buckhead, flashing lights hit my rearview. The cops. Great. I know I wasn't speeding. Not on this side of town. It's a real hot spot. My tags are up to date. So what the hell do they want?

I pull over anyway, and he does the same, parking behind me. I lean over to get my purse and pull out my driver's license. If he tries to give me a speeding ticket, I'm going to dispute it and demand to see the evidence that I was driving over the speed limit from his little laser gun—or whatever they call it—'cause this is some bullshit. But when I sit back up, I can't believe my eyes. Marco, dressed like a damn ghetto RoboCop, is stomping toward my vehicle. He's wearing tall, laced-up black boots, black pants, a tucked-in wife-beater, dark sunglasses, and a serious face. I get the urge to lock my doors, but I don't.

What the hell? This man is really doing a lot to get my attention.

He taps the glass. I roll down the window while trying to stay calm.

"What's up?" I say, like I was about to have a normal conversation.

"License and registration, ma'am," he says, all official.

"Excuse me?" I blink at him.

"License. And. Registration," he repeats slowly, like I'm hard of hearing.

"What the hell did I do?" I snap.

Wrong move. He opens the door and tries to yank me out, but my seatbelt snaps me back. He leans in and unbuckles it, then drags me out and slams me stomach-first against my car. He jerks my arms behind me, cuffing me so tight that it feels like the metal is slicing my wrists.

"What are you doing?"

"Shut the fuck up," he hisses in my ear. "Before I throw your ass in jail with your sister."

He pushes me into the back of his squad car and then goes around to the other side to get in the back with me. I feel tears welling up but fight them back. If he sees me cry, it's over.

We sit in silence for a while. He just stares at me, shaking his head slowly like I disappointed him.

"Let me ask you something, Essence," he finally says. "Do I look stupid to you? Like some punk-ass bitch you can play like you did ole' boy."

I know he's referring to Resident McCall.

"Of course not," I mumble, my voice trembling. "What's this about, Marco? I thought we were cool?"

"Yeah, me too." He shrugs. "That's why I pulled strings to get you that loan. And now you're ignoring me? Making me look stupid?"

He's leaning in so close to my face that I can feel the heat from his breath against my eardrum.

"No—"

"Well why the fuck have you been dodging me?"

"I've just been busy. I've got a lot going on with my family. You know what's going on with my sister."

"Fuck your sister. Karma's a bitch. Your daddy ruined my family's life, now it's payback."

"I'm sorry," I whisper, wrists throbbing.

He leans in closer. "You lucky I'm a generous muthafucka!"

Spittle flies from his mouth and lands on the side of my cheek. I want to wipe it away, but I can't with my hands cuffed behind me.

"Turn around," he demands.

Doing as told, I turn my back to him.

He fiddles with the cuffs, then stops, turns me back around to face him, and kisses me aggressively. He kisses me so hard that his teeth scrape my chin. His tongue invades my mouth, forcing mine to move. I don't kiss him back, though. When he finally pulls away, I feel sick.

"I'm sorry it had to go this way," he says, then finally takes the cuffs off me.

I massage my wrists, trying to get the blood circulating through them again.

"Thanks," I whisper, still not meeting his eyes.

"Uh-huh," he grunts. "Stay here."

He climbs out and opens his trunk, pulling out a black duffle. He throws it in *my* trunk, then returns.

"It's a hundred grand," he says like it's nothing.

"Well…you know…I really don't feel comfortable taking the money. I don't know when I'll be able to pay it back, and I don't want to mess up your business," I say, looking up at him for the first time and flashing him an uneasy smile.

He glares at me like he wants to choke me.

"There ain't no turning back. If I solicit this money, you take it and find a way to repay it. Like I told you before, there's no interest. Just favors. If we need you, you do whatever we ask. Got it?"

I don't say anything.

"Get the fuck out my car," he snaps, opening the door for me. "And answer when I call!"

I nod and run to my car, crank it up, and speed off. Badge or not, that man is no cop.

I'm so upset I almost turn around and head back home, but I don't. I need to see Kwame. I need to tell him everything. Maybe he can help me out of this shit, but then again, Marco is a real head case. I don't want any of my family involved. If he could pull me over like that, he could do a lot worse and get away with it. I played with fire—and now I'm burnt.

By the time I pull up to Kwame's, I'm all cried out. As I'm wiping my face, I see the realtor's sign in the yard. Now, I'm no longer shaken; I'm pissed.

He's doing the same shit again. He couldn't wait a few days for me?

I take a deep breath and storm up to the door, knocking and ringing the bell a dozen times. No answer. I peek through the glass window, and the house is completely dark. I don't know if anybody is home or not because they usually keep their cars in the garage. I almost start to feel relieved that no one is home because I'm really not in the mood to visit anymore. Just as I turn to walk away, I hear the door open. It's Levi.

"Hi, Aunt Essence," he says in a somber tone.

That child always looks like the saddest boy in the world. Never smiles, never laughs. He barely speaks above a whisper. I wonder what the hell is going on in that little head of his. I hate to say it, but the kid looks like a serial killer in the making. Honestly, he gives me the creeps.

"Hey, baby." I step inside. It's pitch black. "Why you sitting in the dark?" I ask, searching for the light switch. "And close the door, sweetie."

He does what I say and flicks on the foyer light. He looks even sadder underneath the light.

"Where's your dad?" I ask, eyes scanning the room.

"He's dead," he says flatly.

"What did you say?"

"My daddy is dead. At least I think he is. Yeah, I'm pretty sure he is."

"Levi, why would you say something like that?"

"Because I seen it."

"Seen what?"

"When Daddy came to pick me up from school, the ambulance had to break his window to get him out. They put him on a stretcher, and he wasn't moving. His eyes were halfway open, and his tongue was hanging out of his mouth with spit foaming up and running down the sides. He looked dead—like in the movies."

My knees give out, and I grab hold of the banister to keep myself from falling.

"I'm gonna miss him," Levi says, then starts walking down the dark hallway.

"Wait, baby. Where's your momma?"

"She left after the police dropped me off. She was crying and screaming. Told me not to answer the door for anybody. That's why it took me so long to let you in. I'm sorry. Are you gonna tell on me?"

"No, baby. I won't."

My lip trembles. I try my best to control my outburst, not wanting to break down in front of Levi.

"Do you know what hospital they took your dad to?"

He shrugs.

"You have your mommy's phone number?"

"Yeah, but she said not to tell anybody what I saw today. Are you going to tell on me?" he asks again.

"No, sweetie," I whisper again, handing him my phone for him to dial Tammy's number.

By the time he grabs the phone, I crumble under the weight of this news. I couldn't take it anymore. I collapse onto the floor, screaming at the top of my lungs, punching the ground, and kicking my legs at the air. I never knew pain like this. Never. All I wanted was to tell Kwame that I forgave him. But now...it's too late.

33
EBONY
"The Deal"

Sitting in front of this man, I wish I'd plotted two murders instead of one. If I had a second chance, I'd shoot Sir Zion in his lying mouth.

When one of the guards told me a man was here to see me, I thought it was Kwame or Malichai with an update on Zena. I'd gotten Kwame's letters in the mail. They were sweet, but I haven't had time to write back. Believe it or not, prison keeps me busier than I ever was on the outside. Funny, right?

They might as well put me on payroll with all the counseling I'm doing in here. Now they're talking about me teaching an art class, saying it will help ease inmates' minds and relieve stress. Like I can say no. I turn down one "favor," and all that special treatment they've been giving me will be over. I'm getting used to it.

When I'm not playing counselor, I'm playing lawyer. These girls ask me the dumbest questions about the simplest things. Half of them want to plead guilty when they're innocent. They were just in the wrong place at the wrong time, like Tweety. The other half are guilty as hell but want to plead innocent, which only makes their sentencing worse. Meanwhile, I've got my own decision to make—

plead guilty and face the system head-on, plead innocent and hope for leniency, or plead insanity and possibly get off. I promised myself I wouldn't plead insanity. I wasn't crazy for shooting Kenton—I was justified. But Sahara thinks the jury won't see it that way. I know I'm not innocent, but I don't feel guilty either. I'll figure it out when the time comes. Right now, I gotta deal with the scumbag sitting across from me, smirking like he's getting a kick out of my current situation. I bet he felt the same way when my father was arrested. The snake!

"I'm sorry I didn't come sooner," he sneers.

"Thank you for that," I shoot back.

He laughs, leaning back in the chair.

He's dressed like a damn fool—green smock, yellow slacks, his carved African walking stick, and a giant knit hat covering his lint-filled locs that now dust the floor. He smells like cheap cologne, and it's making me dizzy.

"What do you want?"

"This thing you did is getting big. Everybody's talking about it. Might even be bigger than your father's mistake."

"The only mistake my father made was trusting you. Just like I once did."

"That wasn't long ago. You used to love me, remember?" Sir Zion says snidely.

I snicker and shake my head at him like he's pathetic. "When I was a child, I thought as a child. Now that I'm a woman, I've put childish things behind me."

"Except plots of murder."

"There was nothing childish about what I did."

"You're a little late trying to protect your daughter."

"You mean *our* daughter," I remind him.

He falls silent, then gives me a serious look. Zena's existence is proof of his true character. If the news gets out, especially now, it'll ruin him. That's why he's here—I know it.

"That's never been confirmed. I only laid with you once, and even in your young age, you seduced me. You got me drunk and victimized me."

"I was sixteen. You were a grown man. You poured the wine and called me beautiful. You bought me my first paintbrush and guided my hand on the canvas. You kissed me with those foul lips, then lowered me to the bed and climbed on top of me. Zena is the only good thing that came out of that mishap."

"You're lying. You and your mother are really made from the same cloth. She tried to get me, too, but it didn't work." He applauds himself.

"The world's going to know the truth about you. And so will my father."

He snickered sarcastically. "You sure about that?"

"I'm positive. Just leave my family alone. Disappear."

"I made your father a promise."

"And broke every single one."

"What do you know about me and your father's promises? You were just a kid."

"Just like I was a kid when you gave me a child at only sixteen and then denied us both. I've kept your secret long enough. No longer will these secrets consume me. I'm telling Zena about you, and then I'm going to tell the world. I couldn't think of a better time—with everybody being so sensitive about child molestation these days."

He clenches his jaw, lips pressed tight. I know that look—he's trying to hide how nervous he is.

"I knew this day would come," he mutters. "Your siblings are busting their asses to keep you out of jail. Too bad when you get out, half of them are going in—and there ain't shit you can do about it," he scoffs.

"What are you talking about?"

He leans forward, clasping his hands together and smiling like the ball is back in his court.

"I've been ordering my steps—planning for this very moment. Kind of getting insurance. Kwame will definitely get locked up once word gets out that he threw that last game. He's done. You don't mess with white Americans and their football. They'll nail his sorry ass to the cross. And Essence, boy oh boy... she's been involved in money laundering. I got people who are willing to testify about that dope dealing brother of yours. Sahara and her husband? They are at my mercy. And Balanah? I'll just leave her to herself. I don't need her. You fuck me, I fuck them," he says with a wink.

I stare at him, trying to figure out how much of what he said is true. If *any* of it is true, I'm not calling his bluff on anything. Sir Zion has a snake-like character and a heart made of stone. He cared nothing about us or our father. He always envied my father—tried to walk in his shoes, but the people never loved him the same. Now he's out for revenge. Taking down my father's children will give him a twisted sense of power. I know how much my siblings did for me. They've gone hard for me, and I don't want what I did to affect the rest of their lives. It's too much of a gamble, and I'm not willing to gamble with the lives of people I love.

"What do you want?"

"Call off this madness. It threatens to bring too much attention to too many unnecessary things. You know the press. They'll start digging and digging until they reach straight through to hell. I don't need that. Tell your sisters to stand down. Say you want to pay for your crime. Take the noble route...like your father." He shrugs.

"Then what?"

"I'll leave them alone. Forever. You have my word."

"Your word is mud."

He shrugs like my statement doesn't faze him.

"Deal or not?" He offers his hand.

I think for several minutes, then decide I won't make a deal with the devil.

"The only thing we share is a daughter—and she'll never be yours like she's mine. Do what you need to do. Who's gonna believe a child molester?"

"You were almost seventeen. Legal in this state."

"But I wasn't seventeen. And for all anyone knows, I was thirteen the first time."

I stare him down, letting the threat hang in the air.

"You liar!" he shouts, slamming the table with his fist.

"Stay the fuck away from my family, and I might not tell the world you started fucking me when I was only thirteen. Deal?"

I hold out my hand for a shake, but he doesn't take it. Instead, he jumps up, knocking over the chair, and storms out.

What a scoundrel of a man he is.

* * * * *

Before I can step into my cell, Tweety's flagging me down.

"Ms. Ebony! Ms. Ebony!" she yells like she just hit the lottery.

She rushes over to me, panting hard. She leans on my shoulder to catch her breath.

"What now?" I ask.

"Whew." She fans her face and blows out air. "I just got off the phone with my lawyer."

"What he say?" I roll my eyes.

"She," she says, grinning.

"She? You got a new lawyer?"

"Yep. Guess what her name is?"

"Girl, don't play with me. Am I supposed to know her?" I ask, exasperated.

I turn to walk into my cell, and Tweety follows close behind.

"You should. It's your sister."

I stop dead in my tracks.

"What type of games is somebody playing with you? My sister ain't no lawyer. She hasn't even finished school yet."

"Well, I just got a call from her. She said you recommended her. Sahara Sedah. She said if I listen to everything she says, she can help me. She's even bossier than you.

I know she's telling the truth now. What did Sahara have up her sleeve? If Sahara's representing Tweety, I'm pretty sure she's representing me, too. That means I really got a chance at coming out of this.

I smile. "Congratulations!"

"That's not all. She found my baby, too."

"That fast?"

Tweety nods. "Uh-huh."

"Where was she?"

"Right where you said she was—next door with my neighbor and her daddy." Her face twists with anger. "You was right about everything, Ms. Ebony. I'm turning his ass in, and he better pray I don't shoot him for trying to steal my child. Both of them better pray."

"Don't do nothing stupid. Don't be like me. Be better than me. I'm proud of you for making the right choice."

"Yeah…me, too. Feels like the first time I've done something right. Well, the second time. First was when I didn't let my baby daddy force me to have an abortion," she says with pride.

"Good for you. Keep it up." I sit on my bed.

"Your sister said I might be out of here in a week. Can you believe that? When I first got here, I thought my life was over. Then I met you. Now I feel like I'm getting a second chance."

I don't like taking credit for Tweety's growth, but if she's grateful for my help in getting her there, I suppose I did something good.

She stretches out her arms for a hug. I give it to her, then kick her out—I need rest. But that wasn't going to happen. As soon as she walks out, in walks the girl who killed her baby.

Her name's Antonia Washington. The news told me that much, but I got her to tell me her nickname—Toni. I hope I'm not letting Officer Rachel down, but I don't know what to do with Toni. I think I'm making some progress. Toni's talking more, and she's stopped wandering the halls like a zombie. I think the picture I sketched on a piece of notebook paper of a mother holding her baby helped. She stared at it so hard, I thought she'd burn a hole through it. Then she held it against her chest like the picture was her own child. That's when I knew she wasn't crazy; she's just hurt. She regrets what she did, and if she has regret, that means someone else probably pushed her to do it. She hasn't told me that part yet, but I feel that's the case.

"Hey, Toni girl. Tell me something good," I say.

She doesn't respond.

"You wanna know what I did that was good today?"

She looks at me and answers yes through her eyes.

"I told a lowlife to go to hell. Should've done it years ago. How about that?"

Toni smiles for half a second, then curls up on her bed and pulls the covers up to her neck.

"Sometimes, the bad things we do—or let happen to the people we love—can possess us like demons. They can haunt us, eat us alive, until we got nothing left but hollowness. But thinking about the good we've done? That helps. I was missing my child today, but when I told that man to go to hell, I felt...better. Balanced. You ever done something good?"

She shrugs her shoulders from underneath the sheet.

"Come on," I coax. "Give me something. Anything. It could've been saving a cat from a tree or helping an old lady cross the street. Tell me what you did? I know you did something good before."

"I helped my grandmama when she got sick," she whispers.

"Now that's a real good one." I swing my legs around and sit at the edge of my bed. "How'd you help her?"

"She got this illness that not even the doctors could explain. She couldn't hold down no food, got confused, and needed a bedpan. The church fasted and prayed, but when she didn't get healed, they said God was punishing her for past sins. Mama told us to stay away. Said a demon had her. But I couldn't. I felt bad for my granny. I started sneaking into her room to clean her up, keep her company, and whatnot. Two minutes before she died, she looked at me, said thank you, that she loved me, and that God would bless me good for what I did. First words she spoke in weeks, but she said them to me."

"Wow," I say, thinking to myself that kind of heart doesn't kill a baby for no reason.

I felt sorry for her. Ignorant religious people can be worse than the devil when they're full of judgment. If they really knew God's love, they wouldn't weaponize it. They wouldn't use God's words to evoke fear and spread hate. God ain't in none of that. But I saw God in Toni the way she helped her grandmother.

"God ain't gonna bless me no more, though. I messed that up," she says, looking like she's about to slip into a daze. I don't want that.

"Why you say that?" I ask.

"You saw the news. You know what I did."

"You went to church a lot, right?"

"Every day except Tuesday," Toni responds.

"Then you should know God forgives. He'll forgive anybody who means it and who can forgive themselves. He's not like the rest of us humans. He forgives and forgets. He doesn't hold grudges. Didn't they teach you that?"

She shrugs.

"They taught that sex before marriage sends you to the lake of fire."

"Is that all they taught you?"

"How to dress, not reveal too much of myself. Not to grow up a Jezebel. But I had that baby."

"A baby is a blessing, no matter how it got here. Just look at it as God's mercy."

"I know. He was merciful enough to forgive me the first time, but the second time, I was playing with His mercy. If Mama or the church found out about that second baby, I would've been doomed. They'd send me to the repentance chamber."

"The what?"

"A program my pastor started. Said it's to chastise us, the youth, for our sins. Once you go in there, you don't wanna do nothing to go back. He says if we think the repentance chamber is bad, imagine hell."

I've heard of abusive churches, but this...

"What happens there?" I ask.

She doesn't answer. Just stares at me like she exposed a secret.

"People don't understand my pastor. He loves us. Calls us his flock. He ain't bad."

"I didn't say he was," I say, hiding my contempt for the man. "I'm just curious about it, is all. I've never heard of that method before."

"We ain't supposed to talk about it. It's sacred. He said an angel gave him the vision one day. It has saved so many lives. One boy was gay. After a few weeks in the chamber, he came out straight. He's married now with children."

Poor woman married to a still-gay, traumatized man, I think to myself.

"Why's it called a chamber?"

"Because it's underground behind the pastor's house. Used to be a bomb shelter. He prayed and fasted over it forty days and forty nights before he started using it. Now angels protect it."

"You been in it?"

She hesitates, then nods. "After I got pregnant with my first baby."

"What was it like?"

"Scary. Dark. Cold. Painful," she whispers. "I had to walk on hot coals to prove my faith. Do a dry fast. Got whipped with a horse whip across my back. Slept in a pig pen. Pastor says that's how God views sin—like filth. So, he makes us lay in it so we can feel what God feels when we sin. Those pigs are nasty. I had to lay my head in their mess. I never wanna go back!"

I'm stunned. People can be so dangerously ignorant.

"How long have you been a part of that church?"

"Since I was born. My mama went there when she was a young girl. So did my daddy."

"Have they been in the chamber?"

"Mama has. Daddy hasn't."

"How long was you in there?"

"Two weeks," she says in a faint voice.

"Two weeks without food or water?"

"I deserved it," she snaps. "Just like I deserve this now. I tried to hide the second baby. I couldn't let Mama know I was pregnant again. Hid it for nine months. Then, I gave birth to her in the bathroom all by myself. Had that baby a month, and nobody ever knew. Sometimes I had to leave her by herself for hours while I attended church, went to work, or cleaned the house. I would hide her in my closet. When I came back, she would be hungry and soaking wet in her own mess. But what could I do? I couldn't stomach the thought of going back to that chamber. I still have nightmares about it."

She starts crying.

"When I returned home one day, my baby was such a mess that my whole closet smelled. So, I snuck and gave her a bath while Mama was downstairs cooking. Daddy was still at work, and my other little one was napping. My baby was fussy from being hungry and wouldn't stop crying. So, I dipped her in that water and tried my best to keep her quiet. Then Mama called for me. I knew if I didn't go see what she wanted, she would come up the steps. I couldn't chance her hearing the baby crying. So, I jumped up and rushed downstairs to the kitchen. Mama needed me to run out to her garden to pick a few tomatoes and cucumbers for the salad she was making for dinner. I did what she said and got back as soon as I could. But one of the tomatoes wasn't good enough for Mama, so she made me go pick another one. By the time I got back upstairs, my baby wasn't crying anymore. She was floating in the water. She was dead."

I run to her and wrap her in my arms, rocking her like she's a baby herself.

"It's okay, Toni. It's okay," I whisper.

It's the only thing I knew to say. What do you say after hearing a story like that? I don't blame her for not wanting to go back to that chamber. She was desperate and delusional. She didn't purposely kill her baby either. I knew there was more to her story.

"I put her in a trash bag and threw it out with the garbage. That's how they found out. That's how I got here. I didn't mean to. I let my sin kill my own child. I didn't mean to," she wails.

"I know you didn't."

I hold her tighter. She don't need judgment. She needs help.

I've got to make another deal with Sahara. If she wants to save me, she's gonna have to understand I'm a package deal. I came with Tweety. Now I'm coming with Toni. We all need saving.

I guess that's what Officer Rachel meant by trying to get through to this girl. But she didn't need anyone to get through to her. She needed someone to listen and not judge. She's had enough of that in her lifetime. Poor girl. Poor baby. And that poor congregation—led by a pastor who doesn't know God at all.

Yeah, I have one more deal to make with Sahara. And hopefully, this'll be the last one.

34

SAHARA

"It's Not Easy Being a Bitch"

I'm sitting behind the ash-colored desk in my study, flipping through case law similar to Ebony's when John walks in and looks over my shoulder. I quickly cover the open books with blank sheets of paper so he can't see what I'm doing.

"So you passed the bar?" John asks, holding an envelope addressed to me.

I found out I had miraculously passed the grueling exam a few days after taking it. The results were computerized, allowing me to access my score online. John is just now catching on.

I couldn't believe I passed. I mean, I prayed to pass. I hoped to pass. I crossed my fingers and kissed the sky. But the fear of failure haunted me once the test ended. I couldn't sleep, torturing myself with ill predictions of my results. Some questions were familiar, things I had learned in law school. Others seemed like they came from outer space because I hadn't seen or heard them in my life. It felt like one big coin toss. But I passed—and I have God to thank for that. Faith carried me through. I gave myself a quick pat on the back and got straight to work. No time to celebrate. Ebony's hearing is a week away, and I have a case to win. A few cases. Ebony added another girl to my workload. I hope she doesn't make a habit of this. I don't have time to save the world. Just her.

"Oh, yeah...I didn't tell you?" I say with a vindicated smile.

John looks stunned. For once, he doesn't have a smart-ass comment or sarcastic smirk. He's completely thrown.

"No...I didn't even know you finished law school. When did all this happen? Though your sneaky behavior doesn't shock me."

"Sneaky behavior?" I laugh. "That's funny. You're the one whose been doing a lot sneaky shit. I mean, I'm not the one cozying up with Becca and paling around with scum like Sir Zion. Now *that's* sneaky. I'm sure your constituents would agree."

"Excuse me?" he snaps, trying to hide the fear in his eyes. "I wouldn't advise you to try and blackmail me."

"Blackmail you?" I pout mockingly. "You're my husband. What type of wife would blackmail her own husband?"

John studies me, like he's trying to read my mind—or should I say the calm, calculated look on my face. But I don't let him see the plans I have for him. That would take all the fun out of it and ruin the element of surprise. I can't wait to see his face when I betray him the way he betrayed me.

"I think you misunderstood what you saw the other day at the Chocolate Bar," he begins. "I was having lunch with my personal assistant—a devoted campaign volunteer. She'll attest to that herself. And Sir Zion just happened to come in randomly. You know how many people a senator-elect runs into daily basis? It meant nothing."

"Of course it didn't, John." I smile sweetly, like the Stepford wife he tried to mold me into.

"I've worked too hard on this campaign to let it fall apart. Too hard, Sahara. You, of all people, should know that."

"I do. You worked very hard," I nod and smile.

"I hope I have your continued cooperation and support with helping me win this thing."

"Anything you need, dear."

"Why are you doing this? Is this about Becca? Because if it is, I told you—"

"No," I say, cutting him off. "I actually like Becca...and so do the kids."

I give him a cold stare.

"They've only met her once! She's my assistant, for crying out loud. I can't have a female assistant now?" He waves his hands in the air.

"A busy man like you? Of course, you need an assistant. There's nothing wrong with that. It's not like you're fucking her...or promising to marry her...or parading her around your high-powered friends like some trophy, right?"

I raise my brow at him, waiting for his response. He just nods, clearly deep in thought.

I turn back to the papers spread across the desk. Funny, I've lived in this house for years and never used this desk. The study was one of the main reasons I wanted to buy the house. I pictured myself here—researching, working cases—but it never happened. Until now. And John no longer fits into that vision. Just like I don't fit in his.

"People are asking about the Christmas party," he says. "Folks from the office, a few neighbors..."

He needs me. I'm the reason those Christmas parties were legendary. They boosted his social and corporate climb, brought life to his boring colleagues, and became the unofficial kickoff to the political holiday season. But this year? He can go to hell.

"Why don't you ask your assistant to help you plan it this year? I'm sure she knows what you need."

"She's not paid for that."

I shrug. "Then give her a raise. She's put in enough *overtime*."

"There you go again." He starts pacing. "Insinuating."

"I'm doing no such thing. I just assumed you'd rather have Becca by your side this year. Will she be attending the party?"

"Will you be attending your sister's trial?" he blurts, folding his arms across his chest and looming over me like I'm a misbehaving toddler.

"Front and center," I reply proudly.

"What?! I thought we agreed that you were going to stay out of that mess!"

"No. *You* agreed. I never said anything."

"So you're going to get your face and my name on the front page of every newspaper in this city—right before my campaign?!"

"I'm not just attending. I'm representing her, John."

"What?!" His eyes bulge, and he throws his long arms in the air like he's about to fly.

Right then, I start to tune him out, focusing more on my notes than his ranting. I remove the papers covering my books. I'm done hiding it. Every now and again, I catch bits of his rant—"ingrate," "humiliation," "ghetto"— and a bunch of other choice words he's using to try to bait me into responding, but I'm over it...and him.

"You finished?" I ask. "I have work to do."

"If you do this shit, we're done! Remember what I told you?"

"Yeah. Now you remember what I'm about to tell you."

I push back in my rolling leather chair and lock eyes with him. I need him to know that he can't scare me into being his puppet anymore. I take a deep breath while John looks like he's holding his breath, fearfully anticipating what I'm about to say to him.

"You threaten to take my kids again, and I swear...not only will you lose this bullshit election—you'll never work in this city again. I talked to Sir Zion and your little precious ivy plant, Becca..." I lie, but it lands. His eyes widen and his brows lift so high I think his face might split. "And I know everything."

"What? You're being ridiculous—"

"Shut up." He obeys. "I'm doing the talking now. Here's how it's going to go: I'm going to help you win this election, and you're going to help me get my sister out of jail. Then we're going our separate ways, which means you're getting your white-washed, phony ass out of my house. Oh, and you're going to pay me for every damn year I spent being your wife, your prop, your caretaker."

"You…I'm not…" John huffs like he's having an asthma attack.

He knows the deal, and the look in my eyes tells him I'm dead serious.

"Now if you don't mind, I have work to do."

"What about the announcement? It's next week. And the Christmas party? I *need* that party to happen to win."

"It'll all be arranged once you get behind me with Ebony."

"I can't touch that case. It's too…messy. Child molestation? Taking someone's manhood? It's too much!"

"I just need contacts and promises. That's all. You don't have to go public with anything."

John stares at me, considering what I said. That's when I know he *really* wants to win. And that's exactly why I'll win, too.

"I don't know what I can do."

"You'll figure something out. I'll let you know what I need once I'm done with all my research."

"What about the announcement?"

"I'll be there." I give him a serious look.

He nods hesitantly, then storms out the front door.

I smile at my boldness—just for a second—then get back to work.

It's not easy being a bitch. But sometimes, it's not hard at all.

35
MALICHAI
"The Body"

I have to identify a dead body today. Of all the shit I had planned, this wasn't one of them.

I'm sitting in this freezing room at Grady Hospital, numb. It feels like I'm dreaming, but strangely enough, it doesn't feel like a nightmare. I don't even know what it feels like. I guess I won't know until I see the body.

The body. That's what the nurses, examiners, doctors—or whatever you call the people who deal with dead folks—keep calling the person I've loved for almost all of my life.

"Mr. Sedah, please sign here to view 'the body'."

"Mr. Sedah, someone will walk you in soon to see 'the body'."

"Mr. Sedah, any special instructions on how you would like us to handle 'the body'?"

That body is a person—well, *was* a person—I gave my life for. I keep waiting for the moment this all hits me, but for now, I just feel numb.

Why the hell do they have it so cold down here? Feels like I'm sitting in a freezer. Maybe that's why I'm so numb, inside and out. I'm too cold to feel. Or maybe I just don't want to feel it. Maybe they keep it like this to preserve the bodies. I ain't never seen a real dead body before. I've seen dudes shot, bleeding out, but they survived. And I didn't know or care enough about them to give a fuck.

The call came an hour after I got a lead on Zena. I was with Natasha at the time. We've been hanging real tight lately. Only on a friendship tip, though. Zach was with us, and she practically begged me to let her keep him. I was in a rush to get to the club and find my niece, so I took her up on her offer.

When I found Zena, I also found Zionah. I didn't even know she was missing. I guess I killed two birds with one stone by finding them together. I tried stopping by Mama's house on the way to Balanah's so she could see Zena, but she wasn't home. Hasn't been answering her phone lately either. Now that I think about it, I don't remember the last time I heard from her. Balanah said she stopped by her place the other day, too, and couldn't find her. Before I could get worried about Mama missing, the hospital called.

I didn't explain anything to Balanah. Just sped off, like my presence could somehow undo what happened. I hated leaving Zena so soon, but she didn't say much anyway. When I hugged her, she felt empty. Barely looked at me, and I barely looked at her. With Zionah in the backseat, talking a mile a minute about everything except for what was going on, I started to feel awkward. I didn't know what to say to Zena. What could I say? What happened to her happened under my nose, and I failed her. I was too wrapped up in my crooked lifestyle to be the uncle she needed. I can see in her eyes that she knows I failed. She looked exhausted, too—like she hadn't slept in years. Maybe she hasn't. If I could rock her to sleep again like I used to, I would. But she's too old for lullabies. I'll have to figure out another way to ease her pain.

My legs are stiff, so I stand and stretch. When I do, I hear a popping sound in my knee. I roll my neck, shake out my legs, and stretch my arms. Then I walk over to the door and peep out into the hallway. I feel like I'm in an indoor cemetery—a temporary cemetery for *'the bodies'* that are claimed. A lady in blue scrubs is standing in the hallway, talking with another, then glances in my direction. When I make eye contact with her, she gives me a weird look and whispers something to the other lady, who looks up at me with the same weird expression on her face. I don't know what the hell that was about, and honestly, it doesn't matter. Nothing ever will again.

A heavy wave of emotion hits. Pressure builds in my chest. I breathe in deeply, trying to hold it together. I sit back down, crack my knuckles, and start fidgeting with my phone—anything to distract myself from the reality of what's going on right now. The truth is, I feared this would happen, but I buried that fear the way I bury everything else.

I wonder what the family will say. I don't want to tell them. I want to pretend none of this is real. Pretend Ebony's not locked up. Zena was never sexually assaulted as a child. Mama's not missing. That pretending feels easier. I entertain that way of thinking for a few seconds, but then I realize grown-ups don't play pretend. We have no time for it.

I think about Zach and how Natasha is managing with watching him. I'm pretty sure she's got her hands full. She's been helping me get my business plan together and even signed me up to take my GED online. I don't know why she believes in me the way she do, but I'm blessed that she does because she's finally got me believing in myself, too. She makes me feel like I can conquer the world. If I had paid her more attention back then instead of chasing the street life, who knows where I'd be now? Can't cry over spilled milk, though. All I can do is wipe it up clean.

I think about texting Natasha to tell her where I am. I don't want her thinking I'm some bum who abandoned Zach. So, I pull out my phone and start pressing buttons. I only meant to tell her I would be running a little late picking up Zach, but before I know it, the words "the body," "hospital," and "dead" spill out. She texts back immediately, but I don't bother to read it. Before I can put the phone back in my pocket, she calls. But I send it straight to voicemail and then turn my phone off. I don't feel like talking—at least I don't think I do.

I stuff my phone deep in my jacket pocket. When I pull my hand out, I'm holding the scratch-off ticket Essence gave me—the first gift she's ever given me and the most thoughtful one. I almost forgot about that card. I don't know why I collect them. Maybe I believe someone else's hope will rub off on me, and I'll catch a break.

Usually, the cards I find have already been scratched, but this one is new, unscratched. To keep my mind occupied, I read the card, even the fine print on the back. Then I start feeling anxious and crumple the card into a ball, tossing it around like I'm playing ping-pong. Then I hear footsteps.

The ball drops near my foot. My heart stops. Is it time?

No. The footsteps pass.

I exhale, part relief, part frustration. I'm not ready, but at the same time, I want to get it over with.

I pick up the balled-up ticket and smooth it out with my index finger. It's still creased, but not ruined. I stare at it for a while. The $250,000 prize catches my eye. What would I do with that kind of money? If I could, I'd spend every dime just to bring the body back to life. But I can't.

I fold the ticket up and stuff it back inside my pocket. Then, I pull out my phone and power it on, thinking maybe I'll listen to Natasha's voice message. I wouldn't mind hearing her soft voice. I almost call but hang up before dialing the last two digits.

I stand and stretch again. For some reason, I have the urge to punch something. I ain't punched nobody in years, but one person I wouldn't mind punching is Kenton. I see myself knocking the hell out of his sick ass, punching him so hard that somebody will have to identify his body. Then I think about Sir Zion. Yeah, I can give him a good one-two hook to the chin. Next, I think about punching myself. I see it so vividly. I almost want to act it out right here in this room. I'm so angry at myself that I just want to punch myself and bang my head against the block wall. I don't know why I'm so mad at myself, but I am. I feel like I deserve to be punched.

I clench and release my fists. Breathe deep. And suddenly, I'm crying.

Tears stream quietly down my face—neat, manly tears. I don't sob. Just cry. When I stop clenching and releasing my fists, I wipe the tears from my cheeks and sniff. Then I sit back down. But as soon as my butt hits the cushioned seat, I feel crushed. My head hangs. The tears are flowing again—but this time, I feel myself sobbing. I try to stop myself by taking a quick deep breath. I breathe in too quickly, though, because I swallow a tear and start choking on my saliva. Now I'm coughing while sobbing uncontrollably.

Enough, I tell myself.

I jump up, fists tight, and start pounding my chest like I can beat the pain out of me. I hiccup, then breathe. Finally, the tears stop, and I sit back down. Using the neck of my shirt, I wipe away the tears. I feel numb again, like I pressed pause on everything. Then—footsteps. This time, I count them. There were approximately twenty steps before the nurse from earlier, who was giving me the weird look, stops in front of the door and calls my name like I'm an inmate.

"Malichai Sedah?" she says, looking at the clipboard she's holding.

I don't look up. I figure maybe if I ignore her, she'll go away—and so will this whole thing. But she only calls my name again, sounding a little annoyed with me. This time, I look up at her.

"We're ready for you to view the body."

I stand without realizing. I count our footsteps—mine slow, hers rushed.

"Wait here," she says.

I think I nod.

I'm in another room—bigger, colder. The floor looks the same, though. White linoleum tiles. I won't look up. I can't. I start counting the floor tiles by twos and then threes. A man's voice interrupts me.

"Mr. Sedah?"

He looks Middle Eastern. Or Indian. I don't know. Does it matter?

I follow behind him, counting his footsteps, as well. When he stops, I stop counting.

"Mr. Sedah, do you know why you're here?"

"Yeah," I snap, annoyed.

Unmoved by my attitude, he doesn't waste any more time. He pulls back the white sheet, revealing 'the body.' My eyes zoom in on the stiff corpse. Face frozen in fear. Fingers curled like it was trying to fight death. I can't believe who I'm looking at. When my tear drips onto 'the body's' forehead, I realize I'm crying again.

"Sir, I need you to—"

"It's her!" I yell without taking my eyes off the body. "Tameka Smith. My fiancée."

I turn to leave. I can't look at the horror trapped on the face of the woman I have loved for years—a horror I couldn't rescue her from. It was too late.

"Sir, you need to sign—"

He rushes by my side and shoves his clipboard in my face. I scribble my signature, not even reading it. I could've been signing over my soul—I didn't care. I just want to hurry and get out of here.

"Will you be back for the body?" he asks flatly.

"Her name is Tameka. Tameka!" I snap, storming off down the hallway.

In the elevator, I try not to think of how she looked on that stretcher—skin gray, lips cracked, hair a mess. She looked like a bag of bones with flesh dangling off of her, so frail and helpless. And her face? She had a grimace like she had seen the Grim Reaper right before dying.

When did this happen? How did this happen? Was she calling for me? Was she afraid? Did she suffer? I hadn't seen Meka since she left the new house. I told myself I wouldn't chase her this time. I let her go. And now she's gone. I should've gone after her. If I had gone and gotten her like I always did, she wouldn't have overdosed. I should've protected her. It's my fault. My fault she got hooked; my fault she overdosed. That's what I get for dreaming—thinking I could have the different life that Natasha painted for me. If you sleep on a situation for one minute, you might wake up and find everything is fucked. I deserve to be on that slab. Not Meka!

As I'm getting off the elevator, I hear somebody call my name. Am I hallucinating? No. It's Essence. She was getting on. Eyes red, she falls into my arms. I start sobbing with her. How did she know about Meka? I wonder if Natasha told her.

"How did you know?" she cries. "I've been trying and trying to get everybody on the phone, but nobody answered my calls."

"Wavy called me. How did you—"

"Wavy? Who? What?" Essence pulls away and wipes the tears from her eyes while giving me a confused look. "What are you talking about, Mal?"

"Meka."

"What about Meka?"

"She's…she's dead," I force myself to say. "Ain't that why you're here?"

Essence gasps, covering her mouth. She gives me a sorrowful look and shakes her head regretfully before bursting into more tears.

"I'm so sorry, Mal. But that's not why I'm here. This is…this is going to be too much for you."

"What are you talking about, Essence?" I ask, staring into her tearful eyes.

"I…I can't. It's too much," she sobs.

"Tell me!"

She chokes on the words, then blurts out, "Kwame!"

She collapses to her knees, crying uncontrollably.

She was right. I *couldn't* take it.

I think I'm falling to my knees to console my little sister, but it turns out, I'm just too weak myself. We both hold each other, crying. People rush over to calm us.

Shit! Another body.

36

THE MAMA
"It's Time"

I always wondered what it felt like to be a paraplegic—to have your body betray you, refusing to move no matter how many times you beg it to. Now I know. It's awful.

For the last two weeks, I've been telling myself to get off this bed, move, go home. But I can't. My brain and body are no longer on one accord. I'm paralyzed by grief so deep it knocked the breath out of me. How do I breathe again? How do I get out of this bed? How do I deal with the reality that my king, the great Akimbo Sedah, is dead?

I don't move. That's how I cope. But now, it's time.

By now, I should realize life rarely goes as planned. I never imagined my daughter would be in jail for attempted murder. Or my son selling crack. Or that the dream my king had for his family and his people would turn into a nightmare. Yet, here it is—reality. Reality that is so crystal clear, it can't be mistaken for anything else. It is what it is. No pretending. No excuses. No reasoning. Still, the news of his death shocks me. I really have my nerve. I've been optimistic to a fault. Now, I have to face it. But how?

When I walked into that prison, I was anxious. Hopeful. Naïve. Boy, did I set myself up for failure. I didn't know three words—*He was killed*—could hit harder than a ton of bricks. Now I'm paralyzed with pain, drowning in fear, and hopeless beyond measure. Some might say, *What's the big deal? You haven't seen him in years. That's just like him being dead.* But it wasn't. Not to me. Just knowing he was out there—breathing the same air, looking up at the same sky—gave me peace. I drew strength from the idea that his soul, his heart, his mind were still alive. But now, he's gone. And I never got to say goodbye.

I should've known something was wrong when they put me in that small, hot room with cinder block walls. I sat alone for almost thirty minutes before a white chaplain came in, holding a Bible and wearing a look of scripted sympathy. However, even then, I remained optimistic. I thought maybe my king sent him to turn me away. Or maybe it was protocol. Maybe he was there to warn me that Akimbo may not be the same person I remembered. But deep down, I knew. I just didn't want to believe it. I still don't.

He began by saying he had both good and bad news. I was confused. However, I was crying long before he confessed what he thought was good and bad news. Inside, my spirit knew a truth my flesh wasn't accepting.

"The bad news is Mr. Sedah has passed on to the other world," the chaplain told me in a soft, even tone. "The good news is he's in paradise forever." Then he gently squeezed my hands and asked if I wanted to pray with him. I don't remember my answer. My mind was stuck, refusing to register that my king was gone.

He read Psalm 23. I tried to focus on the scripture, anything to block out the horror that was starting to seep into my spirit. Then he stopped, patted my shoulder, and left. At that moment, I felt like I was having some sort of out-of-body experience. For a while, I told myself I was dreaming. That I'd wake up in my cheap hotel room, go back to the prison, and laugh with my king about my nightmare. Then he'd give me a profound interpretation of my dream, and we'd kiss like the first time. But I never woke up.

Two officers came in, holding a medium-sized box with Akimbo's name in bold lettering across the top. They placed it gently on the table in front of me. I couldn't stop staring, like the box itself was him.

I think the officers were nice to me. I really can't remember. They removed their hats upon entering the room as a sign of respect. One picked up my hand and shook it like it was an honor to touch me. Then they explained what happened. I don't know how, but I remember every word they said.

Somewhere between their explanations and apologies, I grazed my hand across the box, and with my index finger, traced the lettering of his name. I felt his energy through the box. I placed my palm on it, and warmth radiated back. I closed my eyes, captured the energy in my fist, held it like a lightning bug, and felt it spread up my arm to my chest—strengthening me and starting the slow healing of my heart. At that moment, I felt like my king's spirit was in the room with me. I swear I smelled the sweet aroma of sandalwood and patchouli oils that he bathed his body in daily and felt the weight of his hand on my shoulder.

The two officers spoke highly of him. Said he brought honesty and integrity to the prison, changing the way it operated. He even helped expose the inner corruption that was occurring among some of the prison guards. Maybe that's what got him killed. They didn't say he was murdered. They used the term *assassinated*. My king—killed like a dog on the street. When I asked how, they paused—uncomfortable, shifting their weight around in the chairs, and avoiding eye contact with me. I could tell they didn't want to tell me how, but I needed to know. I deserved to know. But when they told me, I regretted ever asking.

A makeshift knife. Throat, chest, side. In the shower. That's what ended my king's life. He must have choked on his own blood after they slit his throat. He probably fell to his knees when they stabbed him in the chest. As he was on his hands and knees, gagging and fighting for his last few breaths, he probably watched the water rinse his blood away, sweeping it down the drain like sewage. He must've felt so alone. Or even worse, defeated and hurt. But even then, I know he forgave his killers. Even though I would like to think his last thoughts were of me and his children, I know he prayed for them with his last breath. That's who he was. And it would be an insult to him for me to assume otherwise.

I closed my eyes tightly, trying to fight away the bloody image I had in my mind of my king. It was hard; it still is. I clenched my fist tighter, nails digging into my palm. I needed his energy now more than ever, but it wasn't enough. I took a deep breath, and when I finally exhaled, my sobs poured out like his blood. One officer wrapped his arm around my shoulders as I cried. When I calmed down, I wiped away my tears, placed my hand on the box, and gathered myself. I had to be strong. He wouldn't want me broken.

The officers finished their statements by saying they thought I knew he was dead. But the department that was supposed to inform family members of deceased inmates had failed to do their job, claiming a clerical error. More corruption. They naturally assumed I didn't want to claim his body. Who could blame them? Years of no visitors, no outgoing or incoming mail. They assumed I abandoned him. So, they burnt his body like it was trash and stacked the ashes on a shelf with the rest of the unclaimed and unloved. They assured me there would be an investigation, but what difference does it make now? I guess they were just trying to make me feel better.

My king has been dead for two years. Two years. Nobody knew. His death—hidden like a state secret. If the media knew my king had died, it would've sparked all kinds of outrage from his supporters. There would've been a public investigation regarding his death, and the corporate coward involved would have been forced out of hiding to face a world of anger. But that didn't happen. Not yet.

Before the officers left, they told me someone wanted to see me—his cellmate. I didn't feel like entertaining my husband's protégé and being strong for him. But I had to. I had to do it for my king.

Not long after they left the room, a young man about Malichai's age and height walked in. He was wearing the staple prison gear—an orange jumpsuit and shackles around his wrists and ankles—and carrying a box that caused me to raise a curious eyebrow as he placed it on the table before taking a seat. At first sight, I felt an instant mix of remorse and love for this young man. The moment he saw me, tears slipped down his cheeks. I gently wiped them away. He said he'd heard so much about me that he felt like he personally knew me—like I was his mother. My heart warmed. Even after all these years, my king still spoke of me as his queen.

The young man's name was Adisa, meaning *"one who is clear."* I didn't need him to explain. I knew it was my king who inspired this young man's new name. His name told a story of the new beginning my king helped him achieve.

Ten years ago, Adisa had been hired by gangs and guards to kill my husband. But when he went to strike him, Akimbo grabbed his hand and embraced him. Adisa said the hug was so healing that he dropped his shank and embraced him back. From then on, he followed behind my king like a school child, soaking up his energy and learning all he could. My king provided protection for him and a slew of others, especially the new inmates who were subject to meaningless inductive brutality and even sexual assault. It became a joke that Akimbo had nine lives because he survived so many assassination attempts. They didn't look at him like he was a kitten, though. No, he was a bold, roaring lion. Once the inmates who ignorantly hated him started to love him, he changed their lives for the better. Even the warden took notice and allowed him the freedom to start programs, give seminars, and counsel inmates. Everybody trusted him.

Under his guidance, many of the inmates earned their GEDs. Some took it a step further and received college degrees—even law degrees. He solicited the state for money to build libraries and gave seminars, motivating men to be fathers to their children and husbands to their wives, even while behind bars. He raised fathers, healed broken spirits. The prison became a life-coaching boot camp. He changed lives. White men. Black men. All of them. And then— he was gone.

Adisa shared that my king was well loved and that his death was a shock to everyone—a hurt that traveled from cell to cell. Then came the confession.

"I think I know who killed him," he said, a tear slipping from his eye as he lowered his gaze to the floor.

The name he gave me almost knocked me out cold.

"Sir Zion."

I gagged at the mere mention of his name and the thought of his treacherous betrayal. Then my mind flashed back to the horrific moments when I allowed that man to touch me. I felt sick. Adisa called for the guards, but I sent them away. He had a story to finish, and I needed to hear it.

"It had to be him," he said. "Two days before he was up for parole? And he gets killed? That's too much of a coincidence."

My heart dropped at the thought of my husband returning home to me without warning, just as I had dreamed so many nights. But Sir Zion took that from me. He took so much from me.

"I knew Sir Zion from back when I was on the outside. I used to make runs for him. Drop-offs, pickups, you know the deal."

I nodded. I knew what he meant.

"He wanted me to kill Malichai," he said, speaking my son's name like he knew him personally. "But I shot the wrong person. I killed a good friend of his."

I knew who he was referring to.

"People on the street began to talk, and eventually, I got caught. But Sir Zion gave me one more job—to kill Akimbo. I didn't want to do it, but he threatened my family. Then I learned the truth from the guy who was my cellmate at the time. He told me why Sir Zion had been out to get Akimbo all those years. I didn't know anything about Akimbo at the time. I was too busy ripping and running the streets to take note of a hero. Back then, my hero was my nine-millimeter. But he told me why Akimbo was a hero to some and how he *really* ended up in prison. Your husband was innocent."

Then he confirmed what I knew all along. My king was framed. Set up by the same man who pretended to be his partner.

The body found in that building? Already dead. With the help of the county police department, Sir Zion planted it there. Crooked cops approached Sir Zion, offering him dirty money and status if he framed my husband for murder. My husband's partner was working against him the entire time. It all makes sense now. Even now, Sir Zion lurks, trying to gather enough dirt on my family to use as leverage to maintain his innocence. He's not strong like my king and couldn't survive a night in prison. That's why he wanted my king dead—because he knew the truth would come back to haunt him. Even now with all of this media surrounding Ebony's case, he fears his days walking the earth as a free man are numbered...and he's right.

Adisa went on to tell me that Akimbo spoke of me every night, during his seminars, and even drew pictures of my image and hung them on the walls of his cell. He said he never knew a man could love a woman the way my king loved me. Adisa revealed that my king felt much regret for not allowing me and his children to see him, but he feared for our safety and initially thought the visits would weaken him and cause more damage than good in our lives.

Before leaving, Adisa slid the box to me. Inside: drawings, books, pictures of him and inmates, and letters that he wrote to me and the children. One for every day he was locked up. I now understand why he never mailed the letters or wanted us around. He was trying to protect us. It was dangerous. He made many sacrifices to keep us safe. That's who he was.

I pulled the box into my chest and held it just like it were him.

"I'm so sorry, Mrs. Sedah," Adisa told me genuinely, as if everything was his fault.

I got up and hugged him. He gave me a gentle squeeze and kissed the back of my hand.

"It's been an honor," he said, slightly bowing his head at me.

Mustering up all the strength I had, I smiled at him as he left the room.

I still haven't opened the box yet. I don't know why. At first, I thought I'd be anxious to open it—ripping through it and sifting through its contents like it was a Christmas present. But when I got back to the hotel, I just broke down. I placed the box on the bed, wrapped my arms around the corners, and hugged it like it was my king.

Too many emotions were flowing through me. Mostly hurt. But hate, too. Deep hate for Sir Zion. But I can't let it consume me. He's taken so much from me and my family already. I won't allow him to take any more. His day will come. Justice will be served.

As I lay here, I think of Coretta Scott King and Malcolm X's wife, Betty Shabazz. Were they so broken from grief that they couldn't move? Maybe. But they didn't stay broken. They rose. If Coretta hadn't stood up, Dr. King's dream might've been forgotten. Will my king be forgotten because I stayed down? No. I won't let that happen. He won't go down in history as a murderer. His death won't be in vain. His legacy—inside and outside prison—will be known. His message will live on. Stronger than ever. It's time for me to take the torch and finish his works. There's a lot to do. It's time for me to get up.

On that note, I send the signal to my brain to move my legs, and

I don't know how I do it, but I swing my legs to the floor and sit up. I take a deep breath and then exhale all the sorrow. It's time for me to make a move. It's time for me to fill my husband's shoes. Come out of hiding and take his message to the next level. But first, I have to face my children. I have to let them know that their father fell in battle. That he died with honor. That's the most beautiful death a soldier can have.

It's time for me to go home.

37
ZENA
"No More Running"

E verybody's been pushing me to see my mother, and I've been pretty hesitant about it until now. This morning, I got up and left without saying a word. I hope nobody panics and thinks I'm on the run again. That's the last thing they need with everything going on lately. With Uncle Kwame in a coma and the news of my grandfather's murder, I don't want to add to anybody's burdens.

I've been staying with Grandma. She's been on the phone nonstop, tirelessly working on Mama's campaign and starting the process to vindicate my grandfather's name. When she's not doing that, she's right at Uncle Kwame's bedside, holding his hand and talking softly in his ear. She read somewhere that it might help him wake up sooner; he's been unconscious for two weeks now. It's weird to see him lying so helpless in a hospital bed, hooked up to all kinds of machines. I'm used to thinking of my uncle as a superhero, not a vegetable slowly wasting away. The whole thing is frightening and another emotion I'd rather avoid.

Grandma's been the main one encouraging me to go see Mama. I don't know where she draws the strength to take time out and concern herself with me, but that woman is one strong person. She even makes me feel stronger. Maybe she's drawing her strength from that Bible I see her toting around. Every so often, when she's not on the phone, at the jail, or at the hospital, I see her wearing her reading glasses and looking down at the Bible intently, silently mouthing the words as she reads them. If it's not her Bible giving her strength, it's definitely coming from the box on her bed with grandpa's name written across it.

I guess they gave her the box before she left the prison. I'm not sure, and she's not saying anything. She's even keeping it secret from my aunts and uncles. It would've still been a secret from me if I hadn't barged into her room one night and caught her drinking red wine, blasting a Marvin Gaye record, and thumbing through the box with a melancholy smile on her face. As soon as she saw me, she jumped like she was doing something wrong, closed the box, and put it behind her, out of my sight. When I asked her what it was, she told me now is not the time to know.

Every night at 11:00 p.m., I hear soft music playing, and Grandma closes her door, which she never does. I already know what's going on; she's getting reacquainted with years' worth of lost images of my grandfather. I don't pressure her about it because I know the news of his death had to be crushing for her. There's not a day that goes by that I don't remember her not talking about my grandfather. All of us grandchildren know him even though we never had the chance to meet him. But, with everything going on, she can't be weak. Not, at least, until after 11:00 p.m.

Even with everything that's going on, being at Grandma's house feels like therapy. It has such a peace about it, it's indescribable. When you step outside, you almost forget you're in the heart of an urban city. I've been waited on hand and foot, and although I told her she doesn't have to cook for me every night, I've grown to look forward to our intimate dinners on the floor of her dining area, complete with burning candles. I feel so safe that I don't guard my emotions or my tongue—I just talk. I let the hurt pour out of me, and Grandma listens without interruption. She keeps an even tone, a straight face, and an open mind—just what I need. Then she says something so profound that I have an epiphany, or at least a deep realization. She always closes our dinner sessions with the same question: *When are you going to stop running?* I never respond to her question; I just ponder it. Then, this morning, I woke up and had the answer. I decided that today is the day I stop running. So now, I'm here, waiting for my mother to enter the private room the guard so kindly offered us.

Everybody here knows who I am, prisoners and guards alike. But I guess that's no surprise given how often my face flashed across the TV. Strangely enough, I'm not getting the looks I dreaded. The looks that had me considering leaving the state to avoid them. Instead, people are encouraging me with their smiles and even looking at me with eyes of admiration. I instantly start to wonder what they're seeing in me that I'm not. Either way, it makes me feel respected and stronger to face my monsters.

It's been almost fifteen minutes, and there's still no sign of Mama. Does it really take this long? Maybe I'm calling Mama's bluff by being here, or maybe not. This room is freezing, too. I shudder and warm my goosebumped arms with my hands. I should have brought a jacket. Luckily for me, my surprise visit didn't tip off the press, and I was able to get in undetected, but I'm sure leaving will be another story. This room is small and stale. Everything about this place is so drab that it's no wonder there isn't a gray cloud hovering over the building. On second thought, I'm sure there is; it just can't be seen, only felt. I wonder if Mama's cell looks like this. It's definitely no place for an artist to be inspired. It's not even a place for a stray dog to live. With all that said, I'm starting to feel some kind of way now. My chest begins to swell, and my insides are swarming with pent-up emotions. I think it's just now starting to hit me that my mama is in jail. This ain't no movie or bad dream. It's real. She's living like this, and all because of her love for me.

Just when I start to fight back the very determined tears that are starting to fill my eyes, in walks Mama, all chained up. As soon as I see her, I instantly try to look away, but I can't. I just can't avoid her anymore. *No more running.* To my surprise, she doesn't look like all the things I assumed she would. She doesn't look crazy, deranged, or pathetic. The best I can describe her appearance is as a beautiful mess. There is something about that look in her eyes that draws me in. She's speaking to me without saying a word. She's saying *Forgive me, I'm sorry,* and *I love you* all at one time, and she's not asking anymore, but begging. Then I remember something. This look isn't new to me. I've seen it several times before. It was there when I first told her about Kenton, and it has been there every day since. But why am I reacting to it as if it's the first time I'm seeing it? Why is it only now that I'm starting to feel the intensity of it?

The chains jingle as the guard unlocks Mama. When they remove the cuffs from her wrists, she rubs them. I wonder how much the cuffs hurt against her skin. They must hurt a lot. The guard gives her a supportive pat on the back, then looks at me and smiles before walking away. I don't know what to do. Should I stand up or stay seated? Mama seems unsure, too. She's just standing in the same spot, staring at me as I stare at her, but she's not crying like I am. Somewhere between the staring and the tears, I have a flashback. I remember something else, as if it happened yesterday.

It was my first day of school, the first time I had been away from Mama for so long. I spent most of my time watching the door, waiting for her to come back. I wanted to see her face so badly. I wanted to hug her and feel her warm lips against my cheek. I missed her. And right now, I realize I still do.

I jump up and run toward her, feeling five years old again. I stretch out my arms and reach to embrace her, but before I can, she grabs me first and pulls me into her chest. She's hugging me so tightly, softly, and endearingly that I melt in her arms. Then she says it again—something I've heard her say a million times: "I'm sorry," but this time, I listen. I really, really listen. For the first time ever, I respond to her apology, telling her I forgive her, and now she's melting in my arms. Who would have thought that one hug and an "I forgive you" would end it all? Finally, after all these years...it feels like it's over.

No more running.

38

BALANAH

"The Difference a Year Makes"

December 2011

Time has flown by, and so much has changed. We're on our way to meet the family for dinner at Mama's favorite restaurant, Soul Vegetarian. It's within walking distance from her new house. It was thoughtful of Kwame to buy that house for Mama. It's beautiful, with a spacious kitchen and many windows that let light shine in from every corner. And it's still in her neighborhood—the West End. Buying Mama the house was the first thing he did as soon as he got up from the hospital bed. Well, the second. The first thing he did was divorce Tammy, but it's all for the best.

A few days ago, Ebony received a not-guilty verdict. I was shocked. I figured they'd get her for something, but no, the jury had mercy on her. I'm pretty sure they heard Sarah's powerful closing statement at night when they slept. I know I did. No one would have ever known this was her first trial. She defended our sister like her life depended on it. She pretty much had the prosecution tongue-tied, and the state's star witness, Kenton's receptionist, who witnessed the whole thing, was more like her witness. Especially on Sarah's defense of insanity. The way the receptionist described Ebony that day painted a perfect picture of an unstable woman who wasn't capable of reasoning. I could tell she actually felt sorry for Ebony. When Ebony took the stand, she confirmed the receptionist's theory of an insane, deranged woman. Especially when she talked candidly about the thoughts of her daughter's abuse, torturing her all the way up to the moment she pulled the trigger. Then, the girls who I found from the PI report showed up and cooperated. All of them. They had people in there sobbing when they described their experience with Kenton. A few of them said they fantasized about doing the same thing Ebony did. Kenton really was a disease.

Zena took the stand and sealed the deal. She stood up bold and beautiful. She spoke with authority and strength as she recounted the events of her abuse, and she wasn't ashamed either. Days before she took the stand, she was interviewed on live radio and TV. She really was the best advocate for the cause. When she came to court, carrying the soiled panties she wore the day Kenton raped her, the entire courtroom gasped. When they took the underwear for testing, the truth was revealed—officially. It worked out even better that Kenton's sorry ass wasn't there to take the stand as a witness. A few days before the trial, while he was still recovering from the single shot that blew off that weapon he called a penis, somebody finished Ebony's job and shot his ass dead on the street. Good riddance, scum! I hate to celebrate anybody's death, but he had it coming, and in my opinion, justice was served.

I thought I would never stop hugging my sister on the day she was released. Supporters flooded the courthouse, holding up signs, releasing balloons and doves into the air, and chanting Ebony's name as she walked freely down the street. I imagined this is how it would have been if my father had been vindicated before he died. A real celebration. But his time is coming. Mama and Sarah won't have it any other way.

For years, I considered my father to be dead, even though I knew him to be alive. It was how I coped with it. But I didn't realize how much I was fooling myself until I learned of his murder. I grieved for him all over again. I was hurt, especially by the way he died. But then, I forced myself to be strong because I knew he was watching from heaven, urging me to be. Right after Ebony was released, we had a beautiful memorial service for him. The place was so full that they had to shut down two or three roads. Helicopters hovered over the church, and new reporters flooded the area. His vindication was already beginning. Sir Zion was nowhere to be found. Some said he fled the country. He knows what's coming for him, and the coward in him wouldn't allow him to stay. I'm not worried about that, though. He can't run forever.

I wonder what Mama has for us. That's the whole point of us meeting for dinner. I'm a little anxious. To be honest with you, I feel like a kid who is hours away from Christmas morning. What could it be? I hope it's something we all could use, and knowing Mama, that's exactly what it is.

Stephan is driving. He knows I'm deep in thought and doesn't disturb me. I appreciate that. I'm sure it's taking a lot of effort for him not to take over my thoughts and allow me some personal time. He's really trying. We both are, and the family counseling we've committed to twice a week is helping. He and Zionah are also going through counseling. It's working with lightning speed. I can already see the change in their behavior. Stephan isn't ridiculing her anymore, and Zionah hasn't said anything disrespectful to him in weeks. They even go on dates—just the two of them. At first, it was at the counselor's advice, and Zionah acted like it was going to kill her, but now she looks forward to it, and so does Stephan. When I see them chatting or laughing about something they saw together that day, it warms my heart. After all these years, they're finally starting to get to know each other. Peace is approaching, but we still have to work hard to maintain it. We have a long way to go.

Almost a year ago, when I received the phone call about Ebony being in jail, I was in such a low place. Hearing that bad news was just the icing on the cake for me. I could never see myself going from there to where I am today. I guess that's just how life is. Be careful how you judge the worst day of your life; it might turn out to be the best day of your life. Eventually. My phone keeps ringing non-stop. I've got clients booked months in advance, and I'm making twice what Stephan makes, with half the stress. Stephan is so supportive. He keeps asking me to let him close down the property management business so he can work for me full time. I like how he said that. He didn't say help me; he said work for me. I told him I'd think about it, but for now, I need to continue doing this on my own.

When I'm not working for clients, I dedicate my free time to getting the Akimbo Sedah Family Life Center off the ground. Creating the nonprofit organization was a no-brainer. After fighting so hard for Ebony and Zena, I figured that instead of taking a water break, we should gear up even stronger. More people need us, and I know it's something my father would be proud of. It really embodies his spirit. That's why I named it after him. My vision for the Akimbo Sedah Family Life Center is a place where families can come for healing, where people can get free legal advice courtesy of Sarah, life coaching classes courtesy of Mama, and assistance with clothing, food, and job training—all the essentials. Ebony even volunteered to give free art classes for the youth. Kwame is going to coach a Little League team, and Malichai will be the center's big brother. He'll share his story about why selling and using drugs ain't where it's at. Essence will help with finding affordable housing, and Zena is willing to give seminars on life after sexual abuse. We all have our roles, and it's wonderful. Building strong families is what my dad sacrificed his life for, and it won't be in vain.

Donations have been pouring in. Just last night, we received the largest cash donation yet—someone anonymously deposited fifty grand into the account. That practically seals the deal. Now I don't have to hustle the government as hard for funding and grants. Not that it was difficult; they even want to support this center. All we need now is a location, and ironically, the building my father blew up years ago is looking more and more like the perfect spot. We're going to rebuild it from the ground up. It's going to be great.

The thought of the new direction my life is taking and the center makes me smile. Stephan sees me smiling, grabs my hand, and squeezes it supportively. He's smiling now, too. I squeeze his hand back, and we continue to hold hands until we pull up to the restaurant. It feels good to have him by my side, holding my hand.

Who would have known what a difference a year can make? You just gotta get through it.

39
MALICHAI
"New Car Smell"

"**C**ome on, Zach," I say to him, holding out my hand, but he won't take it. He's stuck to Natasha's side like glue. He shakes his head and gives me a mischievous smile. "It's all right, Mal. I told you I got him."

She puts her arm around Zach and guides him to my brand-new Cadillac Escalade. When they get close enough to the door, I use my automatic keypad to unlock it. The alarm beeps, and Zach screams, but he's more excited than scared. He loves the new vehicle as much as I do. It's something about the new car smell and the leather seats that sedate him.

I watch Natasha carefully help Zach into the back seat and buckle him in. When she finishes, she holds out her hand, and he gives her a high-five and a smile. I don't know how she works her magic on that boy. I guess it works the same way it does on me. Being around her just makes me feel happier, like a new and improved version of myself.

Natasha looks at me and smiles before getting in. She knows how much I admire the way she handles Zach. I can't thank her enough for being here for me, for both of us. I could watch the two of them interact for hours, but I can't. I've got to get to the restaurant to meet with the family. I can't wait to see us all together at one table. It's going to be beautiful.

The restaurant is about ten minutes from my condo. Now that Mama moved, I got my place back. She kept all the furniture in it, too, so I didn't have to worry about bringing as much as a pillow with me. It's really nice to have a stable home life for me and Zach, and not have to worry about paying a mortgage. I never have to worry about being kicked out of any place again. I don't think I've ever slept so soundly.

As soon as I open the door, the new car smell rushes at me, and I inhale deeply, taking it all in. It feels like a dream. Believe it or not, I have Essence to thank—that and my obsession with scratch-off tickets. The ticket she found as a gift for me actually turned out to be a winner. I thought I was seeing things when I scratched the ticket and saw I had all the matching numbers. I came across $150,000 in a matter of seconds. To me, the ticket was about more than money, but a second chance. And it couldn't have come at a better time in my life. A time when I need it the most. A time when I'm ready. I know exactly what to do with it, too.

I had to give some to Mama. I didn't spend a second thinking about it. I wanted her to be comfortable in her new house. I tried to give some to Essence for finding the ticket, but to my surprise, she declined the money. I don't know what the hell got into her, but I sure as hell wasn't about to beg her to take the money. After that, I bought the Escalade. I still got the Chevy, and I plan on keeping it forever. That car has gotten me through hell and back. I plan on dolling her up the way I always wanted and parking her in the garage, only taking her out on Sundays.

The Escalade was the only splurge I made, and it's the only one I plan on making. I bought it secondhand for under twenty thousand dollars. It has low mileage, and whoever had it before me took really good care of it.

I'm glad Natasha encouraged me long before I had the funds to work on a business plan. Now, I'm ready. Just like she said, *You never know what can happen, Mal. You've got to be prepared for the best.* And she was right. I've already made a down payment on a car wash not too far from my house. The place has been abandoned for years, but I still remember when it was open. It was the hottest spot to wash your car. Everyone who was anybody was there at least three times a week—if not to clean their car, then just to show off. I plan on making money off those showoffs, too. They're the ones who'll be playing pool and buying CDs and accessories for their precious cars. That's why the lot is so perfect. It has a good-sized building, big enough for a store and a lounge area. People can wait, buy, and chill all at the same time. I can't wait.

Natasha helped me find a good architect to sketch out my plans for the place. She also assisted me in obtaining a loan, specifically a small business loan for minority-owned businesses. The government provided me with a special fixed interest rate, so my payments are less than my car note. This will pretty much be an all-cash business. I plan on making all my money back in less than two years. All I had to put down was twenty thousand dollars and about another fifty thousand to fix it up the way I want. I can't believe this is really happening to me.

I don't really know what's going on between me and Natasha. We're more friends than anything, but I can see the way she looks at me. Just like she notices how I look at her. We kissed the other day, and it was so sweet, I almost cried. She apologized shortly after. She made the first move and felt like she was out of line because of how close it was to Meka dying. Right now, I want to keep moving at a slow and steady pace, just like it is. I've got to really get myself together before I get involved in another relationship. I know how I am in relationships— I'll look out for that other person so much that I neglect myself and Zach. I want to be better equipped this time and be a better provider.

Besides, it's too close to Meka's death for me to jump into something new. I mean, I done had a real history with that girl. So many ups and downs that I can't count them all. I spent almost my whole life with Meka. She was my best friend, my lover, my everything, and before I move forward with anything new with Natasha, I need to make sure I'm ready and done grieving so that I can love Natasha just as wholeheartedly as I loved Meka. It's the right thing to do and the fair thing to do. I can't say how long that will be, though. It's not like I'm looking at a clock or watching a calendar. It could be two days from now or two years from now. Who knows? Right now, I just can't call it. But when I'm ready, I'll know, and if I'm lucky, Natasha will still be here. Just like she's here now.

Natasha's been by my side through it all—Meka's death, Kwame's coma, and even when I found out my father had been dead for two years. I could cry, just felt numb. Maybe deep down, I always knew he wouldn't make it out of prison. Still, it hurts—he came so far, only to be taken before he crossed the finish line. I like to believe he's in heaven now, rallying for us like he always did. Maybe he fought for Ebony's freedom, for Kwame's full recovery, even for Meka's peace by asking God to put a permanent end to her addiction. Maybe he's up there rallying for my second chance, too. He's our angel now—doing more for us from above than he ever could behind bars.

I pull into the restaurant and see Balanah and Stephan walking toward the door holding hands. Zionah looks happy. She's yelling at the girls about something, but she appears carefree, and so does Balanah. I honk at them, and they wave proudly. Stephan gives me a thumbs-up. I know he's thumbing up to my truck, and Balanah is probably giving a thumbs-up because she sees Natasha with me. They really care about that girl, but they need to tone it down right now. They make her nervous. I invited her to the family dinner today because I need her support. I wanted her with me when Mama gives us whatever it is she has for us. She really is a good shoulder to lean on, and I can't wait to return the favor.

I park my truck and take one last sniff of the new car smell before getting out to join Balanah and Stephan. As I step out, I notice I still smell it. Then, I realize that the new car scent isn't just inside my vehicle but also lingering around everything new in my life. I can smell it on Natasha and Zach. I smell it at my condo. I smell it in the air while at the car wash, checking on the renovations. I smell it everywhere. I'm so grateful for it. Every now and then, everyone needs a little new car smell in their life.

Natasha comes around the car, holding Zach's hand. When I see them, it only feels natural for me to reach out my hand for her to grab. She flashes me a girlish smile and takes my hand to hold. Then I smell the new car scent again. As we walk into the restaurant as one unit, I start thinking I could get used to this.

40
SAHARA
"It's Over…But Not Finished"

I'm surprised when I pull up to the restaurant parking lot and realize I'm not the first one here. Mama only lives a few seconds away, so I figured I'd beat her here. I spot Malichai's new Escalade shining next to Balanah and Stephen's car. I wonder if Ebony and Zena are already inside. They've been staying with Mama for a while now.

Ebony lost her house, but I'm not worried. The way her paintings are selling, she'll have a mansion in a matter of months. Publishers have been calling about her writing a book, but she's still on the fence about it. She considered giving all the proceeds to Zena but said the book had to serve a purpose beyond just making money. She'll only write it if it can empower somebody. That's Ebony—still a rebel.

Zena has been doing well. Her band has been touring and performing at charity events, and she's drawing again. Imagine that. She's even been speaking at events. I never knew how powerful her voice was until I heard her onstage. I've been trying to spend as much time as I can getting reacquainted with her—well, I've been getting reacquainted with all my family. Now that John and I are done, I actually have more time.

He's supposed to announce his candidacy for U.S. Senate next month, and I truly wish him well. After everything we've been through, we finally came to a mutual agreement and got a speedy divorce. When we first got married, we didn't anticipate evolving into two totally different people and growing apart, but it happened. Instead of accepting that, we punished each other for it. That's over now.

After Ebony's trial, John came to me with a fair divorce settlement. I kept the house, he paid alimony and child support, and we parted ways. He married Becca a few weeks later. I didn't feel any kind of way about it. I understood the rush. It wouldn't look good with his right-wing constituents if he were going through a divorce during his campaign.

The day before our divorce was finalized, I cut off my perm and felt so light on my feet and free in my spirit—like a new woman. I stared at my reflection in the mirror and felt something I hadn't felt in years. I felt beautiful.

Now I'm selling the house and moving closer to my family. I need to be close to the Akimbo Sedah Center anyway. I plan to do as much pro bono work as possible. Helping others feels more rewarding than anything I've ever done. I felt that most when I helped that young girl who was charged with killing her baby. That girl wasn't a killer, and thankfully, I was able to convince the jury of that. After that, I caught the charity bug. I plan to help as many people as I can through the center.

I also need to find a building for my law office. The home setup just isn't cutting it anymore. I need more space and a full staff. John offered to help me get started, and I might take him up on it. But I'm sure he's not offering help out of generosity; he sees it as a networking opportunity. Ever since I won Ebony's case, law firms have been calling nonstop, offering me partner roles. Can you imagine that? Me—a first-year attorney—offered partner. At first, I thought that's what I wanted: the high-rise, tailor-made business suits, big-name clients. But that's not me anymore. Those firms care more about the cash than the purpose. And honestly, I don't need them.

Everybody wants to know how I did it—how I pulled off a not-guilty verdict. They expect some brilliant legal theory, but it's simple: I cared. I fought with my heart, not just my mind. Love for my little sister carried me through that trial. Loving people is the key to defending them—truly caring, not just chasing a check.

I didn't do it alone, though. I had a lot of help. Ebony had so much support that the case was almost over before it even began. I'm happy it's all over, but something new is starting. And I think that beginning looks a lot like bringing that snake, Sir Zion, to justice.

With all the evidence I have against him, I can charge him with all kinds of crimes—murder being the biggest one. There's also fraud, money laundering, racketeering, drug trafficking, and whatever else comes up. Every day, I find out something new about that lowlife. His face is all the news. There's a manhunt underway for him, and it's only a matter of time before he's caught and locked away for life––right where he belongs. When they're not airing his dirty laundry, they're remembering my father and bringing new life to his cause. Mama has been working tirelessly, doing interviews on TV and radio, picking up where my father left off and preserving his legacy. They're even talking about naming a street after him.

My father had a collection of essays and poetry that he wrote while he was incarcerated. Mama's already planning to publish them. She's determined to keep his name alive. I think doing all this makes him seem more alive to her than when he was in prison. She's still grieving, still strong—but different. I know she'll be fine.

I loved my father. I think I took his death the hardest out of all my siblings. But I pulled myself together because I know justice has to be served. Besides, I know I'll see him again—if not in the faces of the people our center will help, then I'll see him in heaven. It may be over, but it's definitely not finished.

41
EBONY
"I'm Free"

Sahara storms into the restaurant like the doors owe her something, phone glued to her ear. She's walking in her true calling now, and it's beautiful to see it manifest. She's a damn good lawyer— and she did it. She got me off. I knew she wouldn't rest until she did, but truthfully, my real freedom came the day my daughter wrapped her arms around me and cried in my arms. On that day, I released myself from the internal bondage that had held me captive for years.

Zena and I are inseparable these days. I see her in a new light, and she sees me the same. Our mother-daughter relationship is blooming, growing stronger with each passing day. I've never seen her look so free, so alive. I finally got back what was stolen from me——and so did she. Zena found herself again, and this version of her? She's stronger, bolder, more whole than ever.

My career's taking off again—hotter than before—but I'm not the same artist. My art's evolved. It's deeper now, more layered and intentional. I sold a few pieces I created while I was inside. Other? I won't let go. Suddenly, everybody wants to hear from me, dying for interviews, but I'm not in the mood to talk. People approach me on the streets like I'm a superhero, but I'm not. I'm just a woman who took back her life with necessary force and courage. And through that courage, I learned I don't always have to be strong. Weak moments can be just as powerful. Coming to that realization humbles me to the point of silence, and I don't talk much anymore. Instead of verbally expressing myself, I let my art speak for me. I paint. I draw. I release.

Zena reads all my work. She gets me. She's painting again, too—picked up that paintbrush like she never put it down. Watching her heal through the gift she inherited from me melts parts of me I thought had frozen forever.

We finally had our heart-to-heart. I told her everything, including who her father was. It hit her hard, but she knows better than anybody that truth stings before it sets you free. She understands me better now. She knows why I didn't say anything before. Although our experiences were different, we both suffered at the hands of men who took advantage of us. She finally admitted Kenton didn't turn her gay. Honestly, I kind of knew it all along, but I forced myself to believe it was because it gave me another reason to be tortured.

All in all, it's good to be home, although I sometimes miss prison. Not the place, but who I was to those women. I'm excited about the Akimbo Sedah Family Life Center. I'm eager to get started and make a difference. I still talk to Tweety, and she's doing good. She's in school, working, and staying focused. I remind her often: watch the men you bring around your daughter. Don't let loneliness, lust, or love cloud your intuition. That kind of blindness can cost your daughter more than you realize.

I told her it's not just men that can distract you—sometimes it's your career. When you're a single mother raising a girl, you have to move through life carefully. Your daughter should come before any and everything. Always. Because when you think your choices don't affect her, that's when the damage creeps in. Next thing you know, you're out here shooting somebody's dick off. Which, depending on the circumstances, may not be such a bad idea. But the point is that it could have been avoided.

Don't fall for society's fake definition of family. Sometimes, family is just mother and daughter. If there's no father, so be it. Don't go searching for somebody to fill a role that was never theirs to play. Instead, you fill it yourself. And if someone decent does come along, ease into it. Don't dive in headfirst. I don't care if he claims to be Jesus—sleep with one eye open and keep it open for the rest of your life. Love him, trust him, but watch him like a hawk. Always. You don't have to let him know you're watching—but never stop. Ever.

I spent a lot of time in prison thinking about Daddy. Gave me insight into his life. I understand now why he wanted to distance himself from us. It was how he coped. I spent so many years judging him, and it took me to be in the same situation to finally understand him. I promised myself that if I made it out, the first thing I would do was visit him. I didn't care about his demand that we stay away. I needed to see him. I needed to talk to him, to digest his wisdom. But that ain't never going to happen. He's gone.

Prison ain't no place to live or die, but at least he died standing for something. I was never really inspired by what my dad did until I stood up for what I believed in: my daughter and justice. Now I get him. But it's too late to tell him. I forgive him, but he'll never know it.

I spent years hating Sir Zion. And after learning how he ended my father's life—and I mean way before he ever killed him—that hate has turned to loathing. But I'm trying to tame that hate. Trying to let go of those violent thoughts. I got lucky once. You don't get that type of luck twice. Besides, he ain't worth the bullet or my freedom. I'm free now, and I plan to stay that way. Even if it means forgiving Sir Zion and Kenton. My freedom is worth more. My daughter's freedom is worth more.

I'm free. Finally, I'm free.

42
ESSENCE
"Change Ain't Easy"

"**M**a'am, you got twenty-five cents?"

I look up from my cell phone and see a smelly junkie holding his hand like I owe him something. Instead of getting mad, I reach into my pocket and drop a crumpled dollar bill in his hand—at least I hope it's a dollar.

"Thank you, ma'am," he says quickly and is off to solicit the next person.

I hope I can get through this door before another one approaches me. I'm already late to the family dinner, and I don't feel like hearing no shit from any of my siblings, especially Sahara.

With everything that's happened this past year, I've been doing a lot of soul-searching. Honestly? I don't like what I see. I can be selfish, self-centered, and more than a little self-absorbed. I really never noticed before, but life has a way of humbling you. Now, I'm not perfect by a long shot, but I'm trying. My first step to change is learning to give more—not just money, but time. Time is more valuable than money. You can earn money back, but you can't buy back time.

Speaking of time, I haven't left Kwame's side since he got out of the hospital. I'm probably getting on his nerves, but he'll never say it—and I don't care. I'm making up for lost time. Seeing my brother laid up in that hospital bed hooked up to a ventilator really woke me up. If he had died, I wouldn't have been able to live with myself. I often get so caught up in my own life that I neglect the needs of everyone else around me. That's not okay. I wonder why nobody ever said anything before. Or maybe they did, and I just didn't hear them—too busy being caught up in my own life. That's me: if you ain't saying what I want to hear, then I ain't listening. But not anymore. I'm trying to change. Really trying. Who knew change would be this damn hard?

Kwame isn't the only one I almost lost. Ebony almost got a life sentence, and her being in prison would've been like she was dead— just like my father. I was the youngest when he went to prison, so my memories of him are few but sweet. I remember feeling safe when he held me, swinging me in the air like I weighed nothing. I used to think he was a giant. I also remember the day Mama told us he wasn't coming back for a long time. I felt sad and confused, much like the way I felt when she told me he was dead.

That mix of emotions weighed on me. I felt more disappointment than anything else, kind of like how a child feels when they find out Santa Claus isn't real. I had to reprogram my way of thinking. I didn't miss my father as much as I could have because deep down, I knew there would be a day when we would rekindle our relationship and start fresh. I believed he would come home one day, and just like I needed him when I was a little girl, I would need him as a grown woman. I looked forward to that day, but now, it'll never happen.

I feel worse for Mama. She was more patient and anxious than all of us. She ritually counted each day he spent in prison by making marks on her calendar. The more years that passed, the more anxious she became because she knew it wouldn't be long before he walked through the door or the phone rang for her to go and pick him up. She's been strong for us and for him, but deep down inside, I know it's killing her. I've never seen a woman love a man as much as she loved my dad, and from what I hear, he loved her just as much. I visit Mama twice a week now. No exceptions. It kind of hurt my feelings when she seemed so surprised to see me at her door, but I can't complain. I understand her shock. I just want her to give me a chance to prove I've changed. All of them.

I didn't help out as much as I could with Ebony's campaign. I was so caught up with Marco and all that foolishness that I missed my chance. I hate that I wasn't part of the bond that brought us back together, but I plan to make it up by doing my part at the Akimbo Sedah Family Life Center. Balanah and Sahara don't trust me. They don't think I'll follow through with my role, but I can't wait to prove them wrong. I'm really excited about helping others. It's my way of making up for not helping Ebony and officially stamping myself as a true Sedah. My father would have been proud of me for giving back to the community like I intend to. It's the least I can do. I already donated fifty grand, but they won't know it was me because I did it anonymously. That's a big deal for me! Change surely is hard.

I used the money Marco forced upon me to make the donation. I thought about giving it all, then I decided I shouldn't be foolish and just give a quarter. But as I was making the wire transfer, I ended up giving half because it felt right. I plan to use the other half to start my business. If I do it smart, it should be more than enough. I was surprised when Balanah and Sahara consulted with me about finding a place for the center. I had the perfect location—the building Daddy blew up. At first, they said no, thinking it would be too hard, but I kept at it and finally got a deal. I can't wait to tell them today. I believe it's the perfect spot. It's symbolic and the very place he sacrificed his life for.

I don't have to worry about Marco. After Sahara pushed to get Sir Zion charged with murder, the press dug up so much dirt on him that Marco's name came up along with a slew of other crooked cops and politicians. His ass is in jail, awaiting trial. So, I look at the whole thing as a blessing. I didn't know what I was going to do about Marco. I was probably going to have to break down and tell Malichai, but I avoided that because I knew he would probably kill him if he found out he was harassing me. I didn't want to do that, especially since Malichai is getting back on his feet. Before Marco got locked up, that fool broke into my house, stalked me at grocery stores, and held me at gunpoint. Thank God it's over, and I'm a hundred grand richer. Well, actually fifty grand, but who's counting? Wow, that's a lot of money I gave away, but it's for a good cause. That's my story, and I'm sticking to it.

Anyway, things have really come full circle. The family is back together. I'm alive, beautiful, and still have enough money to pay my bills and start my own brokerage agency.

"Excuse me, ma'am, you got a dollar?"

Another junky catches me so off guard that he startles me. I jump and breathe hard. I dig in my pocket for more loose change and then start to think, *what the hell am I doing?*

"No. Now get your begging ass the hell out of my face," I say and walk into the restaurant.

Change ain't easy, but I'm trying.

43
KWAME
"Fight, Fight, Fight…"

I'm starting to see the beauty in everything. It must be a gift I brought back from the other side. I'm sitting in the restaurant with my family, watching Levi patiently show Zach how to color. Zena and Zionah are giggling among themselves, and it's so beautiful I can't help but smile. Balanah and Stephen are acting like newlyweds, and Sahara is looking radiant with her new hairstyle and ethnic gear. Malichai sits proudly beside Natasha, genuinely happy. Essence is beside me, giving me extra attention and carefully watching her words as she speaks to people. Ebony looks like she's finally found peace. Then there's Mama—at the head of the table, dressed in an all-white linen dress with a matching scarf tied elegantly around her head. She looks like a queen. She silently admires each of us, smiling with pride. This is my family. This is my second chance at life.

Mama called us here today to give us something, but I think it's more than that. I think she called us all here today because we need this time together. It's been a rough year, and we need to celebrate the fact that we all made it through it alive. We're fighters. Survivors. Soldiers.

I'm grateful to be alive. There was a time when living and dying felt the same to me. I let myself go—slipped so deep into depression, I was just as good as dead. There was no life in me. No motivation. No ambition. Nothing but emptiness.

Sadly enough, the only time I felt alive was when I raised my hand to Tammy. In a warped way, feeling her flesh against my hand gave me...energy. But afterward, I sank lower, drowning in guilt. It wasn't her fault I didn't love her, and it wasn't mine that she didn't love me. That's why the first thing I did when I woke up from being in a coma was divorce her. I had to—mainly for Levi.

Turns out, all that vomiting and nausea was induced by an allergic reaction to Nyquil. I was being drugged—but not by Tammy, like we first assumed. It was Levi. Doctors found so much Nyquil in my system I could've opened a pharmacy. He'd been slipping it into my smoothies and Kool-Aid. Because I was dangerously allergic to something in it, it nearly killed me.

My family interrogated Tammy so much that she almost had a nervous breakdown, but Levi stood up like a man and told the truth. He drugged me—to keep the peace. He didn't want me beating on his mother, so he gave me Nyquil to sedate me. That was his solution.

I didn't feel angry. If anything, I felt ashamed. Ashamed that my son had to resort to something so extreme. I never thought about how Levi felt, watching me slap her around. Kids see everything. They don't miss a thing. They feel it all, deeply.

After Levi confessed, everybody wanted him to go through psychiatric counseling. Everybody except me. He didn't need counseling. I did. So, I forbade it. What he needed was to see me in a different light. What he needed was to see his father become a man, not remain a boy. And I'm going to be that for him. That's why I devote all my time to him now. He comes first. Blood or not, he's my son. Levi gave me the wakeup call I needed, and I owe him my life for that. He didn't almost kill me—he saved me.

Divorcing Tammy was the best thing I ever did for him. She didn't put up a fight either, especially after I gave her the house and agreed to pay the mortgage, child support, and alimony. But she had to let me adopt Levi and give me joint custody. Now he spends six months with me and six months with her. I hate splitting him up like that, but I have to be in my son's life. I have to teach him how to be a man, just like my father would've taught me. Having a child is a huge responsibility. But the real honor comes in owning it. I often wondered what my father would've thought of the man that I turned out to be. But I figured what he didn't know couldn't hurt him. Boy, was I wrong. He saw everything, but most importantly, he forgave me. How do I know? Because he told me.

Everybody asked me if I could hear them when they whispered in my ear while I was in a coma. The answer is no—I didn't hear their voices, but I felt their presence. It was strange. I knew when they were in the room, even without seeing them. But one presence was loud and clear—my dad. He was with me the entire time. That's why I didn't feel alone. I never told anyone, because they probably would say I was hallucinating. But it was real.

We spent hours together talking. He opened up about his regrets—the ways he felt he'd failed us. That shocked me. I spent many years thinking my dad was infallible, but the truth was that he was no different from me. He was a man who grieved his mistakes. He said that if he could turn back time, he would have put us before his cause. Family always comes first, he told me. He also said he would have let Mama come and see him from time to time and that he didn't give her enough credit all those years he was in prison. He also told me to watch passion because it can be dangerous when it's unfulfilled or deferred. Then he told me that forgiveness is the key to a peaceful life. He said I needed to forgive myself for what I did to Tammy and what she did to me. He said I had to forgive myself for throwing that game and neglecting Levi for so long. He said forgiveness was my true second chance at life, and once I achieved it, I should help others find their second chances.

To tell the truth, I didn't wake up as soon as I could have because I didn't want to leave him. I finally got the chance to know him for who he really was, not just the man Mama told me he was. He told me it was time to get up and make a change. He told me to fight, fight, fight until that change came. I told him I didn't want him to leave me—that I needed him—and he told me he never left us. He said he was always with us. Then he told me, "Kwame, you got to fight. You got to fight..." Then he started to chant it: "Fight, fight, fight." Somehow, I felt my eyes flutter and then pop open as if they were never closed. The first face I saw was Essence, then Mama. I didn't see Daddy anymore, but I knew he wasn't gone.

Mama spent weeks trying to figure out how to break the news to me that Daddy was dead. Ironically, I spent weeks trying to break the news to her. I guess she thought that after everything I went through, I was too fragile to hear the news, but she felt obligated to tell me. When she finally did, I just smiled at her and told her that he's dead, but not gone. She smiled back at me like she knew exactly what I meant.

After the waiter takes our orders, Mama pulls a bulging manila envelope out of her bag and places it on the table. Everyone falls silent. We can't take our eyes off the envelope. We know it's what she said she has for us. She's smiling at all of us. She looks genuinely happy and seems even stronger today than she did yesterday. Then, she leans in close to the table, takes a sip of her water, and begins to talk without pause. We listen intently to what she's saying, feeling like life and death are on her tongue.

"I told each of you that I have something for you, but really, it's from your father. I just want you to know that although he was gone for so many years, there wasn't a day that went by that he didn't think about you."

Mama lifts the envelope, and we can't take our eyes off it.

"Every day...he thought about us every day," she whispers loudly, then smiles proudly. "It gives me great honor to give this to each of you. A letter, a message, a note for each day that he was away from you. Take this and get to know your father for yourselves. Catch up on lost time. Forgive him. Honor him. Remember him."

She starts passing out stacks of envelopes to each of us.

"I can't tell you what to do, but if I were you...I'd start with the last letter he wrote you and then go to the first. Sometimes, starting at the end can give you a better understanding of the beginning. It's what I did, but it's up to you."

We all look at Mama, truly considering what she told us.

Each of us holds our envelopes like it's gold. Essence starts crying, then Balanah, then Sahara. Ebony doesn't cry; she just smiles. A tear of masculinity drops from Malichai's eyes. He wipes it away before anyone can see, but I caught him. Mama's eyes start to get watery at our reactions, but she doesn't let any tears fall. I don't cry because I know he's with us today. I just wish he could give me a sign. The table becomes so quiet. Everyone is in their own world, flipping through the letters, smelling them, and holding them against their chests. It's almost like we're not there together anymore. Everyone is in their own world.

I'm so distracted by the papers I'm holding in my hands that I don't notice the familiar face approaching our table. *Where have I seen this man before?* He's looking right at me and smiling humbly. He walks with his chest out, shoulders back, and head held high. Confidence radiates from him. He's wearing a purple and silver smock with a matching ethnic skull cap. Tendrils of his silver locs fall gracefully on his shoulders. He carries a long, hand-carved stick. He appears regal.

"Shalom," he says to me, and then I remember him. He's the man who sold me the beautiful African-shaped collage that I still admire to this day. It had a theme of a black family on it. What was his name? Clock-Man. I remember now.

"Clock-Man," I say and stand up to shake his hand. His handshake is firm.

He respectfully greets Mama with a kiss on the hand and nods to the rest of my family.

"It's good to see you with your family, young man. I've seen you all on the news, and you are true overcomers. Your father was a great man. Continue to *fight*."

He pumps his fist in the air, and my heart skips a beat. My dad is giving me a sign that he's here.

"*Fight, fight, fight*," he says with authority.

All of us straighten up our posture and nod at him, considering his words.

"Blessings," he says before walking back to his table.

We all stare at him like we're mesmerized by the simple words of encouragement that felt so powerful when spoken through his deep voice. He takes a seat at a table on the other side of the restaurant. There is a beautiful woman with him and six young adults that I assume are his children. How ironic. There are six of them, just like there are six of us, except instead of four girls and two boys, there are five girls and one boy. Poor guy. I watch Mama smile as he takes a seat at the head of the table. He gently kisses the woman sitting next to him on her cheek and then opens his hands, initiating a family prayer to give thanks before they eat.

After the prayer, he catches us staring at him and pumps his fists again while mouthing the words...*fight, fight, fight.*

The End

If you enjoyed this novel, please leave a review.

Keep in touch.
Follow me on:

IG: @authorzee.w
FB: @thiswriterslife
TikTok: @authorzee.w

www.ingramcontent.com/pod-product-compliance
Lightning Source LLC
Chambersburg PA
CBHW070544030726
47505CB00001B/147